the Wardrobe Mistress

D1057733

The Dress Thief was winner of the 2014 Festival of Romantic Fiction's 'Best Historical Read' Award, and shortlisted for the 2015 Romance Writers of America (RWA) RITA Awards and the 2015 Public Book Awards.

The Milliner's Secret was shortlisted for the 2015 Romantic Fiction's 'Best Historical Read' Award.

Also by Natalie Meg Evans

The Dress Thief
The Milliner's Secret
Summer in the Vineyards

NATALIE MEG EVANS

the Wardrobe Mistress

Quercus

First published in Great Britain in 2017 by

Quercus Editions Ltd
Carmelite House
50 Victoria Embankment
London EC4Y 0DZ

An Hachette UK company

A CIP catalogue record for this book is available
from the British Library.

PB ISBN 978 1 78429 938 5
EBOOK ISBN 978 1 78429 939 2

10 9 8 7 6 5 4 3 2 1

Typeset by CC Book Production

Printed and bound in Great Britain by Clays Ltd, St Ives plc

To my Dad, John Douglas McKay.
A fine Yorkshireman and an even better friend.

PART ONE

In the Beginning . . .

December 1925, London

What if she died too?

What if she, Vanessa Quinnell, were put into a hole as dark as this theatre, as cold as the night outside? She reached for her daddy's hand but his eyes were on the stage.

He was yelling, 'Come on, Billy-Boy, show us an ankle!' His voice cut through the laughter and the music. Daddy had been an actor once and Mum often said that from inside their home he could be heard all the way to the churchyard.

The Bad Fairy had cursed the baby princess, before flying up off the stage with a cackle. The King and Queen were wailing because one day, their little Briar-Rose would prick her finger and die – unless the curse were lifted. Vanessa knew what it meant to die. You were put underground and never came up again.

The princess's nursemaid had been summoned. Broad as a carthorse in a stripy dress and a jelly-bag cap, she was shaking her yellow ringlets and kicking up her dress to display red-spotted drawers. In a disturbingly deep voice, she bellowed, 'Children, we'll save Briar-Rose from doom, if with noise we fill this room!'

The Lilac Fairy could reverse the spell. Did that mean there was hope for her too, Vanessa wondered? Earlier that afternoon, a doctor had shone a light down her throat and tutted, before telling Daddy that she must have an operation. Vanessa's Uncle Victor had had an operation, and now he was in a hole in the churchyard. But the Lilac Fairy would make everything all right. They must call her name, the fat nursemaid told them, particularly the children.

'Raise your voices as I count *one, two, three* – '

All the children bellowed, except Vanessa.

The nursemaid cupped a hand to her ear and told the children they weren't shouting loud enough. She strutted along the front of the stage, displaying her drawers, and seemed to stare right at Vanessa. 'Is there a little girl in the audience who isn't shouting at all?'

Vanessa let out a choking sob. She'd tried but her throat hurt too much.

Daddy lifted her out of her seat and held her level with his shoulder. His breath smelled funny. They'd both had their medicine before they came in to the theatre. Hers came in a glass bottle and tasted peppery. His came from a silver flask. 'Come on, Toots,' he urged, 'make a wish! Make it happen!'

So she clenched her fists around the playbill he'd bought with their tickets, and projected her will towards the brightly-lit stage. Moments later, child-fairies in shimmering tunics floated down. Their wings sent out diamond explosions around Princess Briar-Rose's cradle. Next, a lady in a puffball of lilac and silver net descended. Her hair was a cloud of moonlight curls and the audience drew in an awed breath. Vanessa's heart slid back to its proper place. The Good Fairy had come. All would be well.

Daddy thought so too. 'See, Toots? When you want something badly enough, it happens. It's not wrong to want something so much it hurts.'

'Do you want something that hurts?'

'I do.'

She asked what and he chuckled, 'Never mind.' The handsome prince would come on stage after the interval, he said.

'What's the interval?'

'When the curtain drops so the sceneshifters can change the set. Got to make the stage look like a forest has been growing for a hundred years.'

'Where is the handsome prince?'

'In his dressing room, struggling into his fleshings.' Fleshings go on your legs, Daddy explained. 'They're murder if you don't put talcum powder on first. You have to shave your legs three times a week. It's called "paying your dues" but it's still the best job in the world.'

'Shaving your legs?'

Daddy laughed, and told her she was priceless. 'I don't know about you, Toots, but I'm thirsty.'

The curtain dropped and Daddy asked a stranger, a lady, if she'd 'escort his little girl' to the lavatory. Afterwards, as Vanessa washed her hands, the lady touched the dried tears on her cheeks.

'How old are you, dear?'

'Five-and-a-half.'

'I'm sure you're much younger than that.'

'I *am* five.' As if Vanessa would be wrong on such an important matter! 'I'm small. I was made from the last bit of pastry, when there wasn't enough for a whole pie.' For some reason, the lady thought that was funny.

When Vanessa was back with Daddy, his breath reeked of medicine. He handed her a choc-ice. 'Don't tell Mum, eh?'

She did her best with the ice cream but in the end, Daddy

finished it off. A bell rang and they took their seats again. The
second part was much nicer. After the now-grown-up princess
had been kissed by the prince, everybody joined hands and sang,
including the Bad Fairy and the nursemaid. Then the curtain
came down for the last time and Daddy whispered, 'We'll skip
the National Anthem. Grab your coat, Toots.' People tutted as
they left, but Daddy only laughed.

'We're going backstage,' he told her. 'Know what backstage
is? If the theatre were a clock, backstage would be its workings.
It's where the real fun is.'

He led her through a side door that seemed to be part of the
wall. Then they were in a different kind of passage, this one
with a hard, grey floor. There were lots of doors and people in
a hurry. One man stopped, though, saying, 'Johnny Quinnell,
blimey, how's tricks? Gotta dash. We have to reset Scene One
for tonight's house. Full till January. You can't go wrong with
Sleeping Beauty at Christmas!'

'Your name isn't Johnny,' Vanessa said as her dad helped her
up a steep flight of stairs.

'Now, here's the thing,' Daddy answered. 'You're called Vanessa
but I always call you Toots. Anyone can have extra names.'

'Is Johnny your extra name?'

'That's about the size of it.'

Upstairs, Daddy tapped on a brown door and walked straight
in, calling, 'Parcel for you!' At first, all Vanessa saw was the edge
of a long table. When Daddy sat her on it, she noticed that the
room was full of rails, slung with white sheets like aprons. Velvet
curtains, the colour of Victoria plums, covered the window. A
woman with the darkest hair Vanessa had ever seen was sewing
at the table. She looked up and Vanessa saw her mouth tighten,
as if somebody had gathered it up behind.

'Johnny. My God.' Getting up, the woman backed away as the princess had done before she and the prince started kissing. She wore a red dress with buttons and pockets. Lots of pockets.

'Still the undaunted mistress of the wardrobe, Eva?'

'I'm still working, if that's what you mean, Johnny.' Her hair was bound across her head in plaits thick as the poles on a steam-horse carousel. Tucked into them, a pencil and a pair of gold spectacles. She said, 'You're going to tell me why you're back after all this time?'

Vanessa might have listened, not least to find out why everyone here called her Daddy 'Johnny' and not 'Clive' as they did at home in Stanshurst – when they weren't calling him 'Quinnell' or 'Mr Quinnell', that is – but she was fascinated by her end of the table. Shuffling towards a stack of white objects, she discovered wings like the ones the child-fairies had worn. Except these were dull as the paper that the Stanshurst butcher wrapped his bacon in. Checking to see that the grownups weren't watching, Vanessa put her arms through the loops of one, and flapped her arms.

The grownups talked on in low voices.

'. . . not a word and now you come? After all we endured? You tore my heart out.'

'I had to bring the girl to have her tonsils seen by a specialist. She's had bad throats since she was a baby. I wanted to bring her to see her first play too, and I could hardly take her to *King Lear* at the Criterion. Besides, I need a service.'

'You *need* me? You inhuman—'

Vanessa broke in, calling, 'Daddy, I'm trying to fly.'

The lady came towards Vanessa. Her eyes matched her hair, dark as liquorice. 'What's your name, precious?' She turned to Daddy. 'Mary or Margaret?'

'I call her Toots.' Daddy sang, '"She's my Tootsie-Wootsie"—'

'What's her name?' the lady interrupted in a different voice.

'Vanessa Elizabeth Quinnell.'

The lady jerked as if somebody had stuck a pin in her. Vanessa jumped off the table and looked down at her hands. She'd kept the playbill Daddy had bought, only now it was crumpled.

'Don't be afraid.' The lady scooped her up, wings and all. Her arms felt soft – unlike Mum's which were all hard knobbles – and she smelled of roses. Setting Vanessa on her feet, she crouched so their faces were opposite. 'Did you like *Sleeping Beauty*, *Vanessa*?' She spoke the name like powder-puff dabs.

'After the Good Fairy came. Why are the wings not shiny?'

The lady helped her take the wings off and held them up to the light. 'They're covered in sequins which glitter only when the luminaires strike them.' Vanessa hadn't a clue what 'luminaires' were. 'The magic of theatre, my love. Did you like the costumes? I mean, the clothes the people wore?'

'I like the Lilac Fairy best.'

'Ah, yes. But how muffled you are! Sore throat?'

Vanessa nodded. The lady said, 'Let me tell you, the theatre is the best place in the world, and the wardrobe room is the best place in the theatre. When you get better, come back and play here. Will you?'

'I don't know.' The lady made her feel warm and interesting but – 'I would get lost in London.'

'When you're older, then. I shall make sure you come back.' The lady went to a cupboard as big as the one in the room at The Hall where Mum worked. She found a length of ribbon which she held against Vanessa's hair. 'Sea green, perfect against brown.' She wove it into Vanessa's curls, showing her the result in a mirror that reflected the room in reverse, including Daddy who watched them, arms folded. The ribbon made a green-blue butterfly on Vanessa's head.

'It's pretty,' she whispered.

'And very old, little one. French silk-satin. Take care of it.'

Daddy came over. All day, he'd been full of fun, cracking jokes, but now he looked as he did on Sundays when they went to church. 'Eva, she's bound to lose it, or her mother will object. Take it off.'

'Never throw back a gift, Johnny. Haven't you learned that?' Bending to Vanessa, the lady asked gently, 'What will you give me of yours?'

Vanessa whispered, 'I haven't got anything.'

The lady – Eva – took scissors from her pocket. She lifted one of Vanessa's nut-brown curls. 'Can you spare one?'

Vanessa nodded.

Snip. The lady closed her palm around the curl. Then, from the neck of her dress, she pulled a strand of ribbon that had a gold key hanging from it. She kissed the key, saying, 'We'll lock your curl away in a special place. That means you will come back.' Leaning across her table, she pulled a round, wooden box towards her. It made Vanessa think of a chocolate cake, the sort the baker made when Lady Stanshurst held a party. The little key flashed, a lid was lifted and the curl was placed inside the box. After locking it, the lady turned to Daddy. 'So, Johnny, what d'you want of me?'

'You need to bear witness while the child signs a document.'

'She can't sign at her age!'

'You watch.' Daddy took something from his pocket. It was the ink pad from his office. He'd let Vanessa play with it sometimes, stamp bills with the word 'Paid' which made her feel grown-up, though if she came home with inky fingers, Mum would scrub them with kitchen soap.

Before she knew what he was doing, Daddy was pressing her fingertips to the pad. From inside his waistcoat, he fetched a sheet of paper and laid her fingers to it, one after the other. 'There's a good girl, every little piggy, including the thumb. Done. That didn't hurt, did it?' Daddy lifted her up beside the sink, and cleansed away the ink with soap that smelled of flowers.

The lady asked, 'What's my part, Johnny?'

'Get you-know-who's signature against those dabs.' Daddy winked. 'Post the form back, but not to my home – to the Hall. It'll find me.'

He meant Stanshurst Hall, where his office was.

'What are you up to?' the lady wanted to know.

'Planning for the future, Eva.'

'Yours, naturally.'

'*Hers*. Though now you mention it . . .' Daddy looked around the room, at his reflection in the mirror. 'I miss this place. So much, it hurts. I miss you too, Eva.'

Within minutes, they were walking down a side alley. The night was cold but bright as silver because it had snowed again. The pavements were mushy with footprints. 'It'll be All White in Kent,' Daddy joked. Kent was where they lived, in a village called Stanshurst, like the Hall, near the town of Hayes. It wasn't far from London.

On the homeward journey, she half-slept against Daddy's side while he sipped medicine from his flask. She could feel his throat swallowing. It was the smell of peppermint that told her they were about to draw in at Hayes station. Daddy always kept mints in his pocket. Lifting her off the train, he said, 'We won't tell your mother about the show, Toots. Or the ink. Our secret?'

She promised. 'Our secret.'

He took the playbill from her reluctant grip, and the ribbon from her hair. 'I'll look after these. One day, I'll take you back to see my lovely Eva.'

Only he didn't. Some months later on her sixth birthday, Clive 'Johnny' Quinnell left home. She didn't see him go; she was in the cottage hospital having her tonsils out. Her mum and Lady Stanshurst had taken her there in the car, Daddy waving them off. Vanessa didn't set eyes on him again for nearly nineteen years and the, only a fleeting glimpse. All through her childhood she was convinced that her troublesome throat, her habit of whispering, had sent him away.

Chapter One

When war broke out in September of '39, Vanessa was living in southeast London, a year into a commercial design course at art school. Her father, now a professional actor, lived on the other side of the river and occasionally, she'd see his name on the billboard of one of the smaller West End theatres. 'Johnny Quinnell' played support roles. The butler, the crusty policeman, the jovial landlord. Though she often 'went west' for an evening out, she did not seek him out.

Vanessa kept to her art studies through the winter of '39 –'40 while the so-called 'phony war' ticked along. London had fallen still, theatres closed. The streets gained a masculine aura, flowing with khaki, navy and smoky blue. Vanessa never went out without a gas mask bumping against her hip. But life went on as usual until the day after her twentieth birthday, on May 30th, 1940, when she joined the Women's Auxiliary Air Force. Putting on the WAAF uniform gave her the courage to admit that commercial design had been a mistake. That brush with fairy's wings had planted a desire to study theatre costume, something her school teachers had discouraged. Theatre was a dicey profession, they'd warned her. 'You can be in work one day, and sacked the next if the show closes.' Her mum had been equally down on the idea: Ruth Quinnell loathed everything theatrical. Fear of bumping into Johnny had done the rest. Vanessa had shelved her dream.

She hoped the WAAF would send her somewhere exotic – or at least far from Kent. But with the endemic contrariness of the services, they posted her to Biggin Hill, four miles from her mother's front door.

The remnants of youth sloughed from her when she donned the slate-blue uniform of an Aircraftwoman third Class, learned how to march and salute, and was baptised into the world of wireless operation. She forgot about theatre, London and her absent dad – until Germans bombers raided Biggin Hill. The shock of being in direct fire loosened the hard-packed anger within her. Her dad had fought in the last war, the one that had ended two years before she was born. He even had a war wound, nerve damage to his right hand that forced him to write with his left.

She decided she must make contact with him, otherwise it might be too late. The trouble was, she didn't have his address and her mother claimed not to know it. 'Near the theatres,' Ruth Quinnell said when Vanessa pressed her. 'That's all I know. All I want to know.'

But Vanessa didn't believe Ruth. Her mother had told her aged five that having her tonsils taken out 'wouldn't hurt a bit.' It had been horrendous. Ruth had also warned Vanessa that in London, 'Men prey on single girls.' That hadn't happened either. The Fressenden Art School had taken good care of its female students. Separate accommodation, chaperoned life-drawing classes. Their rules had been so restrictive, Vanessa had been knocked sideways by Biggin Hill, which teemed with highly sexed, available men. Or 'demi-Gods in blue' as some of her fellow WAAFs regarded the fighter pilots.

One afternoon when she was visiting home, Vanessa searched Ruth's bureau and found an address book. Under 'Q' was a single entry: Clive J. Quinnell. As if he were a solicitor or the insurance man. There was an address for Long Acre, WC2.

She wrote and after a delay, her father replied with three lines.

Splendid to hear from you, Toots. I think about you often. Have you finished school yet?

Still at school? Had the years become a blur to him? They began a cautious correspondence, no mention of Stanshurst. In November 1940, Vanessa wrote that she was married. A whirlwind romance, typical of the age, love and commitment conducted in six-eight time. Leo Kingcourt was a Spitfire pilot with corn-coloured hair. One kiss, and Vanessa had become a liquid version of herself. He'd proposed to her on October 15th, 1940, and they'd married two weeks later.

Her dad's reply addressed her as 'Mrs L Kingcourt' and he'd enclosed five pounds for a wedding gift. In his jerky left-hand script he wrote, 'Tell my son-in-law I'll look up and wave next time there's a dog-fight over London. Bring him up, I'm keen to meet you both.'

There never was time. Within hours of marrying Leo, she knew she'd blundered. There followed twenty-four days of wretched shame, and then Leo was killed..

At her own request, she was posted to an airbase in the Midlands. A few months after that, she was sent to Waddington, Lincolnshire, and after that to Yorkshire. Moving every ten months or so, she drifted ever further north. She greeted New Year 1945 at RAF Banff on Scotland's Moray Firth, north of Aberdeen. The airfield was white as a wedding cake.

It was from Banff, after four years of correspondence, that she set off to London with the intention of finally meeting Clive

'Johnny' Quinnell once more. He had written, urging her to come and see him, and not in his usual bantering tone.

'Toots, I've something to tell you which can't wait. I'd best not write it. Can you get leave?'

February 9th, 1945 came wrapped in whirling snow. Winter-scoured hills were the unbroken view through the train window as Vanessa made the long haul south. A gruelling over-nighter, she was woken at every stop by trackmen breaking the ice on the train wheels. She'd been granted forty-eight hours' leave and travelling would eat up most of it.

As the locomotive steamed through the fading, Friday afternoon, Vanessa got her first view of the capital in nearly five years. It was a city raped.

A giant flatiron had been randomly slammed down and familiar shapes were razed from the skyline. Windowless factories made her think of ruined monasteries. Where once there'd been residential streets, gable ends stood forlorn. Doorways remained absurdly upright, the homes they'd served vanished. Facades had been ripped away, leaving interiors naked to public gaze. Rubble lay everywhere. Gangs of men rammed pick-axes at the frozen ground, their faces lit by fires in dustbin incinerators.

By the time Vanessa stepped on to the platform at Euston station, it was dark and she was stiff with cold in spite of her thick, WAAF greatcoat. Thanks to innumerable hold-ups, she had only three hours in which to find the White Hart on Drury Lane. Three hours in which to recognise her dad and attempt to sew up nineteen years of separation. The prospect terrified her.

The White Hart had been Clive's choice and he'd telegrammed directions, though actually, she knew where the pub was.

Presumably, it was his local, Long Acre being only a short hop from Drury Lane. She wasn't keen on entering pubs alone, but he'd be waiting for her. And it would be warm! She was looking forward to a glass of port or ginger wine . . . anything to stop her teeth chattering. London cold was different from the dry, Scottish cold. City air tasted acrid, like a frozen cough from infected lungs.

As she walked as fast as she dared along the unlit streets, she pictured her dad waiting. Tall, with slick, black hair and twinkling eyes. A joke on his lips.

Clive had joked, but did Johnny? Clive was like the new moon, a sliver of a memory. Johnny was the dark of the moon.

London still retained the blackout, its street lights doused, windows, blanked-out with card or thick drapes. White squares painted on the kerb guided her feet, but she still got lost. It was like going blindfold. Only on her third tramp down Drury Lane did she look up and see the White Hart's unlit sign. Tugging the door with numb fingers, she was almost hurled off her feet by a man rushing out. His black cloak hung open to reveal old-fashioned evening dress including a starched waistcoat and white tie. He was ramming on a felt hat, as if he had hardly a moment to lose. As they moved in unison, unintentionally obstructing each other, the pub's door let light on to the pavement.

To Vanessa, the careless act felt like an insult to her dead husband and those of his comrades who had given their lives defending the approaches to London. She hissed, 'It's illegal to show light! If the bastards ever come back, this place might cop it.'

With contrary gallantry, the stranger pushed the door wider so she could pass through. Doing so revealed that his cloak was lined with red silk. 'Are we referring to the Luftwaffe?' he asked pleasantly. 'You're out of touch, gentle nymph. They don't fly over any more, they launch rockets at us.'

'Out of touch? I speak to men risking their lives in the air every day!'

'Ah; I suppose that beneath your coat is a uniform?' His voice held a deep vibrato. 'Are you going in, my dear, or patrolling the street for our protection?' His was an aging face with sagging jowls and an off-set dimple. Vanessa couldn't see his eyes, but she imagined them creasing with amusement. For some reason, she wanted to laugh too, but resisted and said with controlled exasperation, 'If there's such thing as fate, you're tempting it!'

'Fate? Of course it exists and I'd enjoy discussing the premise with you, but time has the better of me. I must run. Curtain's up in twenty minutes.'

The tang of cigar smoke and bay tree oil lingered after he'd gone.

Curtain's up. She'd been conversing with an actor. Calling her 'Gentle nymph' was flattering but hardly accurate. At just over five foot, Vanessa was short enough to qualify but her hair did not hang in tresses. It was neatly turned up under her cap. Nor was there any drapery about her person. Even her handkerchief was folded away in the webbing bag slung across her double-buttoned chest. Her coat had locomotive smuts and smelled of second-class carriages; stale cigarette smoke, mainly.

Inside the pub, she chose a door marked 'saloon bar'. From the doorway, she looked for her father. For Clive. A spotty boy in overalls leered at her, as did old men in caps, their rough cheeks attesting to a daily skirmish with blunt razors and second-rate soap. A tired-looking ARP warden glanced her way, then went back to nursing his pint.

There was a greying man with an old, chequered coat slung

across his knees, bashing out a tune on the piano and a barmaid levering the top off a bottle of stout. No dark-haired giant stood at the bar with a joke on his lips.

The pianist broke off as Vanessa swayed in the doorway. She didn't hit the ground, she tumbled into reality.

Her father had been an inch away from her, wearing a red-lined cloak and a deep-brimmed hat. She'd been looking for Clive, but Johnny had flitted past.

She would find herself back in London sixteen days later, crying tears she thought were locked hard away. And her return brought her into the orbit of a man more unfathomable than Clive – or was it Johnny? – Quinnell.

Chapter Two

Sunday, February 25th, 1945

'The Coffin Train, Miss?' The railway guard shook his head. 'Too late. Five years too late.'

It shouldn't have come as a shock to learn that the station serving London's biggest out-of-town cemetery had been flattened by a bomb early on in the war. This time, she was at Waterloo station, wrung out from this second trek from Scotland in a little over two weeks. It seemed as if London were hell-bent on obstructing her. She said as much, her voice grating because winter always summoned back her childhood hoarseness.

'Shout at Adolf Hitler, Miss, not at me,' the guard grumbled.

'I'm too exhausted to shout.' Inside her sturdy, flat shoes, her chilblains throbbed. Her stomach cramped for lack of breakfast. She'd hoped to find a tea stall, but the station concourse was deserted. It wasn't just early morning, it was Sunday. 'How would *you* travel to Brookwood Cemetery? I'm due at a funeral at nine.'

'Not a chance. It's already twenty past seven.' The guard seemed to draw satisfaction from the fact.

'I can't be late. It's my . . . Look, please, I have to get there.'

'Take the Woking service.' Moved by her distress, the guard led her to the correct platform. 'You won't need a ticket, I'm guessing?'

She was wearing uniform: a mark orf respect.

'I do.' The telegram had arrived late on Friday, leaving her no time to apply for a military travel warrant.

'This way, then.' The guard shepherded her to the ticket office, saying, 'I understand there's a branch-line from Woking that connects you to the cemetery proper. Good luck, Miss.'

At eight-fifteen, Vanessa boarded a two-carriage train and sank down on a bench seat. She rubbed her knees through her lisle stockings, achingly cold because in rushing for her train, she'd left her greatcoat behind. Her fingers were chapped because she'd also left her gloves on the last train. At least the Woking-bound locomotive pulled away on time. She'd make the funeral if everything went right from now on.

At Woking, she learned that trains no longer ran on the branch line. 'Haven't for years,' according to a porter. The cemetery, he informed her, lay five miles outside town. Vanessa cupped her hands to her temples. 'Bus?'

'Not for another hour. You've just missed one.'

'Taxi?'

The porter scratched under his cap. 'I saw one draw up to collect a military gent. As you're in uniform too, he might just—'

Vanessa was off. On the station forecourt, she looked vainly for a black car with a 'for hire' sign. A woman was parking a bicycle by the railings, and a farmer's cart was dropping off passengers. With stringent petrol rationing in force, people had returned to old methods of transport. The horse was stamping, its breath cloudy. She moved towards it and saw a motorbike and sidecar parked a little distance away. An orange pennant fluttered from the sidecar's roof. 'Taxi'.

The motorcyclist was buckling on his helmet but seeing her running towards him, he removed it. 'Sorry, love—' then, noting the silver wings and her propeller sleeve badge, he amended 'love' to 'Miss.' 'I've already got a passenger.'

'I can see that.' The sidecar was a double one, with space at the back for luggage, or a child. She was good at cramming into small spaces. Once, after a night at a dance, she'd travelled from Keith to Banff in the footwell of a troop truck. Squeezing under the dashboard had seemed preferable to sitting on the knee of a sozzled aircraftman. 'I'm hoping your passenger's inclined to share.'

'I shouldn't think so, Miss. Doesn't seem the sort.'

Vanessa looked in at the egg-shaped window. The occupant sat with his profile averted, neck muscles tensed as if he was checking a map or reading notes. Dark brown hair was cut bluntly around his ears. She tapped on the glass. 'Hello?'

Sidecars were not sound-proof containers. He must have heard.

She tried again. 'Excuse me!'

He was ignoring her and she wasn't surprised. The sleeve of his coat had three rings of gold braid, the innermost ring forming a loop. The coat was deep blue, and the peaked hat on his knee had the insignia of an anchor and gold leaves. This naval officer was a long way from the sea, probably on official business and with no time to humour a mere Leading Aircraftwoman. What she was about to do would cross a line.

But the line must be crossed. Vanessa opened the sidecar door. 'I'm terribly sorry, sir, I really wouldn't normally . . .'

'What?' More reprimand than question.

His eyes matched the day. So cold they stung her.

'I need a – I mean, I'd appreciate –' she lost her way under the austere gaze. He was quite young. She cleared her throat. 'I – uh – I have to get to Brookwood by nine. The burial ground? Only the branch line has closed. It's a funeral . . .' it would hardly be a party. 'It would save my life – ' What was wrong with her? 'I mean, it would help – '

'You need a lift.' The man removed his cap and papers from his lap and got out. Not easy for him and when he straightened up, she could see why.

He was over six foot, and powerfully built under his figure-skimming frock coat. Not far into his thirties, she reckoned. War promoted the young. Pushed men up the greasy pole. The greasy mast, in his case. His sparrowhawk gaze made her feel as if she was being dissected. Whenever she was anxious, she over-talked. 'I'm so terribly sorry to be a pest.'

'So you said.' He stood aside. 'You'll have to sit at the back.'

'Of course. It's very kind of you.'

'Not really. We're going to the same place.'

'Brookwood? You can't be going to my funeral – I mean, the one I'm—'

He levelled a brown-leather hand, cutting her off. 'Shall we get on with it? You're late already and I don't want to be.'

Like a chastened gundog, she lunged into the bullet-shaped vehicle, anxious not to expose too much thick, grey stocking. Scraping her cap on the ceiling, she plumped down on a shelf-seat, knees up against her chin.

A moment later, the officer took his place and she felt the chassis sink a little. She said without thinking, 'I hope the bike can haul our joint weight.'

'If it can't, you're getting out.'

He rationed his friendliness, for sure. But of course, this was a solemn journey for them both. Vanessa hugged her knees and felt the crackle of the latest telegram in her pocket. The one that had reached her as she sat down to supper in the cookhouse. A blow from an invisible cosh.

At the cemetery gates, the Navy officer eased himself out and held the door for Vanessa. As she stepped out, cramp zipped up the back of her calves and she pitched forward. He shot out a hand to catch her.

Inhaling two-stroke exhaust, she spluttered on his coat sleeve. 'Sorry.' To hide her chagrin, she searched for her purse inside her shoulder bag. 'You'll let me pay, Sir?'

'Certainly not. You'd better run. Do you know where you're going?' His voice was deep, but flat as though giving an order, and she realised that he wasn't seeing her at all. And it wasn't a map or a newspaper scrolled in his hand, but some kind of document. At some point during their journey he'd exchanged brown gloves for a pair of formal white.

She said, 'I'm going to see my father buried.' Without waiting for a reply, Vanessa ran through the cemetery gates, holding her skirt above her knees so it didn't hamper her. Guessing she'd missed the chapel service, she took a straight line into the landscaped grounds. Brookwood was a necropolis, a city of the dead, built in the Victorian age for London's surging numbers. It covered acres, and Vanessa understood why it had once had its own dedicated railway, the mournful sounding 'Coffin Train'. Intersecting paths cut through glades of conifer and birch, silvery in the frozen air. She stopped running when her throat hurt.

She dug out the telegram her mother had sent. 'Regret C J Quinnell dead. Funeral nine a.m., Sun 25 Feb.' It gave basic directions, and 'Interment at London parishes' ground, near columbarium.'

Columbarium? Didn't that mean a dovecot? Being the Sabbath, few funerals were taking place and she saw nobody she could ask for directions. When she met her own footprints in the frosty gravel, she knew she'd completed a hopeless circle.

'Press on, Kingcourt,' she muttered. Trying a different direction, she eventually stumbled on a domed and columned folly. A reasonable bet for the columbarium. A funeral was taking place close by.

Vanessa checked her telegram again. London parishes' ground? She wasn't convinced. The monuments in this section had a grandiosity to them. Some were miniature stone mansions – not for the likes of C J Quinnell, unless he'd enjoyed a success his letters had never let on. A horse-drawn hearse drew up, bearing a coffin whose brass fittings glinted. Men in black top hats lifted it to their shoulders. Joining the crowd of mourners, Vanessa saw that a tribute had been placed on top. Not flowers. Hothouse blooms were impossible to get, of course. No, the coffin was adorned with a heavy-bound book and a folded white opera scarf. A writer? A singer?

'What's the book?' she whispered to a woman next to her.

The woman was heavily made-up and swathed in chocolate brown fur. She glanced down at Vanessa, her leaded eyelashes fluttering. '*The Complete Works*, of course. Who are you, a niece or something?'

Vanessa ducked the question. 'Complete works of . . . ?'

'Shakespeare, who else? I'm sure we've met. Where would that be?'

Vanessa shook her head, and skirted around the crowd to get closer to the graveside. Where was her mother and her dad's friends? He'd had friends, surely? They weren't here, at any rate. This was a gathering of strangers. Most of the women wore furs and hats like black butterfly cakes. One or two of the men wore fur too. Nearly all wore silk scarves. Edwardian echoes.

You've messed up, Kingcourt. She'd have crept away had not her eye alighted on a man whose outer garment made her heart stutter. It was a black cloak, one side dandily turned back on itself to reveal a crimson silk lining. He wore a felt hat pulled forward. She gasped, 'Dad?'

People turned. The man turned. He was young, with light brown hair greased flat against his neck. Why wasn't he in uniform, a man of his age? And were black cloaks fashionable London-wear these days? She itched to know if this one smelled of cigars and bay rum. But somebody stepped between them and Vanessa was confronted with a different pair of shoulders. Navy blue shoulders, an athletic neck above a white collar. Her naval officer. He was wearing his cap and his white-gloved hands were loosely clasped behind his back.

He'll suppose I've stuck to him, like chewing gum.

The coffin was placed on the grass by the grave. Mourners surged forward, pushing Vanessa along with them. She felt her balance go and grabbed at the nearest support – the half-belt of a Navy frock coat.

Her officer turned. Vanessa heard him say, 'You?' but by now she was on her backside, on the ground. She held out her hands and he pulled her up.

His coat was closed with eight brass buttons, with ribbons and orders to the left lapel. The leaves and crown on his cap were gold bullion, the anchor worked in silver. This wasn't any old officer. The three cuff rings marked him out as a commander. Captain of a vessel? Had she run into him visiting her base or on board his ship, she'd have saluted.

He looked at her as he might at a coffee stain on an otherwise pristine cloth. 'Do we really belong to the same funeral?'

'I don't know. Whose is it?'

'Mr Wilton Bovary's. Did you know him? He is – was – an actor and theatre impresario.'

'I never met him,' she said miserably.

The officer's voice gained a rasp of distaste. 'Not a sightseer, are you?'

'Here for fun? Believe me, no.' She wanted to rub her bruised backside but her well-trained body insisted on standing to attention. 'I'm looking for the "London parishes" bit of the cemetery.'

'This is the actors' corner.'

'Then I'm in the right place, but it's the wrong man.'

The young man in the cloak turned at this moment, making a 'shush' motion. He'd pushed his hat back, revealing that he was good-looking in a full-lipped way. A Roman nose kept him from effeminacy but his light-brown eyes held a sulky expression. Extinct acne craters hinted at a troubled adolescence. He drawled, '*Artistes* are buried on Sunday, as are those of a more ordinary caste.' He pointed toward a path leading away through a spinney. 'Cut-price burials that way.'

'You've a vicious tongue, Edwin.' For the first time, Vanessa's officer showed warmth. 'The best tribute to pay Bo would be to imitate his kindness.'

'I never imitate and kindness is for fools. And don't patronise me, Commander. I'm Wilton Bovary's heir. What are you, exactly?'

'Twice your size, and his godson, so shut up.'

The young man shrugged, then scraped Vanessa again with his eyes. 'Couldn't you put on your best blues, dear?'

This Edwin was 'a cocky little snot' as Joanne Sayer, her best friend at base, would phrase it. What he couldn't know was that in spite of being small and wrapped in apology, Vanessa King-court grew steelier the deeper you dug. She said quietly, 'You won't mind me asking which of the services *you're* in?'

The scarred cheeks reddened. 'Flaming gall! Who are you? Have we met?'

'Never.' She leaned towards him and inhaled the tang of tobacco and bay oil. 'But I know that garment, *gentle nymph*.'

The young man's mouth twitched into a strange shape before he hurried away.

The man referred to as 'Commander' said heavily, 'I apologise. In my opinion, snobbery is the last resort of an empty mind.'

'You don't have to stand up for me, sir. I know I'm a mess.' Vanessa had left Banff in a tearing hurry, only throwing bare essentials into her bag. No eye makeup, no eyebrow pencil. Nothing to sustain vanity or protect her skin from the chill. She guessed her face was bluish with unnaturally rosy cheeks. 'I'm sorry to have intruded.'

Cutting through trees, following cocky Edwin's directions, she emerged into a sweep of ground devoid of headstones.

A little way off, three figures stood by an open grave. Two graveyard workers in mufflers and flat caps waited nearby with shovels. Vanessa knew she'd finally located the right funeral.

Chapter Three

'I'm so sorry, Mum, I got lost.' Vanessa took her place next to the woman in a slab-grey hat and raincoat and forced herself to look at the pine coffin at the grave's edge.

Welcome to third class, for cut-price burials.

There was no priest and the man and woman standing a respectful pace behind Vanessa's mother, were strangers. Strangers to Vanessa, anyway. The man nodded when he met her eye. He looked to be seventy or thereabouts, broad-faced with a heavy serving of jowl. Tufts of grey hair above his ears suggested a neglectful barber. His black, discreetly mended suit matched the worn bowler hat in his hands.

His companion was about the same age as Vanessa's mother. She wore a long coat that reminded Vanessa of pictures of her grandmother and great aunts. A black shawl enveloped her head like a mantilla, secured under her chin by an enamel brooch that gleamed like a jewel in a coal scuttle. At first, Vanessa thought she was seeing the woman in profile but no, there was a missing side to her face. The 'good' side showed that she must once have been handsome. The left portion was crushed inward and tram-tracked with burns. A horrifying mess. Vanessa looked away, confused by the interest that flared in one dark, undamaged eye.

'Who are those two?' she whispered to her mother. This was their first meeting in four-and-a-half years. Vanessa's postings since 1940 had been too distant for home visits.

'Shush. Friends of Clive's, they said. Except they call him "Johnny".'

'Stage friends, then. I won't forgive myself for missing the ceremony.'

'You didn't miss much. Whoever paid for this kept it plain and simple.'

'Who *has* paid?'

'The theatre he was working at. The vicar's fee, the coffin, everything. Now shush!'

The workmen lowered the coffin with the aid of ropes. Vanessa heard it bump on the bottom of the pit; they'd let go too soon. The men glanced towards Vanessa's mother as if to say, 'That's your lot, Missus.'

'Couldn't you have brought flowers?' Vanessa asked.

'February.' Ruth Quinnell had a 'no-waste' rule when it came to words.

'I don't mean florists' blooms. A bunch of Christmas roses . . . the Hellebores must be out at the front of the cottage by now.'

'Not this year. I can't garden as I used to. I'm not getting younger.' Ruth unlinked her arm from Vanessa's. 'Nine o'clock start, my telegram said.'

She's already edging away, Vanessa thought. As a child, she'd been afraid of her mother. Never a patient woman, her husband's desertion had sharpened Ruth's temper and made her hands itchy. Growing up, Vanessa had fantasised about her dad swooping in and fetching her away from Stanshurst. She'd imagined them together in a garret, he acting, she helping out in the wardrobe room . . .

Things had improved when Vanessa joined the school sixth form and taken a Saturday job in a Hayes greengrocer's shop. Ruth had mellowed as if Vanessa's accession to adulthood had removed a splinter or turned off a maddening background noise. Ruth had even occasionally called her 'dear'. They'd do puzzles together in front of the fire, go for walks. But when Vanessa announced her plan to go to London and art school, the 'off switch' had flicked back.

'Just like him, leaving me for The Smoke.'

Ruth had greeted her daughter's reappearance in uniform with studied lack of interest: 'You should have gone for nursing. Nurses are useful. What does the Air Force want girls for?'

Vanessa's hasty marriage had widened the rift. 'Who is he? What d'you know of him?'

As for her brutal tumble into widowhood . . . Silence. No questions, no sympathy.

Vanessa wanted badly to cry right now but a glance showed no similar gleam in Ruth's eyes. If she'd imagined her dad's death would bring them together, she must think again. 'There will be a headstone, won't there?'

In answer, Ruth gestured at the flat campus, where graves showed as unmarked hummocks. Early snowdrops and yellow, inch-high aconites were the only break in uniformity. 'This is what a person gets when they don't put anything by or plan for the future. When they give up an honest job for a life of self-indulgence.'

Vanessa sighed. The men clearly wanted to begin shovelling dirt on the coffin. It must have been back-breaking, digging this earth. 'Are we going to leave without saying anything?'

'Say a prayer if you want to but be quick. I'm half perished.'

A prayer. Or maybe a line from a play . . . But all that came were the most inappropriate words imaginable: *'We may save Briar-Rose from doom, if with noise we fill this room!'*

She turned towards the strangers, thinking that perhaps one of them might have a memorised line – but they had gone.

The men picked up their shovels. A moment later, the skittering of soil on wood signalled the ritual's end. Ruth Quinnell turned to go, wordlessly inviting Vanessa to follow.

'Not yet!' Heedless of the frost, Vanessa snatched a handful of aconites and snowdrops. Gold and silver rained down like charity on the unadorned coffin. Too little, too late. She asked the gravediggers to give her five minutes, and they retreated.

The coffin was of the cheapest, knotty pine. No gleam of a nameplate, just C J Q stencilled at one end. The red-lined cloak and dashing hat must have been to feign the appearance of success. 'Oh, Dad.' She'd had years in which to rediscover him and hadn't bothered. Too angry. And now, too late.

'Bye, Dad. You followed a dream. When this war finishes, I'll move you to a more befitting corner, with a headstone.' She dragged out her handkerchief. When the convulsion of grief was over, she looked around and found the woman in the long coat standing close by, watching her. 'What's your business?' jerked in shock from Vanessa.

The answer was unintelligible because the woman's mouth was a mess of scarring. Vanessa had seen badly damaged men crawl out of planes. She'd seen burns a-plenty, but this woman's flesh had been seared to the bones of her skull.

The woman made a gesture and Vanessa realised that she was being asked to hold out her hand. Most reluctantly, she did so and cold metal was placed in her palm. A key, a slender spike of gold.

'Yours – by right,' the woman said hoarsely.

'Mine? I've never seen it before.'

'Farren.'

'Is that your name?' Vanessa had heard of Nellie Farren, a burlesque actress of the late nineteenth century, but she was long dead, she was pretty sure. She tried to give back the key but the woman gestured in frustration.

'Wardrobe – hair ribbon. Child.'

'You're the lady at the theatre! You're . . .' the name shied off her tongue. Vanessa remembered ebony plaits, and the hair-ribbon the woman had tied into her own curls. Sea green. What had become of it? '*Sleeping Beauty*, Christmas. My father took me to meet you.'

A disturbing meeting. Ink on her fingers.

The woman replied by stroking Vanessa's cheek. Ignoring Vanessa's horrified start, she pointed to the grave and made a dumb show of ripping out her heart and throwing it to the ground.

A memory sprung at Vanessa, of a beautiful woman declaring, '*You tore out my heart, Johnny.*' This woman had loved her father. Loved him still. 'Eva! Your name's Eva!' It popped out, like a ripe pea from a pod. 'Did he abandon you too?'

The woman rasped, 'Johnny followed money.'

'What money?' Vanessa gestured to the grave. 'And please, his proper name was Clive.'

'Must go back.'

Vanessa looked past the woman, hoping to see the man with the bowler hat. 'Is your companion waiting?'

Wrong question, said the woman's ferocious gesture. '*You* go back. Farren.'

'Never.' Vanessa turned away, thinking that Eva of all people should know you can never go back. When she finally gar-nered the courage to face Eva again, she was alone but for the gravediggers wanting to resume their work. 'Where did that lady go?'

The elder of the two pointed towards the path Vanessa had come down earlier. 'Back to her cave, I should say. I wouldn't bother chasing her. This place is a wilderness if you don't know your way about.'

'She gave me this,' Vanessa said weakly, holding up the key. 'I don't want it.'

The man looked at it and grunted. 'Looks like proper gold. Hang on to it, sweetheart. It might unlock a treasure chest.' He looked down into Johnny Quinnell's grave. 'I don't suppose *he* left you much, did he?'

Vanessa found her mother at the pillared gates on Bagshot Road. Cars lined the kerb – private vehicles, a rare sight. Some people evidently had access to fuel. The mourners who'd been at the wealthy actor's graveside massed in small groups. A woman's confident voice rang out: 'I shall ride back in the Riley with Miss Shadwell and Miss Eddrich. See how I sacrifice my comfort, Patrick, so you may go in the Minx? Your legs are long, like George Washington's.'

'Abraham Lincoln's, I imagine you mean. Thank you, Noreen, but your sacrifice is not necessary. I shall ride in the Continental. We're giving the Commander a lift into London.'

Patrick, author of the resonant jibe, had fair-to-grey hair, worn a little longer than convention. He reminded Vanessa of the actor Leslie Howard, to whom she'd lost her heart in a country town cinema in '43, thanks to the US Airforce. USAAF planes had imported movies like *Gone with the Wind* along with chocolate, gum and nylons. She'd preferred Ashley Wilkes to Rhett

Butler. She had a weakness for fair men. 'Patrick' was tall and slim. He wore a rakish Homburg hat.

The woman trying to organise his journey was the one who'd earlier insisted that she knew Vanessa and once again, she wasn't giving up so easily. 'Impossible, Patrick dear. I'm taking the Commander back with me!'

'Not a chance, Noreen. It's all decided. See you at the wake.'

Vanessa turned away, disturbed by her ability to be amused while her father's body was even now being covered by stones and soil. She and her mother would take a bus to the railway station. For Vanessa, there was the pilgrimage back to Banff while Ruth would head home to Stanshurst.

'Can I arrange a lift for you?'

Vanessa jumped, though she was growing familiar with this imperious voice. Looking up into the solemn face, she thought, *He's handsome, but not in a comfortable way. I like how his cap squares off his face.*

She looked down, afraid her eyes were bleary with crying. 'No, thanks. I'm with my mother.'

'We can find space for two. Our car convoy will pass the station, if you're going back that way.'

'Yes, but . . .' her mother was already at the bus stop on the opposite side of the road. How to explain that the company of actors was anathema to Ruth? 'Rotten, stuck-up theatrical types' was Ruth's kindest epithet for them. *Actually*, Vanessa thought, I don't want to ride in an expensive car either, leaving my dad in a pauper's plot. 'I hate imposing on strangers.'

A smile moved the forbidding lips. 'If you ask me, they're the best people of all to impose on. Once you say goodbye, you never have to express gratitude again. Don't freeze for the sake of good manners. You can squeeze into one of the vehicles bringing up the rear.'

She knew he meant no insult, but it was sounding more and more like crumbs from the well-spread table. 'As I said before, sir, I hate imposing.'

'It isn't imposing while you're in uniform. Compassionate leave, I take it?' He answered himself with a nod. 'Where are you based?'

'RAF Banff, on the—'

'Moray Firth. I know it, though from offshore rather than land-side. You've come a long way.' He swept a hand towards his fellow mourners. He'd changed back into brown leather gloves. 'These people can put themselves out for you.'

'But not for my mother. And really –' emotion was working its way to the surface. He'd seen through her stubborn refusal, had unbent a little . . . sympathy was a killer. 'A car-ride will make the rest of my journey intolerable.' Giving a sharp salute, she tried to go but his hand wrapped round the crook of her elbow.

'Where are your gloves?'

She looked at her blue-red fingers. 'On a parcel shelf of the train I came down on. With a bit of luck, they'll make their way to Lost Property.'

Taking off his own supple tan pair, he enveloped her hands, passing on his blood heat. Her mind clogged with a profound sense of loss. Of missing something she'd never had. When she finally raised her eyes to his, her yearning slipped out. 'I wish I could take you on my journey with me.'

He didn't look affronted. 'I go only as far as Liverpool, a long way short of Banff.' He slid his gloves over her cold fingers, one hand then the other. He anticipated her objection. 'I have other pairs and yours are probably in the pocket of some heartless traveller, irretrievably lost.'

And so was she, she realised. Part of herself had split off, and was drifting towards this stranger. Her heart was a vacant lot and he'd taken possession. She could never have him. Not only was he wildly above her in status and rank, but by removing his gloves, he'd revealed a gold band on his wedding finger.

'Good luck, sir,' she said, her voice sticking in her throat. 'I hope—'

'Vanessa!' Her mother called from across the road. 'I don't want to miss our bus, thank you very much.'

This time, the man made no attempt to stop her but he said, 'Your name's Vanessa? Unusual. Pretty, too.'

'Vanessa was my dad's whim, though for some reason, he always called me "Toots".' She walked away.

'What were you up to? Who was he?'

The weather had deteriorated and needle-sharp sleet hit them slantwise because the bus stop had lost its roof. Vanessa sighed. 'He's a sea captain at an actor's funeral. You work it out, I can't.'

'Are those his gloves? You'd better post them back to him. He might make out you pinched them.'

'Why would he do that?'

'Never let a man think he can call in a favour. You have a way of looking at men. You peer up through your lashes.'

'Because they're so much taller than me! I don't like addressing their buttons.' *Please stop.*

'You rush in. That daft marriage should stand as a warning.'

'A flighty bit of goods, am I? Don't start on my marriage,

Mum.' Ruth had never once asked if she'd been happy with Leo. Ruth never asked anything that might open doors to intimacy. 'I can speak to a respectable naval officer without being called "fast".'

'He's almost certainly married,' her mother said as the bus drew up, its windscreen wipers lashing noisily back and forth.

'He is, and what does it matter? I'll never see him again.'

They found an empty compartment in the London train. As it huffed out of the station, Vanessa showed her mother the gold key. 'That poor woman wanted me to have it. Have you ever seen it before?'

'Not that I recall.' Ruth turned it over, a frown digging between her brows. 'It could be a theatre prop.'

'Far too small. Nobody would see it beyond row three.'

'Those two were theatrical types. *Her* coat came out of a theatre wardrobe and *his* smelled of lavender.'

'What does lavender prove?'

Ruth sniffed, as if to say, *Everything*. 'That face.' She shivered. 'Awful. I'd wear a veil. Two veils.'

'Who were they?'

'No idea.'

'I won't believe you stood in silence until I arrived, Mum. They must have said something, if only "Good morning".'

'The man came from London. I heard him saying that the mist was thick as onion broth this morning, and he walked smack into Covent Garden thinking it was Long Acre.' Finding nothing of interest in the key, Ruth handed it back. 'If this unlocked anything more valuable than a tea caddy, that woman would have emptied it by now.'

'She's Eva, not "that woman". But I think you know her. You *do* know her!' They were facing each other and Vanessa leaned forward, invading Ruth's space. 'Is she why he left us?'

When Ruth turned her face against the question, Vanessa tried a different attack. 'How did Dad die?'

'His heart stopped.'

'That's how everybody dies, when you think about it. What caused it?'

Ruth spoke as if the words were grit on her tongue. 'He drank himself dead. Two bottles of whisky and he fell unconscious on the floor. Nobody knew for days. Clive never drank the hard stuff when he was with me. That'd be her doing.'

At Waterloo, after the briskest of hugs, they separated. No time for a cuppa. Vanessa took the Northern Line tube for Euston. Sitting in a second class carriage, she ruminated on what she'd learned about her father's death. Halfway through their silent journey, Ruth had finally cracked and given her the details. The real cause had been the cold weather. Clive, it seemed, had inhabited a rented room. 'An ice-box by all accounts.' His electricity meter had yielded the grand total of eight pence. 'Nothing put in on the night of his death.'

The building's landlord had discovered the body on the Monday evening, three days after Vanessa had failed to meet her dad. The thought of it lacerated her.

As did the fact that she'd been writing to him at 'Room 7, Old Calford Building, Long Acre' without ever questioning why he was reduced to that single room. *I'm like Mum*, she whispered under cover of the rumbling train. *I don't ask the big, grinning question*.

She slipped off the Commander's fleece-lined gloves. They were quite worn, with a whitish scuff on the palm that might be salt and they smelled sweetly of leather. She dropped the gold key inside the thumb and wondered about Eva's face. A terrible road accident, a fall, a bombing?

Arriving at her stop, she told herself that Eva and even her father's death were secondary to the real business of her life – being a Radio Telephone operator in the Watch Room at RAF Banff. It was her job to relay radio messages from Coastal Command's strike wing, work that demanded intense concentration over long shifts. To take grief and confusion back with her would be unprofessional. Unpatriotic.

In time, she'd unwrap her father's last days. She would discover where he'd been rushing off to the night they nearly met. She might even push the little gold key into a lock somewhere and hear it click.

At Euston, she received the dispiriting news that her train was delayed. She slid the key into her pocket and pulled the gloves back on. A four-hour wait was predicted, and she knew well enough that such predictions had elastic sides. She bought tea and a wad of bread and margarine at a WRVS van outside the station, and was so famished she drank the tea down in half-a-dozen gulps and queued up for a second mug. After that, she sat in the station hall and allowed herself to think about her sea captain.

Not hers. Somebody else's.

At that exact same moment, Vanessa's captain was leaving the theatre where Wilton Bovary's wake had been celebrated. He flagged down a taxi and asked to be taken to a street near St James's Park thinking he'd snatch some time at home with his wife, Fern, before catching his train back to Liverpool where his ship waited. Getting out on Ledbury Terrace, he paid the fare and asked the driver to come back in one hour precisely.

Letting himself in with his own key, he was surprise to discover Fern in the hall, arranging winter leaves in a vase. She looked up. A little uneasily, he thought.

'You're early,' she said. 'Was it all right?'

'As much as a funeral can be. A good-enough send off, though I wish my godfather had died at the close of a long life. Sixty-five seems a paltry innings for someone who approached everything with such zest. I didn't stay long at the wake.'

'Was it at the Hungaria?'

He looked at her, puzzled. She'd asked the same question that morning and he'd told her, as he did again now, that the wake had been held on stage at Bovary's own theatre, The Farren. 'A throng of thesps, numerous agents, backers and critics. Elbow-to-elbow, drinks in hand, trying not to fall over the set.'

'Actually on stage?'

'Yes, though there was spillage into the orchestra pit and the front row stalls. You'll remember that The Farren's stage was built for intimacy.'

'In 1780. Darling, I'm not that old.'

'You know what I mean.' He kissed her, inhaling the perfume she'd eked out, drop by drop, since their last Paris trip in the spring of '39. 'It's set for tomorrow's matinee and before you ask, the show goes on, albeit with some re-casting. My godfather's sisters demanded it.'

'The redoubtable Sylvia and Barbara. I lunched with them once. They chewed their pork chops to the bone.'

'Good for them. I must say, *The Importance of Being Earnest* is a good play for a wake.'

Fern looked blank, so he explained, '"Scene: Morning-room in Algernon's flat in Half-Moon Street."' He evoked the setting with a sweep of the hand. 'It includes a sofa, several chairs and lots of little tables. Somewhere for the older folk to sit down, and those who dived too deeply into Uncle Bo's claret. What of you?' His eye fell on a vase filled with russet stems. 'How have you passed your day?'

'I've just come back from a stroll in St James's. I dusted off my Voigtländer and got some good shots.' Fern patted the nose of the compact camera poking from her cardigan pocket. 'The shadows inspired me.'

'I cut through the park this morning and everything looked pretty grey. Was it wise to go out in this weather?'

'Worried I might collapse from the cold, like your godfather? Incidentally, I wish you'd call him by his proper name. "Wilton Bovary" was a fitting name for an actor-manager. "Uncle Bo" sounds like a character from a nursery rhyme. You shouldn't claim him as your uncle, either. People will gossip.'

'Godfathers are honorary uncles. "Bo" was what my father called him from when they were schoolboys together. This morning you thought you were coming down with flu.'

That had been Fern's reason for missing the funeral. Alistair had wanted her to come. Though she hadn't known Wilton Bovary as long or as closely as he had, her mother had been Bo's very dear friend. 'You were feverish, you said.'

'So I was, but now I'm better.'

Alistair unbuttoned his coat. He had time for a bath and he wondered if Fern had prepared anything to eat. No tell-tale smells suggested that a quick dinner for two was on the cards. Yellow cheese and day-old bread, then. He was hanging his coat on the hallstand when her abrupt, 'Darling?' made him turn.

A stem of red dogwood quivered in her hand. His attention was hooked. He waited for her to continue.

'Darling, if you were ever to be unfaithful – you know, a

strange girl in a foreign port sort of thing – I just want you to know that I'd understand.'

'What?'

'I'd understand.' She was all fluid curves in a day dress of soft Burgundy wool, the long cardigan belted around her waist. Then, oblivious to the fact that she'd casually violated something sacred, she added the dogwood to the vase and sighed, 'I can't wait until we have roses sent up from Stanshurst again. When I think of the flowers I had to play with— good lord, Alistair!'

He'd stridden across to her and turned her to face him. In a voice that stripped the colour from her cheeks, he said, 'If you've ever imagined me standing in line outside a port brothel, cast the thought out. When I'm away for weeks, missing you, it's hellish. And yes, vows are tough but if they weren't, they'd mean nothing. How about you?'

She tried to wriggle away, but he kept hold. 'If we can't believe in loyalty, what the hell are we fighting for? What are *we* for? Have you any idea how many Navy wives have been left widowed? How many letters I've sent to mothers, wives and daughters, telling them their men won't come home? Have you ever considered the girls in uniform, younger than you, who are risking everything?'

He recalled the WAAF girl, whom he hoped was making good use of his gloves. Father buried, mother put on the train home, herself off to Scotland without breaking step. 'Surely, we owe them a little sacrifice in return? Fidelity is the base line, Fern. Where it all starts from.'

'Yes, yes, blanket agreement, Alistair.' Pulling free, Fern stalked across the hall and faced him from a distance. 'Stop glaring at me like a primitive head on show at the British Museum. I was simply saying—'

'That you imagine I sleep with prostitutes.'

'Oh, let's forget it.' She rubbed her shoulder. 'You hurt me, though why should I be surprised? We all know you have no conscience.'

'What do you mean, "we all know"? Who is "we"?' His tone would have shaken most men. It undoubtedly shook Fern, but she'd gone too far to retract.

She touched her upswept hair, bright as a polished sovereign against her pale skin. 'Ask the crew of the *Monarda*.'

Later, paying off the cabbie and passing under the Euston arch to get his train, he replayed the domestic scene and knew that a line had been crossed. That nonsense about infidelity was Fern being provocative and of course it disturbed him. But her final jibe was a kick below the belt. By referring to the HMS *Monarda*, Fern had passed judgement on his actions at sea that as a civilian she had no competence to make. And as wife, no right. '*Everybody says.*' Who did she know in London who was fit to offer an opinion on something that had happened in the North Atlantic, in a force-seven gale with forty-foot troughs and a wolf pack of German submarines closing in? Gut instinct said 'everybody' was in fact 'somebody'. *But who?*

Striding through Euston's great hall towards the platforms, his gaze cut through the milling crowds. He wanted no contact – until a pair of slim legs encased in hideous cotton lisle caught his eye. He'd seen those legs close-up today, as their owner squeezed out of a motorcycle sidecar. She was sitting on a bank of seats, looking half asleep. Still wearing his gloves.

'Are you all right?'

Her chin shot up, and surprise made her eyes large. He'd

noticed their colour at first meeting, light brown, like tide-washed amber.

She stood. 'My train's delayed. Freight stuck on the line in Hertfordshire. Fate wants to make my time in London as rotten as possible.'

'You believe in fate?'

'Actually, I believe in . . . very little.'

Her simple cynicism sliced through to his core. Meeting her in the cold outdoors earlier, he'd set her down as, 'A nice girl, somewhat scattered.' He now discovered the intelligence in her expression and a subtle beauty. Her face had the light strokes of a da Vinci – something her habit of looking away had hidden until now. Her mouth, undaubed by lipstick, was full and sensual, but turned down so unhappily he stepped out of character to offer comfort. 'Things will get better, you know. In the end.'

'I'm not sure they will. I'm drowning and the only ship that can rescue me is steaming away.'

So soon after Fern's accusation, her response struck like a blade. This girl must surely recognise a naval uniform when she saw one. At best, her drowning comment was grossly insensitive. He walked away.

'I'm so sorry.'

For two or three strides, he ignored her. Then, like an actor hearing booing from the stalls, he turned for a confrontation. She'd followed him, and looked devastated.

'I don't know what made me say that. I'm not myself. You have a ship somewhere—'

'I do, the *Quarrel*. She's at Pier Head.'

'And you've seen drowning men.'

'Too many.' He nodded a farewell. 'Good luck.'

'And you, Sir. The best of British.'

Vanessa arrived back at RAF Banff at six the following evening, having exceeded her leave by several hours. Her commanding officer was inclined to sympathy, however. Everyone knew what the trains were like.

As the weeks passed, a veil of unreality thickened between Vanessa and those London visits, until she imagined her father was still alive, doing six evening shows and four matinees a week in one of the lesser theatres. One day, they might meet somewhere between Shaftsbury Avenue and Trafalgar Square.

Another figure strayed in too. A figure who had no place in her imagination. A married man who might not survive the coming months, given that his profession was one of the most dangerous going. She didn't send back his gloves but kept them in her locker, with the golden key and her dad's letters. Life – and war – went on. Until . . .

On the 8th of May, 1945, Germany surrendered to the Allied forces. Victory unfurled throughout Europe. As Britain went wild with joy, the threads that linked Vanessa to her married captain – invisible to both – tightened. The same bands tied them to Clive 'Johnny' Quinnell, to a dissatisfied wife and to a dreadfully maimed woman. These threads were anchored to the stage of The Farren Theatre.

Chapter Four

Monday, May 28th, 1945

The white ensign of HMS *Quarrel* made a chalk line against the dawn sky.

Returning from her final voyage, she'd enjoyed swift passage and a stiff, onshore wind was pushing her faster than expected towards Liverpool Bay. As she passed between the Bar Lightship and Formby Point, the dusty shoreline hardened into the familiar sweep of their home port.

'Looks like we're a bit early, Pilot. Reduce engine speed,' the captain instructed the navigator standing at the compass on the bridge. 'Drop down to eight knots.' The ship was entering the funnel-mouth of the River Mersey, cutting a creamy arrowhead. Seagulls wheeled out to greet them, celestially white against pink, crabmeat cloud. A fine morning for a homecoming. Would it bring what all returners crave – a welcome?

The captain, Commander A W Redenhall, RN, flipped the question into the air like a philosophical coin. Will-she-won't-she? He'd been sailing in and out of Liverpool on convoy duty since the opening month of war. Not once had his wife met him or spent his shore-leave with him here. Fern was always too busy with her welfare work.

'Darling, there's a war on in London too, you know.'

With VE Day behind them, her one-sided rationale had run out. Alistair Redenhall was sailing towards a personal moment of truth. Two days ago, during the *Quarrel*'s refuelling at Londonderry, he'd sent a telegram:

To Mrs Redenhall, 12 Ledbury Terrace SW1

    Home Monday. Please be at POL — Port of Liverpool — Take suite at the Leasowe.

    Confirm arrival by message at Admiralty Office, Gladstone Dock. New beginnings.

Standing apart from the navigator and the officer-of-the-watch who shared the bridge with him, Alistair stared across the water to the city he'd last seen fourteen weeks ago. Its ragged outline reminded him of surviving teeth in a punched-out mouth. Roofless walls, the paralysed arms of cranes . . . Like London, Merseyside had been relentlessly bombed. Beyond Pier Head, devastation telegraphed itself in muzzy outlines with irrational gaps. Alistair felt a lacerating affinity for the place. Battered but alive. Ready for the next phase.

Over the coming weeks, the *Quarrel* — his *Quarrel* — would be sent for refit before being assigned to some new function. He didn't know where he would be this time next year, or even next month. It was why he wanted so badly to see Fern at the dockside. Her presence among the wives and sweethearts would prove that something was permanent. Actually, he just longed to see her.

'Sir? Sir?' The navigator had been trying to get his ear for some time, by the look on his face. 'Sir, the port authority can't spare us a tug. We've caught them on the hop — we'll have to dock unaided.'

The crosscurrents in the Mersey were devilish, but it was a devil they knew. Alistair broke into a faint smile as he answered, 'Good. We don't need to hold nanny's hand, do we?' The berth that had been signalled to them lay midway along the furthest of Gladstone Dock's three prongs. With the navigator happy with their speed and course, Alistair went to the bridge wing to watch the fo'c'sle party laying out wires and readying the anchor in case of an emergency. These ratings, overseen by their petty officer, would secure the ship when she came alongside. He would watch, but not interfere.

He'd always held to the belief that a captain's job was to train his men so well that he himself became superfluous. This ingrained standard did not stop him analysing every pulse and vibration as the ship's engines were thrown into reverse in preparation for docking. Nor did it stop him logging each order that passed between his First Lieutenant and the fo'c'sle party. Alistair listened, then moved his attention to the world beyond the ship's rail.

Gladstone Dock was where the anti-U-boat convoys had clustered throughout the war and Alistair took stock of every vessel in his sightline. Gun-grey decks, battle-scarred hulls, rivets bleeding rust . . . Destroyers like his own and any number of frigates. Recognising a couple of Flower Class corvettes, he was instantly pitched back on board the *Sundew*, a ship he'd joined as First Lieutenant and whose remains lay at the bottom of the Atlantic. From the *Sundew*, his mind jumped to her sister ship, the *Monarda,* whose destruction had taken him to the threshold of despair. After the *Sundew* was sunk, the Admiralty had given him the *Quarrel*. His first command, aged thirty. A shave young, some had suggested. Now thirty-two, he had many years at sea ahead of him. But it wasn't that simple any more. Entire, exhausted convoys had come home. He had come home. But did Fern want a husband with a shore job, or did she prefer him perpetually away?

'Sir?' This time, it was Crawford, the coxswain, barging into his thoughts. 'Sir, do you want us to "up-spirits" at the usual time?' The man was referring to the customary measure of rum doled out to the crew at eleven forty-five each morning. They'd be tied up by then, but the ship would still be manned.

'Your call, coxswain. Soon as we dock, I have to present myself at the Admiralty Office.' What he really meant was, 'I have a date with my wife.' Alistair conjured a seductive shape on a hotel bed, in a silk camisole, her rich hair spread over the pillow –

Recalling himself, he told Crawford – who seemed anxious at being handed a decision on the sensitive matter of rum – 'In general, I advise holding to routines.'

'Aye aye, sir.' The coxswain hesitated. 'Perhaps as it's our last trip, you'll join us in the Chief Petty Officer's mess for a tot? A toast to a successful homecoming, sir?'

'I'll join you if it all goes right.' Berthing a ship the size of the *Quarrel* was no piece of cake. Plenty of time to collide with another vessel or the dock wall. 'And I accept your implied criticism, Crawford. A captain who won't touch alcohol may be giving a moral example to his men, but it isn't necessarily one they want or ask for. I do have my reasons, however.'

'We get through tough times the best way we can, sir.'

Out of earshot, Crawford confided to the Chief Engineer, 'I don't get the captain. Doesn't drink, doesn't smoke. Doesn't you-know-what either, as far as I can tell. "Faithful unto death." His wife must be something special.'

'She's a titled lady,' replied the engineer. 'They're a demanding species.'

'Aye, well, I've often wondered if the captain's entirely human himself.'

Alistair's demeanour as the *Quarrel* nosed into her berth played into such doubts, but it was a false impression. He was not immune to the passions of ordinary men, he just hid them better. The light irises that pointed to Scottish ancestry held a piercing quality and some in the lower decks fancied that their captain could peer into men's souls. The prosaic truth was that Alistair knew how men were put together, could measure their courage and fear. He also knew every job on board and how it should be done. He was ice-cold with slackers. That, combined with a tough physique, had allowed him to imprint his personality on his ship and turn an ill-assorted tribe of men into an effective crew.

As they came alongside, the navigator stepped over and offered his hand. 'Home and dry, Sir.'

The fo'c'sle party cheered and waved their caps in reply to the greetings from the jetty. It was eighteen minutes past six on a Monday morning and Alistair Redenhall and his crew had survived five-and-a-half years of hell. He scanned the quayside crowd. There were many female figures but not the one he longed for.

He handed over to his second-in-command and went ashore. He was welcomed at the Admiralty office by a petty officer, who informed him that no message had arrived.

'In that case, may I make a telephone call? Long distance.'

He was shown into an office where he dialled the operator, gave the exchange as Whitehall and recited his four-digit home number.

'We'll put you through as quickly as possible, Sir.'

He settled down to wait. A city-to-city call required the cooperation of multiple exchanges to set up a line. It could take an hour or two. Or all day. Tightness crept into his gut. Minutes ticked by and when a staff member brought him a cup of tea, it tasted metallic. He got his line in just over an hour.

'Putting you through, sir.'

His mind's eye filled with the elegant interior of Ledbury Terrace. He saw the hall table with its vase of artistic twigs, a side-console studded with silver-framed photographs where the telephone would be screaming like an angry baby. He didn't count how many rings, but surely there were enough for Fern to put on a dressing gown and come downstairs. He was about to hang up when somebody picked up.

Three words later, Alistair's hopes of a happy homecoming were dead.

Chapter Five

Gilmore & Jackson, Solicitors
South Audley Street, W1

May 30th, 1945

To Cdr Redenhall RN
C/o Colonial and Overseas Club

Dear Sir,

We write in connection with the recent death of our client, Mr Wilton Bovary, for which we offer our heartfelt condolences. As a friend, he will be much missed. Your godfather died in February at the theatre bearing his name and it is in respect of the same that we request you attend our offices as soon as may be convenient to you. We have information of a beneficial nature to pass on.

Yours faithfully,
P Jackson

A week after receiving this letter, Alistair called in person at South Audley Street. Reeling from what he'd just been told, he walked from the solicitors' officers to his club where he'd been staying since returning to London. Long. Evening light breathed gold over the weary streets, and he stopped to admire a magenta clematis that coiled around the brick pillars of a bomb-site. Today was the 7th of June. It would be a summer of peace. Would he find it hard to live without the single-minded pressure of war? He cut through Green Park, where the vege- table plots that were cut into the lawns threw up ripe farmyard smells. An hour ago, Mr Jackson had informed him that he'd inherited 'The freehold of The Farren Theatre, Farren Court, London and the controlling share of "The Farren Theatrical Company".' A leasehold property in Cecil Court WC2 was now his, along with chattels and residuary estate. In short, everything of his late godfather's 'with the exception of certain monies held in trust'.

To prove it, a heavy set of keys jangled in his pocket.

As he walked, Alistair tried to unravel his godfather's motives. If you're going to die and bequeath a theatre, who do you choose? Your sisters who were born backstage with you? Your nephew, a little shit, but also born to the greasepaint – or somebody who spends three hundred days a year at sea and doesn't know one side of a stage from another?

'Bo, your sense of humour lives on.'

At Pier Head, Alistair had evoked the heavenly powers to restore his marriage and had been given a theatre instead. What the hell was he going to do with it?

Two hundred miles north, at RAF Banff, Vanessa Kingcourt made her way to the cookhouse where she and her friends,

Joanne and Peggy, groaned in unison at the familiar smells of boiled brassica and sweated meat.

'Half-a-crown says its rissoles.' Peggy Williamson's voice was like a ribbon stretched tight, its edges folding inwards. They'd all had the day off, having completed an eleven-and-a-half hour shift on the previous one. The effects were still with them.

Vanessa agreed, 'It's Friday. Bound to be, unless it's fishcakes from yesterday.'

A group of pilots made room for them at a table and, over a meal of mashed potato and the inevitable rissoles – fried corned-beef fritters – they talked about the NAAFI dance that evening. Finn Karlstad, a Norwegian pilot of the 333 squadron, with hair the colour of ash wood shavings, asked Vanessa to come as his partner.

She told him she needed to catch up on sleep. It wasn't strictly true. Someone from the Control Office had given her a letter and she recognised her mother's writing. Ruth's letters were usually as spare as her conversation, but this one contained more than just paper. Hearing her intention to 'grab an early night,' however, her friends howled in protest. Kingcourt, missing a dance? The squadrons were disbanding now that the coastal and anti-submarine patrols were winding down and in a week, the Norwegian boys would fly home.

'This will be the last dance ever,' Finn said sadly. 'It is your duty to be my date.'

'I reckon she's got another fellow.' Joanne Sayer subjected Vanessa to close examination. They'd arrived in the same troop-van during the summer of '43, and for a while, had been the youngest females on the base. Theirs wasn't always a comfortable friendship. Joanne had been an actress before joining the

WAAF; she had poise by the bucket, and liked to tease. 'A new man is the only feasible explanation.'

Vanessa blushed. A reaction to being stared at, but that just made them press harder. 'Can't I curl up and read a letter in peace?'

'Not on Friday night.'

'Peggy stays in sometimes.'

'Special dispensation.' Joanne always had an answer. 'Hair-washing is a religious duty for Peggy these days.'

Peggy Williamson was to marry soon. She preferred to stay in and knit socks for her fiancé, a pilot from nearby RAF Leuchars.

Vanessa caved in. 'Fine. You win. But I'll meet you there.' Quickly finishing her meal, she made her way to the 'Waffery', the fenced-in huts that housed female personnel. As a Leading Aircraftwoman, she was spared dormitory living, sharing a room with one other. Flashing her identity card to the guardhouse sentry, she entered her quarters. Quietly. Her roommate was catching up on sleep.

Vanessa opened her letter and extracted one flimsy sheet and a piece of eggshell-blue card, folded in four. The card was a theatre playbill for *The Importance of Being Earnest*. The room was too dark to see any detail.

Walking over to the admin block, she knocked at her head of section's door, saluted and asked to borrow a reading lamp. She was offered the use of the desk for five minutes. The head of section tactfully withdrew. Vanessa sat down and shone the lamp on the playbill.

'Mr Wilton Bovary presents Oscar Wilde's enduring and enchanting masterpiece . . . opening 27th January 1945 at – '

The hairs rose on the back of her neck. *At The Farren.* Eva had whispered the name by her father's grave, invoking memories of *Sleeping Beauty*, and a fairy in crow's feathers and another in lilac gauze. Laying down the playbill, Vanessa read the accompanying letter which was every bit as brief as her mother's usual offerings.

'This was with your father's things. Thought you might like it as a memento.'

Returning to the playbill, Vanessa scanned the cast-list. 'John (Jack) Worthing . . . Patrick Carnford.' The fair-haired man at the Bovary funeral had been called Patrick.

'Algernon Moncrieff . . . Ronald Gainsborough. Lane, man-servant to Algernon Moncrieff . . . Mr Wilton Bovary.'

Her scalp tingled as she read: 'Rev Canon Chasuble . . . Johnny Quinnell.

Something finally made sense. Her dad had rushed out of the White Hart because he'd been due on stage at The Farren. 'Curtain's up in twenty minutes!' He'd been performing alongside Wilton Bovary, who, according to the credits on the back of the playbill, had owned The Farren as well as taking stage roles. How had both men come to be buried in the same cemetery on the same day? If she'd been on time that fateful Friday, would her dad still be alive? If she learned nothing else in her life, she'd have the answer to that. But how?

Returning to her billet, she discovered her roommate was up and dressing. The girl eyed Vanessa's crumpled uniform. 'You'd better get a wiggle on if you're going dancing. Can't you hear the music?'

Vanessa hadn't heard a thing. Which was inexplicable as the wail of saxophones played to a swing beat swelled across the compound, piercing the hut's walls.

Her roommate made an offer. 'Do my shift if you like; I'll dance in your place.'

'Sorry, I've a date.' Vanessa grabbed her towel and tore across to the ablutions block where she washed and dashed cold water on her face. Dashing back to her room, she put on the shirt she'd washed and ironed earlier. Everyday clothes were forbidden on base, putting style beyond the reach of any servicewoman who hadn't the good fortune to be tall and slender. They all did their best, shining their buttons, starching their collars, so that by the night's end, they would all have chafed necks.

After knotting her tie, she put on her least-worn skirt and her parade jacket with its wings insignia and the 'props' badge that had come with her most recent uplift in rank. Breathing in, she pulled the belt as tight as it would go. Next, she drew on silk stockings. A violation of uniform, silk – whether as stockings or underwear - could get you put on a charge but it was worth it to fling off suffocating passion-killers for an evening. Black court shoes replaced her regulation lace-up "beetle-crushers".

Using her powder-compact mirror, Vanessa teased curls on to her brow before pinning her cap at an angle. Eye shadow and a slick of cherry lipstick finished her preparations. She was ready to dance, grateful to the friends who had vetoed her night in.

'Where were you?' Finn demanded as she wriggled through the crush in the sergeants' mess. A raucous trumpet proved that tonight they had a real, live band. He took her through the boiling mass of airmen, pilots and WAAFs to the bar where the reek of beer was stupefying and the floor was sticky.

'What to drink?'

'Whatever you're having,' she yelled and discovered she'd said 'yes' to a pint of beer. No such thing as 'ladies' measures' at this bar. She wasn't mad about beer, but a small sherry wasn't going to hit the spot tonight. When Finn took her to dance, she surrendered to the heat, to the music, to his arms, but couldn't rid herself of the idea that, just as her life here was ending, another crucial choice was beckoning.

When the band took a rest and they all spilled outside, Vanessa located Joanne. 'There's something I want you to look at.' Vanessa shone a borrowed torch on the playbill.

Joanne squinted. '*The Importance*— oh, The Farren! I worked there . . .' she raided her memory, '1938, a spit and a cough part. "Very good, milady" and "At once, milord". The critics went wild. Why am I looking at this?'

'I'm hoping you'll remember my dad. He's in this play. *Was*, I mean.' Joanne knew of Vanessa's father's death, though not the seedy circumstances.

'Ooh, which part?' Joanne accepted a cigarette from her dance partner, lifting her chin so he could light it over her shoulder. Dark-haired with slanting eyes full of the quality people call 'it', Joanne Sayer cut the most glamorous figure on base. She enriched the image with a gold cigarette holder between lilac-painted nails. Nail varnish was strictly forbidden, but apparently nobody had informed her.

Vanessa said, 'He played Canon Chasuble.'

'Miss Prism's love-interest. "My metaphor was drawn from bees". What was your dad's name again?'

'Clive Quinnell, stage name "Johnny".'

'Johnny Quinnell . . . of course. I've definitely heard of him.' Joanne's smile was a little too tactful. Vanessa knew she was lying.

She asked, 'What's The Farren like?'

'Cosy – seats four hundred, which is nothing. Tucked away, you have to know how to find it. The same actors go back time and again because Mr Bovary, who owns it, is a sweetie. An old-fashioned actor-manager. A dying breed.'

A dead one. Joanne clearly hadn't heard the news about Wilton Bovary. Staring out across a dark pelt of grass to where the concrete runways reflected the rising moon, Vanessa smelled the heady cocktail of moorland heather, sea salt and aviation fumes. Would she miss this place? Or just the friends? 'Is it easy to get a job in theatre?'

Joanne laughed. 'Are you burning to act?'

'Not a bit. I'd want to be behind the scenes.'

'You could get work as an ASM, Assistant Stage Manager. Lousy pay. Don't you want to go back to your studies?'

'No. What pays better?'

Joanne exhaled a stream of smoke. She was moving her hips because the band was playing again. Any moment they'd re-join the dancing. 'If you claimed your widow's pension, low pay wouldn't matter so much. Why don't you?'

'I can't. It's complicated . . . what other jobs are there, ones I could live on?'

'Props, lighting, set design, though those can be very "jobs for the boys". There are women scene painters. Yes,' Joanne peered at Vanessa, as if struck, 'I can see you daubing away in a pair of natty overalls, up a ladder. It would have to be a long ladder.'

'Scenery . . . right.' It wasn't ringing bells for her. 'How would I start?'

'I'm joking! You're an educated woman. Go back to art school, finish your degree. Then at least you could teach. Theatre's so precarious; you can easily spend thirty weeks out of fifty-two not being paid. I see you teaching in a nice girls' school, with a regular salary and a pension attached.'

'How odd. I can't. What about –' Vanessa prepared for Joanne to laugh – 'theatre costume? Wardrobe.'

Joanne looked dubious. 'Trouble with Wardrobe Mistresses,

they die in harness. Or when they finally retire, they hand their jobs on to their daughters or nieces. It's deeply nepotistic . . . is that a word? Though I know you can wield a needle, because I'm wearing the parachute-silk knickers you made me.'

'My mother says I'm a terrible seamstress. But she judges me on things I made at infant school. It was always me who put the costumes together for school plays and carol services.'

'If you're serious, start writing letters, because all the old theatre hands will be demobbing soon and you'll get knocked down in the rush.'

'I *am* serious . . . My dad dying the way he did— Joanne?' But her friend had gone away to dance. Vanessa followed, looking for Finn. As she went, she touched a cord around her neck, looped through the head of a golden key. Something told her that whatever it unlocked lay in a small, hard-to-find London theatre. Which, by hell or high water, she'd revisit some day.

On Joanne's advice, she took out a subscription to *The Stage*, the newsprint bible of the theatre industry. She was prepared to grab the lowliest opportunity to get her foot in the door.

High summer arrived, and with her demobilisation date set for autumn, she scanned ads for a position in wardrobe. Whenever one jumped out, she wrote, enclosing a reference from her commanding officer.

It was a failure. Mail travelled so slowly, the jobs were filled by the time she made contact with whoever was recruiting. She called those theatres that included a telephone number in their ads, telling herself that if she could survive an air attack, she could survive a chat with a brusque manager. One after another, they dashed her hopes. They all wanted someone with 'credible experience'. That meant at least one season as a professional, paid wardrobe mistress. On one occasion, as she described running up costumes for school plays, the man at the other end laughed. 'Didn't we all, darling. Try am-dram.'

She had to ask Joanne what that meant.

'Amateur dramatics. Nessie, are you sure you want to put yourself through this?'

The short Scottish summer passed, and on September 3rd, 1945, Vanessa became a civilian again, six years to the day since war was declared. She returned to Kent with her discharge papers, a suitcase containing items of uniform she'd been allowed to keep and a small wad of clothing coupons, courtesy of a grateful government. Rather than sign on to the unemployment register, she became personal secretary to Lord Stanshurst, her dad's former employer. His Lordship's late wife had employed Vanessa's mother for many years. The Quinnells had occupied a grace-and-favour house within Stanshurst Park, until Johnny's defection. It was almost too much history, and Vanessa's throat became inflamed the day she took up her new job, as if at some level, she'd assumed the collar of servitude.

And it was dull work, letter writing and administering his Lordship's much-diminished payroll. Her predecessor, recently retired Mrs Mancroft, had run the estate office in a state of inspired muddle. She'd left no instructions or briefing notes and for the first month, Vanessa waded through files until her eyes swam. At least she had a typewriter at her disposal, and plenty of good-quality pre-war paper. On quiet afternoons, she'd write application letters to London theatres. Once, she wrote directly to The Farren, using the address on her father's playbill, offering herself in any backstage capacity they might require. For that letter, she used her maiden name, thinking 'Quinnell' might chime with somebody and improve her chances.

Within a few days, she received a reply: 'Thank you for your letter, which has been placed in our files. We regret that The Farren is closed and there are no immediate prospects of its reopening.'

It was signed 'Miss B Bovary'.

Her mother was pleased to have her home. Not because Ruth particularly enjoyed her daughter's company – Peach Cottage was so tiny, they couldn't help but intrude on each other – but because it gave her a window into Stanshurst Hall. Ruth Quinnell had been Lady Stanshurst's social secretary. She still referred to 'My Lady' as if her late employer were eavesdropping from the next room and not buried in the family mausoleum. At each day's end, Ruth greeted Vanessa with, 'Who did you write to today? Did you speak with his Lordship?'

Something in the way Ruth said 'His Lordship' hinted at admiration. Adulation, even.

Lord Stanshurst was overwhelmed by debt. During hostilities, his home had been commandeered for use by the RAF's School of Navigation, and had been handed back bearing the scars of occupation. He had no money to make repairs, and was crushed by the idea that after his death, he would leave his son a bankrupt title.

The election of a Labour government in July had knocked a final nail into the coffin of his world. 'It'll be a life of taxation with only death duties to look forward to,' he told Vanessa one afternoon. It was by now November, and the absence of central heating at the Hall had turned from a mild joke into a danger to health. For days now, Vanessa had been typing in woollen gloves with cut-off fingers. Finally, unable to concentrate, she'd lugged her typewriter down to the kitchen, dragging the table close to the coal-fired range which was the only reliable source of heat. Lord Stanshurst came down in search of a cup of tea and Vanessa made a pot for them both.

He drank his leaning against the range. He was a lanky man in worn but bombproof tweed. 'Chris should be here, lending a hand,' he complained. 'Not hanging about in Paris.' His son, Christopher, had been a prisoner of war in Germany but instead of coming home on his release, he'd accepted a post with the British Embassy helping to process British citizens making their way back from various corners of Europe and North Africa. 'Apparently every lost soul heads for Paris. A sort of homing instinct.' Lord Stanshurst shook his head in bewilderment. 'And poor Fern . . . Did you know, her husband has moved out of their home and is quitting the Navy?'

'No, sir.' Despite the difference in their education and social status, Vanessa and Fern had been great friends throughout their childhood. Lady Stanhurst, Fern's mother, had encouraged the friendship, declaring that 'little Nessie' brought out her headstrong daughter's kinder side. Vanessa's departure to art college and Fern's to a Swiss finishing school had separated them but they'd met again after Vanessa was posted to Biggin Hill. At the time, Fern had been escorting evacuee children from London into rural Kent. Several of them had ended up at the Hall.

'I never met Fern's husband,' Vanessa said. 'When you say "moved out" . . . ?'

'Quit. Packed his bag. I wish her mother were still here.'

'Wasn't it Lady Stanshurst who introduced Fern to her husband?'

'In Malta, yes. Margery liked to match people, but I'm not sure that marriage was her finest hour. Still, she'd have got the two of them together for peace-talks and there'd have been no scandal.' Lord Stanshurst stared hard at Vanessa. When a tear slipped down his cheek, she realised he was giving way to emotion. She pretended to type so he wouldn't know she'd noticed.

'Perhaps they'll see sense,' she said bracingly. 'Give them time to adjust to each other.'

'Everything's crumbling. Manners, tradition . . . Redenhall, leaving *my daughter*. I can only suppose the *Monarda* business did something to his brains. Having his first ship torpedoed under him couldn't have helped either. The *Sundew* sank in under twelve minutes, he told me.'

'*Sundew*?'

'His corvette. Blown up by a U-boat in '42, all hands drowned bar a dozen. Fern thought it might put the brakes on his promotion, but they gave him a new command within weeks. A destroyer, HMS *Quarrel*. Who thinks up these names? A blessed bad omen.'

Vanessa's fingers stilled on the keyboard. Comprehension arrived in formation, several thoughts at once. Her sea captain had been on his way back to board the *Quarrel* at Pier Head. There couldn't be two ships with the same name. She knew that Fern had married a sailor in Malta. 'He's strong and doesn't smile much,' she'd written to Vanessa after the wedding. 'We're setting up house near St James' Park. Smart, no?'

'Heaven help me, I think I've fallen for my oldest friend's husband,' Vanessa whispered as Lord Stanshurst noisily swallowed his tea, oblivious. 'But now I know, I can avoid him.' Then it burst on her. He'd survived the last weeks of war. Alive. And that was wonderful.

Vanessa applied for theatre jobs up until Christmas 1945 but Joanne's prediction had been spot on. Thousands of former theatre employees had left the services and were competing to get back into an industry that was struggling in an atmosphere of rationing and gloom.

The year turned. 1946 arrived.

As the snow melted on the Kentish Weald, Vanessa took solitary walks and whenever she was a mile clear of the nearest habitation, she'd scream into the sky, 'Let me live the life I'm supposed to be living!'

She needn't have worried. Becalmed existences always start moving eventually.

Lord Stanshurst inadvertently put the wheels in motion by writing to his daughter and son-in-law separately, inviting them to Kent to give their marriage another go. 'There has never been a divorce in this family.' He heard nothing from either at first. Fern was currently in Paris, 'resting'. Commander Redenhall was serving out his time in the Navy, on Baltic patrol, captaining a sister ship to the *Quarrel*.

To Vanessa, Lord Stanshurst expressed disbelief that Redenhall was leaving the services. 'I had him down as a career sailor.'

It was late summer before Lord Stanshurst's invitation was accepted by both parties. On August 14th, Alistair cabled that he'd be at Stanshurst by the 20th. Fern arrived a day earlier, bursting into Vanessa's office, her coppery hair falling in curls over her shoulders.

'Darling Vanessa, Pops told me you were here. Some sanity at last! Poor Mrs Mancroft would have signed her own execution order if someone had put it in front of her. Oh, I was so sorry to hear of your dad, by the way. Did you get my card?'

''Fraid not, but thanks.'

'Bloody post. Shall we run through the orchard together, like old times?'

'The orchard's full of wasps raiding the fruit.'

'Ugh. Like life! I can't tell you how much I'm dreading these next few days. I suppose Pops has told you, Alistair and I are estranged. Isn't *estranged* a ghastly word?'

Vanessa observed her old friend closely. She saw a chic outfit. A coiffeur charmingly ruffled from a long journey. Meticulous makeup and professionally shaped brows framed hazel eyes that showed no trace of recent tears. Fern was like her father, putting on a good face for the world.

Vanessa thought, I owe her whatever comfort I can give. In the days following Vanessa's widowhood, Fern had called at Peach Cottage. Rather than sit with Ruth fussing over her, she'd dragged Vanessa out for a walk. Once clear of the village, she'd said, 'Nothing shocks me except for cruelty to animals and dirty nails. If you want to talk, my ears are at your service.' For a mile or two, Vanessa had said little. But, encouraged by Fern's silence, a dam had broken, and things she'd hardly admitted to herself poured out. Fern had listened without passing judgement.

It would require finesse, supporting Fern while avoiding Fern's husband. Vanessa cringed, imagining Alistair Redenhall's reaction should he discover that she was a spectator at yet another harrowing moment of his life.

Fern fanned herself with her kidskin gloves. 'This heat! I'm going outside. Join me.'

'I'll just finish off.'

She found Fern on the loggia, pulling weeds from between cracks in the paving stones. It was wiltingly hot out here as well, and Vanessa suggested they try the woods bordering the park.

Chapter Six

As they walked through Hunter's Copse, a patch of ancient woodland bursting with dog violets and honeysuckle, Vanessa expressed her long-stored gratitude. 'You gave me my life back, Fern.'

'After your husband died? No doubt I was the only person who didn't say, "Pick your chin up, Kingcourt, and press on!" I never have done "stiff upper lip" very well. I know the healing power of letting it all blub out.'

'I did blub, didn't I? I couldn't cope with the fact that I'd lost Leo in the blink of an eye. But that wasn't the first time you came to my rescue. After my dad left, my mother went to pieces and my Aunt Brenda came to stay.'

'I remember her.' Fern exaggerated a shudder.

'Whenever I asked for Daddy, she'd tell me I was naughty little girl, plaguing my mother. The village children snickered; their mothers stared. I felt utterly bewildered, abandoned, and I stopped speaking. If you hadn't called round and asked, "Can Vanessa come out to play, please?" I'm not sure I'd ever have said another word.'

Fern made a self-deprecating gesture. 'I heard your silence was because they'd botched your tonsil operation.'

'No. I stopped talking because I thought Daddy leaving was my fault.'

'How could it be? You were five.'

'I was just six.'

'So grown up!' Fern draped her arms over a low bough, fixing Vanessa with cynical humour. 'Marriages are not made in heaven, they're made by well-meaning amateurs and some break sooner than others. My parents bamboozled a show of phony happiness for years.'

'I thought they adored each other!' Vanessa could still picture Lord Stanshurst watching Lady Stanshurst riding out to join the local meet on a raking hunter, murmuring, 'Best horsewoman the London stage ever produced,' a reference to his wife's time as a West End actress before her marriage. 'I thought your parents adored each other,' she said. True, she'd heard hints over the years that Lady Stanshurst's passions and foibles clashed with the customs of rustic aristocracy, and that in marrying her, his Lordship had allowed love to cloud wisdom. But if their happiness had been a fake, then it had been a good fake.

Yet Fern seemed to be saying exactly that.

'I dare say it started well enough.' Fern tipped her mouth wryly. 'But once my brother and I were away at school, their marriage became a polite dance, and I doubt she and Pops spent more than a month in each other's company in any year. Marge would go to London or up to our Scottish estate at every opportunity. Or to Malta, which suited her best. Malta is out of gossips' range, d'you see? What do parents like yours do, stuck in one home?'

'Endure. Or split. Did you always call your mother "Marge"?'

'I started off calling her 'Miss Bowers'. Her stage name was Margery Bowers, but it upset her because she missed the stage so badly. We settled on "Marge", which amused her. Actually, it was her lover's idea.'

'She had a lover?'

'Oh, listen to that song thrush! I love this wood. I love Stanshurst, never more so than now when it's so fragile.'

Vanessa wanted to ask, *Must every good memory crumble?* but Fern's revelations made that seem insensitive, so she murmured instead, 'Things change without our permission.'

'New beginnings.' Fern sighed. 'How I long for them! But to have a new beginning you have to crash through the inevitable ending.'

She reached for a springy branch. Tall, with the curves of a long-pattern violin, she'd reached a new level of beauty since Vanessa had last seen her. The elder by three years, but miles ahead in sophistication. Her complexion defied the privations of a ration-card diet, while her eyes reflected the greenery around her. So many boyfriends had clustered about Fern, Lord Stanshurst had joked about charging a fee to receive them. Her choice of a naval sub-lieutenant from an untitled, northern family had shocked some.

Vanessa had heard that at the wedding reception, Lord Stanshurst had announced his certainty that his son-in-law would one day be 'Admiral Sir Alistair Redenhall'. Not now, he wouldn't be. Vanessa couldn't imagine Redenhall in anything but uniform, but then, she shouldn't be imagining him at all. 'You *will* give things another go, won't you, Fern? After what your husband's been through, he deserves another chance.'

Black-tipped ash pinged and wagged as Fern let go of her branch. A smile crept to her lips, which were painted a terracotta shade. 'Did you enjoy being a WAAF? I never quite knew what you did. I know it was Signals.'

'Changing the subject? I was one of the golden-voiced lovelies who kept radio contact with pilots or their wireless ops while they were flying. If they were in trouble, we'd guide them home.'

'Did they swear?'

'I'll say! Not *at* us, not usually. Only when they were really in trouble. Engines crippled, a rear gunner dead, a fire on board or not enough fuel to get across the water . . . You could hear the fear in their voices. We took notes verbatim so if they didn't make it back from an operation, we had a chance of knowing if they'd completed the mission or not and where they might have crashed.' Talking and writing, ears full of crackle and echo, it had been hell at times. Reading the notes back when you knew a crew wouldn't return had felt like eavesdropping on death.

'I'd have liked to have been a WAAF plotter.' Fern swung under her branch and they continued walking. 'They were the glamour girls, weren't they, leaning across the tables like croupiers at Monte Carlo.'

'There was a little more to it than that. What stopped you?'

'Marriage. It stops a lot of things.' Fern became serious again. 'Look, you know Alistair and I are a lost cause? I know Pops is distraught, but I can't help that.'

'What went wrong?'

Fern gave a defiant shrug. 'I'm not the only woman who has discovered that six years' conflict has reshaped her husband's character. And sailors are notorious, aren't they? Apparently, to some women, the Royal Navy uniform is a walking aphrodisiac.'

Vanessa privately acknowledged that uniforms made some men heroic, or just honest-to-God desirable. She loitered to pick a handful of woodruff, burying her face in it as she relived assertive fingers slipping gloves on to her hands.

Fern waited for her, saying, 'An acquaintance who's a barrister expects a surge of divorces this year. All those "Let's marry because I might die tomorrow" unions grinding to a halt . . . Oh, God, sorry. That was tactless. I still speak first and think second.'

'So you do.' Vanessa softened the reproof with a smile. 'How long will you stay?'

'Here? A few days, then back to Ledbury Terrace.'

'And Alistair?'

'He's inherited property of his own. A flat above shops, somewhere in central London. I can't see how we could ever live together again.' Panic showed, replaced just as quickly with pleasure. It was a habit Fern had displayed from childhood, trapping ideas in her expression as they flashed past. 'Why don't you come and stay?'

'In London?'

'Yes, and make it soon. I'll be scooting back to Paris at some point. It's a good place to hide.'

Vanessa raised her eyebrows. Why must Fern hide? 'Is there anyone else in your life?'

'A man? Golly, dozens. I danced my way through the war. Oh, look. Poor house!'

They'd come out from the wood. Across a meadow stood Stanshurst Hall, a Palladian building of buff stone. Its front windows were boarded and a scar on the roofline showed where a section of the pediment had gone, like a piece broken off a biscuit.

Vanessa said, 'It was a secondary casualty to Biggin Hill.' Buildings in a five-mile radius of the airbase had felt the effects of German raids.

'There's a crack to the east flank shaped like a villainous smile, as if it knows how much money it's going to gobble up in repairs!' Fern used laughter like a rolled-up newspaper. If something disturbed her — swat! 'Pops hoped the RAF would make us their permanent School of Navigation because they paid the electricity bill. Somebody else will have to pay it now.'

'Who, Fern?'

'The butcher, the baker, the candlestick-maker. I'm glad you're back. You belong here.'

Did she? Vanessa stole a look towards another house, a diminutive version of the Hall which nestled among trees. Ash Lodge was the first home she'd ever known, where she'd lived with her mum and dad. She remembered herself and Ruth moving out on a summer's day – not as hot as this one – everything piled on farm carts. Ruth defaming the husband whose selfishness had scythed down her world. Had her dad felt as trapped here as she, Vanessa, did? 'Fern, I'm not planning—'

But Fern was already away into the meadow, swinging her arms.

At the door of the Hall, they were met by the butler, the last resident member of household staff.

'A telephone message from Commander Redenhall, Madam.'

'He's not coming tomorrow?' Fern sounded hopeful.

'He's coming tonight, Madam. He dealt with his London business quicker than anticipated.'

Fern turned to Vanessa. 'You'll dine with us?'

'I'd better not. I'll finish my typing, then go home.' There had been a moment in the woods when Vanessa could have mentioned to Fern that she'd met Alistair Redenhall already. *We bumped into each other when I intruded on a funeral.* The moment had passed, and now she couldn't admit to knowing him. Not with the butler standing by. 'I'm here if you need advice, Fern, or even a slug of gin fetched from the Queen's Head. But I won't insert myself between you and your man. In fact, I'll stay right away until he's gone.'

True to her word, Vanessa stayed home the following morning. Before leaving the previous evening, she'd left a note for the butler saying that she had a bad migraine, and would be off until it went away. In other words, she'd be ill until Alistair Redenhall had left again for London.

Unused to idleness, however, she put on gloves and a straw hat and took secateurs to the climbing rose that smothered the front of Peach Cottage. There was an abundance of blooms this year, and their weight was pulling away the weatherboarding. She took an armful indoors, and offered to take the rest up to the church. 'It'll save you a toil uphill,' she told her mother, whose habit was to traipse every day to St Anne's to tend the family graves. 'It's stifling out there already.'

'Be sure you give the stones a thorough wash, back and front,' Ruth instructed.

Vanessa arrived at the church gate with her blouse sticking to her. Putting down her bucket, she rested in a yew tree's shade and stared up at the square tower. She'd been married in this pretty, Norman church whose tower had been a sight-marker for Spitfires and Hurricanes returning to Biggin Hill. Its leaden weather-cock was still missing its tail-feathers because 'spinning the rooster' had been a favourite pastime of the pilots. Leo had claimed the tail feathers as his own 'kill', boasting that he'd flown so low over the church that a man edging grass around the graves had thrown himself flat.

That had sparked their first quarrel. Leo had seen it only as a prank that he, as a fighter pilot putting his life on the line, had the right to play while she'd viewed it as an act of disrespect. 'How would you like it if some mad airman put the fear of God into your grandfather?'

They were heroes, Leo and his brothers-in-arms, and through the critical summer and autumn of 1940, they'd died like flies. But . . . the danger and fatigue had blunted some of them to others' pain.

Vanessa filled her bucket at the outside tap. Her bright yellow-green blouse was attracting a plague of bugs. She slapped at them as she washed her grandparents' gravestones and those of her Uncle Victor and Aunt Brenda, and put fresh roses in each pot. The water she tipped away was clean; her mother washed these graves obsessively. Collecting her tools and the remaining roses, she went to the south door where a memorial had been erected to the dead of Biggin Hill's squadrons. Five squadrons were inscribed, though no individual names. There would have been too many. She ran her finger over '64 Squadron' and for a chilling moment, was back in the Watch Room on a squally November afternoon.

She was on duty at her wireless when Leo came thorugh screaming into her earphone. 'I'm on fire, I'm burning!'

Half out of her chair, she was shouting into her mic, 'Bail, Leo, bail! Darling, ditch the bloody plane! We can start again. Darling, please!'

Colleagues looked on in horror.

'I'm so sorry, Leo.' Vanessa fanned out the roses at the base of the plinth.

After a silent vigil, she took respite inside the church where, in her mind's eye, she saw two young people in uniform making hurried vows. There had been four others at her wedding. The vicar, her mother, Leo's best friend and one of her WAAF colleagues who'd been off-shift at the right time. Afterwards, they'd eaten a cold meat salad at the Queen's Head, then walked back to Peach Cottage, where she and Leo had spent their wedding night while her mother slept over at a neighbour's. The following morning, Vanessa had returned to base for the eight a.m. shift. Leo had been scrambled to action that afternoon and she hadn't seen him for forty-eight hours. Her heart had spent every minute of it in her throat. Between her legs, she'd felt sore.

She glanced through the visitors' book and put a two-shilling bit in the collection box. Must she spend all day nursing an imaginary migraine? If she went home, her mother would nag her but she couldn't hang about here. Humidity and sorrow exhausted her.

As she closed the church's mighty oak door behind her, she heard voices. Loud and very near.

Someone was shouting, 'No! You will not,' while a deeper one contradicted, 'There's no going back.'

The first voice had been Fern's. Vanessa was pushing back against the church door, intending to retreat inside, when the smack of a hand against flesh and a sharp cry sent her racing forward. She found Fern with her back to the porch wall, her palms flat as if drawing protection from the stones. A man stood beside the Biggin Hill memorial, his hand pressed to his face. Blood leached between his fingers, on to his white cotton shirt. Vanessa's scalp prickled. She'd walked around this man too often in her night-time fantasies not to recognise the muscular neck with its wind-bitten texture. And the hair, dark with an auburn gloss. He'd cast a stubborn shadow across her life. Seeing 'her captain' blooded and primitively angry ignited a need in her to appease, to comfort – until she saw that he was standing on the roses at the base of the memorial.

Fern noticed her then. 'Vanessa! Stay and witness. My husband lost control! Vanessa?'

'Your husband hit you?' Vanessa saw no mark on Fern. 'Or you hit him?'

'He went for me first!'

Alistair Redenhall lowered his hand, unveiling a red streak from the corner of his eye to the hollow of his cheek. He stared at Vanessa. 'What the hell are *you* doing here?'

'Alistair!' Fern snarled his name. 'You're in a churchyard, not on board ship.'

Alistair ignored her. His eyes burned cold at Vanessa. 'I can accept the occasional coincidence, but you're like a postage stamp stuck to my shoe.' He turned to Fern. 'Why is this woman lurking here? What's going on?'

'Vanessa lives here. She works for my father. What d'you mean, "stuck to your shoe"? Have you met already?'

Vanessa said, 'Not really,' as Alistair said, 'Unfortunately, yes.'

'At a funeral,' Vanessa stammered. 'Um – Mr Bovary's.'

'Bo's? I didn't realise.' Something in Fern's expression warned that she'd question Alistair about it later.

Alistair gave Vanessa a succinct once-over. She'd put on her coolest clothes that morning, but her blouse, which had once been white, had been accidentally put into soak with a yellow duster, which explained its bilious colour. Nobody threw away clothes these days. Her gypsy skirt was homemade from hand-kerchief cotton. The chip-straw hat and rope-soled sandals must add to the impression that she'd wandered out of a rustic water-colour. He said, 'You're going to claim you were polishing the brasses in the church?'

'I have my reasons for being here, Captain Redenhall.'

'"Commander",' Fern corrected. 'He never made the rank of Captain. It's why he's chucked in the towel. It's why he's planning to ruin his life and mine.'

'Commander Redenhall,' Vanessa amended. The bitter looks that passed between the couple roused a searing anger. Had they nothing better to do with their lives than inflict pain on each other? She couldn't shout at both of them, however, and Fern had stuck up for her. So she directed everything at Alistair. 'I might ask why you're bullying your wife in a churchyard. And would you kindly move your feet.'

'I beg your pardon?'

'Move your bloody feet!'

Even Fern looked shocked. Vanessa pointed to the bruised roses. Alistair instantly stepped away. As she bent to recover them, Vanessa knew he was reading the citation carved on the stone. She heard Fern say quietly, 'Oh, Nessie, what must you think of us? You'll let us replace the roses? There are stacks in the garden.'

'No, thank you, Fern.' Vanessa fluffed up the petals and removed one broken pink head. *Rosa 'Madame Alfred Carrière'*. They looked bruised but they wouldn't have outlasted the day's heat anyway. As she straightened up to go, she felt a firm touch on her arm.

'I hadn't noticed the memorial, but that's hardly an excuse. I'm sorry.'

'Anger blinds us, but you're right, it's no excuse.' She walked away, chalking up a victory. She'd shut them both up.

At home, Vanessa found her mother hemming dishcloths, when not swiping at flies. In place of 'hello' Ruth said, 'Borthwick called.' Borthwick was Lord Stanshurst's butler. 'His Lordship's anxious about you, but I said you looked perfectly well this morning.'

'That's my cover blown!' Vanessa changed into something more formal and went to the Hall. She could turn out a cupboard or two and with luck, nobody would know she was there.

In her office, the latest issue of *The Stage* was waiting for her. She put it to one side, thinking she might as well cancel her subscription. The cupboard she turned to first was stuffed with leather-bound wage books going back to before the Great War.

She opened one that started in September 1925, knowing it would cross into the year when her father left.

There he was: 'Sept 25th Quinnell, C J. £14.8s.'

Fourteen pounds and eight shillings per month had been a high wage, back then. The estate's employees had been paid on the last Friday of every month, as they still were. The entry for the 28th May 1926, eight months later, showed that 'C J Quinnell' had received his salary as usual. The following day, the 29th, had been Vanessa's sixth birthday. As she'd lain recovering from the effects of ethylene and surgery in Beckenham Cottage Hospital, Clive had left home.

The following month, Ruth appeared in the records. Prior to that, there'd been no mention of her, presumably because her salary as Lady Stanshurst's secretary had come from another source. From June 1926 onwards half her husband's wage, seven pounds and four shillings, had been paid to 'Mrs R Quinnell, *ex gratia*'. *Out of kindness*.

Seven pounds a month back then had been no bad sum, and Lady Stanshurst had paid for Vanessa's schooling and medical care. It still was a better wage than many of Ruth's neighbours had to rely on, yet Ruth sliced her bread no thicker than her little finger. She spread on margarine and scraped it off again. Vanessa suspected her mother's addiction to poverty was rooted in disappointment. Ruth had hoped for a substantial bequest when Lady Stanshurst died but a bedspread and her Ladyship's treasured Staffordshire porcelain dogs were all that had come her way. Ruth had subsequently instilled in Vanessa an obligation to support her.

Turning the ledger back to May 1926, Vanessa spotted a margin note recording that C J Quinnell had been paid five hundred pounds. A rush of anger threatened to choke her. Five hundred pounds? For what – for bolting to London?

Emotion left her parched and she went to fetch a jug of water from the kitchen. She returned to find that the desk she'd left covered with old ledgers was now strewn with saffron-yellow roses. 'Fern?' she called, mystified.

It wasn't Fern who answered.

Chapter Seven

Alistair sat in the window seat. She jumped; she hadn't seen him there when she walked in. He'd opened the sash to its highest extent and a breeze was lipping at papers on her desk.

He said, 'Fern told me about your husband. Is his the face you see as you fall asleep and the first you see when you wake?'

Taken off guard, she answered with the unvarnished truth. 'It was, for a year. When I started seeing somebody else's face, I was mortified.'

'Whose face replaced your husband's?'

'Ray Pocklington's. Rear gunner, Lancasters. We met at Waddington, my third posting. He was terribly persistent, very sweet and stole a corner of my heart until . . . would you like a glass of water?'

She'd noticed perspiration on his upper lip, and on the spearhead of skin where his throat disappeared into his open collar. 'Yes, thanks,' he said.

She handed him her glass, shaking pencils out of a tin mug for herself. After gulping her water down, she said, 'For almost five years, men's faces have haunted me. If I can claim any courage, it's that I've dared to love over and over. Loss doesn't seem to put me off, I don't know why. What about you? Is it Fern's face you see?'

'I see too many to count.' As he got up, she saw a deep welt running from the side of his nose to his cheek. He gave a spare smile. 'The roses are a peace offering. Fern advised that if I were to ask pardon for trespassing on you this morning, you'd forgive me out of good manners. I prefer to be forgiven freely.'

The roses came from a bush in the tangled parterre where Vanessa often sat during her lunch hour. The Hall's rose beds had once been renowned throughout the county but these days they had a more Shakespearian tone: *Crowned with rank fumiter and furrow-weeds*. 'It was kind of Fern to pick them.'

'I picked them. Fern's gone back to London.'

'Oh.' Vanessa retired to her desk, wishing she hadn't closed the door behind her. She'd sworn to have no contact with this man!

He came to sit opposite her. 'I didn't hit her.'

'She looked petrified.'

'She did, didn't she? I will only say this once more. I did not strike her.'

For a minute, neither spoke until Alistair brought up the gaping issue between them. 'Are we going to be falling over each other for the rest of our days?'

'I shouldn't think so.' After he left here, their lives could have no future touching points. Not if he and Fern lived apart, as seemed likely. 'It is odd that we keep meeting but the common denominator is Brookwood Cemetery. Oh, and Euston Station.'

'It's this place. It's Stanshurst.'

'How does that work?'

'Fern told me that your family served hers for generations.'

Vanessa's teeth came together. Fern hadn't mentioned that, for seven years they'd been as close as siters? Perhaps finishing school and marriage had diluted Fern's memory.

Alistair's quiet smile acknowledged her reaction. '"Served" was not my word. Your father, I understand—'

'Assisted the estate overseer. Until the bright lights seduced him and he left.'

Alistair picked up her copy of *The Stage*. The action was a question, but Vanessa remained still. No confidences, no explanations.

Alistair said, 'My godfather, Wilton Bovary, owned a theatre, but in the twenties, he'd bring companies of actors here and produce plays for Lord and Lady Stanshurst's house parties. On occasion, he cast members of staff in small roles – until Lord Stanshurst stopped him. He was turning servants' heads, I believe, giving them dreams of a life they hadn't been born to.'

'I didn't know that.' Vanessa wondered if her father's head had been one of those turned by the theatricals. Clive's thirst for acting must have stemmed from something.

Alistair carried on with his story. 'When, many years later, Lady Stanshurst became unwell, my Uncle Bo – Wilton Bovary, I mean – lent her his house on Malta. He'd often stay there with her. Malta is where the British Mediterranean Fleet is based, which is how I came to meet Lady Stanshurst and in due course, Fern. So, you see, Stanshurst is the key to our repeated meetings.'

'It's the key to your meeting with Fern. I've no part in your life, Commander.'

'No?' Alistair opened *The Stage*, folding it to the last-but-one page and turning it so Vanessa could read an announcement:

'The Farren Theatre to reopen in November.'

She gasped, 'The Farren? That's where . . . where my friend Joanne played a chambermaid.'

'And is that all?'

'Yes.' *No*. At The Farren, a Wardrobe Mistress had snipped off a lock of her hair and invited her to come back and play. Mystery radiated from that place, like spikes of light from a star. 'It was Mr Bovary's theatre?'

'Correct. Now it belongs to me and I've quit the Navy to run it. One of the reasons Fern is so angry with me.'

Vanessa nodded. Fern claimed to be a free spirit, but she enjoyed the status of being a Baron's daughter. Once, Vanessa had asked her why the village shopkeeper called her 'Miss Fern' while addressing her as 'Young Missy', to which Fern had replied, 'Because I'm the Honourable Fern Wichelow, of course. You're just Vanessa Quinnell.' To Fern, a naval commander would be an acceptable husband, while a theatrical manager . . . But it was Alistair who was leaving Fern, she reminded herself.

'How did the Navy take your decision to run off to join the stage?'

'I will leave you to imagine.' Alistair thanked her for the water and got up. 'Fern accuses me of jettisoning a fine career for something without social worth. But I'm looking for a new beginning.'

'So is Fern!'

He gave her a scouring look, and carried on with his earlier point. 'I consider theatre to be a pulse of civilisation. We've had so much war, we should surely create the best peace we're capable of. Do you wish to act?'

'I want to work in wardrobe.'

'It's a tough profession, long hours with little glamour.' Glancing at the chipped furniture, the whitewashed walls, he continued, 'Fern would love you to stay on here, and why shouldn't you? You'll meet a pleasant man soon enough and make a life.'

'I'll decide what adds up to a life, thank you.' This would be the moment to ask if he was hiring and to put herself forward.

But if he was in charge of The Farren, she'd spend half her time hiding from him; she wouldn't want a job there. Would she? 'Will you be an actor-manager, in the footsteps of your god-father?'

His eyes creased at the corners. 'I wouldn't inflict my acting talents on the paying public. I'll be at the helm, but out of the spotlight.' He held out his hand. 'Goodbye. We won't meet again.'

As snubs went, that one was shoot to kill. Rebellion flashed and Vanessa called loudly after him, 'Who knows, I might bump into you in Ledbury Terrace. Fern's invited me to stay.'

She had the impression that he hesitated, but a moment later, she heard him striding away.

When next week's copy of *The Stage* arrived, Vanessa turned straight to the classifieds and suddenly, her heart was going mad.

REQUIRED IMMEDIATELY
The Farren Theatre, Farren Court, WC2

WARDROBE MASTER
Must have War Service.

Must also have knowledge of period costume
and be able to cut and make.

Apply by letter to Mr Macduff, Company Manager.

Wardrobe *Master*? The swindler! Was this an example of what her friend Joanne called 'jobs for the boys' or was Alistair Redenhall trying to checkmate her?

That night, she dreamed she was flying above a theatre stage on white wings. Soaring alongside her were her father and a woman with plaits so long, they swept the boards. Vanessa woke with the name 'Farren' on her lips.

She climbed out of bed and lifted one of her floorboards, taking care not to let it creak and alert her mother. Fishing about in cobwebs, she located the little key. She'd cleaned it and it shone like a bracelet charm. From the same space, she retrieved a playbill, mended with Sellotape, and studied the cast list again. Wilton Bovary. Johnny Quinnell. She truly believed she was being pulled towards The Farren by unseen hands. Alistair Redenhall may believe that he wanted a man to run his wardrobe department, but he hadn't reckoned with her. He might be a decorated naval officer, but she'd soaked up the spirit of the RAF: *per ardua ad astra*, 'Through adversity to the stars'.

She drafted two letters. The first gave notice to Lord Stanshurst. The second was to the unknown Mr Macduff.

A week later, she got a reply on headed paper, offering her an interview, though not until the following month which condemned her to a period of chafing frustration.

PART TWO

A Broken Pathway

Chapter Eight

London, September 3rd, 1946

In the front hall of 12 Ledbury Terrace, Vanessa checked herself in the oval mirror above the console table. The upper half of her body, which was all she could see, was clad in yellow.

A shop assistant had once told her that yellow not only suited her, it was a colour that made things happen. Yellow pushed you forward.

'As do banana skins on the pavement,' she informed her reflection. Though as bananas had been off the shelves for so long, she had no way of proving the hypothesis. She'd arrived at Fern's the previous day, and from the moment she'd crossed her friend's threshold, her fears at what she was about to do had escalated.

Fern hadn't helped by saying, 'Have I told you that I think you're mad?'

'Yes, twenty times.'

That first night, Fern had insisted Vanessa sleep in the master bedroom, saying, 'I've moved to the smaller room. I can't bear the double bed, thinking about Alistair and what he's done to me. What he's still doing to me.'

Vanessa had asked, 'What has he done?'

'Been faithless. He can't help himself, but it doesn't make it any better.'

Lying where Alistair must have lain many times had ensured that Vanessa got little sleep. Fern had been generous, though, in her casual way. Her second comment to Vanessa yesterday had been, 'Darling, your *hair*. Girl Guide curls won't do here! I'll phone Mr Stephen at once.' Fern then sent Vanessa trotting off to Hans Crescent where her stylist had his shop. He'd stayed open late as a special favour and had spent the first several minutes of the appointment lifting Vanessa's hair before declaiming, 'Your curls have gone into spasm, dear.'

'I used to tuck them into a piece of stocking, tied round my head. It's what we all did, to get the Victory Roll. It looked neat under a cap.'

'The horrors of war.' Mr Stephen had trimmed the tired ends and given her a side-sweep, her hair gathered to the left in a cluster of waves, leaving her right side plain for a 'profile' hat. Everybody was wearing hats side-on in London, apparently. On her return, Fern had opened the doors of her wardrobe and said, 'I can't share a dress – anything of mine would swamp you – but pick out a hat.'

'Do I need a hat?' Vanessa had wondered.

'Hats mean business. D'you fancy straw or felt, plain or colour?'

'One that goes on the side of the head, please.'

'It'll have to be this one, then.' Fern had unboxed a hat of mustard-coloured satin.

Lord Stanshurst had given Vanessa five pounds – a leaving gift, though she still had a couple more weeks to work at the Hall. She'd spent nearly the lot at a renowned dress agency in Charing Cross on a short jacket the colour of Forsythia blossom that matched the triangles on her print dress and squared off her shoulders. The jacket, being second-hand, hadn't required any coupons.

Two shades of yellow ought to have clashed, but the moment Fern placed the mustard satin hat on her head, Vanessa felt like a different person. WAAF-and-Stanshurst Vanessa was packed away. Stylish Mrs Kingcourt had emerged.

Fern came down the stairs just then. She wore a green dress that made her eyes emerald, and her hair was arranged in a sleek chignon. It was only ten in the morning but she looked as though she was going out to dine. She asked, 'What time's your appointment?'

'Eleven.' Vanessa wanted to ask Fern if she'd ever come across Mr Macduff, so she could gauge whether she was heading for a kindly interview or a grilling, but any mention of The Farren irritated Fern, who called it 'that bloody variety hall'.

'I'd better shift.' Vanessa checked her watch and as she did so, her wrist collided with a pile of framed photographs lying face down on the console. She caught one as it fell, gasping, 'Sorry!'

'Nerves?' Fern asked.

'I'll say! They're expecting a man.' She'd written for this interview as 'V E Kingcourt, ex-RAF'. It wasn't exactly passing herself off as male, but it wasn't coming clean, either. Mr Macduff was going to get a shock in approximately one hour. And what if she ran into Alistair?

The thought of it made her unsteady. 'Fern, if your husband—'

'He won't be there,' Fern cut in contemptuously. 'Alistair commands from the bridge. He gives orders and lets the underlings get on with it. He won't know you're even in the building.'

'He'll know soon enough if I get the job.'

'It isn't too late to cry off. They're going to rumble you. The dress, you know.'

'If I went in trousers, I'd be muscling in on false pretences. This outfit says, "I'm female, and proud of it." Do I look all right?'

Fern moved around her critically, and her signature fragrance filled the air. 'Mm. It's a *Javier,* this little jacket, from his spring '38 collection.' She laughed at Vanessa's astonishment. 'I used to go to the Paris shows with my mother. I worshipped Javier because he designed for real women. I wonder . . . no, I don't want to think about it. A Jew, in Paris.' She stroked Vanessa's sleeve, which was polished cotton. 'Don't leave this lying around. Sticky fingers everywhere. Not sure about the hat, though.'

'If you'd rather I didn't wear it – '

'Normally, you wouldn't mix yellows but it looks fine. Just – it has memories attached.'

'Romantic ones?'

'Dead ones. Wear it, it brings out topaz and gold in your eyes.' Fern laughed as an irresistible idea struck. 'If you do meet Alistair, tell him to move his bloody feet again! His face when you said that in the churchyard. Brilliant. Now, what about makeup?'

'That's the next job.' Vanessa gave herself a generous mouth-shape with a stub of Leichner No 2 in poppy red. She'd found the lipstick inside the bag she'd also bought from the dress agency. A smear of petroleum jelly over the top gave a moist look. She declined Fern's offer of a pair of American-import stockings, fearful she'd ladder them. She'd go bare-fleshed but she allowed Fern to apply leg makeup. Not the 'Leg-stick' which had been the emergency recourse during the war, but a homemade potion of talcum powder, liquid paraffin and brown pigment. Fern assured her that the pigment was the highest quality artist's oil paint. The result looked good with the blond suede sandals that had cost Vanessa eight coupons from her 'demob' supply. She checked her watch, and again caught the corner of a framed photo. This time, the picture crashed to the floor.

'Oh, God, I'm so clumsy!' It was a wedding picture, showing Fern in a long lace veil and bias-cut silk, the man beside her in white naval uniform. His eyes . . .

Vanessa felt a flutter of desire followed by shame. 'Sorry!'

'For heaven's sake!' Snatching the picture and shoving it, broken glass and all, into the console drawer, Fern showed the other variant of her smile. The short, irritated one. 'You keep saying "sorry". I don't know why.'

'Because I so often am. I'll have the frame mended.'

'We can't even get glass to repair windows, let alone for family photos. Don't fret, it's not a picture I look at. Though he's handsome, I grant you. I had to fight girls off him in Malta. You wouldn't believe the effect that a white uniform has on women. Wait, Vanessa?' Fern peered down into Vanessa's face. 'This sudden urgency for the "life theatrical" isn't anything to do with him?'

'Not at all.'

Fern narrowed her eyes. 'He told me he was going to pick roses for you to make up for squashing the ones at the war memorial. Did he?' When Vanessa nodded, she gave a sarcastic whoop. 'And gave his performance of the wounded hero, brought low by a fiendish woman? That being me, of course. He did! And you lapped it up. You always were rotten at hiding your feelings.'

'I think I'll go, Fern.'

Fern walked to the door with her, and down the white steps. 'Nessie, *please* don't fall for him. He'll make you miserable.'

Vanessa lingered. 'I have my own reasons for wanting to work at The Farren, and none of them are to do with your husband.'

She kissed Fern's cheek and struggled not to sneeze as she caught a nose-full of perfume. Arpège was potent, more night than day.

'Thanks for everything,' she said from the bottom of the steps.

'Got your map?'

'In my head. Farren Court's between Russell Street and Bow Street and I know the way.'

'Show them what you're made of. Though not straight away.' Fern giggled.

A few yards along Ledbury Terrace, Vanessa turned to wave and saw that Fern hadn't moved. Her gaze seemed to be locked on the end of the street. When she realised that Vanessa was looking at her, she called out, 'I'll beg or borrow some champagne to celebrate, or drown our sorrows, whichever's needed. Good luck!'

Joanne Sayer had told her that The Farren was hidden, and so it proved. Vanessa traipsed down Russell Street so many times she could reel off the stars of the Fortune Theatre's current show and quote the ecstatic reviews. A Delight! Riveting!

On Bow Street, she paused in front of the Royal Opera House. As an art student, she'd queued here for cheap tickets. In 1940, on her way to WAAF training in Blackpool, she'd been lured inside by a group of American GIs. The opera house had been a dance hall by then, a swing band playing behind the proscenium arch. The American boys had taught her how to jitterbug for six hours straight, and one of them had taken her in a taxi to catch the last available train to the northwest. Bending to adjust the straps of her sandals, which were beginning to rub, she listened for those vanished sounds, and instead heard the grind of buses. Life and business chugged on, though she could count the cars on the fingers of one hand. Fuel was being measured out in teaspoons, and thousands of private cars had been commandeered by the government. Behind the snarl of buses was the slam and scrape of far-off building work. It came from the direction of the City, where the bombing had been unremitting.

From the Opera House, she crossed to the magistrate's court and stared at a red telephone box, flat on its back, its panes criss-crossed with anti-shatter tape. Behind it lay an open space where orphaned walls stood at angles, charred cross-beams pointing into nothingness. A row of shops destroyed? On the blackened flank of a surviving draper's establishment, somebody had painted a sign. 'Farren Court'.

This was her journey's end. A bomb site.

Picking her way across the rough ground, she smelled the stagnant breath of rain-flooded cellars. A board on a sagging wire fence shouted 'Keep Out'. Farren Court had, in effect, been wiped off the map. But what of the theatre? She followed a path of broken cobbles, certain this had once been a passage between high walls. Ahead stood a stranded cube of a building.

It had taken war and death to get her back here. Alistair Redenhall had given up his naval career for this place.

The theatre's doorway still had white stucco plaster clinging to its pillars like remnants of cake icing. The name, 'The Farren', was inscribed in black paint which badly needed touching up. Rough cement over the doorway spoke of some architectural detail ripped away. An arched window had lost its glass and boards kept the weather out. How many explosives had fallen nearby, she wondered? A miracle it had survived at all.

The glass-panelled entrance was shuttered and a hand-written notice said, 'All enquiries to stage door.' An arrow directed her around the side, into a narrow walkway called Caine Passage. Recognition flickered. Brick walls and old gas lamps. She'd walked this way after watching *Sleeping Beauty*. Dad had bought her a choc-ice. And later, he and Eva had inked her fingers. Funny, how some details stay, like poker burns in a carpet.

Scaffolding marred this side, while from the roof came a repetitive hammering. Repairs must be underway. The stage door was unlocked and she went straight in. The first thing she saw was a leather armchair backed into a niche, suggesting a doorkeeper was employed, though there was no sign of him. By instinct, she turned left, the wooden soles of her sandals scuffling on the concrete floor. Doors either side of the corridor were labelled 'Dressing Room' and one boasted a dog-eared bronze star. Another had a gold sign saying, 'Green Room'. She was heading towards the back of the theatre, but the corridor ended in a locked door where a notice proclaimed, 'Crew and performers only beyond this point.'

She knew she could access the auditorium from here because she'd done it with her dad twenty years ago. But what if she barged in on a rehearsal? She'd try the next level up, she decided. A pointing hand etched on the stair wall advised 'To Chorus Dressing Rooms, Props, Understudies' Room and Wardrobe'. The stairs were painted flame-retardant silver, which meshed with her memory. She'd locked her hand in her dad's because the rises had been too steep for her.

The corridor above was identical to the one below, except that this one ran unhindered to the end of the building. As she passed the wardrobe room, she trailed her fingers against the door mouldings. Time to try her key? No – she was now two minutes late. At the end of the corridor she found a lift and a further staircase. Both would take her to ground level behind the stage, but the lift was little more than a bird-cage, wide enough for two at a squash. She didn't fancy it.

She went down stairs that were carpeted in canvas to muffle footfall. Was that a dog barking somewhere? She was now in the backstage realms, gazing up between walls of black-painted brick. Eighty or ninety feet above, the stage-house roof disappeared in shadows. Ethers of paint, fish glue and wood resin set her sneezing and she trod carefully over trailing wires. It would be easy to go flying in her new sandals. Or bump into one of the stage flats, or fall over the sawhorse protruding from a carpenter's bay. She moved towards the sound of male voices.

They came from the stage. Double doors took her into a walkway that must allow the actors to get from one side of the stage to the other. A backdrop of scrim fabric was all that separated her from the stage itself where bright lights glared. She heard a man ask, 'Can you see what you're doing?'

She pushed through the scrim and found herself on a compact stage. In front of her was a proscenium arch where curtain linings shone unearthly white under an arc light beam. Pinching her eyes against the dazzle, she walked towards a male silhouette. Cleared her throat. 'Good morning. I'm looking for the Company Manager.'

A voice, impatient, came back, 'We're not calling yet. Not even the secondaries.'

That was as clear as Mandarin Chinese. 'I'm sorry?'

'We're not casting yet. And when we do –' the voice climbed in exasperation, 'we'll use an agency. I'm sure you're very talented, dear, but you're wasting your time. And ours.'

She walked towards the man, her wedge heels clumping. Every sound was amplified because the stage was a box within a box. Joanne had described The Farren as 'intimate', but to Vanessa, it felt as functional as an engine shed with its darkly varnished boards and layers of scrim defining the wings. She looked down at her yellow sleeves. The lights had turned them phosphorescent. 'I have an appointment with Mr Macduff.'

The man continued staring upwards into the fly tower. Finally, he swung round. He had reddish hair, savagely cropped, and was a few years older than her. A sucked-in belly suggested he hadn't seen a square meal in a while. Taking in her outfit, the hat, the black-leaded eyebrows and crimson lips, he pasted her with loathing. 'I said, buzz off. We're busy.'

'No, you aren't.' If she let herself be scared, she'd never come back. 'I haven't seen you do anything yet.'

While the man gawped at her, Vanessa peered out into the auditorium, at raked seats draped in ghostly dust covers. They dwindled into blackness after the first ten rows but in the middle section, next to the aisle, was where she'd sat with her dad. 'I'm here for the wardrobe post. My name's Kingcourt. So – the Company Manager?'

From above the proscenium arch came a sound like somebody cleaning a blackboard with wire wool and she cringed. The red-headed man went stage front, calling, 'Ready for me to let it down?'

A voice drifted down from the dark zones; 'Let me get my hands clear of the cable.'

A long ladder was propped in the corner and she made out a figure balanced two or three rungs down from the top, stretching forward into the arc light beam. She heard, 'The line-shaft drum has seized. Moisture's got in. All right, Cottrill, lower away.'

This time, the hideous rasp had Vanessa covering her ears. The ropes and pulleys of the fly tower put her in mind of a sailing ship, while its lighting rigs stared down at her like frog eyes. Thirty feet up, a steel catwalk spanned the empty air. A hole in the roof showed a flash of blue sky. Dust trickled down through the arc light beam to join a circle of debris on the stage. She could hear men high above, bashing with hammers. She took her hands from her ears. Somewhere, the dog still barked. From up the ladder came, 'She's stuck! Switch off, Cottrill.'

Fruity opinions floated down, followed by, 'I hope it just needs greasing. I could use my old engine-room chief right now.' Then, 'Sod it.' A rag flopped on to the floor. 'Chuck that back up, would you?'

Unthinking, Vanessa beat red-headed Cottrill to it. She made a ball of the rag and hurled it upwards.

An hand shot out. 'Thanks. Start it up again.'

Once more, the mechanism protested and Cottrill killed the electricity. 'Stuck fast, sir. I'll fetch another ladder so we can attack it from both sides.' As he strode by, Cottrill hissed, 'Make yourself scarce, dearie. Women on stage before rehearsals are bad luck.'

Vanessa subdued the urge to pursue Cottrill and whack him. Nobody had called her 'Dearie' when she'd been wearing uniform and kept to her post during a devastating air raid. She yelled into the air, 'Can somebody please take me to the Company Manager's office – or shall I ask the dog?'

Coming down the ladder, favouring his left hand because he'd caught his right on the sharp edge of the pulley drum, Alistair Redenhall wondered if he'd just heard Tom Cottrill giving an unscripted reading of one of his plays-in-progress, battling out male and female parts. Cottrill's ambition was to be a playwright, but his work was too raw for The Farren. For now, he was better employed as Stage Manager. Alistair called out, 'The first job for the fly men will be to strip down the safety rig. That curtain should float up and down. Tom, are you hearing me?'

Balanced on his ladder, Alistair saw somebody who definitely wasn't Cottrill. *She* was staring at him, her jacket a searing, chrome yellow in the arc lights. She wore a golden halo on one side of her head which stirred a memory. Malta, a walk above Spinola Bay on a summer evening. 'Fern? Is that you?'

She stepped forward and he saw that she was nothing like his wife. Lots of brown curls. Lipstick, very red. Short. He climbed down and walked towards her, wiping his hands on his trousers. 'Who are you?' he asked, squinting into the light. He expected her to retreat at the same pace. She didn't and he bumped into her.

For a precious moment, he'd thought his wife had come to make peace and in the clawing disappointment, anger got a toehold. 'Did I hear Mr Cottrill ask what you were doing here?' He waited for her to wilt.

'Of course you heard him. He was impersonating an offended foghorn.'

'Oh! It's you, Mrs Kingcourt. I ought to have realised.' Alistair turned the arc light around, cancelling its glare. 'You've changed your hair.'

'It is allowed.'

Staring down at her, he reacquainted himself with eyes that could widen and soften or flash with irritation. The wrong eyes, because they were not Fern's. Though she sounded composed, he saw that his appearance disorientated her. Well, she did the same to him. At Stanshurst, he'd assumed she must be a closet actress. He'd continued to think so, even after she'd written in requesting an interview for the wardrobe post. He'd felt baffled, then suspicious. And, he had to admit, intrigued. 'It's your interview this morning, isn't it? Sorry. Things have run away with me.'

'How fortunate one of us remembered. Is Mr Macduff going to interview me on stage?'

He considered telling her that there would be no interview, that this situation was a cockup. He'd intended to advertise for a Props Master, and had dictated the wording to someone on the classifieds desk at *The Stage*. When the ad appeared, it said 'Wardrobe Master'. His mistake or theirs, he wasn't sure. Strange things happen when you're tired, and he hadn't been sleeping well.

He now had a dozen hopeful men to interview – and Mrs Kingcourt. She was beginning to feel like the spider that keeps reappearing in the bath; every time you put it out of the window, it creeps back in. Although to be fair, nobody had forced him to invite her in. 'Look, this is all a bit of a mistake. Come to my office and I'll write you a cheque to cover your expenses.'

'To cover your embarrassment, you mean? Like the fig-leaf that covers the nudity of David in the V&A?'

His experience of young women was that they talked to a fairly predictable script. Vanessa Kingcourt steam-rolled that convention. She stirred something dangerous in him that he could not afford to give way to. 'We're looking for a Wardrobe Master with frontline war service. A man. I'm sure you have many great qualities, but there are a couple you entirely lack.'

He presented his most freezing demeanour and waited for her to make her habitual apology and shuffle off.

She instead retorted, 'I'm Leading Aircraftwoman Kingcourt and you need to know that last night, I slept in your bed.'

He'd thought the capacity for his jaw to drop had been erased by war, horror and a torpedo slicing into the bowels of the *Sundew*. Hauling his features together, he said curtly, 'You'd better explain that remark.'

What had she meant to say? Alistair was dressed like a naval rating in belted blue trousers and a serge blouse the same colour. The shirt was cut into a V at the front, plunging down to where dark chest hair began. The simple rig made sense for going up ladders, but how, Vanessa asked herself, did you deal with a Commander dressed as a deck-hand? Or an angry man who allegedly mistreats his wife, but from whom you want a job?

There was no job, she reminded herself.

'Meant to say what?' Alistair looked on the point of exploding. Two weeks on, the marks of Fern's fingernails had healed to calamine pink. It reminded her of Fern's scornful appraisal, 'the wounded hero.'

She ordered her thoughts. 'Last night I stayed at Ledbury Terrace, and I realised how deeply I've missed Fern. We were as close as sisters once, and she was with me at my darkest hour. I'm telling you so you know who and what I am. A *bona fide* friend of your wife's, not an imposter or a hanger-on.'

'What did my wife say when you told her about this interview?'

'Um, that I was mad, though she conceded you'd be unlikely to bother with me. Oh, and last night, we drank wine from your cellar. I wobbled upstairs, actually.'

'I hope my bed was comfortable.'

As a cloud. 'This isn't a conspiracy, Commander Redenhall. My being here, I mean. I want the wardrobe job and I happen to know your wife.'

'Well enough to borrow hats. I bought that one for her in Malta.'

Oh, Fern. 'I – I didn't know. I wouldn't have worn it if I had.'

'I expect she was making a point. You must ask her –' He looked up. Dust peppered his shoulder. He brushed it off. 'We've already decided, haven't we, that our continuous meetings are no coincidence? But what do you reckon to "fate"?'

'Isn't fate just coincidence with strings attached?' She felt a dry tickle against her exposed ear. Dust was falling more thickly. 'Perhaps we should move.'

Alistair led her to the front of the stage. A moment later, the shriek of splitting metal burst above them and without knowing why, she was flying backwards. She hit the stage as a canon-fire crash shook the building. Afterwards, came silence reeking of engine grease and rust. Fern's hat flopped over one eye and her nose was buried in Alistair's chest. She felt his ragged breathing and the roughness of body hair against her cheek, the warmth of his skin. It sent a needling tide through her.

'Are you hurt?' he asked.

'I walloped my elbow.' Her lips grazed his skin. 'What the hell was that?'

'The Iron. Iron safety curtain. By law, it has to be capable of being lowered within a few seconds of a fire starting, but it's rusted. Rain got in this summer after part of the roof caved in. It just proved it can move fast when it wants to.'

'As did you.'

'Is anybody hurt?' Cottrill called from the rear of the stage. Seeing them locked together on the ground, he swore pithily. 'I thought the building had caved in. You could have been crushed!'

'At least then there'd have been one less annoying woman in the world,' Vanessa answered. 'If I hadn't seen you leave, I might have imagined you'd deliberated dropped it, Mr Cottrill.'

'Don't be a bloody ignoramus!'

'Why not? I'm female, aren't I?' She started laughing and couldn't seem to stop. She laughed against Alistair's breast bone and through her convulsions said, 'I'm not sure this is the moment to say it, but I intend to have the Wardrobe Master's job.'

'Then you'd better come to my office and persuade me.' Alistair helped her up and they stood close as the shock of their near miss drained out of them. Tom Cottrill looked on sourly.

Alistair's office lay on the opposite side of the theatre to the wardrobe room. It resembled a club lounge with its brown furniture, brass lamp stands and deep carpet. It even had a fireplace, though this was closed off with a screen. The jarring note was the modern portrait hanging on the wall behind the desk.

'My late godfather,' Alistair told her.

Vanessa was curious to see the face of her dad's employer. For some reason, she'd imagined Wilton Bovary as a fleshy *bon viveur*, fat and rosy. Perhaps with a monocle. The reality was a narrow-shouldered man, long faced, with eyes that goggled behind metal glasses. The face of a left-wing writer, not of a theatrical entrepreneur and actor. The painter's brush style was vigorous. This was an impression of the man.

'It's a shame the artist didn't capture Bo's humour.' Alistair seemed to read her disappointment. 'His smile made his face. He enjoyed all the vices; drink, tobacco, affairs. Oh, would you like a drink? You're not in shock, are you?'

'Thank you, I'm fine.' Taking a seat on the interviewee's side of the desk, Vanessa removed her jacket and unpinned her hat, which was definitely in shock. It would need the attentions of a milliner.

Alistair slipped into the chair behind the desk, and leaned his weight on his forearms. Papers were stacked in wire trays, crowding out a blotter and a desk diary. 'Excuse my casual appearance. You'll have gathered we're still at the fitting-out stage. Why do you consider yourself qualified to take on wardrobe?'

Gosh, he didn't hang around. 'Aren't I supposed to be explaining this to Mr Macduff?'

'Of course. I'll fetch him.'

By leaving the room, Alistair allowed her a moment to rehearse her qualifications. Her art studies. Her WAAF responsibilities, naturally. Her innate love of colour . . . perhaps she should put her hat and jacket back on? She heard him shouting in the corridor, 'Macduff? Where are you? Come on, old man. Shift yourself.'

Was that how he'd ordered his ship's crew around? 'Commands from the bridge,' Fern had said, and Vanessa prepared herself for an aged lackey to hobble in at his heels. She wasn't expecting Alistair to return with a large, brown dog, which made a direct line for her, mouth wide and panting.

She got up fast. *Thank goodness I'm not wearing nylons.* It was only as the dog cannoned into her, using her knees as a runaway train uses a buffer, that she saw he had only one leg at the front. Where the left one should be was a lump like a tennis ball, healed over with scar tissue. 'What happened to you?' She stroked his muscular shoulder. 'But you're a lovely boy.'

The dog's tongue sought the palm of her hand. He looked like a Labrador, big-headed, with silky ears and dark, trusting eyes, only she'd never seen a brown-coated one before. Lord Stanshurst had kept a few, blacks or light golden. 'Is he a war casualty?'

'He was hit by a car in the first week of the blackout. He slipped his leash to chase a cat.'

Alistair was watching her closely and she stopped stroking. Some people hated their dogs being petted, believing it spoiled them. She sat down and the dog sat too, its head seemingly glued to her leg. 'What's his name?'

'Macduff. Chief Macduff of Banchory, to give him his full title.' Alistair returned to his seat, telling Macduff to stop bothering Mrs Kingcourt. The dog settled under the desk, resting his nose on his single front paw. 'He was hoping you might have a cream cracker in your pocket.'

'No such luck. Your dog?'

'He is now.' Alistair indicated Wilton Bovary's portrait. 'Nobody wanted him when Bo died – three-legged dogs aren't on many people's wish-list – and he ended up dependant on the goodwill of the janitor. That's the first part of the story. The more complex part is that Mr Bovary has two sisters. Had. Do you say "has" or "had" when the man is dead but the sisters very much aren't?'

'"Had", I think.'

'One is Mrs Rolf. She and her husband are big names in the theatre world. You can blame them for Edwin. Remember Edwin, at the funeral?'

She did, the rude young man wearing a cloak very like her father's. *Cut-price burials that way.*

Edwin was the Rolfs' son, Alistair told her, and an actor. He had assumed 'Bovary' as his stage name.

'The other sister, Barbara – or Miss Bovary as she chooses to be known – is the administrator here. Highly efficient, yet blisteringly angry. Should I be telling you this?'

'Of course you shouldn't. Is Mrs Rolf the nicer one? There's usually a good sister and a bad one. A Good Fairy and a Bad.'

'Yes, Sylvia's the softer of the two. They fought bitterly after their brother died, over who should run this place.'

Vanessa remembered snotty Edwin's challenge to Commander Redenhall: *I'm Wilton Bovary's heir. What are you, exactly?* 'I'd like to have been a fly on the wall at the will reading.'

'Me too. I inherited everything but my godfather's money, and decided *I* should like to run The Farren myself.'

'And instantly, they all became allies against you.'

'There you have it. *The Wars of the Roses* in a few lines.'

'I bet you have the best office and the biggest chair,' she said. 'And the dog. Who gets the money?'

A smile cut across his lips, though it had been an impudent question. 'Nobody. It's in trust. I've installed Miss Bovary in the room next to this. She knows everything about this theatre, every cobweb and heartbeat.'

'And the name of everyone who ever worked within it?'

He gave her an inquiring look. 'Probably. But she has two incurable failings: Miss Bovary dislikes dogs and Wardrobe Mistresses.'

'That's why you advertised for a man?'

'That was an error. But I won't deny, a man with military service behind him will be better able to stand up to her.'

'What do you think, Macduff?' The dog's eyes met hers with gentle entreaty. She bent to stroke his nose and he strained forward to lick the flesh around her sandal straps. She tucked her feet back as far as she could. 'Why put Macduff's name on the advertisement?'

She fancied Alistair's expression had softened but it was a fleeting impression. He gave his explanation tersely.

'"Redenhall" isn't a common name and many of my former colleagues don't yet know I've left the Navy. I didn't want anybody seeing my name in *The Stage*, and setting off a chain of telephone calls. Not before I've written to them all individually – a job I keep putting off.'

'I'm not sure I like being tricked into writing to a dog.'

Macduff eased forward. Something about her legs attracted him.

'The alternative would have been to put Miss Bovary's name,

but "LACW", being a WAAF-only rank, would have set the sirens off. Miss Bovary knows her aircraftmen from her aircraftwomen.'

It crossed Vanessa's mind that Miss Bovary knew too darn much. 'She hates women?'

'Just Wardrobe Mistresses. She believes they wield too much power behind the scenes and don't die when they ought. So – would you like to tell me why you feel you're qualified for the job?'

Vanessa laid down her strongest card, two years' study at Fressenden Art School. She'd ended both years with high marks. Nobody could argue with her reasons for cutting her studies short.

'Any experience in period costume making? The Farren is famous for its eighteenth and nineteenth century productions.'

'None, I'm afraid. But life isn't all about getting from A to B in a straight line, is it? I never imagined I'd end up enrolling in the WAAF, or getting involved in a war.'

Fair point, said his sparing smile, but not quite good enough. 'We're looking for someone who knows their way around costume, and around a theatre.'

What could she say? 'I know nothing, but I'm willing to learn'? *If I were him*, she acknowledged, *I'd want somebody who already knows the ropes*. He was waiting for her answer. In defeat, she said, 'Years ago, my dad brought me here to see a pantomime and afterwards, he took me backstage. I met the then-wardrobe lady; she smelled of roses. Her name was Eva. She told me I'd come back one day. I suppose I've always believed it.'

'Eva St Clair? That's going back to . . .'

'1925. Christmas.'

'*Sleeping Beauty?*'

'Yes!' Her excitement started Macduff barking. The dog planted himself by her right leg and began licking her foot. This time, when she moved, he moved too.

Alistair folded his arms. 'I was staying with my Uncle Bo that Christmas, and I saw the run of *Sleeping Beauty* from dress rehearsal to its final performance. We were probably here on the same night.'

'If you imbibed this place as a child it explains why you came back.'

'I'm not sure. I didn't approve of *Sleeping Beauty*. At the time, I was far too sophisticated for fairy tales. You, I suppose, were enchanted.'

'I was terrified! The Dame! She – *he* – looked straight at me and told me off for not shouting loudly enough.'

'He did that every night. Always looked towards the mid-right-hand stalls.'

'Why?'

'It was where his boyfriend always sat.'

Her hand shot up to her mouth. 'I didn't realise – '

'One would hardly expect you to. You couldn't have been more than six or seven.'

'I was five.'

'Then your lack of worldly knowledge is forgiven, but you need to broaden your outlook if you're to survive in this world. May I be blunt? An assistant wardrobe post would be more up your street. That requires somebody well-organised to curate the costumes. Cleaning them, ironing, hanging them – '

She butted in. 'Look at me – do you see a laundress? A woman good only for folding clothes? Good thing the WAAF saw more in me than that.'

He continued as if she'd not spoken. 'The person we're looking for needs pattern cutting and tailoring skills. You haven't.'

'Neither have you. And frankly' – she carried on because her only chance of surviving five minutes more in his company lay in making an unarguable point – 'you must have been out of your depth as the war progressed. They threw new devices at you all the time, I should think. Radar, better sonar, bigger guns. You must have learned to use them as you went along. You got on with it.'

'True, but I had engineers, specially-trained officers and gunners.' Don't push me, said his unbending mouth.

'I would need engineers too, in the form of cutters and seamstresses.' Macduff started on her left ankle, his muzzle like whiskery velvet. She had to admire the dog. He embodied triumph over adversity. 'As for bustles, bodices and guss—' for some unearthly reason, she'd been about to say 'gussets' – 'galligaskins and suchlike, I'd find an old theatre-hand to show me how.'

'How many assistants is that so far?'

'As many as I'd need, no more.'

'Mrs Kingcourt, have you never heard of "tactical retreat"? Consider a lesser post and you might learn all these amazing arts yourself.'

Put simply, an assistant's wages wouldn't allow her to live in London. She rose, pulling her jacket off the chair, struggling to get her arm into the sleeve. Looking down, she saw that Macduff had licked all the liquid stocking from her feet and ankles. Her legs were luminous white below the shin. She burst out, 'Fern didn't say her leg-mix was irresistible to dogs!'

'Her given name is Frances. Did you know that? Her father called her Fern after she played an elf dressed only in fern fronds in one of Bo's Stanshurst productions. The name stuck. And if you're talking about the liquid stockings my wife mixes up, she puts cocoa powder in with it.'

Alistair held her jacket for her. Vanessa couldn't stop herself saying, 'We didn't talk about you, if you're wondering. No private stuff.'

'Well, that's good to know.' It was said with deadly lightness. 'How much do you understand about my marital situation, Mrs Kingcourt?'

'Only that you're living apart.'

'*Only*.' Cynicism spun off the word. 'If a couple live apart, where's the point in remaining married?'

'None, I suppose, if there are no children.'

'We haven't been blessed. And yet I would give my eyes and half my soul to have her back. I'll let you know tonight what I've decided.'

'Look, I already know – '

'You know a great deal less than you imagine. I'll call you. The Ledbury Terrace number?'

She nodded, and told him she'd see herself out.

Joanne Sayer had kept in touch since their demob, so Vanessa knew that her friend was in rehearsal at The Rondo, a theatre in nearby Shaftsbury Avenue, for a production called *High Jinx*. Joanne knew nothing about her interview today, or even that she'd left Stanshurst, and Vanessa was looking forward to seeing her friend's expression.

The Rondo's doorkeeper directed her into the auditorium. 'Creep into the back row,' he told her, 'they'll be breaking for lunch soon.'

She watched a strenuous dance routine conducted by a man whose trousers were held up by scarlet braces over a tight vest. Some of the girls kept breaking time, and he was losing patience. Joanne was one of the more confident ones, Vanessa noticed.

After twenty minutes or so, the man in red braces clapped his hands and informed the troupe that they were an utter shower and to be back in forty minutes. Vanessa hurried forward and hissed, 'Joanne, it's me!' Her friend spun round.

'Nessie? Glory be, I'd have walked past you on the street. Which magician did your hair?'

'Mr Stephen of Hans Crescent.'

Joanne's eyes boggled. 'Found yourself a sugar daddy? He costs a fortune.'

'My friend Fern paid. But you should try him out.'

'He's already my stylist, but I have to practically sell myself to pay his prices. Have you time for lunch? I could use a break away from this mob. ENSA rejects calling themselves dancers . . . let's go.' Changing her tap shoes for flat pumps and throwing a coat over her cropped jersey and shorts, Joanne hurried Vanessa along Shaftsbury Avenue to the junction with Coventry Street, to the famous Corner House. They ordered grapefruit followed by fish and salad, which cost one shilling and sixpence. Vanessa related her morning's experiences, beginning with Tom Cottrill.

Joanne laughed. 'Pin on some medals, that'll show him.'

Vanessa then tried to sum up her meeting: 'The interview could hardly have gone worse. For a start, I pretended to be a man just to get my foot in the door, only he knew all along . . . it's rather complicated. Also I got lost and blundered on stage in wooden-soled sandals.' She swung her foot out for Joanne to see.

Joanne made a pained face. 'A hanging offence. Get some rubber soles.'

Glossing over her reaction to Alistair in his rating's uniform, Vanessa described the safety curtain smashing down. 'Like a giant guillotine.'

Joanne gaped, a forkful of salad paralysed by her mouth. 'It could have decapitated you both! Those things weigh tons.'

'I can still feel the noise in my spine.' Vanessa then sketched her interview replies, noting every grimace on her friend's face, and finished with the story of Macduff and the liquid stocking.

By this time, Joanne was in creases. 'Most of us make do with Bisto gravy powder in our leg makeup. Mind you, a Labrador would be just as happy with that.'

'Fern promised me it was artists' pigment.'

Joanne turned serious. 'Probably for the best you don't get the job. I've heard things about your Commander Redenhall.'

'He isn't mine. What have you heard?'

'NSIT.'

Vanessa shook her head.

'Not Safe In Taxis. A womaniser. Threw off his wife and abandoned the Navy in much the same fashion. There are worse rumours, too.' Joanne lowered her voice, making Vanessa crane closer. 'He was on convoy protection, and a ship in his group was hit by a torpedo. It went down within sight of him, but he turned away his own vessel and left the other crew to drown.'

The words unleashed cold spiders but also angered Vanessa. The entire war had felt like an exercise in mass murder. 'Eleven convoy ships a day were being lost in the middle years of the war. Every captain made horrible choices.'

Joanne shrugged. 'Rumours start somewhere.'

'With malicious people. Alistair Redenhall was awarded the DSO, the Distinguished Service Order. They don't hand those out for being an idiot.' Though they might hand them out to men who were not safe in taxis. And to men who intimidated their wives. Fern had looked terrified in the churchyard at Stanshurst – but the blood had been on his face.

'Vanessa, everyone in the business says The Farren will fall flat on its backside. Redenhall's out of his depth and will get his fingers burned.'

'That's a criminal mixing of metaphors.'

'You're defending him, which means you like him.'

'In a way. I'm not sure.'

'People say The Farren's a creepy place.'

'It's empty and dark. Even aircraft hangers are creepy when the lights are out.' Vanessa was glad when Joanne glanced at the wall clock and gasped, 'I have to run. If we're a second late, we get sacked.' The meeting had left her deflated, making her wonder if the shared hardships of camp life had been the glue in their friendship. Still, outside the restaurant Joanne assured Vanessa, 'My sofa's yours, if your posh friend gets tired of you.'

Vanessa was tempted to take a taxi to Ledbury Terrace, but mindful of economy, rode buses instead. Leaving Lord Stanshurst's employment had been a leap, minus parachute. In two weeks' time, she'd be unemployed. She hoped Fern hadn't gone to the trouble of finding champagne. There was nothing to celebrate and there was the matter of the flattened hat. If she could find the words, she intended to ask Fern, 'Do you have any idea just how much your husband adores you?'

In the event, Vanessa was spared both pains. A note wedged under the front door knocker informed her, 'Had to leave, so sorry, darling. My brother's secretary rang from Paris. Chris broke his ankle falling down some museum steps yesterday. He's in agony. The key is at number fourteen. Help yourself to anything you like. Went the day well? Leave your news on the hall table for when I come back.'

The house telephone rang as Vanessa boiled the kettle for tea. Running up from the basement kitchen, expecting Fern, she snatched up the receiver and said, 'If I sneak a half-bottle of wine from the cellar and leave the money on the table, will your husband mind?'

'Not so long as you appreciate what you're drinking,' said a firm, male voice. 'And by the way, I've come to a decision.'

Chapter Nine

'You have the job.'

Her thoughts split like atoms, creating a hundred simultaneous responses. The Farren wanted her. Alistair Redenhall wanted her. What she said was, 'Oh, damn it.'

'You don't want the position?'

'Oh, I do! The "oh damn" is because I have to serve my notice at Stanshurst when all I want to be doing is spring-cleaning the wardrobe room. Can I come in and see it?'

'I wouldn't bother, it's smothered in dust sheets for painting. Can you be back at The Farren on the sixteenth? Be here at ten sharp and you'll meet your new colleagues. What about lodgings?'

'I'll sort something.'

'Good. Could you fetch Fern, please?'

The vocal alteration had been minimal but Vanessa had spent years interpreting scratchy radio transmissions. She knew the subtle cadences of elation, frustration, fear. In Alistair she detected a guarded hurt.

'Sorry, she's not here.'

'D'you know when she'll be back?'

'Um, no. She left a note saying she was on her way to Paris. Her brother had an accident yesterday. It sounds serious.'

'And she's gone to his bedside . . . how did she hear about Chris?'

'His secretary called.'

'What time?'

This was coming close to interrogation. 'It must have been while I was with you. The neighbour said a taxi came at about midday.'

'I wonder why Chris' secretary didn't send a telegram. Placing a call from Paris to London can take days and if the other party won't pick up, you've wasted all that time.'

His obvious scepticism nudged her to a foolish lie. 'The call came from the British Embassy, actually. They get put through pretty fast.'

'Ah, of course. What has Chris done to himself?'

'He broke his ankle tumbling down museum steps.'

'Wasn't yesterday Monday?'

Vanessa sensed she was being backed into a corner, but couldn't locate which one. 'Um . . .'

'I always understood Parisian museums closed Mondays,' Alistair said. 'Well, thank you for passing on the details, Mrs Kingcourt.' He hung up.

Vanessa stood holding the receiver for a long time. She reckoned he'd detected her lie from the moment she'd said 'British Embassy'. Far from helping Fern, she might have widened the rift – and lost Alistair's respect.

From the console drawer she took the wedding picture. Shattered glass formed a lethal rosette around the good-looking couple. 'Damn,' she said again.

Alistair took Macduff for a walk. He'd clung for months to the belief that there was hope for him and Fern. One bloody telephone call too many, and he finally knew that his marriage was over. He'd have liked to walk ten miles, getting up a sweat, but Macduff had limitations. They made it only as far as Trafalgar Square, where the dog had a fine time scattering the pigeons.

'Let's take you home.' Alistair could see a familiar stiffness developing in Macduff's shoulders. He led the dog slowly past the National and Portrait Galleries. The grand steps were peppered with visitors entering and leaving. Lights glowed within. The art collections had been shipped out before the bombing began, and were being brought back in dribs and drabs. London's cultural life was rising, an exhausted phoenix from deep ashes.

He wanted The Farren to be part of that rise. He needed to believe in something. He didn't, however, believe that Christopher Wichelow had broken an ankle. Had little Mrs Kingcourt knowingly lied? She'd quavered, telling him about the phone call from the embassy.

At the theatre, he fed Macduff and passed him into the care of the night janitor. The dog lived at The Farren, sleeping mostly in Alistair's office; he found the stairs up to the flat in Cecil Court too steep. Alistair left for home – a ten-minute walk away – where he washed, changed and set out for his club. This wasn't an evening to spend alone. It was, however, to prove an evening when truth overturned lies.

His father had made him a member of the Overseas and Colonial Club as a twenty-first birthday present. It was popular with military men, civil servants and diplomatic corps. The qualification for membership, other than being male, was to have served one's country abroad.

Walking in, he saw faces he knew. Most were his father's

generation and they offered him nods that implied, 'I know you, young fellow, but damned if I can put a name to you.'

He encountered a former colleague as he crossed the lounge in search of an empty table. Jameson had been a sub-lieutenant on the battle cruiser *Filton* when Alistair had been an eighteen-year-old midshipman.

'Now out with it, Redenhall —' Jameson grasped his forearm as if arresting a thief, 'I keep hearing you've joined a circus. I threatened to thump the last halfwit who said it.'

'Theatre, not circus.' Alistair indicated his civilian suit and offered to stand his friend a drink to assuage the shock. While he was at the bar signing his tab in the member's book, someone tapped him on the shoulder. It was then that the surviving shreds of Alistair's faith disintegrated.

'Thought I recognised the salty silhouette. We both survived, eh? If that doesn't make Fern happy, nothing will.'

Alistair finished signing before he turned. Christopher Wichelow's lean, sunburned face confirmed at last that Fern was lying to him. And that Vanessa Kingcourt was dishonest, too. It pained him more than he could have imagined, and pain with nowhere to go turns rabid.

Soaking in hot water, scented with Yardley's bath salts, Vanessa asked herself at what point of Fern's marital drama had she intruded. Not at the first rift. Fern's weary bitterness, combined with Alistair's simmering anger, suggested a lengthy estrange-ment.

Turning the hot tap on with her big toe, she blew lather away from her chin. Such luxury. Blood-warm water, in a setting that could have come out of *Home Magazine*. She'd bundled her expensive new curls under a silk-jersey turban that she'd found hanging on the bathroom door. There was a robe of the same fabric and the shelf beneath the mirror was spread with makeup, tweezers, combs, razors and pots of skin cream. It had been a draining day and an important one. She had a job, starting September 16th. Her eyelids surrendered. Dreams stole in. Menacing dreams. She was in a coffin, somebody hammering hard on the lid. She sat up with a yell, splashing bathwater over the rim. The knocking was real.

Somebody was at the door, waking the dead.

Chapter Ten

The last time she'd been yanked from sleep this way was by a military policeman, alerting her accommodation block to an imminent air raid. She gave herself a rough towelling, pulled off the turban and grabbed Fern's bathrobe. She ran to the stairs, shoving her arms into it as she went. The slippery fabric resisted her wet limbs, and she was knotting the belt around her waist as she arrived at the door.

The unseen hand attacked again. 'Hold fire,' she called out. At last she got the door open. 'Oh – you.' She stepped back, her hand rising to close the last inch at the neck of her robe. One look at the Commander's face and she knew that lying for Fern had caught up with her. Had she been dressed, she'd have ducked round him and run for it.

Walking straight past her, he picked up letters from the centre table, looking at them one after another before slamming them down. He turned to her. 'Have you any idea how angry I am?'

'Yes.' His eyes had a glassy look, humanity rinsed from them, which told her that excuses were pointless. 'I don't know why Fern has gone to Paris, or if her brother's hurt or not. That's what her note said and I wanted to protect her.'

'From what?'

Vanessa pointed – *from you*. 'Have you any idea how you appear when your temper's up?' As he took a step towards her, her arm shot out. 'Don't! I've already admitted that I shared her lie. Wipe the floor with me verbally, but if you raise your hand to me, I'll scream until the neighbours come.'

Alistair did indeed raise his hands, but not aggressively. 'I've never hit a woman and I'm not going to start with you. But I mean to know why you've turned into Fern's accomplice. Why are you even in our lives? What and who the hell are you?'

'Vanessa Kingcourt, Fern's friend and your employee – unless, of course, this changes things.'

'It changes every damn thing. I've just come away from a conversation with Christopher Wichelow, and I wasn't in Paris. He was trying to shake my hand and I just wanted to thump the poor bastard.'

She hung her head. How could she blame him? 'I'll go and dress,' she said, fumbling the words because she wanted to cry and it was paramount she did not. 'I'll leave.'

'It's too late for you to be out, looking for a place to stay.'

'I'll get a train back to Kent.' She kept her eyes low as she passed him, jumping in shock as he caught her wrist.

'You thought you were helping, I suppose. I can accept a clean lie, out of loyalty, but why the artistic detail about Chris falling down museum steps? That was just insulting.'

She nodded. 'I liked the image; it had drama.' She dug through the pile of mail he had briefly rifled and found the note Fern had left her. She handed it to him. He read it through with a short laugh.

'I can see that. Christopher Wichelow is every Frenchman's stereotype of a privileged Englishman. The crowd would have taken great delight seeing him rolling on the cobbles. Except it didn't happen. No, don't go upstairs. Come.' He released her hand and went into the lounge. She followed reluctantly.

When he'd arrived, she'd seen only his anger. Now she realised he'd undergone another transformation. His hair looked freshly washed and lightly oiled. His single-breasted suit was of mid-grey wool. It looked new, though in line with the diktats of austerity, it had no pocket flaps and no excess fabric except on the shoulders, which were wide. The trousers with their single centre pleat had no turn-ups. His white shirt was conservative, his tie dark. A silk pocket handkerchief made three yacht sails at the top of his breast pocket.

Vanessa cleared her throat. He hadn't actually told her not to turn up at The Farren in thirteen days' time, and his tone had softened considerably in the last half-minute. One glance would tell her if the thaw had reached his face. Frustratingly, he went to a drinks cabinet and fetched out a bottle. 'Somebody's been at the Plymouth gin.'

'Not I,' she assured. 'Look, I have to ask – '

He seemed just then to notice her state of undress. Fern's robe licked every swell and curve of Vanessa's form. What she saw in his face silenced her.

His voice was different too. He asked, 'Ever tasted a pink gin?'

She shook her head.

'Would you like to?'

'A thimble-full.'

'No, that doesn't work.' He took out crystal tumblers and a small bottle with an outsized white label. Adding a few drops from the bottle to each glass, he swirled until they were stained carmine. Uncapping the gin, he filled one glass well above the halfway line.

'Lord, not that much,' Vanessa protested. 'I'll be . . .' *on my back*. 'Head over heels.'

'I'll give you a midshipman's measure.'

That was about half what he'd poured for himself. He held the glass towards her, making her come to him. He was looking at her now without anger. Gin vapours had stimulated something closer to hunger. His lips showed the first lift of arousal. He waited for her to try her gin and she wondered, *Is this an attack by other means? Or is he trying his luck?*

Something was happening to her too. A treacherous heart-thrust, desire curling deep in her stomach. She wanted him. That madness was unchanged, but this other side of him scared her. She wanted closeness and protection and he was offering something riskier, colder.

He said, 'You're trembling.'

'I jumped out of a hot bath.' She put her glass to her lips, tipped, and spluttered. 'My word, that's strong.'

'That's the point of it. Actually, tonight's the first time I've had a real drink in months. Gin and bitters are pretty much all you have on board ship in the tropics. It wards off fever.'

'I'm not feverish.'

'No?' He tested her pulse. 'Hectic.'

She took a desperate slurp.

'No, like this.' He downed his drink, and when she didn't follow suit, took her glass and put it with his on the cabinet. Then he drew her towards him and kissed her. The kiss tasted agonisingly sweet – and misplaced. This was Fern's husband, in Fern's sitting room, with an appallingly comfortable sofa two paces away. She pulled free.

'We can't do this. Please. It's wrong.'

His hand moved to the belt of her robe. One clever twist

would undo it. He found her lips again, persuasively, and she knew that if she opened her mouth to him, they'd both be lost. His breathing was gaining intention, as were his hands.

We want different things of each other, she wanted to tell him. *Different yet mutually destructive.*

She did the only thing she could to save herself: she opened a gate in her mind to let in a memory that was guaranteed to quench her passion. It had been the fourth night of her marriage, the second she and Leo had spent together. Leo had come in, exhausted from a sortie, high on adrenaline and he'd wanted her. Before anything − drink, bath or meal. He'd wanted her with a carnality that frightened her. Her body hadn't been ready; she'd needed reassurance he wasn't prepared to give.

Driven by the memory of what had followed, she elbowed Alistair in the ribs. He hardly seemed to notice and soothed her with a whisper. When he linked his hands around her waist, she slapped him hard across the cheek. She'd never done that before, and she tensed, waiting for the riposte.

Rosehip patches bloomed on his cheek. The same cheek that Fern had injured. He said, 'You're meant to give a warning shot. A word would have done, ideally "no". Just a suggestion.'

'You came here, knowing I was alone in the house. What was your purpose?'

'What was *your* purpose, opening the door in a damp bath-robe?'

'You were bashing the place down. Drunk.'

'Nowhere near drunk. Just enough to take the handbrake off.'

'Put it back on again! You can't get at Fern by using me.'

A smile hovered on Alistair's lips, but not a compassionate one. 'That smacks of a disappointed past. What freight do you carry, Mrs Kingcourt? Did some glamorous pilot officer breach your widowhood then throw you over?'

'There's been no one – though it's none of your bloody business, actually. Next time Fern thwarts you and you seek diversion, remember the bereaved millions who don't have the luxury of marital discord.'

He went to stand by the empty fireplace. 'Did Fern take much with her?'

'Luggage? I've no idea. You know Fern. She throws things into a bag and dashes off.'

'To Paris, but who with? That's the point of all this, isn't it? The wart on the princess's nose that nobody likes to mention. My wife has a lover.' He said 'lover' like a tiger tearing flesh from bone.

Vanessa said, 'One of us should leave now.'

'And of course it must be me. There's something I might as well find while I'm here. Then I'll leave you in peace.'

She stayed in the lounge long enough to re-tie her belt. When she joined Alistair in the hall, he'd opened the console drawer and was staring at the smashed wedding photograph. His expression lanced her. *Why*, she demanded silently, *did you kiss me when it's obvious that Fern's behaviour is tearing your guts out?* He returned the photograph, rooted around in the drawer and located a red booklet.

'My driving licence. I've asked Fern to send this several times but all she sends is bills.'

Vanessa came to a fast, painful decision. 'Commander Redenhall, I'm afraid I can't work for you. I can't work *with* you. Not after . . . I mean, with Fern being . . . I don't want to be forced to choose sides. I'm sorry.' It came out in a blind rush.

Alistair was already at the door.

'Sir, did you hear me?'

'No. I'll see you on the sixteenth. Ten o'clock. Our opening production is to be Wilde's *Lady Windermere's Fan*. You'll find a second-hand copy easily enough on Charing Cross Road.' Opening the door, he added, 'Thank you.'

'For what?'

He touched his cheek. 'For sobering me up. What happened a moment ago will not be repeated. You have my solemn promise.'

She returned upstairs to find her bath had gone cold. 'I hope you keep your promises.' He'd be the type who did, who completely missed the effect he had on a hurt and lonely young woman. The respect he'd accorded her by giving her a job in his theatre had allowed her to make an emotional leap. From defeat to success. From shyness to sexual readiness. He'd roused an ache in her, then retreated and that was a crying shame.

Chapter Eleven

Monday, September 16th, was drizzly and Vanessa put up her umbrella as she stepped out on to Shaftsbury Avenue. She'd been staying with Joanne, whose flat was above a bookseller's on Phoenix Street. The street had once linked Shaftsbury Avenue and Charing Cross Road but was now cut off at its eastern end by the devastation of a neighbouring road. Joanne paid just ten shillings a week for her two-bedroom, blast-damaged flat. She seemed on top of the world. Her show had opened to positive reviews and she had a new boyfriend whom she referred to as 'The Gorgeous Specimen'. She'd invited Vanessa to live with her permanently and Vanessa was happy to accept: from Phoenix Street, she could reach The Farren in under twenty minutes.

Wanting to look her best on her first day, she was wearing new shoes. They weren't ideal for the rain, but she comforted herself with the thought that each splashy step printed her into the London pavements. She'd reignited a friendship with this maimed city, with its cracked walkways, boarded-off bomb sites and buildings plundered of the railings, gates and tracery that had once beautified them. Today, she'd finally enter her own, personal domain at The Farren. She touched her talisman key and her heart felt like a crab busily shedding its shell.

She cut down Neal Street, between dead-eyed warehouses that stored the fruit and vegetables for Covent Garden market. From Neal Street, she took Long Acre and her heart gave a sideways scuttle. A few days ago, as she left Peach Cottage for the last time, her mother had handed over a wad of letters with the words, 'You never said you'd planned to meet him the night he died.'

The letters were those Vanessa had sent to her dad in Room 7, Old Calford Building, Long Acre. He'd kept every one.

She'd answered, 'I don't expect you to understand, but I wanted to see Dad again. Besides, he had something important to tell me.'

'Oh?'

'He wouldn't say what, he didn't trust the post. We exchanged a few words in a pub doorway without recognising each other. I have to live with that.'

Ruth had pondered Vanessa's admission, then said, 'If ever you find yourself on Long Acre, pop in and ask about his clothing coupons.'

'I'm sorry?'

'A person who dies suddenly always has coupons left over, and I reckon some rascal stole your dad's. The landlord, most likely.'

Not knowing whether to laugh or cry, Vanessa had promised to inquire if she stumbled across the Old Calford Building. She fervently hoped she wouldn't.

Today, she did so within a minute. First, she was brought to a stop by a glorious aroma. A café's doors stood open and she leaned in, like a cat to catnip. If these people had discovered the alchemy of turning chicory and roast barley grounds into real coffee . . . *Get up early, have breakfast here tomorrow*, she ordered herself. It was then she looked to the other side of the road and saw a functional three-storey building. 'Calford Press' was painted under the pediment in faded capitals. Vanessa counted nine windows. Some were boarded over, some were curtained and all were filmed with dirt. Crossing the road, she discovered that a second storey window had a 'To Let' sign taped to the glass. Room seven? She moved quickly on.

As she entered The Farren by the stage door, a man in a commissionaire's uniform tilted his clipboard.

'Good morning, Miss.' A campaign medal was pinned to his chest, while a mermaid tattoo swam suggestively around his throat, ending at the base of his ear. Or what would have been his ear had that side of his head not been reduced to a scorched cauliflower. A naval casualty, she guessed. He asked, 'Are you on my list, Miss?'

'Kingcourt, Wardrobe Mistress.'

'Right you are, ma'am.' She noted the uplift from 'Miss' to 'ma'am' and hoped she looked the part, in her dress with the yellow triangles, worn this time with a short, beige jacket and matching hat. Hats needed no coupons, and she'd bought two felt berets. She really ought to have bought jumpers and winter skirts, but advice from Joanne had branded itself on her brain.

'Wear a hat or everyone will think you're a typist or the box-office clerk. Heels, too, even if they hurt, and tailored shoulders because you *must* show that you're the equal of any Wardrobe Master and not the second-reserve-substitute female version.'

After ticking off her name, the doorman introduced himself. 'Leading Seaman Doyle, Jacob Doyle, ma'am. Commander Redenhall was my captain on the *Sundew*. Come to me for anything you need. Messages taken, errands run, awkward so-and-sos dealt with.' He pointed up the corridor. 'Take the OP pass-door, then up to the wardroom, ma'am.'

'Wardroom?'

'Commander's lair, ma'am. His office.'

'And what do you mean by "OP"?'

'"Opposite Prompt". Right-hand side, when you're standing on stage. "Prompt" is left-hand side. What we call port and starboard in the Navy.'

'Why not call it left and right?'

Chuckling, Doyle conducted Vanessa to the door that led into the stalls. He said, 'Commander Redenhall's given me a sheet of theatre jargon. I'll let you have a gander at it some time.'

'Please do. You – you respect Commander Redenhall?' According to Joanne, the entertainment world was still a-buzz over Alistair's nerve – temerity – in running the theatre he'd inherited. This morning, drinking her morning tea in her curlers and dressing-gown, Joanne had said loftily, 'Redenhall will find that Navy rules don't apply in the West End. For one, he'll have to deal with trade unions. You can't just give orders and expect them to be obeyed.'

Doyle's opinion of his former captain was plain as soap. 'He's the best, ma'am. I served with him from day one, until the *Sundew* went under. He saved my bacon. I can say that with feeling, as at the time I was frying.' His voice shook, and not with humour.

'Are we all new boys and girls here?'

'Clean sweep, excepting Miss Bovary. Oh –' Doyle winked, 'and the one they call Back Row Flo, but she don't appear that often.'

Once in the auditorium, Vanessa remembered how colossal this place had seemed to her as a child, and her awe at the dimming lights, the congealing hush. For the first time, she saw the interior for what it was: an intimate Georgian theatre, miraculously preserved. Walls were iridescent jade, with marble inset panels. The ceiling was painted to resemble an ocean, waves foaming over the torsos of mermaids and mermen. Neptune with his trident pierced the waters, his fiery gaze shooting up into a clouded sky. Bow-fronted boxes, once reserved for the gentry, resembled split oyster shells with their creamy mouldings. Waterfall chandeliers filled the lofty space. These weren't illuminated – by the look of them, they still had their original candle holders – but they reflected light from all sides. Dust covers had been removed from the seats, which were sea blue, matching the carpet. The effect was of being under the ocean, looking up to heaven. Rather appropriate for Alistair. 'Beautiful,' she murmured.

'Unique, too.'

Alistair must have entered from the back of the auditorium. His tone suggested he had no intention of referring to their scene in Ledbury Terrace.

Perhaps it was foolish of her to tease, but she couldn't resist saying, 'I'd love to have seen your face when you learned this was to be yours.'

'You wouldn't, I promise. Nor will I repeat my comments when I walked in the first time. She'd been dark long enough for vagrants to find shelter inside, and rats.'

She. Appropriate. There was a soul to this place. 'At least she survived the Blitz.'

'Only just. The pub on Farren Court and six shops went. We're patching up, but the materials we need are reserved for rebuilding more vital institutions.'

'How did you get the scaffolding and the men on the roof?'

For the first time, she detected something other than guarded formality. *Help me,* she called out to the invisible guardians of her heart, *I still feel his body against me. I can taste his skin.*

'What scaffolding? What roofers?'

'So I imagined hammering when I first came here?'

'I'm afraid so.'

'What you're saying is, you have your secret suppliers. What about the safety curtain?'

'See for yourself.' He shouted towards the stage, and to somebody she couldn't see, 'Bring the house lights down, footlights on.'

'Aye, aye, Sir,' came the return shout.

The auditorium slid into darkness. A moment later, footlights cast an upward glow on the iron barrier. Vanessa had previously only seen its rear side, which had been as plain as an oil tank. By contrast, the audience-facing side was exquisite, with 'Safety Curtain' in shapely lettering and wreathes of flowers framing a brown-haired woman leaning against a plinth. She wore an ivory, Georgian-style gown, her tresses dressed in courtly style. Her expression was composed of sorrow.

'Who is she?'

'Elizabeth Farren, the actress and tragedienne, born mid-seventeen-hundreds. This theatre was named for her. She became the Countess of Derby.'

'She married well!'

'Assuming the Earl of Derby was worth spending time with, I suppose she did. A daughter of hers became Countess of Wilton.'

'Wilton, as in "Wilton Bovary"?'

'Bo was a descendent, reputedly. It's why he and his father felt this theatre to be a family possession. Ready to start work? Crew meeting in my office.'

'Can I sneak a look at my room first?'

In reply, Alistair handed her a black, iron key. 'Yours. I have one and Doyle has the other.'

*

The wardrobe room walls had been painted pale green, the ceiling cream. An industrial-looking light hung above the long cutting table.

Her fossilised memory was of a forest of chair and table legs. The room was brighter than she'd expected, thanks to a wide metal window set high in the wall. Hadn't there been curtains across it before? Of course, she'd come here as a child in the depths of winter, when it would have been dark by three-thirty. She ran her fingers over the table, frowning because it was chipped. She must find some baize or American Cloth to cover it.

The wardrobe stood where she remembered it, near the door. It was eight feet wide, built of sombre oak. It wasn't locked and didn't seem to have a key of its own. She tried Eva's gold key and it almost disappeared.

She poked around the shelves and found white cotton, hat ribbon and assorted buttons. On the top shelf, her fingers dislodged a reel of ribbon. It was soft as moleskin and faded in the middle, but at the edges a rich sea green. 'Hello!' How long had her baby curls survived in Eva's possession? Her dad had taken the bow Eva had tied in her hair so as not to upset her mother. Had he lost it, or deliberately dropped it as they stepped off the train?

A movement caught the edge of her eye and she turned in fright. A figure was watching her from the opposite end of the room. A disconcerting, dismembered figure. Her heart stopped – until she realised that it wore a cotton dress with yellow triangles and a beige jacket. She was looking into a mirror.

It must have been broken. Somebody had cemented it back together with window putty, to crazy effect. The frame was painted in the same green as the walls. She went over and nicked a corner with her fingernail and saw gilding beneath. That's how she remembered it, as a golden, scrolled frame mirror. She would need a new one. She couldn't imagine actresses accepting Cubist versions of themselves.

Perhaps she should take an inventory? She looked inside wicker skips, which presumably were for storing costumes. All they contained were calico cotton dress covers. When she pulled the covers off the hanging rails, she discovered men's lounge and evening suits, late Victorian or Edwardian. They looked about right for *Lady Windermere* which was set in the 1890's.

Would she have to measure actors' waistlines and inside legs? How did one measure a man's inside leg? Efficiently, of course. You wouldn't want to have to ask to do it again. But which end did you start, thigh or ankle? She decided to ask Doyle; he seemed to know a lot.

Rummaging along the shelves, she found flat irons and crimping irons. Cravats, bow-ties, spats and monocles in labelled boxes. But though she searched every corner, she discovered nothing her little key would unlock.

And something else . . . unless female costumes were stored elsewhere, there was nothing for the actresses. They'd have to be dressed from scratch. '"Must have knowledge of period costume."' *Crumbs.*

As she moved hangers on the rails, a sweet smell filled the air. Her mother's voice made an unwelcome intrusion in her thoughts: '*Her* coat came out of a theatre wardrobe and *his* smelled of lavender.'

'Eva, I'm back,' Vanessa whispered. 'I'm going to need help and more luck than I'm used to.' But for now she'd better get to the crew meeting. Chancing the cage-lift, she descended to the back-stage area and took a similar lift up to Alistair's corridor. As she approached his office – his wardroom – she whispered, 'OP is the left side as you look out from the stage. Wait. No, it isn't!' She stopped, copying Doyle's hand-movements. 'OP is the *right* side when you're on stage, because "P" is "prompt side", which is on the left. Isn't it?' She sighed. 'How will I remember all this?'

Alistair was setting out chairs and nodded in response to Vanessa's 'hello,' then said, 'I forgot to ask earlier, did you find accommodation?'

'Phoenix Street, above the Russian bookseller's. With my actress friend.' He was looking at her as if he'd just discovered a new flaw. 'What have I said?'

'The fact that you aren't staying with Fern suggests she hasn't returned from Paris.'

He didn't know where his wife was? Vanessa didn't know either. While working out her notice, she'd pointedly refrained from asking Lord Stanshurst for news of Fern. She said to Alistair now, 'I always intended to stay with Joanne, sir. It's easier because Jo lets me chip in financially.' The sight of Macduff under the desk gave her an excuse to crouch down, out of Alistair's sightline. 'Hungry, old chap?'

The dog returned solid thumps of the tail.

Getting up, she found Alistair looking at her quizzically. Or rather, at the beret she wore side-on. Was he wondering if it was another of Fern's?

All he said was, 'Don't call me "sir". We stand easy here. Unless you'd prefer "Mrs Kingcourt"?'

'The "sir" was from habit. I'd like to be Vanessa.'

'Good. I like to imagine it was Mrs Kingcourt who slapped me, and Vanessa who returned my kiss.'

'I didn't return –' she began. She almost said, 'You forced

yourself on me,' but that wasn't strictly true, so she leaned back on reproach. 'You promised to forget about it.'

'I promised not to repeat the attempt. I didn't say anything about forgetting.'

They put out the rest of the chairs in silence. Fourteen in all. The room undoubtedly resembled a ship's wardroom, just as the theatre in some ways resembled a luxury liner – the side corridors being the deck promenades, the auditorium the lounges and ball room, and the stage the prow. *OP side is to the right, if you're standing on stage*, she repeated to herself. *Got it!*

She watched Alistair place a final chair on one side of the doorway. Now the door wouldn't close. 'It's a bit tight, isn't it?' she said. 'If anybody smokes, we'll expire.'

He surveyed the room, then looked at his watch. 'You're right. Ten minutes to get these chairs down to the stage.'

For the next fifteen minutes, they travelled up and down in the lift, Doyle off-loading chairs at the bottom. They phased their journeys, travelling one at a time, until the final descent when the creaking lift conveyed Alistair, Vanessa and Macduff. A tight squash, the dog panting between them.

'Is the dog joining the meeting?' she asked when things unsaid became suffocating.

'Of course. He's on the payroll.'

'What's his job?'

'Theatre mascot.'

'He really *is* on the payroll?'

'Twenty guineas a year, most of which goes on food.'

Other staff began to arrive just as she and Alistair finished placing the chairs in a semi-circle across the stage. Cottrill traipsed on and hoisted the safety curtain. This time it rose on buttered wheels.

Alistair put the final chair out front for himself. Vanessa chose one at the end of the row. Joanne's second piece of advice had been, 'Don't ally yourself with crew. Keep a professional distance.' But how could she? The men now filtering in through the OP wings would be working alongside her to the same end, a successful show.

Though of course, she had the extra burden of mapping her father's last days. She pressed her fingers against her breastbone until the gold key bit into her flesh. She'd been in danger of forgetting her mission to find out why her father had wanted to see her so urgently before his death. This job, this company, and above all, Alistair, must not obscure her purpose.

Vanessa soon became aware that the crew were choosing seats at the end opposite to hers. There was nothing overtly hostile in their action; she supposed that these men with their competent, military bearing were conditioned to separateness from women. Then, just as she was thinking of calling Macduff over for company, a young woman strode on to the stage.

She drew whistles because she was wearing a siren suit, the all-in-ones people had pulled on during air raids to protect precious clothes in the underground shelters. Hers was a pattern of faded greens, which shouted 'old curtains', but it was tightly belted, emphasising a pert bottom and breasts. Her sandy hair was bundled under a yellow duster, tied at the front in a knot. With her poppy-red lipstick, she could have been a poster-girl for female munitions workers. Considering Alistair's insistence that his new staff must have war-service, she might well have been a shell-case packer or a dockyard riveter.

Seeing Vanessa, she shouted, 'Hurrah, a sister!' and sat down beside her, shoving out her hand. 'Name's Tanith Stacey. I'm DSM. You?' Her voice had the short vowels of a private school education, but there was a catch to her breath. Scared, Vanessa thought, and hiding it.

'Vanessa Kingcourt, Wardrobe.' Vanessa returned the handshake. Having no idea what 'DSM' meant, she probed – 'Were you in this business before the war?'

'Gosh, no, I was eleven before the war! Though I was an air raid warden for the last year, when I wasn't at school.'

'Who will you be reporting to?'

'Horrid Cottrill.' Tanith spoke in a stage whisper and eyes turned their way. Fortunately, Tom Cottrill was pacing behind the scrim curtain like a sergeant major looking out for stragglers.

If Cottrill was Stage Manager, the 'D' in 'DSM' must mean 'Deputy'.

'You're very glam.' Tanith glanced at Vanessa's bare legs. The legs terminated in soft canvas shoes that, to Vanessa's mind, made her feet look like baby rabbits. The wooden-soled sandals would never intrude upon the stage again.

Tanith sighed. 'Wish I had nice pins. Mine are like sea defences and they never go brown.'

'My friend Joanne, who's in a dance show, makes a leg mixture with cornflour and gravy powder. You just fluff it on. I'll show you how.'

'Would you? I envy every inch of you, because you'll have your own room and no boss.'

'I have a boss.' Vanessa glanced at Alistair who was shaking hands with a dark-skinned man, asking him if his accommodation was satisfactory. The reply, 'Very acceptable, sir, thank you,' came in the back-throated accent of Liverpool.

Tanith laughed. 'We're a mixed bag, aren't we?'

'With one thing in common.' Vanessa nodded lightly at Alistair. 'Him.'

'Mind if I ask —' Tanith's eyes were blue and when she spoke, they moved with a searching speed, 'were you ever an actress?'

'Never. Why?'

'You pack a lot into one word. *Him.*' Tanith's glance towards Alistair was pure schoolgirl. 'You like him.'

'I don't know him.'

'You keep looking at him.'

'I'm getting his measure.'

'They say he walked away from his marriage. So if you're not interested . . .'

Vanessa whispered fiercely, 'He's very much married.' She added privately, *and you're too young to even think of such things!* To shake off the memory of Alistair's mouth on hers, Vanessa counted the number of people on stage. Apart from Alistair, herself, Tanith and the dog in his customary snoozing heap, there were ten men. All shades of hair and one with sleek, brylcreemed waves. Some wore collar and tie, others had waistcoats and rolled shirtsleeves. Many of them wore rubber plimsolls, their footsteps inaudible as they moved about. Her eyes grazed Alistair and she knew he'd been watching her.

He cleared his throat. 'Ladies and gentlemen, welcome.' He was standing, a hand resting on his chair back. His mastery was unforced, implying that he, and everyone with him — Macduff included — was in the right place. 'None of us, apart from our stage manager, has previous theatrical experience.' Tom Cottrill was staring into the fly tower until, with a nervous turn of the neck, he shifted his gaze to the upper circle as if looking for somebody.

Alistair continued, 'Yet here we are, raising a theatre from the ashes. People will say we're mad. How can a bunch of innocents put on shows that will bring in audiences? We've much to prove, and we ought to question ourselves. But we all have one thing in common – '

Tanith nudged Vanessa and whispered, '*Him.*'

'Most of us gave everything except our lives to our country. Think of this as a peacetime challenge that will draw on that experience. The Farren will continue to be a Producing Theatre, which means we'll produce and create plays ourselves, hiring in designers and directors for each show. Money will be tight –' he stopped to allow for the good-humoured groan that issued from a portion of his audience. 'Some of you will be doubling up on jobs but I want you to know –' he stopped again as an apologetic cough cut across him.

'I am unforgivably late but I made a detour via the Charing Cross Road. One step inside a bookseller's and I'm lost.'

The late-comer was a slim young man dressed in loose trousers. His slightly too-small jacket was fastened with a single button. It looked like thrown-on jumble salvage until he came more into the light, when it became evident that the 'impoverished loafer' effect was intentional. Only a red cravat around his throat and a brown beret set at the same rake as Vanessa's showed any substantial wear. Close-cut dark hair framed a face of beautiful structure.

'Sit down,' Alistair told him.

Long-lashed eyes regarded Alistair with reproach. 'Do throw me a life-belt, Captain.' A soft, Irish accent made the provocative comment somehow musical.

Though not to Alistair's ears. 'As you inferred, there are no excuses for being late on the first morning. You are?'

'Hugo Brennan. Production Designer. Where shall I sit?'

The only seat going spare was the one Tom Cottrill would have occupied had he not chosen to stand. Brennan was making for it when one of the burly flymen picked it up, plonked it down beside Vanessa, and tramped back to his own seat. The action said clearly, 'You're with the girls, matey.'

'Why, thank you.' Sitting down, crossing his long legs, Brennan whispered to Vanessa, 'Everything about you shouts "wardrobe". Thought they were going to appoint a man.'

'Shush!'

'Don't you snub me, too. We must be in tight cahoots, darling. With all these sailors around, a person could get violently seasick. How are you with corsetry?'

'Can we discuss it later?'

'Straight or swan-bill, what's your preference?'

Alistair cleared his throat. Brennan shifted his gaze frontwards, the eager innocent, giving the impression that it was Vanessa who'd been gossiping.

Alistair went on, 'Should any of you find yourselves overwhelmed, talk to your supervisor, and if you are the supervisor, talk to me. I am Theatre *and* Company Manager, in charge of the daily grind. I'm also a co-producer. For those of you who don't know what that means, I'll be managing the finance.'

'Busy, busy,' Brennan murmured.

'But I won't be casting the play, so don't send your nieces, sisters, or sweethearts to me in the hope they'll get acting roles. Call me Redenhall, or Alistair, if you prefer. Not "sir" unless you really can't help yourself. Never "Captain". Should you ever meet me on board ship, you may call me "Commander", that being my rank. In this place, however, we leave ranks behind. Fine with that, Brennan?'

'Perfectly understood, and do call me Hugo.'

A hostile buzz rose, an intimation that these men had tastes and opinions, and not all of them liberal. Brennan needs to wind in his sails, Vanessa thought. And what the hell is a swan-bill when it's not on a swan?

'Here's the bit you all want to know.' Alistair shifted his hands on the chair. 'Rehearsals start October 1st and by then, the play will be cast. The director arrives at the end of this month, giving you, Brennan, a shave under two weeks to collaborate with Wardrobe and Scenery on your designs. For everyone else, there's plenty to do getting backstage in trim. As some of you already know, the play we're kicking off with is – '

'You have begun without us!' A female figure was proceeding down the aisle from the back of the auditorium. She walked with long steps. A second woman waddled in her wake, indicating she found downhill progress difficult in heels. A third and fourth figure brought up the rear.

Walking to the lip of the stage, Alistair shielded his eyes. 'Miss Bovary, is that you? Mrs Rolf? This is a meeting for design, technical and stage crew.'

The first voice demanded, 'Why weren't we informed?'

'Because it's none of your concern.'

'On the contrary, Commander Redenhall. It is my right to be informed of all activities affecting this theatre.'

'That's not how it works under me, Miss Bovary. But since you're here, come and join us.' Alistair opened the pass door beside the prompt box. Vanessa heard him exclaim, 'Have we got a coach party? Who else is there?'

Miss Bovary returned, 'My brother-in-law, Mr Rolf, and my nephew Edwin.'

'Ask Edwin to go. Doyle can show him to the nearest Lyons Corner House.'

'There is no call to exclude Edwin,' a reedy, male voice

objected. 'Need I remind you that The Farren has been in the hands of the Bovary family for two generations?'

'And now it belongs to me, Mr Rolf. Edwin,' Alistair's tone was crisp, but not unkind, 'get lost.'

'Well, that's blunt, Redenhall.' The answer came with a sneer. 'Remember Icarus who flew too high? His waxen feathers melted in the sun's heat. Father, you can pick me up at my club.' Moments later, the auditorium door clicked shut, silencing the off-hand laughter that accompanied Edwin Bovary's exit.

Alistair sent two stage crew to find more chairs. They came back with the sofa left over from *The Importance*, which had been stored in the backstage corridor. Once Mr Rolf had dusted it and fussily arranged the panels of his overcoat, he and the ladies settled themselves. Alistair introduced them. 'Miss Bovary, the late Wilton Bovary's sister and our administrator. She works with contracts, promotions and accounts. Along with Mr and Mrs Rolf, she is a minor shareholder of Farren Theatre Ltd, the company that will produce our repertoire. Mr Terence Rolf also runs a production company, Rolf Associates. He is casting and raising investment for us.'

'No money, no theatre.' Miss Bovary gave Alistair an emphatic stare. The stare fell next on Vanessa.

Ah, Vanessa thought. She's the one who doesn't like Wardrobe Mistresses. Thinks they live too long, or something.

In a grey dress, a strip of lace encircling a wrung-out throat, Miss Bovary offered an advertisement for over-preserved virginity. After staring at every human in turn, she aimed her disgust at Macduff. 'Who allowed that dog on stage?'

'Still knows how to charm,' Hugo breathed.

'You know her?'

'Her late brother gave me my first job as a scenery painter.

I daubed my way up the ranks, a rising star in set design, and finally pulled off a triumph in a competing theatre. Bo wished me luck. *They* never forgave me.' Hugo nodded to indicate the sisters and Terence Rolf. 'These days, of course, we're all dim twinkles in an egalitarian sky. All starting anew. Just that some of us don't realise it.'

'So what's the play to be, sir?' someone called out.

Alistair's reply was drowned by an ear-rending sound. Macduff was howling at the sofa's occupants. Nothing could induce him to stop, and Alistair closed the meeting.

As people prepared to go, Terence Rolf announced above Macduff's dirge that the play was one of his 'late, sorely-missed brother-in-law's favourites, *Lady Windermere's Fan*.' Wilton Bovary had planned to put it on in 1939, only to be thwarted by the closure of theatres during the war. 'Our tribute to him will be its revival.'

The call to nostalgia fell flat. Nobody present had worked under Wilton Bovary. Nobody had warm memories to cradle. Terence Rolf was undeterred. Three talented stars had agreed to play the lead roles, he bellowed, which would pull in the critics and public alike. Put off by Macduff's unrelenting vocals, he stuttered on the word 'stars'. A man near Vanessa repeated, 'Three talented tarts? Things are looking up.'

Alistair offered Macduff a cream cracker from his pocket and the howling waned, like the dying notes of a siren. Taking out a ten-shilling note, he beckoned Tanith Stacey to his side, and asked her to take the dog to an eating house on Long Acre called Frimley's. 'He has eel pie and liquor.'

'Liquor?' Tanith echoed. 'Alcohol?'

'Eel juice; he loves it. Have some yourself.'

Tanith called to Vanessa, 'Fancy it?'

Vanessa was longing to get back to her room, to take full ownership of her new workspace. Something in Miss Bovary's stare had made her feel she needed to make her mark, quickly. If Tanith could wait a while . . .

Alistair overruled, saying, 'I want Vanessa with me.' He summoned her and added quietly, 'I need your powers of observation for the next hour or so.'

A select group retired to Miss Bovary's office. Long and narrow like Alistair's, she shared hers with Mr Amery, Head of Promotions. He was out today.

The first thing Vanessa noticed was the framed stills on the walls, so many that the green silk wallpaper was visible only in patches. There were stills of *Sleeping Beauty*, featuring one fairy in black and another in silver-lilac. Between them, a man in royal robes. The caption read, 'Silv, Bo and Babs. A family affair, Christmas 1925.'

Behind her, Alistair asked, 'Can you tell which is Miss Bovary?'

The Bad Fairy, of course. She didn't say it out loud, but Alistair guessed anyway and laughed.

'Miss Bovary played the Lilac Fairy. She was the more beautiful, but both sisters were famous for their trapeze stunts.' Seeing her expression, he laughed. 'We all have a past, Vanessa.'

Miss Bovary swept up to them and Vanessa thought she was going to comment on the photograph, but she pointed to the door, informing Vanessa, 'Tea things are in the office marked "Records". Fresh milk is in the cold box. The jar containing sugar is my personal ration, but you may give some to Commander Redenhall and Mr Rolf. I take one level spoonful.'

'I don't need sugar,' Alistair said. 'And why are you sending Mrs Kingcourt to make the tea?'

'I don't mind,' Vanessa said, deciding that cooperation was the best course, to be followed later by a show of firmness.

Hugo offered to help. 'Come on, we'll let the grown-ups talk about us for a bit.'

The records room was little more than a glorified store-room, a cold-box and a spirit kettle crammed on a shelf. Vanessa pointed to the kettle, asking Hugo, 'Where do we fill that?'

'From the tap in the gents'. I'll take it.'

Left alone, she took her bearings. There were two filing cabinets in the room, four drawers deep, each identified by letters of the alphabet. She went straight to the drawer labelled N-O-P-Q but it was locked.

'You'll find me under "B".'

'Hugo! You nearly gave me a seizure.'

'You haven't laid the tea tray. Some slave-girl you are.' Hugo squeezed past her and lit the spirit stove.

'What's in those cabinets?'

'Why do you want to know?'

She gave Hugo a silent appraisal, yielding to the impulse to trust him. 'My dad acted here, and I want to learn everything I can about him.'

'Name of?'

'Clive Quinnell.'

Hugo reached into the cold-box for the milk. He brought out a set of keys along with the jug. 'I knew a *Johnny* Quinnell.'

'That's him.'

He gave her the keys. 'This is what you need. Have a dig, but be quick.'

As Hugo measured out tea leaves, Vanessa searched. 'Q' was represented by a single hanging-file. In it, she found a peach-coloured card referring to a 'Quarles, Timothy', date of birth 6th March 1908, followed by personal details. 'Clumsy when inebriated. Too fond of public houses, burdened with an ill-natured wife. Do not employ again.' She asked Hugo, 'Does everybody's character get put on record?'

'Even Macduff has a card,' Hugo answered. 'Nobody is spared. I started here in 1934 as a scenery-man's assistant. Have a rifle, see if I'm still there.'

Vanessa had just pulled out a manila envelope labelled 'Quin-nell C. J', but she humoured Hugo, putting it aside and opening the top drawer once again. 'Here you are,' she said after a short search. '"Brennan, Hugh". You're an August baby, born nine months after the Great War ended.'

'My parents knew how to celebrate.'

'Why "Hugh" not "Hugo"?'

'Mr Bovary said that "Hugo" was classier and that theatre was "frightfully, frightfully snobbish." When I turned twenty-one, I made the change permanent. What does she say?'

'She?'

'These records are Miss Bovary's handiwork. When the Domesday Book was written, and English folks' souls were reduced to chattels, she was there with her quill, getting her hand in.'

'She says you're a promising painter, "Willing to learn though can be obtuse."'

'What the hell does "obtuse" mean?'

'Slow to understand.'

'I'm joking, Nessie.'

'"Displays effeminate tendencies." Awful woman!'

'It was the way I held my paintbrush.'

'"Is let down by his time-keeping –"' The kettle whistled,

filling the room with steam. Hugo poured boiling water over tea leaves while Vanessa shut and opened drawers, finding the brown envelope again.

'Your father's file?' Hugo gently rocked the tea-pot side to side. 'Another character assassination?'

'It's empty.'

'As if he never existed.' Hugo's voice lost its teasing note. 'She always did prefer the dead to the living.'

'Miss Bovary?'

'She cannot tolerate opposition – Oops, put your subservient face back on.' Somebody was calling from the corridor. Hugo called back, 'Just counting out the sugar grains, coming in a mo.' Loading the tea tray, he said under his breath, 'The Rolfs and the Bovarys have met their match in Alistair Redenhall, but that doesn't mean they'll go down without a fight. Now close that cabinet and put the keys back.'

Having spent twice as long making tea as they ought, Vanessa expected a reprimand, but only Alistair looked up. He said briskly, 'Put the tray on the desk, Brennan.'

Vanessa tuned in to what Terence Rolf was saying.

'Edwin is an experienced comic actor. Indeed, this being a family theatre, a Bovary must be part of the company.'

Mrs Rolf took over from her husband. 'Our son is perfect for the part of Mr Cecil Graham, in age, stature and natural demeanour. Wearing lustrous furs, and as fat as her husband was thin, she put Vanessa in mind of a she-bear defending her cub. 'You hold a different opinion, Commander?'

'I defer to you and your husband on casting, just as I've deferred to you in the choice of director and designer.' Alistair briefly shifted his gaze to Hugo. 'However, it's my decision that every person working here should have served in some capacity in the war. Unless they were too old or young to do so.'

'Or too fragile,' Mrs Rolf burst in. 'Recurrent pleurisy prevented Edwin.'

'In which case, he's unsuited to the part anyway. Nowhere in the script does it say that Cecil Graham has a lung disorder.'

'We'll talk about this another time, Sylvia.' Miss Bovary spoke, then turned a hooded look on Vanessa. 'So. You are the Wardrobe Master who never was, Mrs Kingcourt. I was most surprised to learn that a female had been employed after all. You must be highly experienced, to merit the position.'

'I'm not very experienced, I'm afraid.' Leaving Hugo to make theatre of pouring tea – he was whistling 'The Java Jive' – Vanessa took a seat to Alistair's left.

Miss Bovary turned to Alistair. 'Commander, perhaps you can explain your reasons for hiring Mrs Kingcourt.'

'She was in the WAAF, where she did a job far harder than that of wardrobe mistress.'

Terence Rolf glanced sidelong at Vanessa. 'We all like a Mistress.' He had removed his outdoor layers revealing a burgundy velveteen jacket, a mushy silk cravat filling the gap between its taffeta lapels. With hair dyed black around a bald patch, he looked every inch the aging rake. 'Naturally, by "mistress" I meant "one in a position of authority".'

'Naturally,' Vanessa echoed.

Hugo passed tea cups around until something seemed to catch his eye. It was one of the photographs on the wall. Vanessa saw him lean forward, ignoring Miss Bovary who had taken a business card from her handbag and was holding it out to him.

'Mr Brennan?' She waved the card to get his attention. 'Daphne

Yorke of Mayfair has been making costumes for us for years. *Mr Brennan*, are you listening?'

Hugo turned around, slowly. 'Sorry. You were saying?'

'Mrs Yorke of Mayfair is expecting a call. She will make costumes to your sketches.'

'Designs. I design, I don't sketch.' Hugo declined the card. 'And I've set up my own *atelier* in Great Portland Street. I will create the originals and Mrs Kingcourt will take them to a manufacturer of my choosing. We'll hire in whatever we don't want to make.'

Miss Bovary made a mouth shape as if sucking a seed from between her teeth. She returned the card to her bag, closing it with a snap. 'The Farren *never* hires. Creating costumes in partnership with fine dressmakers is what we became famous for. Our costume collection was so renowned, we hired it out to others.'

'So let's use it!'

'It's gone.'

'Hitler's fault,' Terence Rolf explained. 'The same bomb that . . .'

'Let's not relive that horrible night.' Miss Bovary held up a hand. 'As we keep reminding ourselves, this is a new beginning.' She trailed Hugo's gaze, which had returned to the wall. She frowned, then happened to look across at Vanessa. She gave a start.

'Is there something the matter?' Vanessa asked.

'I – no. I imagined for a moment that we'd met before, that's all.'

'I don't think so.' Vanessa had no recollection of seeing Miss Bovary at Brookwood among the mourners, though she must have been there.

Terence Rolf took over the conversation, expanding on the

merits of the chosen director. 'Aubrey Hinshaw is an old hand at Wilde. He'll go for the wit and comedy, without trying to wring meaning from every line.'

'I have my doubts about the play,' Alistair said.

'That's nonsense.' Miss Bovary had recovered her composure.

Alistair let a beat or two pass. 'Elegant banter in upper class drawing rooms . . . "Cucumber sandwich, dear Duchess?" Pretty much the only characters who aren't titled are the maid and the butler. What's more, The Farren will have done two Wilde plays in succession. War-sick audiences want something fresh.'

'They want glamour. Fun. Colour.' Miss Bovary beat her hand in time to each point. 'And cucumber sandwiches do not make an appearance in *Lady Windermere's Fan*.' She asked Hugo to sit down, complaining that he made her giddy by towering over her. When he took a seat by Vanessa, Miss Bovary moved her chair so that she sat in front of the wall. There was something she didn't want them to see. 'Oscar Wilde never goes out of fashion,' she said with finality.

Terence Rolf nodded agreement. 'Investors adore a well-trodden old favourite.'

Hugo's snort made everyone stare. 'Sorry. Sorry, Mr Rolf. It's a psychological condition, laughing inappropriately in small rooms.' To Vanessa he whispered, '"Well-trodden old favourite". Thought he was referring to himself.'

'It has a huge cast.' Alistair's tone made it clear he was impatient to be out of this room. 'Twenty characters, even after we cut non-speaking parts. The costume budget will be elephantine, as will the salary bill.'

'Won't matter if we play to full houses,' Terence Rolf got in quickly. 'Irene Eddrich has graciously agreed to take the part of

Mrs Erlynne. Patrick Carnford and Ronnie Gainsborough are raring to go as Lord Windermere and Lord Darlington.'

Mrs Rolf simpered. 'The public adores them. Such red-blooded tension between them on stage.'

'And off,' Hugo said aside.

'For the role of Lady Windermere, we're hoping for Clemency Abbott. She's under contract to a Canadian film company, but a little bird says she won't sail.' Rolf shook his head indulgently. 'She's dying to meet you, Commander.'

'Clemency Abbott is a cow,' said Hugo.

'But so beautiful, one hardly minds. And one must always make allowances for talent.' Terence Rolf's smile acquired a dash of malice. 'Aren't allowances *occasionally* made for you, Hugo?'

Alistair stood, drained his tea. 'As I said, casting is your province, Terence. Choose whom you want, but it's no to Edwin. We'll meet again in a few days. Miss Bovary, any more comments?'

Miss Bovary was tight-lipped. As they all gathered their things, Vanessa heard Alistair say, 'Do *you* wish to add anything?'

It took a few seconds' silence to grasp that he meant her. 'I – I don't think so.'

'Are you happy to work with Hugo, helping him meet his creative vision?'

'Of course she can't help him.' Miss Bovary couldn't resist one last thrust. 'Costume-making is not an amateur pursuit.'

'Would you let Mrs Kingcourt answer for herself?'

Though she'd much rather make a swift exit, Vanessa understood the need to face Miss Bovary down. Otherwise, she'd be treading on tin-tacks for ever. She flashed a smile, bright as a rabbit's tail. 'I'm happy to work closely with Hugo.' She'd probe her father's life and at the same time, become a damn good Wardrobe

Mistress. 'And I want to make it clear that I won't be sent to make tea at every meeting, Miss Bovary. Not until it's my turn again.'

Alistair nodded, satisfied.

Miss Bovary took a notebook from her bag, and a pencil. 'I might as well jot down your personal details while you're here, Mrs Kingcourt. May I know your given names?'

'Vanessa Elizabeth.'

'Your date of birth?'

'May 29th, 1920.'

The pencil dropped from Miss Bovary's fingers. Vanessa bent to pick it up and as she leaned forward, the gold key fell from her neckline. Returning the pencil to Miss Bovary, she saw Terence Rolf's gaze fasten on her throat. He looked almost as shaken as his sister-in-law.

They trooped out of the office, the Rolfs and Miss Bovary on their way to lunch in a restaurant nearby. Vanessa noticed that Miss Bovary locked her office door carefully.

Suspecting Alistair would want to conduct a debrief on the morning's events, Vanessa remained in the theatre and snacked on an apple. Wanting something to do, she begged a roll of sandpaper from the carpenter's bay and spent her lunch-hour smoothing the nicks out of her cutting table. It would have to be planed to remove the worst of them, but that wouldn't be beyond her. Her paternal grandfather had been Stanshurst's estate carpenter and such things ran in the blood.

A brisk knock had her wiping dust from her brow. 'Come in.'

It was Alistair. 'Hugo asked if you could meet him at Anjeliko's on Long Acre. It's easy to find. Follow the smell of good coffee.'

'I know it already.' From outside the door came a muffled whine. Macduff. 'Bring him in,' Vanessa invited.

'I'm not staying.' Yet Alistair made no move to go. 'Sorry about the green paint.' He flicked a gaze over the walls. 'It was the only light colour I could get in any quantity. Feel free to personalise. Family photos and such.'

'We weren't a family for photo albums and I have no wedding pictures. There wasn't time.'

'What year were you married?'

'1940. October.'

'In the thick of it.'

She braced herself for follow-up questions, quickly preparing a bland answer or two. She had no treasured memories of her marriage, only deep hurt and a lingering sense of failure. But Alistair withdrew from the subject. He rested his hands on the table and in a mocking echo of Terence Rolf, glanced at her throat. She'd pushed Eva's key deep inside her clothes and now waited for him to mention it. To distract him, she opened her handbag and removed the gloves he'd given her many months ago, laying them on the table. The tactic worked. Alistair pulled his eyes from her, saying, 'You'll have felt the cross-currents earlier.'

'And you want to know my frank impressions?' A nod gave her the go-ahead. 'I didn't care for Miss Bovary but I don't suppose that bothers her. Her power lies in making others uncomfortable. And Mrs Rolf is her husband's expanded shadow, though her son seems to be her chief concern. She's blinded by partiality. Terence likes to charm and with plum acting roles in his gift, I'm sure he does so to great effect. He doesn't know what to make of you, but he'll chip away to get that part for Edwin and you can't really refuse. A lot of actors avoided joining up. You can't ban them all.'

'I count ENSA as service.' Alistair was referring to the

Entertainments National Service Association, which had toured to entertain the troops. He picked up his gloves with a quiet fondness before pushing them into his jacket pocket. 'What about Brennan, with whom, I believe, you are already in tight cahoots?'

She couldn't hold back a spurt of laughter. '"Tight cahoots" sounds like something Elizabethan gentlemen wore under their breeches. I'd say that Hugo wants to be left in peace to do the job he's paid for.'

'The last show Brennan worked on closed after four nights and he needs a success. He has a reputation for being good, but idle. Can you keep him in line?'

'I'll try. Where did he spend the war?'

'Overseas missions – he can't speak about it.'

'Understood. Miss Bovary won't be able to run him as she'd like.' *Nor will she run you*, Vanessa added privately. At that moment, Macduff pushed the door open. He headed straight for Vanessa's legs. She took hold of his collar. 'Does this boy always howl at the Bovary clan?'

'He's confused. They come to the theatre, but his master doesn't.' Alistair reached down to stroke a silky ear, then lightly covered Vanessa's hand with his. 'Why, when you mentioned your birth date, did Miss Bovary look as though she'd seen her own ghost?'

'I haven't the foggiest idea.'

Alistair's gaze trapped her. 'I think Miss Bovary fears something in you. She seems to know you.'

'Perhaps we brushed shoulders at the gates of Brookwood Cemetery.' If she confessed that she was here because of her father, the bold claims she'd made during her interview would ring false. Keeping Alistair's good opinion mattered.

Mattered ridiculously. She was rescued by her stomach which gave an intrusive gurgle. 'Sorry. I haven't had lunch. I'd better find Hugo.'

Hugo was tucking into a plateful of chicken by the time Vanessa arrived at Anjeliko's, opposite the Old Calford Building. He waved down a moustached waiter and told Vanessa to be quick if she wanted the same. Discovering that the chicken was finished, she ordered percolator coffee and a slice of cheese and spinach tart instead.

'Where does the proprietor come from?' she whispered.

'They're Turkish here. Listen, you saw Miss Bovary beckon me over during the meeting?'

'To give you a dressmaker's business card. To demonstrate her authority.'

'To stop me looking at the picture of a young Wilton Bovary with an even younger Johnny Quinnell.'

'Together?'

'I've no idea what play they were in, but they looked very deep into their roles. From the cut of their coats, I'd say the photo was taken sometime around 1910 or 11.' Hugo shuddered. 'That office is a shrine to a vanished past. I hate shrines.'

Vanessa frowned, working out the timings. Johnny had let Stanshurst for London in 1926 but she knew from her mother that he'd spent time in London before the Great War, trying his luck as an actor before returning home to marry. Perhaps he'd worked for Wilton Bovary then too, crossing swords with a youthful Miss Bovary. She tried the idea out on Hugo. 'She was an actress, wasn't she? Perhaps she had a run-in with Johnny.'

'Perhaps she was in love with him.'

'Not she!' Vanessa's food arrived and she stared at it

despondently. The tart was mostly pastry and the potato salad that came with it was crying out for some kind of dressing, but she was ravenous and ate it anyway. The coffee was divine, but her pleasure was overlaid by the thought of her dad's empty file. Why was The Farren hell bent on erasing Johnny Quinnell?

As the waiter cleared their plates, she leaned down to get her purse out of her handbag, and the cord around her neck slid out.

'Why do you wear that?'

She showed Hugo the key. 'It unlocks something.'

'Really? Never! Have you tried it on Miss Bovary's chastity belt?'

'Can you never be serious? Truth is, I don't know what it unlocks.'

'But you mean to find out?' Hugo took her left hand in his. 'No ring. Where's Mr Kingcourt?'

'I don't know. I mean, his body . . .' she took the breath she always needed at this point, 'is in the English Channel. Leo was a fighter pilot.'

Hugo's humour vanished. 'Now you're trying to put it all behind you.'

'New beginnings.'

Hugo examined her key, turning it round several times.

She asked him, 'Did you ever meet Eva St Clair?'

'Nobody could work at The Farren in the 'thirties and not know Eva. She and Johnny Quinnell were an on-and-off couple. When Johnny was off – and he often was – she kept Wilton Bovary company.' He read her face. 'That shocks you?'

'Yes.'

Hugo shrugged. 'Theatre's a broad church.' His eyes narrowed slyly. 'What does our rugged Commander make of you being Quinnell's daughter?'

'Alistair doesn't know.'

Hugo tutted. 'He'll ferret it out.' Signalling the waiter back to their table, he ordered 'something to ward off the cold'. Then he continued, 'Miss Bovary's on to you. If you don't satisfy her lust to know every corner of your soul, she'll go above your head.'

'To Alistair, you mean?'

'No.' Hugo pointed upward. 'She'll interrogate the higher planes. If there's one woman who can't leave the dead to their rest, it's dear Barbara. The whole family is morbid. No –' he corrected himself. 'Bo wasn't. He was the light in the tunnel.'

The waiter set down two shots of white Sambuca. Hugo lifted his. 'To Lady Windermere and a dazzling triumph.'

'You drink mine, I have to go.' Hugo's ghoulish words disturbed her. There *was* something of the night about Miss Bovary. She paid for her lunch, saying, 'Do we start work today?'

'We don't. I've already peaked. I have to conserve my life-force.' Hugo downed Vanessa's Sambuca.

'Tomorrow, then,' she said firmly. 'I'll come to your *atelier*. Great Portland Street, you said. Which number?'

Hugo scrawled an address on the back of Mrs Yorke's business card, which Miss Bovary had insisted he take. But his eye fastened on Vanessa's golden key. 'Eighteen carat, I'd say. Made to fit a musical instrument case, a jewellery box, something of that sort. Eva was Irish like myself, and we like a riddle.' His voice changed, his accent deepening. 'You're after finding a hole for this key, but what is a hole? Tis nothing at all.'

Chapter Twelve

She found Hugo's *atelier* locked the next morning and stood an hour on the pavement.

Back at the theatre, she waited all day and finally went home, dispirited.

She didn't mean to quarrel with Joanne. She could have held her tongue when, as they drank cocoa in the kitchen before going to bed, Joanne interrupted her anxious soliloquy, saying, 'Everyone's splitting their sides over The Farren's choice of *Lady Windermere*.'

Vanessa had already gauged that Joanne was also in a rotten mood. One of the leads in *High Jinx* had left. 'Pregnant without permission'. Joanne had been touted as her replacement, but in the end, the management had brought in a girl from outside. Realising she'd been hogging the conversation, Vanessa asked mildly, 'Who is everyone?'

'*Everyone!* "A woman wavers on the brink of adultery." What a play for a cuckold! How will your lord-and-master sit through the first night, the world watching to see if he squirms? It'll be toe-curling.'

Cuckold? Joanne's sneering tone triggered Vanessa's protective instincts. 'Alistair deserves respect, for what he is and what he's been through. He's strong. He cares. He's . . .' Vanessa groped for a word, 'significant.'

Joanne gave a tinkling laugh. 'Oh, bless you, poppet, you're overboard for him, aren't you? Poor Nessie, you always do this!'

'What do I do?'

'A passably good-looking man only has to buy you a sherry and invite you to foxtrot and you're his forever. Until he's shot down – '

'Stop it, Joanne.' Vanessa slugged down the rest of her cocoa, swilled her tin mug in the washing up bowl, and then dumped it upside down on the drainer. 'Know what? I think you might be jealous.'

Joanne's eyes flashed and she swiped back with, 'Jealous that you're a skivvy in a tin-pot theatre? Come on!'

The next morning, Vanessa was still seething while Joanne was brittle and unapologetic.

Making toast only for herself, she said, 'Vanessa, did I mention? A friend of mine from the show is looking for a room, so if you were still thinking of getting a place of your own, now might be a good time.'

Vanessa took a room at the Old Calford Building. Not on the second floor where her father had lived and died, that would have been a nightmare in waiting. Her room was number two on the ground floor, and it had just become vacant. It boasted little refinement; its best feature was an industrial-size window that drank in light, and gave a straight-line view on to Anjeliko's awnings.

Heating was a two-bar electric fire with a pay-metre, a brutally ugly object that clicked with patient avarice. A sink, a compact kitchen, a table, two rickety chairs and an iron-framed bed completed the facilities. The bedframe creaked when she pressed down on it. A new mattress was a must.

But . . . she'd lived in worse as a WAAF. The damp would dissipate once the room was warm. She might charm leftover paint from the scenery men and buy a rug. Best of all, she had beat the landlord down from eighteen shillings a week to twelve. As they sealed the deal with a gritty handshake, Vanessa congratulated herself at being an eight minutes' walk from The Farren and finally living on her own. *Nobody will tut-tut at me if I come in at two in the morning. Nobody will be watching my face for signs of worry. Nobody here knows of, or cares for, The Farren.*

She made no mention of her father while striking the deal. The landlord had made no mention of a tenant dying on the premises, either. This was a good decision, she assured herself. Being where her father had seen his last daybreak would keep him at the front of her mind.

On Sunday the 22nd of September, she moved in. The following morning she had breakfast at Anjeliko's, and to her relief and delight, Hugo joined her there. When she demanded, 'Where have you been?' he gave a warning growl.

'You're not my nanny, Vanessa. I don't work to the rules, and scowling at me won't change that.' He waved. 'Darling waiter, coffee please, before I die.'

The coffee was, as usual, superb, though the omelettes they both ordered were like damp face flannel with the pallid bloom of powdered egg.

When she pointed to her new lodgings, Hugo turned around in his chair to gaze across the road. 'That place? Nessie, it isn't decent.'

'It's snug.'

She said the same thing the following Thursday when they finally got to meet in Hugo's Great Portland Street *atelier*. 'My room's cosy, unlike this place.'

The term *atelier* evoked an artist's studio, romantic views over the rooftops. In reality, it was two rooms plus a basement, a sublet from a defunct firm of 'gown and mantle-makers', whatever they were. She said, 'Get some paraffin heaters. In a month or so, we won't be able to work, our fingers will be so cold. I will go on strike.'

'March up and down outside carrying a placard? I'll join you. I fancy a career in politics.'

She growled, 'Please let's do some work. Alistair keeps asking me how things are going. He's worried you'll have nothing to show the director when he arrives. Let's do some quick pencil sketches, break the ice.'

'I have no pencils.' Hugo's previous studio had vanished in the conflagration of the East End, along with his portfolios. Vanessa found a stick of charcoal. Hugo took it and drew a cartoon of the Prime Minister, Clement Attlee.

In exasperation, Vanessa went to the window and stared out at the slick pavement. It was late afternoon, a postcard London scene for those who liked rain. She'd walked here from the theatre – about two miles – protected by her WAAF greatcoat. She'd come expecting to discuss fabrics and patterns. Instead, they'd had a repeat of all their previous meetings. Plenty of talk but no actual work. This was what Alistair had been driving at when he'd said he wouldn't employ Hugo.

Hugo was still harping on about her move to the Calford Press Building. 'It's been derelict since they stopped printing magazines there.'

'It's my nest. Now let's talk about the dwindling number of days before the director wants your ideas.'

'Toads and rats have nests. Respectable Wardrobe Mistresses live in mansion blocks on Dolphin Square. The world will call you eccentric and raffish.'

'You live on Old Compton Street, which is decidedly raffish.'

'But I'm not a single, young woman. Damn it, is that rain again?' A squall pattered against the window. 'Why must you slum it? Ask the Captain for a pay rise.'

'Commander, not Captain.' That wasn't Vanessa. They hadn't heard the door click open and shut.

'Is this an official visit?' she asked Alistair as he shook raindrops off his hat.

'Official, yet friendly. Like a bank manager who happens to be your uncle.' Alistair peeled off his mac and put it over the back of a chair. He looked around, his eye alighting on sheets of newsprint pinned to the wall on which Vanessa had written a list of the play's characters. She'd used a different sheet for each act to help Hugo navigate the task ahead. She'd been reading her copy of *Lady Windermere* each night before going to sleep.

Alistair studied her work. 'I take it you've seen the cast-list?'

'Not yet. Is it true that four characters have been cut, and two roles are doubling up?'

'If I have my way,' Alistair answered. 'Wilde must have had lots of friends to whom he promised walk-on parts. The play's almost fully cast, and I'll have the list copied out for you.' He reviewed her plan again. 'It helps, seeing all four acts mapped out like this. Would you make me one? In fact, do one for the director, too.'

'Right-o,' she said. *Right-o*. Alistair scrambled her brain and Vanessa was never quite sure what would spring from her mouth.

This afternoon, it seemed, she was sounding like a netball captain. Alistair looked the model of a wealthy theatre manager in another stylishly-cut suit. So handsome, it felt like a punch in the ribs.

Alistair asked, 'Would you two like to come for dinner tonight? I'm celebrating. I've been reunited with my first love.'

'You mean Fern?' Seeing his reaction, Vanessa exclaimed, 'Sorry! But you said your first love. I assumed . . . heck, have I –?'

'Fired the guns and sunk the wrong ship? Yes. As far as I know, Fern is still in Paris.' Alistair turned abruptly. He strode to the lobby and Vanessa assumed he was leaving until she heard him saying to somebody at the front door, 'What are you doing here? Well, don't huddle there getting soaked. Come in.'

When he returned, he was followed by a stocky figure in a cape and rain hood, bringing Macduff on a lead. The dog slithered on the lino before shaking himself, projecting raindrops at the wall.

'There is a reason dogs are not allowed in workrooms,' Hugo said menacingly. 'Had I left muslin *toiles* draped about the place, I would want to kill you both. Who are you, oh Caped Stranger?'

When Tanith Stacey appeared from under the waterproofs, he demanded, 'You didn't walk the poor mutt all this way?'

Blue eyes opened wide. 'We came in a taxi. You don't mind, do you?'

'Yes, I do,' Hugo said. 'We're working then going out to dinner.'

Earlier in the day, Tanith had been wearing her siren suit, hair bundled up as usual. Since then, she'd changed into a skirt and jumper similar to Vanessa's. A short skirt, half-an-inch below the knee. The legs she'd described as resembling sea defences were clad in silk stockings and rather shapely.

Alistair asked, 'Did Tom Cottrill send you?'

Tanith shook her head. 'Macduff saw you leave and was desperate to go after you, so I thought it would be safer to bring him. Imagine him following your scent through the traffic.'

'Imagine. Did you let anybody know? Otherwise someone will organise a search party. For the dog, not for you.'

'Doyle knows. He gave me Macduff's spare lead.'

'Did you ask Mr Cottrill's permission?'

'He's having a meeting with lighting and props.' Tanith's hair was set in a lush configuration of back-swept curl, though the rain and a hat made from a remnant of barrage balloon had somewhat flattened the effect. 'Cottrill doesn't need me.'

'*Mr* Cottrill.'

'Whenever he wants an assistant, he asks Pete.' Peter Switt was the ASM, assistant stage manager, subordinate to Tanith.

Alistair sighed. 'And you think absconding will improve your standing? Never walk out, unless you want another person to do your job.'

Tanith cast down her eyes. 'Can I come to dinner too?'

She looked so dejected, Vanessa said, 'Take her along. I need to go home.'

Alistair wasn't having it. 'We all go, or none. Tanith, you must ask your mother's permission. You live at home, don't you? May she use your telephone, Hugo?'

Hugo jerked a thumb towards a door at the far end.

'I'll make tea,' Vanessa said. Tanith was shivering. From the kitchen, as she filled the kettle and put a match to the gas ring, she heard Tanith close the office door; closing it twice as if she needed to be sure it was firmly shut. Fibreboard walls divided the two rooms and the purr of dialling was audible. As was Tanith's request to be put through to a Whitehall number.

Whitehall? Tanith had told Vanessa that she lived with her mother in a flat in Pimlico. They'd had a sandwich together a couple of days ago and had compared travel times to the theatre. Perhaps she was ringing her mother at work; apparently, Mrs Stacey ran a shoe shop somewhere near the river.

As Vanessa warmed the pot and spooned in leaves, she overheard snatches of Tanith's conversation.

'. . . out tonight. Yes, with Commander Redenhall.' A pause. 'No, not alone. A party of four, to a restaurant. I don't know which one. Yes, another girl's coming. Very respectable. Much older than me.'

Much? Thanks!

Tanith concluded her call with, 'I will. Yes, tomorrow. Goodbye.'

Not a cuddly mother-and-daughter relationship, Vanessa reflected. Loading her tray, hooking the door open with her foot, she nearly collided with Tanith, who emerged at the same time.

'Mum happy?' Vanessa asked.

'Oh, er, yes. She fusses dreadfully. Tea, how lovely. Is there sugar?'

'Saccharine only because Hugo forgets to buy his ration, but the milk's real.'

While Vanessa had been out of the room, Hugo's creative logjam had freed itself. She found him regaling Alistair with ideas while pouring tawny liquor into tumblers. He was saying, 'I visualise the gradual evolution from polite formality – the Windermeres' loving but untested marriage – through the chaos of betrayal as the marriage comes under attack, to the finale of love reaffirmed. To my mind, *Lady Windermere* has one of Wilde's less conclusive endings. Questions remain, nothing will ever be quite the same again. The *mis en scène* must delight, yet inspire unease.'

He handed Alistair a whisky. 'I need to find a single, powerful idea. I call it the "tap-root".'

When, after a mouthful of whisky, Alistair said, 'I can't get excited until I see something. It's one of my limitations,' Hugo looked deflated. Alistair shrugged. 'Whatever's brewing, get it out of your head and on to paper. Our first meeting with Aubrey Hinshaw is a week today.'

At the mention of the director's name, Hugo gulped whisky. He then noticed Vanessa pouring tea. 'Fancy a tot, Nessie? It's Old Dublin.'

'Bit early for me.'

'The sun's over the yard arm, isn't it, Commander?'

'The sun's always over a yard arm somewhere in the world.' Alistair went to stand beside Vanessa, holding his whisky in her eye line.

'What?' she demanded, stirring sweetener into her tea.

'You evidently think me a drunkard, unable to get through the day without stimulant.'

'I've formed no such opinion. Nor do I have moral issues with alcohol. I just hate what it does to some people.'

'I was half-cut that day at my house, I confess. Did I apologise?'

'In your fashion.'

'Ah, "my fashion". I was insulted at being lied to. What you don't know is that after you left the theatre following your interview with me, I telephoned Fern at home. I was sure she'd be in because she was expecting you later. To misquote Jane Austen, "I wonder who first discovered the efficacy of the telephone in driving away love!"'

'She answered?'

'A man did. And it wasn't the first time. Last year, just after

VE Day, I docked at Liverpool and put a call through from the Admiralty office there. The same man picked up then, too. He said, "Fern Redenhall's residence?" and I knew.'

'Knew that –'

'He was her lover. Of course, she later explained that it was just a friend passing through.'

'It could have been.'

'At seven-fifty in the morning? It was the way he answered, with a growl of triumph. He knew I was miles away, unable to do a damn thing. "Fern Redenhall's residence." Not, "Commander and Mrs Redenhall's residence", which any well-bred friend would have said. Sometimes, you just know.'

'Who is he?'

'I have absolutely no idea. But I know that on both occasions, it was the same man.'

Vanessa remembered Fern watching her walk away on the morning of her interview. What Vanessa had taken as a projection of good wishes might have been Fern, heady with Arpège, looking out for her lover. Hoping there wasn't going to be an embarrassing overlap. Fern, unfaithful?

Alistair said, 'When the mind can't encompass the next move, the hand often reaches for the bottle, though it may interest you to know that I didn't touch alcohol all the time I was Commander of the *Quarrel*. It's not easy to refuse the daily rum ration, nor the wardroom gin decanter, and some of my officers thought they had a moral reformer for a captain.'

He put down his tumbler and raised a teacup in a sardonic toast. 'I heard Brennan talking about your salary as I came in. I instructed Miss Bovary to pay you the man's rate.'

'I'm happy with what I'm paid but I send half my wages to my mother.' Ruth had accepted the provision with the curt comment, 'That's as it should be.' Vanessa had asked if the *ex gratia* seven pounds, four shillings still arrived monthly to which Ruth had replied, 'Yes, until his Lordship passes away. After that, heaven help me.'

Alistair was looking thoughtful. 'You have a widow's pension as well.'

'No, I don't.'

'Why not? Your husband was killed in action, wasn't he?'

'Yes, but . . . well, I don't have one.'

'Why? Did they fob you off? Do you need somebody to rattle doors at the War Office? I'm trying to understand why you might "slum it".'

'I'm not slumming. Compared with some of the rat-infested quarters I've lived in, my new place is quite swanky.' She raced to change the subject. 'Should we get an early dinner? I have a feeling Tanith's mother is quite strict.'

Darkness had fallen, and it was now just gone five. Once, the idea of dining before eight or nine o'clock would have seemed outlandish, but war had changed social habits. Early dinner, early bed.

Twenty yards along Great Portland Street, Alistair stopped beside a mint green saloon car.

Hugo whistled. '*Bellissima*, an Alfa Romeo. Doyle mentioned that you went into the country last Sunday to fetch something.' He stopped Vanessa and Tanith getting ahead of him. 'As the senior creative talent, I sit in the front.'

Vanessa was happy for him to do so. She let Tanith slide into the back, then helped Macduff in. The dog arranged himself in the footwell with a familiarity that suggested he was a seasoned passenger. Alistair held the door as Vanessa adjusted her coat and skirt so that she wouldn't flash any leg when she climbed in. He said, 'I did say the *first* love of my life. Wilton Bovary bought this car long before I laid eyes on Fern. It became the focus of my passion and envy. All in? We'll drop by The Farren first and offload Macduff.'

From the theatre, Alistair drove to Soho and drew up on Wardour Street, a lane as narrow as a strip of ciné film. Appropriately so, as film company headquarters did business above restaurants with foreign names, basement bars, and jazz clubs. There were also establishments of a more dubious nature. Here, as everywhere, buildings were buttressed by wood cladding, windows latticed with heavy-duty tape. Alistair took them to number seventeen, Pinoli's, which advertised 'Parisian dinners' while a hand-written sign assured 'All for five shillings', a reference to the price cap on restaurant meals. Inside, art nouveau mirrors reflected candlelight, snowy tablecloths and napkins. Vanessa stood in the doorway, dazzled. 'I'd forgotten places like this exist.'

'Pinoli's was one of the first Italian restaurants in London.'

'It says "Parisian" outside.'

'Probably as well. I'd be surprised if some of the staff weren't interned during hostilities. I dined here in 1940 when –' Alistair said no more as the maître d' bowed them to a table.

They started with a rich tomato soup, and then Vanessa and Alistair went for rabbit casserole. Rabbit was an off-ration meat and the portions were generous. Hugo had fried sole and Tanith, whose tastes were conservative, chose roast chicken. Pinoli's was famous for its wines and Alistair ordered French Chablis for the table. Italian wines were off the menu, mired in post-conflict embargos. Vanessa lifted her glass to the light to embellish its bloom. The wine was pale straw with a hint of green. Bottled beer had been the staple at RAF dances. Her 'safe' resort had always been a medium sherry, though she'd tasted champagne once, in the company a well-off RAF officer. A nice man, with whom she had *not* fallen in love, and who had *not* subsequently been shot down in flames. Joanne's mockery still rankled.

'Just an inch or two,' Alistair instructed as the waiter hovered the bottle over Tanith's glass, adding, 'On your next birthday, you can have a glass full.'

Tanith pouted prettily. 'Could I have a Coca-Cola instead?'

'With tomato soup, you savage? Would you bring water,' he asked the waiter.

Alistair knows how to soften the edge, Vanessa thought. *He'll make sure Tanith gets home sober and safe. I wonder if he'll do the same for me.*

Hugo drank fast and dominated the conversation. Ideas for the play were fruiting in his brain, crowding each other out. His fixed fear, they discovered, was how to source cloth.

'Act Two, Lady Windermere's Ball – one cannot conceive of a ball without sweeping skirts, necklines vomiting lace, brutally throttled waistlines and bulbous, elephant sleeves.' He sketched with his hands. 'Underpinnings, corsets – where will I find the acres of fabric?'

'Borovick in Berwick Street,' Tanith said pertly. 'Everyone goes there.'

'Ninny. You suppose they have bales of silk and satin lying about in the quantities I require? I shall need . . .' Hugo worked out roughly on his fingers, 'one hundred and twenty yards for the ball scene alone. And where do I start with whalebone?'

'You'd better hire from Angels or one of the other costumiers,' Alistair said. 'Miss Bovary will understand if you take her to see Borovick's empty shelves.'

Hugo's mouth thinned. 'If I do that, what's the point of me? You'd as well sack me, let Nessie take my job.'

'You should let Vanessa help.'

Hugo's face tightened. 'Like Mr Terence Rolf, I too have been in this business a while.' He piled spinach on his plate and used the salt-pot aggressively. 'Vanessa can't cut through to the critical problem.'

'Which is?' Alistair asked.

'If I knew that, would we be having this conversation?' Hugo was heating up. Vanessa, learning to predict his sudden emotional shifts, wasn't surprised when he reached for his glass and drained it in one.

'Vanessa did two years at Art College. A fresh pair of eyes isn't a luxury; it's a necessity. I want drawings by next Monday, and not back-of-a-fag-packet sketches.'

Hugo turned with glowering formality to Vanessa. 'Madam, will you lend your talents and help a poor struggler?'

''Course. I'm flattered to be asked.'

Hugo made a sound of disgust. He made it again when he shovelled the spinach into his mouth, remembering too late that he'd doused it in salt.

When the waiter removed their plates and brought the sweet menu, Hugo rose, saying, 'This was generous of you, Alistair, and probably exceeds the first meal I will taste on reaching heaven. If you'll all excuse me, I'm cutting along to a club round the corner.'

'Can I come?' Tanith asked.

Hugo laughed. 'Not on your life.' His easy nature had reasserted itself. 'I'll see you tomorrow, Nessie-darling.'

'Eight o'clock sharp at your studio,' she agreed.

'You'll be all alone, then. I don't crack an eyelid till ten at the earliest. Goodnight all.'

With Hugo gone, the atmosphere settled. They ordered crème caramels, which arrived as a sensual wobble in a sea of coffee-dark liquor. Vanessa held her spoon over hers, afraid to make the first plunge. 'It's years since I've tasted anything this good. This is a fabulous place, Alistair.'

'Six years for me.'

'Since you came here last?'

He looked right into her eyes, his own coming alive. 'Six years of pleasure deferred. Six years since I gave love and got it back.' The comment shivered between them. Tanith, scraping caramel sauce from her plate, looked up, oblivious to the undercurrents.

'Can we go to a club?' she asked.

'I was thinking of ordering coffee, then taking you home.'

'Not yet, please. I never go out! Oh, Alistair, please.'

'All right.'

Vanessa thought, *when he's a father, little fingers will tie him in knots*. Would he ever be a father? Fern had often said that she wasn't the least bit maternal. 'I don't feel we should go to Hugo's club somehow.'

'No, we'll give that one a miss. We'll try the Wishbone, a few doors down. An hour, no more, because I'm getting Tanith home by midnight.'

'Me, I can stay out as late as I like,' said Vanessa, then kicked herself because she was forgetting that this was Alistair, out-of-bounds and possibly predatory.

He said, 'Me too. Shame we play by the rules.'

She and Tanith followed Alistair down into the Wishbone's seething belly, where shouted conversation competed with a sob-bing clarinet. Vanessa instantly regretted her skirt and jumper. If she'd known where this evening would end up, she'd have put on a party dress. Within moments, though, she realised that this was a dress-down club: men wore tweed and soft collars, and girls a more erotic variant of her outfit with tight jerseys and thigh-skimming skirts.

Alistair found them a table. 'You can have your Coca-Cola, Tanith. Beer, Vanessa? I wouldn't drink the wine here.'

'Same as Tanith, please.' As she slid on to the bench, something sweet and musky flooded her nose. 'Tanith, did you put your scent on with a ladle tonight?'

Tanith replied, 'Wouldn't you be more comfortable on a chair?'

'I'm fine here.' Clearly, the girl wanted Alistair next to her on the banquette. Unsubtle in every way.

The clarinettist finished to energetic applause. Some people clapped with raised hands, while others whooped their approval. A drummer came on and began a fast riff. The clarinettist joined back in, and other musicians ambled on to the tiny stage. The music became livelier and couples seeped on to the dance floor.

Vanessa peeled off her jumper, glad that she had on one of her more attractive blouses, an apricot cotton with a V-neck that showed a shadow of cleavage. The golden key hung round her neck as was her habit, but she'd changed the cord for yellow silk ribbon.

Tanith also tugged off her jersey, with much arm-waving. Vanessa helped her pull down her blouse, which was bronze silk with a kerchief at the neck. The kerchief was printed with what Vanessa at first thought were daisies, but which on closer inspection turned out to be aircraft propellers. She was intrigued. A souvenir from an operational station?

'The scarves were for a Spitfire Party — to raise money to buy one. I hemmed a hundred of the things,' Tanith explained.

'They feature different fighter-plane propellers. This one's "Hurricane".'

Alistair came with their drinks as Vanessa said, 'No, those are Spitfire props. Hurricanes have three blades, these have four.'

Tanith asked Alistair, 'What do you think?'

He set down the glasses. 'Defer to Vanessa. She saw planes from every angle.'

Vanessa agreed. 'Even from the inside. During one of my Lincolnshire postings, I was taken on a test flight in a Beaufighter. Things were quiet at the station and they offered joyrides to us Watch Room girls. I sat in the navigator's seat, behind the pilot, and saw the world through angels' eyes. I'll never forget it.' For more reasons than that: after they'd landed, the pilot had asked her out to a dance in a nearby village. After a moonlit walk home, he'd kissed her, just out of sight of the WAAF quarters' guard hut. Her first kiss since Leo's death. Her lips had been as cold as the moon and he'd laughed, saying, 'Thank goodness you don't dance like you kiss.' A challenge that she'd taken, astounding him with a surge of passion. She'd fallen a little in love . . . Joanne hadn't lied. She fell too easily. He'd been shot down a week later over the North Sea. How it was, back then. You gulped down the nectar, then the sorrow, and got on with your job. Was it wrong to long to be loved and wanted? To be held . . . danced with?

'I envy you,' Alistair fished her attention from the dance floor. 'I flew once, as a passenger, and so wanted to see my ocean from a pilot's viewpoint, but fog wrapped us up straight away. What is it like to see buildings from ten thousand feet?'

'It's like – '

Tanith squealed, putting her Cola glass down with a bump. 'Bubbles are rushing up my nose!' Resting her chin on the back of her hand, she said wistfully, 'I'd love to dance, Alistair.'

'Then so you shall.'

Vanessa reflected sorely, Can't he say no? But instead of holding his hand out to Tanith, Alistair approached a group of young men huddled near the bar. He exchanged words with one and a moment later, was bringing him over. Vanessa recognised one of Aubrey Hinshaw's assistants, 'third assistant director' or some such. He'd arrived at The Farren a few days ago, to begin measuring and sketching the stage, touring the lighting rigs.

With a little prompting from Alistair, he asked Tanith to dance. It looked as if she might refuse, but in the end she sighed. 'I suppose so. I hope you *can* dance.'

'I hope you can too,' the young man swiped back.

Alistair returned to his seat. The band had settled into a repertoire of old-fashioned melodies, playing a slowed-down 'It Had to Be You'.

He held his hand out. 'Shall we?'

'Dance?'

'I wasn't imagining we'd try a spot of goose-stepping.'

'Can you?' A smile pushed across her face.

'Only one way to find out.'

The dance floor allowed no chance of a light, polite embrace. They were grain in a slow-rolling mill. Crushed against each other, they moved counter-clockwise, other people's heat and perfume binding them. Alistair's hand sank into her waist and they moved in an uncomplicated, swaying walk. Her cheek rested on his collarbone and she caught wafts of shaving lotion. 'It Had to Be You' ended and the band struck up 'Moonglow'. Alistair gathered her closer, looking down at the yellow ribbon between her breasts. His eyes held a smoky intent that warned her he was deciding something. *I'm not falling in love*, she reminded herself. *I loved him by the end of the first day I met him.*

She closed her eyes. Happiness was a mayfly, dead within hours, and she knew in her bone marrow that Fern would ultimately reclaim Alistair. She must make the most of being in his arms.

He asked, 'Are you really what you seem, Vanessa? Free?'

'I'm spoken for, actually.' She felt his step choke, though it might have been because the floor was sticky with spilled drink. 'I'm already in love with my work. I know it's rather soon, but that's how I am. My wardrobe department will be a byword for insane levels of enthusiasm. I'll keep Hugo focussed. You won't have to lose sleep over costumes.'

'That will leave me free to lose sleep over other things.'

'Alistair, your life is none of my business . . .'

'But?' Alistair prodded.

'There's no point digging a hole and sitting in it.'

'Tell that to the infantry. But I get your point. You're suggesting I give Fern a divorce?'

'A new start for you both.'

'There's a problem.' It was like listening to a wireless slip abruptly into another waveband. She opened her eyes. 'You love her too much to let her go?'

'There's an obstacle to divorce that you couldn't begin to understand. It's to do with reputation. Honour. Character. Yes, pride too. You'd have to be a man to grasp it, and a man you most definitely are not.'

They danced twice more, then Alistair danced once with Tanith. Vanessa sipped warm Coca-Cola, trying not to mind that Tanith was draped shamelessly against Alistair. To his credit, he kept scooping her upright. But then, she told herself sourly, he knows I'm watching. He knows that *I* know that the obstacle to divorce isn't male pride, it's that he doesn't want it.

He took them away after that and at her request, dropped Vanessa off first. She had a headache and was craving a darkened room.

Chapter Thirteen

This arrangement misfired badly on Alistair. Following Tanith's directions, he parked on Lupus Street, Pimlico. Opening the passenger door to let her out, he stared at the stars so there was no chance of him glimpsing stockinged leg as she climbed out. He wanted a woman tonight but not this one.

'Which flat?' he asked.

Tanith pointed to a curtained window above a shop. He knocked at the side door, but Mrs Stacey, it seemed, slept like the dead.

'Don't you have your own key?' he asked.

'I'm not allowed.'

'Friendly neighbours, other family nearby?'

'Nobody, I'm afraid. Lordy, what shall we do?'

We? Cursing unnatural mothers and top floor flats, Alistair suggested she get back in the car. Driving slowly along the Embankment to conserve fuel, he considered his options. Her hand, meanwhile, kept moving towards his thigh.

The following morning, he woke with pins and needles in one arm. His initial thought was the one he always had – the moment a German torpedo exploded against the *Sundew*'s stern. Followed by a flicker-book of drowning faces. He threw back the covers and rid himself of the ghosts with a swift walk to the theatre. His phone was ringing; it was Terence Rolf. Their conversation gave him the excuse he needed to walk across to the wardrobe room.

From her doorway, he watched Vanessa. She was perched on the table edge, unpicking the lining of a garment. Sunshine – unsullied this morning by smog or traffic vapours – splashed the table, which was lighter and smoother than he'd ever seen it. Vanessa had done a meticulous job of repairing it.

She, however, was everything he remembered. Curls flopped over her cheek. Her skirt was strained tight around the thigh and her legs were shown to advantage in nylons. Had she joined one of the mile-long queues that sprang up outside department stores whenever a delivery came in? One shoe hung off her heel, displaying the stocking's petal-shaped reinforcement, which rose in a pencil-line seam. A fluttering sensation moved across his shoulders. She had on one of her neat, fitted blouses. Blue, today. Her bent neck had a fragility that made him loath what he was about to do.

She looked up just then and nodded as though his arrival was part of her daily routine. She hadn't woken up disliking him, by the looks of things, but in a moment she would.

'I really enjoyed that meal, Alistair. Thank you for taking us.'

'Think nothing of it. It's Miss Bovary and the Rolfs' turn tonight, then tomorrow, our Promotions Director and his wife. Has to be done.'

'Oh. I see.'

Last night, as they'd danced, he'd felt need crawling through his veins. Driving along Embankment it had stalked him. He wouldn't – couldn't – allow such need to strike roots. Dismantling his world, leaving Ledbury Terrace and the Navy, moving into Bo's flat in Cecil Court, he'd reached decisions about his marriage that he would not go back on, because to do so would blow apart everything he was and believed in.

He would never give Fern a divorce.

It wasn't fair to want Vanessa and it would help if she began to actively dislike him.

When she said, 'I hope you have a good supply of Pepto-Bismol,' in a voice as flinty as his own, he silently praised her. But he had to make sure. 'As we danced together I had a feeling you thought you might organise my future. I just wanted to say that, along with my desk, it's out of bounds.'

Red spots flamed in her cheeks. 'Did Tanith get in safely?'

To his shame, he hesitated, saying after he'd cleared his throat, 'She was fine.'

'Good.'

When it became clear she'd gone back to her unpicking, he turned to one of his notional reasons for being there. 'Any idea what Brennan's up to today?'

'Visiting fabric wholesalers. There's cloth to be had, he says, if you know whom to bribe. He's hoping for offcuts or reject rolls. I'm trying to help, honestly I am.'

'But is Brennan helping himself? So much rides on this production, Vanessa. If Hugo's having some kind of creative seizure, I need to know.'

Instead of answering, she showed him what she was doing – unpicking the violet silk lining from a man's evening jacket. 'We have enough suits to clothe the male characters and luckily, men's fashion doesn't change much decade to decade. They just need cleaning and some new buttons.'

'The lining looks in good condition.'

'That's why I'm stealing it.' She let the fabric spill over her hand. 'If I strip every jacket, I'll have enough for sleeves, bodices, sashes, that sort of thing. Hugo wants a uniform colour scheme, and all the linings are from the same dye lot.'

'I should think they were made by Grunberg's – costumiers who went bust in the Depression. Will you re-line the jackets?' He was chit-chatting, which he never did, but he'd just been struck by the most ludicrous jealousy. Last night, Vanessa had told him that she was falling in love with her work. He wanted to rip the silk from her and take hold of her. He wanted to say, 'Listen, I'm married and it's going to stay that way. But I want you so badly it's crucifying me.' Instead he kept on about coat linings until the mechanical crump of the lift, followed by the rattle of crockery, announced the approach of the tea trolley. The tea lady trundled up to the open door. The Farren employed people on long shifts, and was entitled to serve extra rations.

'Your usual, Mrs K?' the tea lady asked, pouring steaming liquid into a tin mug. She reacted to Alistair's presence with undisguised fascination. 'Didn't spot you there, sir. Usual, is it?' She filled another mug even though he declined.

Perhaps she was a little deaf. Her forearms were powerful and she'd told him once that she'd made munitions casings during the war. Endless machine noise scarred the eardrums. 'Nice buns today,' she bugled at them, shovelling a couple on to plates. They were so dry, they reminded him of fossilised ammonites on display at the Science Museum. They had a lick of sugar topping, but no sultanas and no spice. But they had their use . . . because now he must stay.

He wanted to stay.

He and Vanessa took their elevenses sitting on the table. It took her two tries to break her bun in half and her shoulders shook. Her mirth summed up the awfulness of food rationing, of the same dreary 'make-do'. A loveless ever-after, when even Chelsea buns were robbed of their sultanas.

'I'm keeping mine for Macduff,' he said.

'He can have mine too,' Vanessa said. 'The tea's good, though. Cheers.' They clinked tin rims and anyone looking in would have thought they were fast friends. Her court shoe finally slipped off her heel entirely and fell to the floor. She gazed down at her nyloned foot, evidently unsure what to do.

He picked the shoe up, and then didn't know what to do with it either. To slip it back on would require him to touch the silky arch of her foot and a slender ankle. He could not do it without his mind going further, literally travelling upward. So he handed the shoe to her, saying, 'They must be a size too big.'

'I bought them off a friend of Joanne's, hardly worn. Of course they'll oblige by shrinking to fit. You know how it is.'

Not really. For years, he'd had his shoes made for him at Lobb's. The pair he had on now, bought in 1939, was hardy. He'd spent most of his war in sea boots, keeping a much-mended pair of Oxfords for travelling.

Vanessa replaced her shoe, and the yellow satin ribbon bowed outwards.

He said, 'That key – is it worn to inspire mystery?'

She slipped the ribbon over her head. 'Eva St Clair gave it to me.'

Alistair cradled the key in the palm of his hand. Eva St Clair had been an enduring presence at The Farren. To visit her here in the wardrobe room was to get a hug, which he'd found uncomfortable, and a shortbread biscuit from a tin, far more acceptable. He knew of the tragic end to her career in September, 1940.

Only the other day, he'd asked Miss Bovary about pension

payments made to Eva that showed up in the wage books. Bo, who'd cared deeply for Eva, had been providing her with a retirement income.

Miss Bovary had confirmed it. 'We've been paying for her lodgings too. She lives under the care of the Catholic Church.'

'"*Lives*?"' he'd queried, discerning a fractional hesitation before Miss Bovary answered, 'Indeed, yes. One has to admire Miss St Clair. Can't talk, can hardly eat, but as the poet said, the creaking gate hangs longest.'

He'd thanked Miss Bovary, who had gone away ignorant that she had blundered, that Alistair's ear for voices was acute. Afterwards, he'd studied the wage books and dug deep into the theatre accounts. He'd learned that Miss St Clair had been receiving her pension since December 1940, three months after falling victim to an air raid. The payments continued, though the account into which they were paid had changed recently. A call to the bank had disclosed that the money was now going into an account owned by somebody else entirely. Alistair was still waiting for Miss Bovary to mention the fact. He now asked Vanessa, 'You met Eva here, didn't you?'

'Didn't I say? My father brought me to see her. They were – um, acquaintances.'

'She gave you the key then?'

'No, much later. At dad's funeral. She said it was mine, by right. Take it –' Vanessa tried to pass it over, but Alistair refused it. It wasn't just voices he was good at. What people *didn't* say could be just as informative. To put it charitably, Vanessa was under-explaining.

'Pity we can't ask Eva what it unlocks,' Alistair said. 'You know she was almost killed when the pub next door was bombed?' He pulled chairs up to the high window, and standing on one, he invited Vanessa to join him in looking out over the waste-ground. 'See there?' he pointed. 'Those exposed cellars are the site of the Nun's Head, which for decades was The Farren's unofficial rehearsal space and drinking-parlour. Three hundred pounds of TNT destroyed an historic pub in seconds. This window blew right in from the force of the explosion.'

'Damaging the table and smashing the mirror?'

'I should think so.' He pulled a face at the mirror. 'Make-do-and-mend' was laudable, but that degenerate jigsaw was going too far. He'd tell Props to locate a replacement. Helping Vanessa down from her chair, he continued, 'When the siren went off on the evening of the raid, everyone in the theatre ran down to the sub-stage area. Except Eva, who dashed outside. Her man was in the Nun's Head.'

'Her man?'

'That's how Miss Bovary described him. Only, he'd already got himself to one of the public shelters. Eva was dug out of the debris, crushed and burned, and when this man was called to the hospital he took one look at her appalling injuries and said, "Nothing to do with me, doctor". How's that for betrayal?'

Alistair thought Vanessa was going to tumble forward. He caught her and heard her say, 'Even he wouldn't – '

'Who?'

She shook her head.

'Vanessa, are you here because of Eva, or because of somebody else?'

'I want this job. That's all. Don't ask any more.' For no obvious reason, she added, 'Sorry.'

She spilled the remains of her tea as she tried to drink it, stumbling to the sink to dab at her blouse. Accident, or a manoeuvre away from further questions?

Fine. Patience was another talent of his. 'If you see Brennan before I do, tell him that Monday's design meeting is as inevitable as the rising sun.'

Picking up the buns destined for Macduff, he recalled his second excuse for dropping in on her. 'Terence Rolf phoned. The girl who was to play Lady Agatha Carlisle has broken her leg. Tomorrow is the first full cast read-through and somebody has to speak the part. Could you?'

She turned to him as if he'd asked her to deliver a baby or perform eye surgery. 'I'd rather have daggers thrown at me.'

'No acting is required; we'll be sitting around a table. All you have to do is read Lady Agatha's lines on cue. It helps the others to have somebody of the right age, with the right vocal tone. You'll see another aspect of the job, too.'

'What about Tanith? She's much nearer Lady Agatha's age.'

'Tanith isn't in today to ask. Is this really beyond you?' He didn't intend to sound severe but it did the trick.

'All right. I'll read.'

'I'll get a script over to you. The foyer, tomorrow, ten o'clock. Sorry to ask you to give up your Saturday.' Walking to the lift, he had a strong sensation that Vanessa was staring at the empty doorway, fingering the key round her neck.

Farren Theatre Productions Ltd.
Lady Windermere's Fan by Oscar Wilde
Opening November 28th, 1946
Provisional Cast List

Lord Windermere	Patrick Carnford
Lord Darlington	Ronald Gainsborough

Lord Augustus Lorton	Lawrence T Weston
Mr Dumby	J Victor Pagnell
Mr Guy Berkeley	Arthur Whitworth
Mr Hopper	Roy FitzPeter
Footman / Lord Paisley	Walter Hamilton
Sir James Royston	Simon Greengrass
Mr Cecil Graham	Uncast
Parker, the butler	James Harnett
Lady Windermere	Miss Clemency Abbott
Mrs Erlynne	Miss Irene Eddrich
The Duchess of Berwick	Miss Rosa Konstantiva
Lady Agatha Carlisle	Uncast
Lady Jedburgh	Miss Noreen Ruskin
Lady Plymdale	Miss Maxine Shadwell
Lady Stutfield	Miss Emmeline Perkins
Lady Paisley/ Rosalie	Miss Gwenda Mason
Understudies	Leslie McManus
	and Miss Anne Aisleby

Saturday morning and they were preparing to witness the birth of a play. Five tables made a pentagon in the front foyer, which would be their rehearsal space until the sets were completed, when they'd transfer to the stage itself. The director had arrived, as had the talent – with one exception.

Alistair told the director, 'Miss Abbott isn't here yet.' Vanessa hadn't arrived either. He hoped she was all right. Though why should she be? Yesterday, he'd taken an axe to their fragile relationship and revealed the horror of Eva St Clair's fate. He'd also implicitly questioned her motives for being here. On top of which, he knew she was anxious about reading alongside professional actors. 'Let's give it ten minutes, then start,' he suggested to the director. Vanessa was probably still in her room, summoning up courage.

Noreen Ruskin, the heavy actress playing Lady Jedburgh, showed impatience at Miss Abbott's non-appearance. 'I trust dear Clemency won't make a habit of this,' she said in her powerful vibrato. 'I shall tell her, there are more falling stars in the sky than rising ones.'

'Lateness is hard to forgive in a young actor. In an older one, it is impossible.' Patrick Carnford improvised in a clipped, upper class style. Presumably he was 'being' Oscar Wilde, though nobody really knew how Wilde had sounded. The playwright had been dead forty-six years.

Miss Ruskin called across to the director, 'Aubrey darling, do place a ban on bad Wildean pastiche lest rehearsals set our teeth on edge.'

The director laughed tactfully. 'We will be like workers in a chocolate factory, Miss Ruskin. Day One we gorge ourselves. By the end of the week, we will never want to touch chocolate again.'

From which Alistair derived proof of something he already knew: Carnford, who was playing the emotionally-persecuted Lord Windermere, was a fixed star on the West End stage and would pull in the audiences – in particular the female matinee crowd. Carnford could mangle Wilde as much as he liked off-stage so long as the famous sexual charisma oozed on stage. Noreen Ruskin, meanwhile, could go and boil her head.

Where the devil was Vanessa? Alistair was pushing back his chair, intending to go find her, when a man in a driver's buttoned coat called through the doors, 'This The Farren? Miss Abbott thought you was on Bow Street. I said no, Farren Court. She wants to be sure before she gets out of the car.'

'Why?' demanded Irene Eddrich. Her character, Mrs Erlynne, was a pivotal one but not the lead. Accustomed to being the female star of anything she appeared in, Irene was showing early signs of disliking Clemency Abbott.

The driver mugged an appeasing smile. 'Pardon, ma'am, but she says the location isn't what she was expecting.'

'Would she like us to move the theatre or Bow Street?' Miss Ruskin asked acidly.

The chauffeur appealed to Alistair. 'She don't like the look of the footpath, guvnor.'

Alistair couldn't entirely blame Miss Abbott, but in one vital point the theatre resembled naval life: lateness on board was impermissible.

'It's her shoes, see,' the cabbie said. 'She's fearful about her heels.'

'Advise her to swim up through the drains.' This from Rosa Konstantiva, an ENSA veteran cast as the Duchess of Berwick. It was said so reasonably, one or two people nodded.

Patrick Carnford touched Irene Eddrich's hand in a show of collusion. It was well-known that theirs was a relationship that veered between love and hate, but a bumptious juvenile will always bring older actors closer. 'Tell the dear girl that *we* managed perfectly well.'

'I'll go and collect Miss Abbott.' Alistair paused to say to the assembled party, 'I apologise to you all for the pot-holes outside. We're filling them in as fast as we can. There was a war, you see.'

Ronnie Gainsborough, who had slicked his hair with Macassar oil to express Lord Darlington's fluid morals, murmured, 'A war? So that's what all the banging was about.'

Alistair left with a wry smile that fell away as he followed the driver to Bow Street. The telephone box that had been on its back for many weeks had recently been returned to its plinth. Somebody was inside, making a call. Somebody who made his heart stop briefly, then pump an acid torrent. He kept going towards a parked black cab, however. 'Miss Abbott?'

A peerlessly made-up face gazed out at him. When he opened the door, legs misty with silk stockings stretched out. The shoes that Clemency Abbott was so keen to preserve were Marina blue, as was her hat and coat, unbuttoned to reveal a white lambswool dress. Alistair held out his hand.

She gave a little gasp as their fingers met. Brown, boudoir eyes rose to meet his. Pink lips opened a fraction. 'Are you who I think you are?'

'Alistair Redenhall.' Nothing about her charmed him; she was a spoiled female using other people's time and energy to pad out her self-consequence. 'You can take my arm, Miss Abbott, or if you're determined not to touch the ground, I'll ask the doorman to heave you over his shoulder.'

Chapter Fourteen

Vanessa knew she was late, but an unexpected visitor had sabotaged her. Actually, the day had got off to a lousy start. She was tired, twitchy, forced to accept that Hugo had been right. She *was* slumming it in her new lodgings.

The rhythmic pulse of bedsprings from the room above hers in the Old Calford Building had kept her awake most of the night. The noise had followed a pattern. Fifteen minutes on, twenty minutes off. Every time she'd drifted back towards sleep, she'd been startled awake by the resumption of the squeaking.

Stumbling out of bed at one point, she'd smacked a broom handle against the ceiling. Silence was followed by a muffled obscenity and continued creaking.

'Stop that noise!' she'd pleaded.

'Put a sock in it,' a female voice had roared back. Ten minutes later, feet on the stairs. The front door opened and closed. Then the sound of heels on lino and a rap on Vanessa's door.

'You mind your own business, Lady Muck, and I'll mind mine. Got it?'

Years of operational shifts had disrupted Vanessa's sleep patterns. She drifted off as a clock on some nearby tower struck three a.m., and then overslept.

She'd arranged to meet Hugo for breakfast on Oxford Street, but she'd had to forego it, instead running every step of the way to Farren Court, arriving at the stage door with her curls sticking to her forehead, no lipstick and her stockings twisted. Doyle had called out something about 'letting the lady in' which made no sense until Vanessa took out her key and discovered that the wardrobe room was already open.

Inside, somebody was waiting.

A woman in moss green stood before the fractured mirror. Red-gold hair identified her.

'Fern! When did you get back? Are you all right?'

'She wants to know if I'm all right!' Making a leisurely about-turn, Fern Redenhall walked to the window and they met beside the sink.

Never had Fern seemed so tall. Her shoes were towering, peep-toe wedges. A 'plant pot' hat added dignified inches while her fitted coat-dress had large, square pockets and wildly over-sized lapels. Only French couturiers would dare put so much cloth into an outfit. But this wasn't the moment to ask Fern where she'd done her shopping.

'I arrived from Paris not an hour ago. I went home and straight upstairs . . . Explain this.' Fern thrust a patterned silk square at Vanessa. It reeked of perfume. After a moment's confusion, Vanessa recognised its Spitfire motif. 'Where . . . ?'

'In my bed. Mine and my husband's bed. More to the point — when, Vanessa? I know he still has a house key.'

All Vanessa could say was, 'It's not my scarf.'

'Come off it. You are the only person I know who would wear something littered with fighter-plane propellers. Leo gave it to you, I suppose. What would he have thought of you rolling about with Alistair? You didn't even have the grace to pull the sheets back up!'

Fern's haughty contempt roused something similar in Vanessa. 'It's not mine.' She shoved the square under Fern's nose. 'Sniff it.'

'I already have. It smells tarty.'

'Thank you very much. I have always worn Chanel No 5 – you should remember that. Your father bought me a bottle for my twenty-first. Until it comes back into the shops and I can afford it, I stick with lavender-scented soap.' She extended her neck sideways, giving Fern the opportunity to check for herself.

Fern's fury gained a film of doubt. 'Then who was it in my bed?'

'Do you imagine that's how I'd repay your hospitality?' A mortifying vision spanned Vanessa's mind. A girl and a man, rucking the sheets.

'Oh, Nessie, oh God, how could he?' Suddenly, Fern was in her arms, her body racked. 'How *could* he? You don't know what my life is like. I'm trapped. What am I going to do?'

'Talk to him! He still adores you.' Saying it felt like cracking a nut with an abscessed tooth, but the truth was insistent. Whatever Alistair had done with Tanith, Fern was still first in his eyes. 'I think you love him too.'

Fern stood back. She was pale under a skim of face powder. 'It's too late. And anyway, have you ever tried to talk to Alistair? If he doesn't like what you have to say . . . it's like watching frost spirals form on a window pane.' She dabbed her eyes with the scarf, frowning at the run-off from her mascara. 'He cuts you off with a look, with the inflexion of a word. And he's always right. Alistair could fall into a pit of Bovril and come out bleached!'

Vanessa couldn't argue. Alistair stuck limpet-like to ideals.

'Even when it's a terrible decision, he won't go back on it.'

Vanessa consulted the clock Doyle had found for her and put on a shelf beside the mirror. It was gone ten. The reading would have started. 'Fern, I'm sorry but – '

'He won't lose face. The *Monarda*'s crew paid for that!'

Vanessa recalled Joanne's condemnation of Alistair over a lunch table: *When a ship in sight of his got hit by a torpedo, he turned his vessel away*. The story followed Alistair around. Not safe in taxis. Not safe on the sea. Not safe in a theatre and *not safe with Tanith*.

'How could he?' Fern kept saying. But were those tears real? Vanessa recalled her own reaction on discovering, that Leo had been unfaithful to her in the run-up to their marriage and even afterwards. Raw shock. Anger and that punishing sense of failure. Everything *but* tears. But she hadn't time to massage the truth from Fern. They'd be waiting for her downstairs, or they'd have found someone else to read the part.

'I'll just say this: Alistair believes you've been betraying him since another man answered your house telephone.'

Fern beat her fists together. 'That was Darrell Highstoke. You remember Darrell, who used to come down to Stanshurst for the long holiday? He and my brother made us play cricket with them.'

Vanessa certainly recalled a friend of Christopher Wichelow's coming down for summer holidays. A loose-limbed boy with fair hair and a smile that could be charming or cruel, at whim. Yes, Darrell. She remembered now. In his company, Chris had shown her less kindness. They'd christened her 'Minnie Mouse' and mimicked her whispery voice.

'It was Darrell, popping by to say hello.'

'Before breakfast?' Vanessa shook her head. 'Alistair met your brother in London, the day you left for Paris. Your "emergency dash" excuse fell apart.'

'What about Alistair and his tart?' Fern believed 'when cornered, attack'. 'Who the hell is she?'

'Turn the noise down. For all you know, Alistair might have slept alone at your house hoping you'd come home to him.'

'A perfumed scarf in his pocket?' Fern would have ripped it in two had Vanessa not taken it from her. 'Nessie, I have to get free of him. I have to get a divorce.'

'Consult a lawyer.'

'The only way is for Alistair to admit adultery and let me divorce him.'

'You're right.' Vanessa opened the door. A coarse hint, but she might be here all morning otherwise. 'It's how it's done. The man takes the blame. I'll walk you to the stage door.' She hadn't the time or inclination to repeat Alistair's refusal to end his marriage. Let Fern discover that for herself.

To Vanessa's inexpressible relief, the reading hadn't started. People were lounging, or out of their seats stretching their limbs. 'We're waiting for Clemency Abbott. The Commander's fetching her.' The information was given by a trouser-wearing blonde girl who invited Vanessa to sit by her. 'I'm Gwenda Mason.' The girl had a Yorkshire accent, though she reverted to perfect BBC pronunciation to add, 'I play Lady Paisley and Rosalie – two of me for the price of one. You?'

'Vanessa Kingcourt, standing in as Lady Agatha. I'm not a real actress.'

A moment later, Alistair was preceded into the foyer by an imposing young woman wearing the chicest of hats. A grim hush fell. Oblivious, Clemency Abbott struck an effortless pose. 'Darlings! Don't tell me I've kept you waiting?'

'Miss Abbott,' the director filled the silence, 'I bid you welcome. Gentle players, Miss Abbott has indeed arrived late but will not do so again. Shall we get on?'

As it was Saturday, Alistair had dressed down in a blue crew neck jersey sprayed over his muscles. For the benefit of Clemency Abbott and the other actresses? Several eyed him appreciatively as he took his chair to observe the read-through.

It began, with Lady Windermere and Lord Darlington trading scripted banter. The Duchess of Berwick 'entered' with her daughter, Lady Agatha Carlisle. Rosa Konstantiva spoke her lines and looked towards Vanessa, as if to say, 'Get ready!'

Vanessa's pulse knocked. *Don't let me muff it.*

Nobody laughed or sneered as she gave her simple lines: 'Yes, mamma.' Alistair nodded 'well done'. She radiated disgust at him, and went back to her script. The reading jigged along. *Lady Windermere* was so firmly part of the actors' repertoire that they had lines and intonation ready. Too ready for the director, who stopped the flow several times to say, 'Remember, the line was new when Wilde wrote it. Speak it as if for the first time.'

When they'd read to the end of Act Two, a tea-break was called. As the cast trooped off to the green room, the director thanked Vanessa and told her she might go since Lady Agatha made no appearance in Acts Three or Four. 'Stand by to help on Monday, for the blocking-rehearsals. Getting an Equity member to stand in is too much of a fiddle and I can't ask any of the stage crew. The unions forbid the crossing of the divide.'

'I'm glad to help, Mr Hinshaw.' She needed to get away. Alistair was trying to catch her eye. 'We're also meeting on Monday to discuss set and costume.'

Aubrey Hinshaw laughed. 'Are you one of those women who quietly run the world?'

'I don't know. If I see broken eggs, I mop them up but I don't try to get them back in their shells. Will you excuse me?' She made for the exit, affecting not to hear Alistair calling for her to wait.

Doyle detained her a moment at the stage door. 'That Miss Abbott swanning in half-an-hour late. Tsh! A rum lot, thespians.'

She managed a smile, which vanished when she discovered that it was raining. Her greatcoat was upstairs. All she had to protect her hair was Tanith's scarf. Doyle handed her an umbrella.

'You're a gem, Mr Doyle.' As she made to leave, she heard the auditorium door click, and Alistair call, 'Mrs Kingcourt?'

'Must dash. If anyone asks, I'm tracking down Mr Brennan.'

Vanessa crossed Bow Street and was halfway down Tavistock Street before she acknowledged that she was going fast in no particular direction. If she wanted to apologise to Hugo for missing their breakfast, she should cut around the market and take the Covent Garden tube. If her intention was to avoid Alistair, she should keep walking.

She headed for The Strand and the river. Being the weekend, the trucks, carts and barrows that served the market were absent, but there was still an air of bustle. Delivery boys dashed past on bicycles, pinging their bells, shouting coded greetings to one another. Queues of patient matrons in raincoats and waterproof headscarves spewed from shop doorways. The occasional old man stood in line, or a lad in cap and blazer, but it was hard to escape the evidence that waiting was women's work. If men did the queuing, Vanessa thought, the government would soon simplify its convoluted rationing system. There'd be no more books to stamp, or coupons to tear out. 'A pint of this on alternate Tuesdays, an ounce of the other every third week.' She was lucky, she could take her meals in canteens and the communal British Restaurants.

'Mrs Kingcourt, will you please stop?'

She picked up her step, crossing at Southampton Street just as a double decker bus came along, then cut down a side-street and ducked inside a deep doorway. After listening cautiously for signs that Alistair had seen her, she rolled up her umbrella, opened the door and found herself in a flag-stoned porch, staring at a statue of Christ.

Incense permeated the interior of the church. Vanessa stopped at a marble statue of a bearded man. *The blessed Robert Drewrie, martyred 1603.*

A plaque behind the statue was dedicated to the much more recently deceased Fr Joseph St Clair. Any relation to Eva? 'I wish memorials could talk.'

'I'm glad they don't,' someone said behind her, 'as I'm here by myself quite a lot of the time.'

Vanessa swung round and saw a smiling priest. After apologising for intruding, she asked, 'Who was Father Joseph?'

'The priest-in-charge before I took over here in 1944. Father St Clair served this community for many years.'

Vanessa took the plunge. 'I met a lady called Eva St Clair a long time ago, and then saw her again a few months back. Would you know her?'

'I know of two or three families with that name.'

'You'd remember Eva if you'd seen her. She . . . she was severely injured. Her face . . . you wouldn't forget it.'

'Ah,' said the priest. 'You'll be describing Father Joseph's sister. I never knew her given name.'

'"Knew". So she's –' Vanessa broke off as the church door whined shut. A firm tread approached. Thanking the priest, she went to intercept Alistair. 'Why are you following me?'

'I want to know why Fern called on you within hours of returning from Paris.'

'Did Doyle tell you?'

'He didn't need to. I saw her in the phone box on Bow Street. I was collecting Miss Abbott, so I didn't tap on the glass and wave.' He spoke sarcastically. 'She'd been to see you. Correct?'

'Correct. Why follow me?'

'Call it the chase instinct.'

The priest came over. 'Feel welcome to sit or pray.'

'We're leaving.'

Vanessa had never heard Alistair so close to rudeness and she apologised for him. 'I'm sorry; we've brought our disagreement into church, Father.'

'Which is a good place to leave it.' The priest looked from Alistair to Vanessa. 'The lady you spoke of, I met but once, at a hospice run by this church.'

'What lady?' Alistair demanded.

After silently consulting Vanessa, who shook her head, the priest walked to the door. 'The rain's coming down hard again. You'll need this.' He handed Vanessa the umbrella that she'd left by the Blessed Robert's statue. 'In case you wish to ask for me again, I am Father Mannion and I am always here.'

'Did Fern describe the glories of Paris? Or those of her lover?'

'Alistair, stop doing this to me, and to yourself!' Rain bounced off the pavement, off Vanessa's umbrella. Never in her life had she argued in the street. For her, raw emotions needed four stout walls before they were allowed release. But lack of sleep, combined with the dull presentiment that she never would meet Eva St Clair, had shortened her tether. If he'd just let her walk away! Even so, she didn't fight Alistair when he took her arm and guided her back to Southampton Street.

'We are going to talk, Vanessa, but you can choose where.'

'I need to find Hugo and to be truthful, I don't want to be alone with you at the moment.'

'Yes, let's be truthful. Fern has many sophisticated friends in London, but she confides in you, hot foot off the boat train. Why?'

'Please, let me go.'

'All right.' Alistair flagged down an approaching taxi and Vanessa climbed in thankfully. Propping her sodden umbrella against the driver's partition, she closed her eyes.

Alistair got in and slammed the door.

'Hey – I thought you were leaving me alone!'

'Great Portland Street, please,' he instructed the driver. 'The southern end.' He said to Vanessa, 'We'll see Hugo together.'

'NSIT. Not safe in taxis,' she muttered.

He heard. 'What's life without risk? Was that priest speaking about Miss St Clair, by any chance? Why are you obsessed with her?'

'I'm not.' They had easily fifteen minutes incarcerated together. She might start shouting at him, or she might simply confess: I have lied to you consistently. I'm at The Farren to lay the ghost of my father to rest. I need to know why he deserted me, my mother. And Eva too. And why he didn't hang on to life a few weeks longer. Your marital problems are a diversion – though I confess, a diversion seared on to my heart.

Instead, she dropped Tanith's crumpled scarf on to Alistair's knee.

'What's this?'

'You tell me.'

He groaned. 'Tell me, save time. Is it yours or Fern's?'

'Are you really claiming not to know?'

'I really am. It's a failing of mine, not remembering clothes.'

'You remembered Fern's yellow hat!'

'Because I bought it for her in Valletta, the day after we got engaged. I agonised over it until the milliner chose for me because she was desperate to close shop and go home. When I saw it on you, more than Maltese sunshine flooded back. Though perhaps I'm improving here, because I know I've never seen you in that soft cardigan before.' He stroked a grey, angora sleeve then unfolded the scarf. 'It's Tanith's, isn't it? I remember the propellers. Who mauled it?'

'Fern found it in her – your – marital bed.'

He shut his eyes in what looked like defeat. 'I took Tanith home, as you know.'

Vanessa looked pointedly out of the cab window. 'I don't care to hear more.'

'So very shocked, Mrs Kingcourt? The idea of two adults enjoying each other's bodies can't be *entirely* alien to you.'

'Tanith is seventeen!'

'I know. And we didn't spend the night together.'

'A quick tumble, was it? Where did you take her?'

'To Fern's. But I did not sleep with her. Are you going to sit in armour-plated silence, staring out of the window?'

'I am.'

'Right. Let's get this over with then.' He tapped on the dividing glass. 'Driver? Forget Great Portland Street. Ledbury Terrace, SW1.'

Chapter Fifteen

Fern opened the door to Alistair's knock and turned pale. Seeing Vanessa standing one step down, her wariness deepened. She still managed a quip. 'You look like a pair of Jehovah's Witnesses. Have you come to offer me the Kingdom of Heaven?'

Alistair dangled Tanith's scarf. 'We really do need to talk.'

Fern made to shut the door, but Alistair put his hand against it and resisted. With a cry of vexation, Fern stepped back. 'I could call the police and have you flung out.'

'On what grounds? I'm your husband and this is my home.'

'Yes, home! Not your private brothel!'

'They're peering through the curtains at number fourteen.'

'Oh, come in then.'

Vanessa followed Alistair into the hall. This promised to be the worst kind of eavesdropping, undignified and heart-breaking. She'd stay in the hall, she decided. Only, what was that noise?

'Come down into the kitchen.' Fern opened the door at the top of the kitchen stairs, her eyes willing Alistair into line. But he, like Vanessa, had picked up on the sounds of dreadful distress from the lounge.

Someone crying, 'I didn't do it! Why won't you believe me?'

Vanessa demanded, 'Who's in there, Fern?'

Alistair didn't wait for an answer, but pushed open the lounge door and went in.

Sandy hair flopped over trousered knees. A yellow duster as a handkerchief, a face mashed into it. Anguish like the noise of machinery left to run down.

'Tanith?' cried Vanessa. 'What on earth?'

A blotched face emerged from the duster. Tanith Stacey took a moment to identify who was standing over her. Then – 'Tell them I didn't do it. They're blaming me and they hate me. But I didn't do anything.'

They?

Then Vanessa saw: there was a man by the window. He was slimly built, wearing a conservatively-cut suit.

Alistair gave no impression of having seen the man at all. He was more concerned with Tanith. 'Miss Stacey? What the hell?'

Vanessa snapped, 'Show a little compassion, Alistair. This may be a murky barrel, but you're well and truly at the bottom of it.'

Alistair showed anger for the first time. 'I'm sick of being cast as everybody's favourite lecher. I'm no seducer. Nor am I an adulterer.'

At the window, the suited stranger slowly turned to face them. He was piercingly handsome, with something of the Plantagenet in his narrow face and sensitively modelled lips. Hair, thick as summer corn, was slicked back. Without its grease it would flop over his eyes. Limbs formed to wear cricket whites and a glint of highborn contempt nudged Vanessa to recognition. 'You're Darrell Highstoke, aren't you? I remember you.'

'Unfortunately, I can't return the compliment.'

'Vanessa Kingcourt, but you used to call me Minnie Mouse.'

'I can see why I might have.'

His insolence goaded her into asking, 'How was Paris?'

Highstoke shot a glance at Fern, who had remained by the door. Fern said, 'Darrell was never in Paris.' At the same moment, he said, 'Depressing and chaotic.'

Vanessa gave a superior sniff. 'First rule of deception, get your stories straight – oh, and never pick up another person's telephone.' To Fern, she said, 'I believed you when you said you were going to Paris to look after Chris.'

Fern sighed, genuine regret in the sound. 'Before you accuse me of taking advantage of your obliging nature, let me remind you that it was your choice to work at The Farren, and your decision to stay here.'

'After you gave an open invitation.'

'I thought it would be fun. It was. You were not used.'

'Somebody was.' Alistair moved to block Fern's view of Highstoke. 'How did you get Tanith in your claws?'

Fern extended her fingers, tipped with immaculately painted nails. 'I never saw this girl in my life until she knocked at my door an hour ago. You explain her, Alistair.'

'I brought Tanith here on Thursday night, after she was locked out of her home.' Alistair ignored Highstoke's snort. 'We'd been out, a party of four. I took her home but we couldn't raise her mother. When it became clear she had no relatives, no friends to take her in – '

Fern jumped in with, 'My double bed was the obvious solution.'

'My bed too, Fern.'

In a voice dry as millet, Vanessa asked, 'Why didn't you bring Tanith to me, Alistair? I'd have given her my bed and slept on the floor.'

'She wouldn't hear of it. Correct, Tanith?'

Tanith nodded. 'I heard someone talking about where you live. I couldn't go there!'

Vanessa couldn't hold back. 'Bloody cheek!'

Alistair went on, 'My next thought was to take her to my flat – '

'So much more respectable,' Fern mocked.

'– while I would sleep at the theatre. Then, I had a better idea. Here. *My home*, from which my wife was absent. I had my keys, I let us in, showed Tanith to the spare room and told her to make her own way to the theatre in the morning. I then left.' He glanced at the girl, then at Fern. 'Has she implied any different?'

After a pause, Fern admitted, 'That's pretty much what she told me. But what's to have stopped the two of you sorting your stories out in advance?'

'How about: because there are no stories. Tanith, why did you return here?'

Tanith used the clean handkerchief Vanessa passed her. 'This – this morning, I realised I'd lost my scarf. It had to be here. I wasn't going to do anything about it – it's only an old thing – but then I called at the theatre to explain why I didn't come in yesterday, and heard Doyle telling Cottrill that a woman had called on Vanessa. She'd been overheard ranting that her husband had slept with a girl, in *her* bed. I thought I'd be blamed, that somebody would tell my – my family. I came to get the scarf and to explain to Mrs Redenhall that nothing happened.'

Vanessa interjected, 'That doesn't explain why you moved from the spare room to the master bedroom, making no effort to straighten the bed afterwards. Bad manners, Tanith.'

Tanith's eyes were swollen almost shut, so there was no flash of blue innocence as she protested, 'But I didn't sleep in the big bed! That's what I keep telling them. He –' she indicated Highstoke – 'keeps accusing me but it would have been a – a –' whatever word Tanith was searching for failed to materialise. 'I don't know who slept in it, but it wasn't me.'

Alistair looked pointedly at Fern. 'The stewing sheets, the enseamèd bed . . . a figment of your imagination, my love, or a squalid attempt to frame me for adultery? I put it to you that Tanith slept in the spare bed, as she claims, and that you invented the rest.'

Fern stared into a corner, at a niche filled with books.

Darrell Highstoke broke the silence. 'The fact is, Redenhall, the girl's seventeen and by her own admission and yours, she accompanied you upstairs. Unchaperoned. You're fatally up a gum tree. Imagine if it leaked to the press: "Former Naval Officer Seduces Child Employee".'

Fern folded her arms. 'You are exposed, Alistair, and I require a divorce.'

Alistair folded his arms in mocking echo. 'Fern darling, your time in Paris in this man's company has compromised you in every possible way.'

'Not at all. Darrell went with me as a friend.'

'But you shared a room.'

Darrell Highstoke denied it. 'He's guessing, Fern.'

Alistair acknowledged it, adding, 'Hotel staff, bell boys and chambermaids can supply the evidence that the courts demand. Why don't I shoot off to Paris, stay at the Polonaise, and ask them myself?'

'The Polonaise – how do you –?' Fern's voice slithered in anguish.

'How do I know that you and Highstoke were there? I didn't, but it's where you and I went in spring '39 when I had a month's leave. You liked that it was near the best shops and the waiters spoke English. You don't speak French, do you, Highstoke?'

Hobbled tongues.

'So all I need to do is show your photograph to the lift boy and I'll have my proof.'

'Alistair?' Fern pressed her hands together, imploringly. 'You and I aren't in love any more. I didn't plan things this way.'

'They simply happened.'

'*Yes*. May I please, please, have a divorce?'

'You absolutely may, Fern.'

Vanessa stopped breathing. Two nights ago, Alistair had assured her it was out of the question, for reasons he hadn't thought her capable of grasping. He'd changed course, three hundred and sixty degrees. Why?

'Thank you,' Fern gasped. 'Oh, thank you.'

Alistair continued, 'On one clear understanding – that I will bring the action on the grounds of your adultery with High-stoke.'

'No! That's infamous! Alistair, you wouldn't be so vile. I'd be finished. The scandal would kill my father!'

'What else did you expect? Am I not capable of the worst actions any human being can commit? Did I not leave men to drown, just for the hell of it? If you want Highstoke, stand up in court and tell the truth. If that's beyond you, stay married to me until one of us drops dead.'

In the street, Vanessa asked Tanith, 'Are we going to your mother's or to The Farren?' They'd reached one end of Led-bury Terrace, and must either go east towards the river or north towards Shaftsbury Avenue.

'I'll find my own way.' Tanith had recovered remarkably

quickly. Perhaps she lived in the moment. She had her scarf back and nobody was glowering at her any more. All was well.

For Vanessa, all was wrong. Alistair had left ahead of them, destination unknown. Moreover, it was still raining and Vanessa had left Doyle's umbrella in the taxi. Her cardigan was dripping a dark tide on her skirt. Inside, she felt broken.

She was taking her pain out on Tanith. 'I want a word with your mother. Which direction? Pimlico? Or do you actually live just around the corner?'

'What makes you say that?'

'You phoned a Whitehall number from Hugo's office. I was in the kitchen, I overheard. Now I'm wondering if you were calling Fern. Were you spying for her? Trying to trick Alistair into an affair?'

'Oh, no, honestly, I was calling home. I admit I don't live in Pimlico.' At Vanessa's look, she defended, 'Well, I had to say I lived somewhere!' Tanith spread her arms: *what else could I have done?* 'I told Alistair to take me to Lupus Street on Thursday night, because I used to get my school shoes from a shop there. It's closed down, and I knew the flat above would be empty.'

'You duped Alistair into thinking you had no bed for the night so he'd be forced to play Sir Galahad. Did you want him to take you to his home?' Vanessa shook her head incredulously. 'And to think I accused him of behaving like a rat!'

'That's not my fault, is it?'

'And this phantom shoe shop . . . did your mother ever work there?'

'Did I say she worked in one?'

'You did!'

'Then I suppose it was. Only, she doesn't.' Tanith tipped her head sideways. 'I wanted Alistair to be the first, you see.'

'The first— oh, by God, Tanith, I hope your father tans your backside when I tell him.'

'I don't have a father.'

'Mother, then. Just lead the bloody way to wherever it is you live. And don't talk, because I may snap and wring your neck.'

'The bloody way' took them through St James's Park, which they left by the barracks gate, passing the bomb-shattered Guards' memorial. They crossed Whitehall, seat of government and many illustrious institutes, but of few private homes. Just as Vanessa was beginning to think she was being led in a deceptive dance, Tanith turned into a street of neo-classical terraced houses, and stopped in front of an imposing front door.

A hotel? Vanessa wondered.

Tanith mounted the steps and rapped a dolphin's head knocker. The door was opened by an elderly man in formal tails and wing collar.

'Miss Tanith, we wondered where you were.' His eye moved to Vanessa. 'Good afternoon, Madam.'

Tanith shot a nervous grin back at Vanessa, before asking, 'Is Granny all right, Tucker?'

'Her Ladyship is resting in the day room.'

'Better face the music. Come on, Vanessa,' Tanith invited.

The entrance hall was palatial, its walls studded with fine portraits. All but one seemed to be of the same woman, an Edwardian stunner in a pearl choker, her hair piled up in a voluptuous pouf. Vanessa pointed to the single male portrait, of a man in military dress uniform, shoulders draped in ermine. 'Is that who I think it is?'

'King Edward the Seventh.' Tanith led the way up sweeping stairs, pointing to a pen-and-ink sketch of a lady in a cream-coloured evening gown with a plunging décolletage. 'That's my Granny too. The dress came from Worth and she still has it.'

'*The* Worth, of Paris?'

'Yes, Granny went everywhere. She was a PB.'

'A what?'

But Tanith had reached the landing and was knocking at a closed door. 'It's me, Gran-of-my-heart. I have a friend with me. May we come in?'

A fragile voice answered, 'No light, you understand?'

'Roger Wilco.' Tanith led the way in, whispering, 'Granny abhors daylight.'

Why, then, was this called 'the day room' Vanessa wondered as she sent a footstool flying. Heavy blinds cast gloom on lavish clutter.

'Granny, I have to put some light on.' Tanith upped a bud of lamp flame, allowing Vanessa to make out a prone figure on an ottoman sofa, a mask over her eyes.

'Where have you been?' The voice scraped like a badly-oiled latch.

'Here and there. Say hello to my chum, Vanessa.'

'She may make herself known to me.'

The butler had used 'her Ladyship' so Vanessa said, 'Good afternoon, Lady Stacey.'

'Lady Ververs. "Stacey" was this child's good-for-nothing father.' A gnarled hand pulled away the eye mask. 'Who are you?'

Vanessa gave her surname and explained her role at The Farren.

'Back-stager,' Lady Ververs sniffed. 'You will have heard of me, I daresay, as a celebrated beauty. My stage name was Dido Meredith. Tanith's mother wanted to act, but she had no talent. Ravishing but stupid. You cannot act if you're stupid. I tell that to Tanith when she asks to go to drama school.'

'Tanith isn't stupid, Lady Ververs.'

'There are no roles for thickset girls. None that I can think of. Is she good at her job?'

'You'll have to ask her.'

'I'm useless,' Tanith said, collapsing on a stool. There were many to choose from. Leather ones, plaid ones, others covered in animal skins. Vanessa wondered if Lady Ververs hosted gatherings of worshippers.

'I'm going to quit The Farren,' Tanith said. 'Cottrill hates me. So will Alistair now. Plus Cottrill gives all the decent jobs to Peter Switt.'

Vanessa felt caged in this over-heated room. Her head swam, having shared a portion of Fern's shock and distress. But she took a moment to reprove Tanith. 'He is "Mr Cottrill" and merits your respect. However, that doesn't give him the right to steamroll you. Walk in on Monday with your head high and stop running away.' She dropped her voice. 'And stop running after Alistair.'

'But he's blissikins.'

'Deluding yourself over a man nearly twice your age embarrasses him and makes you look an ass. Look where it's got you.'

'I thought he liked me. That night, I really hoped . . . you know.'

'But he didn't, and he won't. I presume your mother never gave you a pep talk?'

'No.'

'Come to my room early on Monday and I'll give you one of mine.' Vanessa stood up. 'Goodbye, Lady Ververs.'

'Are you still here?' her Ladyship enquired with genuine surprise.

On the stairs Vanessa met the butler bearing a silver salver with a port decanter and three tiny glasses. 'May I?' She knocked a measure back in one. It hit the spot. 'Where is Tanith's mother?'

'Dead, Madam,' the butler answered. 'Her father too, though he was only ever a technicality.'

'Are you aware that Tanith pretends to live above a shoe shop in Pimlico, run by said mother?'

The butler cleared his throat. 'It was easier to keep Miss Tanith in check when there was a full staff here, and she was small enough to send up to bed when she was silly.'

'She's no child any more, Mr Tucker. She's heading for trouble.' Something dawned. 'Was it you she telephoned the other night, asking permission to go out?'

The butler nodded. 'Were you the older lady of the party?'

'I was. If you have any influence, get her to come to work looking neat and professional. Make her throw away –' Vanessa stopped, for the first time noticing the full-length portrait that dominated the stair gallery. It was of a young Lady Ververs, wearing a pearl coronet and a purple velvet evening dress. Cinching a minuscule waist, the gown formed a heart-shaped bodice. Throat, shoulders and arms were bare but for strings of pearls. Gliding into a ballroom dressed so, young Lady Ververs must have struck the place silent.

'You were saying, Madam? Throw away?'

'That awful siren suit. Mr Tucker, might I bring a designer to see that picture?'

'Male or female designer?'

'He's called Hugo Brennan.'

'I'm sure her Ladyship would be delighted. She likes gentlemen and so few visit nowadays.'

★

Vanessa brought Hugo over that same evening. At the sight of the butler, he muttered, 'If Harnett needs a night off, we know where to come.' James Harnett was the veteran playing the Windermeres' butler, Parker.

When Tanith scampered down to greet them, Hugo said, 'You never mentioned living in splendour.'

'Because people laugh, or try to borrow money.'

'I'll try not to do either, Tanny-darling.'

The stairs with their filigree balustrades and carved newels seduced Hugo and it took half an hour to get him to the top. As Tanith knocked at the day room, he appraised the painting that had enthralled Vanessa. He pulled a face. 'It's after the Singer Sargent *Portrait of Madame X* but without the impact. I hope the lady's port is a decent vintage so it's not entirely a wasted evening.'

He was polite to Lady Ververs, chuckling when she flirted like a Victorian belle, but he only really livened up when Tucker came in with a tray.

Chapter Sixteen

September's last Monday dawned damp and grey, but this time Vanessa got to The Farren refreshed from a good night's sleep. The woman in the room above had gone out the previous evening. If she'd brought anyone home with her, she'd done it silently.

At the stage door, Doyle handed her a tissue-wrapped box. 'Arrived by errand boy.' Vanessa ripped into it as she went upstairs. It was a Chanel gift box. From Alistair?

A note fell out.

'Darling Vanessa, you reminded me how much you love No 5 and I'd forgotten I had this.'

No, you hadn't, Fern, was Vanessa's instant response. The packaging was brand new. It smelled of Paris.

The note continued:

'When I came to see you at the theatre on Saturday, I was dreadfully upset, but later I admitted to myself that if Alistair were to take up with anyone, I'd like it to be you. As for that poor, silly girl with the outlandish name, I'm ashamed of imagining for an instant that she and Alistair might have – oh dear, what word can one use? Fill in whatever feels comfortable. All I can think of now is Alistair's determination to hold me to a prison sentence. You promised you would help. Please don't abandon me. Now that I seem likely to lose your friendship, I value it all the more. F.'

Vanessa put the gift box in her cupboard. She should respond right away, before her desires clouded her judgement. Shedding her coat and changing into canvas shoes and a warm, knitted gilet, she worked out how much time she had. The blocking rehearsal would begin mid-morning, when she'd again stand in as Lady Agatha Carlise. Then there was the later meeting when Hugo was supposed to present his designs to Aubrey Hinshaw. Vanessa had seen little evidence that Hugo had begun work. Leaving Lady Ververs' Saturday evening, he'd brushed off Vanessa's pestering.

'Nessie-darling, I'm empty. I'm going home to sleep. I have all day tomorrow.'

She scribbled a few words for Tanith – who might or might not take up her invitation to a pep talk – 'Get the kettle on, I've gone to make a phone call.'

She could have walked to Bow Street and used the public box, but Alistair's office was closer. She'd ask for five minutes' privacy. She could hardly phone his wife with him listening.

He was poring over papers, a pencil loose in his fingers. He laid it down when he saw her in the doorway.

'You mean, can I vanish and leave you to it?' Alistair said in answer to her request. He looked drawn and when Macduff lumbered over to her, she leaned down to stroke him to avoid seeing too much.

'I'll be quick.'

'Take your time. I owe you, for dealing with Tanith on Saturday.' Evidently, there was to be no post-mortem on the scenes at Ledbury Terrace. He took a dog lead off the bookcase. 'I'll take this fellow around the block. Quarter of an hour enough?'

'Plenty. Have you heard from Hugo?'

'I telephoned him yesterday and ordered him to be here at nine to show me what he's got. I don't want horrible surprises with Aubrey Hinshaw looking on. If he's not here by half past, I'm fetching him in a taxi.' Alistair scooped his keys off the desk. She heard them rattling as he went down the corridor.

Vanessa dialled and requested a now-familiar number.

Fern answered after a dozen or so rings. She sounded as fatigued as Alistair had looked. 'Vanessa? Only you would sound so beastly-bright at this hour.'

'That perfume, it's too much. I'm sending it back.'

'What a bore. Darrell said you might.'

'He's there? He spent the night?'

'No, actually. He went to his flat after you all went. I was left alone to cry the rest of the weekend. You realise that my life has collapsed?'

'Look, Fern, you're painted into a corner. You have to give your marriage a second go.'

'You don't know what it is to be trapped. You were released from your ghastly marriage without having to try.' Fern must have realised that she'd gone too far. 'Look, I'm not myself. There's something I need to tell you.' She began speaking very fast. 'I have to marry Darrell. I'm too far in to bail out.'

'You're pregnant?'

'No, a different kind of trouble. Darrell won't put an engagement ring on my finger until Alistair has formally agreed to a divorce.'

'Alistair has agreed. If you take the blame.'

'I might as well tar and feather my own head! You've no idea what it would mean to somebody of my class and position to be painted as an adulteress. The Highstokes would shun me. Darrell and I love each other, but I have to go to him without a stain.'

Vanessa was tempted to say, 'You should have thought of that before.' It seemed to her that reconciliation with Alistair was the only rational course for Fern – but she'd said it once and would not do so again. 'Perhaps there is another way. Live apart, let Alistair divorce you in three years' time for desertion. That way, there's no charge of adultery.'

There was a silence in which the telephone line made mysterious clicking sounds, a mechanical count-down to Fern's grit-teethed avowal, 'I cannot wait three years. Get him to see it.'

'You imagine I have influence with Alistair?'

'You do! He admires you.' At Vanessa's sceptical grunt, Fern grew insistent. 'You're a former WAAF, a war-hero's widow. It makes up for being small and mousy.'

'He calls me small and mousy?'

'When I told him how your father ditched you and your mother and left for the theatre, he said, "Then more honour to Vanessa for coming through so level-headed." "Level-headed" is the greatest compliment Alistair can bestow. When I told him how Quinnell – your father, I mean – put acting ahead of a secure job, his family and his reputation, do you know what he said? Vanessa? Are you there?'

Vanessa had stopped breathing. 'I – I'm sorry. I have to go.'

She hung up, paced around the office until Alistair walked in.

Her voice touched the edge of hysteria. 'I need to tell you something.'

'Go ahead.' He unclipped Macduff's lead.

'I know you probably already know – '

He interrupted, saying, 'You look pale, so either your telephone call turned personal, or it's family matters.'

'Family. My father. I need to tell you – '

'Skip the monologue. You're the daughter of Clive Quinnell, stage name Johnny, who came here in summer 1926 in pursuit of theatrical glory. Yes?'

'Pretty much.'

Alistair gave his godfather's portrait a thoughtful glance. 'Bo would never have induced a man away from his family. Quinnell had several shots at being an actor, and each time, he started well, but he couldn't sustain being in an up-and-down profession. Last time I met Johnny, he was playing Sir Lucius O'Trigger in *The Rivals*. He was good, but so are many others,

Why are you crying?'

She wiped her eyes roughly. 'Dad was Eva St Clair's lover and forsook her in her direst need. I am learning to hate him.'

'Too harsh.'

'You didn't know him!'

'Didn't I tell you? I spent every school holiday here from the age of ten. My father worked for a shipping line as its travel-ling promotions executive, and my mother would accompany him. I was sent to Dartmouth Naval College at thirteen.' He explained that as the family home had been in Kelso, a town in the northernmost county of England, it had been natural for him to spend his vacations in London, a mere three hours' train ride from Dartmouth. 'The Farren became my second mother.' He told Vanessa to open the middle drawer of his desk. 'You'll find a peach-coloured card.'

She located it and handed it to him.

Alistair read what was typed on it. '"Quinnell, C J. Re-joined the company June 1926. Promising comic, fastest actor off the book I have ever met." Miss Bovary is saying here that he learned his lines quickly.'

'I bet he did. Mum sometimes said – never mind. Go on.'

'"Good impressions misleading. Sacked November 1927, cause of dismissal: upsetting backstage staff, distracting the wardrobe mistress in her work. Repeated attempts to borrow money from fellow actors".'

Vanessa stared down at the desk. 'When I met Dad on Drury Lane, I didn't realise who I was speaking to. As a child, I thought him as tall as an oak tree but he was ordinary height. It threw me.'

Alistair smiled. 'Actors aren't lumberjacks, they don't have to be tall. It's obvious from this report that Miss Bovary disliked Johnny, yet Bo kept re-instating him in the company. At the time of his death, Johnny was playing Canon Chasuble in The Importance. His last play. The last for both of them.'

She knew that, having seen the playbill. 'A good part, considering.'

'There are no bad parts in Wilde's repertoire. Now I sound like Terence Rolf.'

'Did you see the play?'

Alistair shook his head. 'By that stage of the war, I was getting very little leave. I'd dash down to London, spending more time travelling than being here. I saw Bo for lunch a couple of times, that's all.'

'I didn't even get to London. I wish I'd tried harder.' She met Alistair's eye. 'I looked for that card in Miss Bovary's filing cabinet. I hoped to find out more about my dad. It's one of the reasons ... No. The *main* reason for wanting to work here.'

'Why didn't you say so at your interview? Or on any other occasion, for that matter. It's fundamental, a material fact, Vanessa.'

'How long have you known?'

'Fern gave me your father's name that sizzling day at Stanshurst.

I recognised "Quinnell". It's unusual. Fern contributed some of the more sordid details.'

Vanessa asked faintly, 'Sordid?'

The telephone burst to life. Without thinking, she picked it up. 'Commander Redenhall's office. May I ask who's calling? Oh, hello, Mr Doyle. Yes, he's here. Right, yes, I'll let him know.' She covered the mouthpiece and looked to Alistair. 'Hugo's arrived and Doyle's helping him take his portfolios to the foyer. The tables are still in position, so they'll set up there.' She put the receiver to her ear again. 'Who else? Oh, that's good to hear.' Tanith had also arrived. Thanking Doyle, she set the receiver back in its cradle.

'How many crippled fighters and bombers did you sweet-talk down to a safe landing?'

'Not as many as I'd have liked.'

'Did you know that when we're in desperate trouble, when catastrophe closes in, a woman's voice is what we crave? It was rare at sea, but every now and again, a Wren would come through on the transmitter. Electrifying. Cold, frightened men stood taller and found their courage.'

'So we do have our uses.'

'You do. We'll return to this conversation.'

He let her go ahead of him so he could shut Macduff inside the office, and they travelled down in the lift. Detouring through the auditorium, they saw Tom Cottrill on stage, consulting a broadsheet plan. The ASM, Peter Switt, and a lighting rigger, a carpenter and two scene painters stood in a separate huddle, scrutinising a similar-looking plan held by the props master. Tanith was by the OP wings. She was dressed in Navy surplus slacks, a crew-neck jersey and soft shoes. Her hair was plaited into short pigtails. She looked like an orphan cabin boy.

Alistair muttered, 'I thought she'd have the grace to keep away for a few days.'

'I told her to come.'

'You had no right.'

'No. But you had no right to take her to a jazz den and then drive her home. Everything that happened afterwards is down to you.'

'My error was to take *you* home first. I thought you were the greater danger.'

Flustered, she asked, 'What's Mr Cottrill doing?'

'Getting his first eye-full of Hugo's set. I hope it's a clear plan and not some kind of Expressionist explosion. I'm beginning to wonder if Miss Bovary and Terence Rolf weren't having a joke at my expense, appointing Brennan.'

'Or sabotaging you.'

Alistair's look was sharp. She confessed, 'Hugo thinks there's something macabre about the whole family. Bo being the exception.'

'Talking of Brennan, shall we go and find him?'

Hugo rushed towards Alistair and Vanessa as they entered the foyer. 'I need walls,' he said, making windmills of his arms to indicate the empty space. He was wearing the suit he'd had on for visiting Lady Ververs, and the reek of cigarettes and alcohol met Vanessa as she went towards him. 'My sketches don't work laid flat.' He hadn't shaved that morning, either. Nor all weekend, Vanessa guessed.

'It's not an exhibition,' Alistair said. 'Aubrey Hinshaw isn't a critic. Talk him through your designs and it'll be fine. Have you had coffee?'

Hugo nodded. 'Far too much.'

'Go take a nap in the green room. I'll wake you when Hinshaw is ready.'

Hugo shook his head. 'Can't risk it.'

'Pull up some chairs, then,' Alistair suggested. 'You can explain your plans for manufacturing the costumes.'

But Hugo paced instead, re-arranging his work, occasionally swooping on something, snarling, 'This won't work. Why ever did I think it could?'

Vanessa recognised a man who had hit a wall. Leo had been the same after flying twenty hours of sorties, four hours off in-between, when sleep was often impossible. Though there the comparison ended. Hugo wasn't facing death. 'I'll ask Tanith to make you some cocoa,' she said.

Miss Bovary arrived for work just then, dressed for a chilly autumn morning in a black coat and hat with a gauze face-veil. She turned a bony shoulder to them, implying that they were cluttering the place.

Alistair said, 'I'd better make sure Macduff has water. I'll be back in a minute.'

Hugo muttered something about needing the gents, and suddenly Vanessa was left alone.

Like a child trying not to peep at the presents round the tree, she straightened the sketches that Hugo had thrown onto the table any old how. She examined only one, the ball gown to be worn by the play's black sheep, Mrs Erlynne, whose arrival at Lady Windermere's birthday ball was a climactic point of Act Two. The audience should by that time be on the edge of their seats.

Mrs Erlynne's drum-roll gown was deep amethyst, fitting like a glove over the hips and with a savagely-corseted waist. A sweetheart neck revealed a spade-full of cleavage. Throat and arms lay bare. It was Lady Ververs' portrait to the last detail. 'Hugo Ruddy Brennan!' Vanessa burst out. Coming back from the gents', he heard her and parted his hands in apology.

'One thing life has taught me, Nessie-darling, is never give too much away. Wear your heart on your sleeve, some bastard will stub his cigarette out on it.'

Aubrey Hinshaw arrived with his third assistant director. Vanessa wondered if there was a second-assistant director as he or she had made no appearance so far. Having little confidence that he'd be able to keep Hugo on the premises for the entire day, Alistair called the design meeting right away.

Aubrey Hinshaw was delighted with what he saw. 'Inspired,' he told Hugo. 'Showing the play's progression through day to night, linking it to the hopelessness of the marital situation. I adore that mauve gown. Very "Helen of Troy" meets "Rule Britannia". Ought to bring the house down. What gave you the idea?'

Hugo swept his hand towards Vanessa. 'She did. She showed me a picture. If life is a play, Nessie is the narrator, keeping it flowing.'

'Ah, the lady that makes omelettes with a mop.' Aubrey Hinshaw smiled at Vanessa.

'I don't understand, Sir.' The third assistant director, Neville Eden, shortened to 'Ned', addressed the director over Hugo's head. 'Mrs Erlynne will undoubtedly steal the scene, yet surely, Lady Windermere is the focus of the play.'

'Isn't it bloody obvious?' Hugo's manner darkened in a heartbeat.

'Good and bad women are one of the themes of the play,' Vanessa put in quickly. There were shades of Leo in Hugo, both quick to flare, quick to turn. 'What society calls a "good woman" may simply be one who has never been tested morally. She's had everything laid at her feet, never having to fend for herself or make difficult decisions. A "bad woman", on the other hand, has made profoundly human choices. Society condemns one and praises the other. Wilde asks the audience to consider if Society is right, and intelligently, he gives the "bad" woman many admirable qualities.' Vanessa felt Alistair observing her, his smile a mite sardonic.

'Flint-edged observations poking through the froth,' Hinshaw agreed. 'We will make this play as bitter and relevant as can be, without losing the fun. Do we have a Lady Agatha yet?'

'No,' Alistair admitted. 'Rolf has turned a few girls away for being too pretty.'

'Can a girl be too pretty?' Ned Eden demanded.

'Yes, if they're sharing the stage with Miss Abbott.'

'Where can I store my drawings?' Hugo interrupted. He'd told Vanessa a few times that actors bored him.

Alistair suggested the models of the set go straight to the carpenter's workshop.

'Put the sketches in my room,' Vanessa offered.

Hugo nodded. 'Perfect. That makes you responsible for mediating with pattern cutters and out-workers. My work is done, Mrs Kingcourt. Having been up three nights straight, I can go back to being an artistic drifter. I'll be napping in some quiet corner if anyone needs me.'

As Hugo strolled off, Aubrey Hinshaw asked, 'Is he playing games?'

'He's playing the role of himself,' Alistair answered. 'He writes the script as he goes along.'

In a few, casual words, Hugo had laid the onus of costuming the play on to Vanessa's shoulders. She caught up with him later, on his way out to smoke a cigarette. Smoking was prohibited backstage, where glue fumes and wood shavings made a volatile mix.

'You must not leave me holding the hand-grenade,' she pressed. At the very least, she needed the names of cutters, dressmakers, fabric wholesalers. But just then Aubrey Hinshaw came out to smoke, along with the lighting riggers. Hugo ignored her and she listened to them discussing The Farren's luminaires, Fresnels, spots, projectors and footlights, and how many coloured gels were still in a useable state. In the end, she hissed at Hugo, 'Come up to my room.'

He did not. An hour later, Doyle knocked on her door with Hugo's portfolios and together, they decorated her walls with his drawings. Vivid and exciting, the sketches were vague in actual detail. How would each garment work as a pattern? What would the pumpkin sleeves of Lady Agatha's visiting gown look like as flat, two-dimensional pieces?

'Darned if I know,' Vanessa muttered to herself. 'Eva, I wish you were here.'

Chapter Seventeen

The following day, October 1st, blocking rehearsals began. They had been put back from the previous day in all the excitement over the designs. Expecting to stand in for Lady Agatha, Vanessa discovered that Tanith had been recruited instead.

'She strikes absolutely the right note,' Aubrey Hinshaw explained, 'of childlike vacuity and latent cunning. A relief for you, no?'

Oddly, it wasn't. Having made a fuss about being asked to read the part, Vanessa had unexpectedly enjoyed it. Tanith must have known what was in store today because her hair was in an extravagant roll and she was wearing a dress and stockings. Now I know why actresses get so catty, Vanessa thought. Competition at all sides. It just proved, backstage Bessies like herself shouldn't develop a taste for the limelight.

'May I stay and watch?' she asked the director. 'I don't have much to do yet.' She'd tried to find Hugo at his atelier yesterday, and later at his flat, without success.

'Tell you what,' Aubrey Hinshaw replied, 'take a script into the prompt box. The cast should be off the book by now, but they're bound to fluff. Blocking interrupts the rhythm.'

In the prompter's cubicle, Vanessa spread out the script. Peter Switt demanded to know what she was doing.

'Your job. Complain to Mr Hinshaw.' She wasn't keen on the young ASM. He'd taken too much obvious pleasure in eclipsing Tanith. She wondered how he'd react when Tanith was demoted from temporary actress back to being his clueless superior.

Patrick Carnford and Ronnie Gainsborough arrived punctually. James Harnett, the butler, turned up next and Miss Konstantiva a few minutes after. Vanessa watched the older woman being introduced to Tanith.

'My new daughter! How lovely.'

In her late sixties, Rosa Konstantiva challenged every notion of aging. Tall, with striking features and supple limbs, she moved with a balletic precision, legacy of a career in Paris many years ago with the *ballets russes*. Her hair was an ice-white chignon and she wore a couture suit. Vanessa noticed that in ordinary conversation, she spoke with a slight French intonation, though on stage she became as English upper class as any actress.

She greeted everyone, including the stage staff, with unforced pleasure.

Patrick Carnford bowed low. '*Madame la Duchesse de Berwick, bonjour.*' He resembled a superlatively handsome scene shifter in his loose trousers, a rolled-sleeve shirt and boating shoes. His fellow male lead was more in character in a dark lounge suit, his hair slicked. Giving Carnford a brisk evaluation, Ronnie Gainsborough delivered a slice of the barely-polite contempt that was known to exist between them.

'Cool and casual, Pat? I shall feel as though I'm performing with my tennis coach.'

'Then I'd better be quick on my feet, Ronnie, to avoid those notoriously low balls of yours.'

'Haven't lost your instinct for the easy laugh, I see.'

'Dear chap, it's only the blocking rehearsal. I shall hone my humour as we progress to the serious stuff.'

'Blocking *is* serious. It isn't only where one stands, it's *how* one stands. How one moves, establishing character, relationships, mood. It was so when I trained.'

'Ah, but so much has gone out of fashion over the decades, Ronnie.'

Noticing Miss Konstantiva observing them with a sardonic eyebrow, the men grinned sheepishly. Rosa looked around. 'Is our little firmament missing a star?'

There was as yet no Miss Abbott. Minutes later Alistair brought a message: Miss Abbott was deeply fatigued and would not be attending.

Aubrey Hinshaw requested Alistair ring Terence Rolf immediately. 'Either she's here in twenty minutes, or he has my permission to re-cast. Miss . . .' he wiggled his fingers at Vanessa in the prompt box. 'Mrs King – um – '

'Kingcourt.'

'Lady Windermere for the rest of the morning, if you please. Bring your script and take your position on stage. Beginners to the wings please, Parker and Lord Darlington. Miss Konstantiva, Miss Stacey, stand by. Lord Windermere, you've time for a cup of tea. Mr Cottrill, lower the curtain. Ned, got your notebook? You,' he waved at Peter Switt, 'into the prompt box.'

Blocking was slow and even though Aubrey Hinshaw directed her gently, the script in Vanessa's hand shook ludicrously. She'd often pondered the exact meaning of 'charisma'. Sharing a stage with Ronnie Gainsborough, she learned that it was the ability of another person to draw eyes and energy from you to themselves.

When Tanith entered with Miss Konstantiva, she felt utterly eclipsed. Tanith made her moves with an ease that must be inherited.

Aubrey Hinshaw remained patient and by raising eyebrows and mouthing directions, Miss Konstantiva helped too, though Tanith tittered whenever Vanessa confused stage left and right. Ronnie Gainsborough made no effort to conceal his affront at being asked to share a stage with amateurs.

When Vanessa accidentally overshot her mark, Gainsborough snapped, 'The audience pays to see my face, not the back of my neck. You're forcing me to turn my back. Come forward.'

'Sorry.' Vanessa shifted quickly downstage.

'Not so far that I have to shout!'

Rosa Konstantiva came to her rescue. 'Ronnie, don't bully. Ask Mrs Kingcourt what you wish for.'

'I wish for her to stand a little downstage of me so I can give the impression of conversing.'

Carnford's voice floated from the wings. '"The impression of conversing." *Bravo*. Ronnie's given us the definition of acting. Perhaps our director will note it down so we can make it our company motto.'

Gainsborough appealed to the director. 'Can't we get through this? I am dying for a pee.'

Hinshaw came on stage and gently moved Vanessa into a different position. 'Perfect. You too, Ronnie, an inch or two back please. No, just an inch. Remember, you love this woman. You are passionate about her and in your desire to have her, you will tempt her to defy social convention. She shows no sign that she will waver. Let me see frustration in your stance, in your face.'

'I'm already in agony! If we could race to the end –'

'Work with it, dear fellow. Mrs Kingcourt, you are doing splendidly. Virtue under siege. Say your line again, please.'

Aubrey Hinshaw took them through Ronnie Gainsborough's exit lines with painstaking, overly-deliberate thoroughness. When he finally said, 'Exit Lord Darlington, let's take a fifteen-minute break,' and Ronnie rushed from the stage, he winked at Vanessa. After the break, she was back on with Rosa and Tanith. Patrick Carnford entered as Lord Windermere. Where Ronnie Gainsborough magnified his stage presence with big movements and an open stance, Patrick moved with the tread of a leopard, seeming to know exactly how and where to place his body – and hers. When he moved Vanessa into place, it was like being led by a good dancer. She realised suddenly that his light colouring reminded her of her Norwegian friend Finn, and liked him all the more for it.

As the discord flashed between the Windermeres, Carnford's mannerisms changed. He retreated into himself, and Vanessa was beguiled into projecting stronger emotions. She felt the pain of a woman losing the love of her life. She didn't have to dig deep. When she spoke of Mrs Erlynne, the supposed cause of the rift, it was Fern's face that swelled in her mind. '". . . if that woman comes here – I warn you –"'

She felt a current drawing her on. *I'm acting. Now I understand. It's like falling off a cliff and finding you're flying.* She left the stage on cue and Patrick Carnford delivered his final, tormented lines.

'"My God! What shall I do? I dare not tell her who this woman really is. The shame would kill her."'

Aubrey Hinshaw called, 'Curtain down. Thirty-minute break, ladies and gentlemen, then all beginners for Act Two. Good work.'

Vanessa went down into the auditorium, still holding her

script. She'd slip upstairs, quickly freshen up. She was walking on air, and hardly noticed the pass-door opening to admit a female figure. A moment later, a hand fell on hers. A slender hand terminating in silver painted nails. 'I'll take that from you, if it's all the same.'

Vanessa clutched her script to her body. 'The director will probably want me to read after the break,' she told the woman. 'Wretched Clemency Abbott hasn't bothered to get out of bed.'

'Wretched *Miss* Abbott has been ordered to rest by her doctor. Nevertheless, she has put her health at risk to be here.'

Cold dismay coursed through Vanessa. The fur-draped shoulders, the upswept hair and pert hat . . . the voice had misled her. Miss Abbott wasn't using the honey-bee tone she'd used during the read-through three day ago.

'I'm terribly sorry.'

Miss Abbott took the script. 'You've had your little moment. Whatever the day job is, I shouldn't rush to give it up.'

Vanessa forced out a smile. 'You're absolutely right, Miss Abbott. For a moment, conceit got the better of me. For a moment, I knew what it was to be an actress.'

She escaped upstairs to her room, shaking the euphoria from her system with each step. Acting was addictive. Becoming somebody else was a drug. She could imagine it possessing her father powerfully enough for him to leave a child and home. She wouldn't be needed back on stage now, so she might as well have another go at finding Hugo. Once again, however, her search was fruitless and she returned to the theatre. Reaching her room, she found Doyle just leaving.

'Beg pardon, ma'am.' He explained that he'd taken the liberty of unlocking her door so a mirror could be fetched in.

'A new, unbroken one?'

'Not new, no. Though it took us an age to find it. You'd think, being a theatre, there'd be mirrors everywhere. There are some in the dressing rooms, but those can't be removed. So the lads searched the sub-stage where the old props are kept, but they didn't find one there, either. Seems actors won't have mirrors on stage. If a play calls for a looking glass, the set-makers paint wood silver.'

'Superstition?'

Doyle shrugged. 'If you ask me, actors don't want the audience having to look at two things at once. In the end, they found you a nice cheval mirror that used to be in the ladies' powder room. What do you want done with the old one? Firewood?'

'Oh, no. The frame is beautiful. Under that green paint, anyway. Could it be stored till I find house room for it?'

'Aye aye, ma'am.' Doyle checked to ensure that nobody was nearby. 'What's wrong with that fellow Cottrill? I saw him on stage before I came up here. One moment, he was with Props and the carpenters, marking out the set. Next time I looked, he was staring up at the upper circle, one knee jerking as though he'd stood on a live cable. I called out, "Are you all right," and he sort of choked. "It's her, Flo," he said. Do you reckon he saw her?'

'Flo being . . .'

'Our ghost, ma'am. Back Row Flo. She always appears right at the top, a girl in Victorian dress and bonnet. I reckon I've seen her a couple of times, but I don't like to think about it. I reckon, if you don't bother ghosts, they don't bother you.'

'Mr Cottrill is quite sensitive. Was the figure actually wearing a bonnet?'

'A hat . . . sort of lopsided.'

'Ah.' Vanessa pondered that, a suspicion forming. 'Worn at an angle?'

'That's right.'

'Come with me.' Vanessa led the way down, and across the auditorium to the foyer, where she took the public stairs. At the top
of the second flight, she paused to catch her breath and take stock.
There were ladies' and gents' lavatories on this level and a bar called
'The Georgian', which was shuttered. Impulsively, she tried her
key in its lock, but like the wardrobe before, the solid door swallowed it. Checking that Doyle was still behind her, she continued
to the upper circle. Softly creeping inside, she heard a sound that
reminded her of the distant hum of fighter squadrons returning
home. Rhythmic droning. She waited for Doyle to catch up.

'There's your ghostly apparition.' She pointed to Hugo,
slumped in the middle of the front row, his beret pulled half
over his face. She hadn't the heart to wake him.

Returning to her side of the theatre as Doyle went back to his
niche, she found the wardrobe door slightly ajar. She jumped like
a cat at the sight of a black figure searching inside her wardrobe.

'Miss Bovary!'

'Oh, you, Mrs Kingcourt. I let myself in.'

'So I see. How may I help?'

Vanessa had the impression that Barbara Bovary was replacing
something, or covering something. When she turned, however,
there was no sign of apology in her demeanour. 'You can begin
by explaining your conduct towards Miss Abbott.'

Vanessa said nothing, instead making for the tea kettle. She
was parched. The sight of Hugo's drawings on the wall gave her
a lift. She asked, 'Will you take tea?'

'No thank you. You were insolent to our leading lady.'

'She was late again.'

'Since when has it been your business to comment on the
conduct of the talent?'

Vanessa filled the kettle. The tap wheezed rudely. 'It isn't, and I apologised. Didn't Miss Abbott say?' Fed up of being yet again on the wrong side of Miss Bovary, Vanessa launched an attack of her own. 'Why won't you comment on Hugo's work? It's all around you.' She made a gesture that implied *gorge your eyes*. 'Hugo was your choice. I'd have expected more enthusiasm from you.'

Miss Bovary looked ready to pop. 'Mrs Kingcourt, you are on your final warning. One more word or look out of place, I'll see to it that you're fired and that you never work in theatre again. Understood?'

The correct answer was undoubtedly, 'Perfectly.' But Vanessa had sat firm under enemy fire, flown in a Beaufighter and slapped the face of Commander Redenhall. Remembering Hugo's enigmatic revelation about the woman's penchant for the dead, she said, 'Did you hear we had a ghost in the house earlier? Seems Back Row Flo is up to her tricks.'

Miss Bovary was suddenly alert. 'What – what do you mean?'

'A faceless entity watched today's proceedings . . . so I heard. Should we conduct a séance?'

The woman tottered. Vanessa leapt forward. *Good God, what have I done?* Firm steps approached and she called out, 'Please, help!'

It was Lord Windermere, or rather, Patrick Carnford, who hurried into her room. He carried a long-stemmed rose. 'Which of you is fainting?'

'Miss Bovary.'

They got her to a chair. Vanessa poured a glass of water.

Miss Bovary's colour gradually revived. She asked Patrick Carnford to walk her downstairs.

'With pleasure, Barbara, but first I have a little speech to make.' Patrick Carnford faced Vanessa and proffered the rose. 'Fairest Vanessa, I humbly apologise for my colleagues' behaviour earlier. Art is nothing without manners. Don't you agree, Miss Bovary?'

Miss Bovary now looked as if she was going to be violently sick, but speech was not beyond her. 'She's an employee, Mr Carnford. Johnny Quinnell's girl, so the Commander says. It's why we feel we know her but can't place her. However, it does not confer special status.'

'Quinnell's girl . . . I wouldn't have known it. He was a strapping fellow, whereas you – ' Patrick bent and kissed Vanessa full on the mouth.

She heard Miss Bovary's gasp. She'd have gasped herself, if she could. When Patrick raised his head, she discovered she had her second audience of the day. Tanith, Alistair and Macduff made a ragged line in the open doorway. Doyle stood behind, his scarred face like a child's drawing of shock. Alistair looked as if he'd swallowed salt water. Tanith giggled violently.

Carnford placed two fingers against Vanessa's cheek, and whispered, 'Don't let the buggers grind you down, darling.'

With a polite 'How-de-do' for Alistair, he loped past them, forgetting his promise to escort Miss Bovary down the stairs.

Miss Bovary asked Alistair instead. He said, 'Of course,' but made no immediate move, too occupied appraising Vanessa. 'Why is Carnford giving you flowers?'

Vanessa looked at the single rose. It was the colour of fresh butter. 'He was being . . . mystifying.'

Alistair's voice gained its brisk quality. 'Tanith is to play Lady Agatha Carlisle.'

As a stand-in, Vanessa assumed. Miss Bovary was faster on the uptake.

'In a professional capacity? Absolutely impossible. For one, she isn't a member of Equity.'

'She will be,' Alistair said patiently. 'These things can be arranged. How else do young performers get their start?'

'The girl has no experience!'

'Saying "Yes, mamma" and flirting wordlessly with a fellow actor is something she's more than qualified for. The newspapers will love the fact that we have Dido Meredith's granddaughter in the cast.'

Miss Bovary said through clenched teeth, 'I have never heard of Dido Meredith.'

'She was a Gaiety actress,' Tanith informed her. 'And a PB.'

'What is that?' Vanessa demanded.

'A 'Public Beauty'. Granny was ever so popular in the olden days. I bet you had postcards of her on your wall, Miss Bovary.'

Alistair buried a cough in his sleeve. His face gave nothing away.

Tanith piped up again, 'And she was Edward the Seventh's mistress when he was Prince of Wales.'

Miss Bovary rose unsteady, then pushed past them all, saying as she went, 'A story that will guarantee an audience of gawping scandal-mongers and outrage the Royal Family at the same time. I congratulate you, Commander. I will see myself to my office.'

'It's no trouble, Miss Bovary.' Before following her, Alistair said to Vanessa, 'The design of Lady Agatha's dress won't suit Tanith. I recall the shoulders are very wide.'

'You came here to tell me that?'

'No.' He leaned very close and said softly, 'Two plain clothes policemen came to my office, asking for Hugo. I said we hadn't seen him for a while.'

'He's up in the Gods, sleeping. What's he done?'

'They wouldn't say. But I'm afraid I can guess.'

Tanith stepped forward. 'Nessie, can we ask Hugo to draw me something that won't make me look like a fairground tent?'

Vanessa nodded. ''Course we can, but don't say "draw me something" – he's a designer, not an illustrator. Come in and look at the pictures.'

With an approving nod, Alistair went. Macduff remained, his mind perhaps on Vanessa's biscuit tin. Doyle seemed in no hurry to go, either. While Tanith was occupied on the other side of the room, Vanessa asked, 'Did you tell Cottrill that his ghost was a six feet tall, exhausted Irishman?'

'I did, ma'am. I went to check on Mr Brennan again, but he'd gone. I too have my suspicions what this police trouble is. We're meant to be a family theatre, but ghosts, dead bodies, now the cops . . .' Doyle scratched his mutilated ear.

'"There is only one thing in the world worse than being talked about, and that is not being talked about." From *The Picture of Dorian Gray*, and I've never believed the sentiment. Sometimes, gossip is poison.' Vanessa went to her cupboard. After a short search, she ascertained that Miss Bovary had rifled among the letters she'd concealed under a wad of material. They were those from her to her dad, which Ruth had passed on. None seemed to be missing, but what had Miss Bovary been hoping to find? *What so disturbs her . . . Am I too much alive for her liking?*

'Doyle, how long have you worked here?'

'I started a week before you did.'

'Who was your predecessor?'

'Mr Kidd, who works nights here, looked after the theatre while it was closed, before Commander Redenhall took over. Any particular reason you need to know, ma'am?'

'I'd like to speak with someone who was here the night Mr Bovary died.'

'That would be Miss Bovary, Mr Rolf and his lady.'

She pulled a face. 'Who else, Doyle?'

'Well, there was one who witnessed the whole night, start to finish.'

'You don't mean Back Row Flo?'

'I wouldn't know about her.' Doyle pointed to Macduff. 'This fellow was found outside the stage door, lying across his master. He's a good dog. His only shortcoming is, he don't talk.' Doyle gave him a pat, then nodded towards the rose that Vanessa had forgotten she was holding. 'A nice, well-mannered gent, that Mr Carnford. Generous. All the ladies say so. Well, best be getting on. I just wanted to mention that it's the Commander's orders that I sign everyone in now, staff, actors, policemen. It takes a bit of time, see, writing down names at the door. Asking their business, keeping them waiting, if you get my drift.'

'I think I do. More to the point, I'll try and ensure that Mr Brennan understands.' She watched Doyle leading Macduff away, then called to Tanith who was studying a drawing of Lady Windermere's ball gown, her head cocked to one side. 'Let's see if we can run Hugo to ground.' After another futile trip to Great Portland Street, they called at his flat. Hugo wasn't there either.

He made no further appearances at the theatre that week.

Three evenings in a row, Vanessa went to Old Compton Street and knocked at Hugo's door, even though there were no lights on in the flat. She even tried an early morning visit, hoping to catch him sleeping. A man unlocking a dance-wear shop below the flat told her in a low voice, 'The police can't find Mr Brennan either.'

'Why do they want him?'

The shopkeeper gave her a considering look. 'Are you a friend of Mrs King?'

'I'm sorry?'

'Never mind, treasure.' They got chatting about matters theatrical and Vanessa explained her costume sourcing predicament.

'Have you thought of Stage-Stock?' the man said. 'They hire anything and everything. They're in the City, Clerkenwell.'

Vanessa went straight there, and spent the remainder of the day being shown around a massive warehouse that contained every period costume imaginable.

A heavy shower fell as she made her way home and when she woke the following morning, her hair resembled a bunch of dried hops. She telephoned Mr Stephen from the phone at the back of Anjeliko's and asked for the earliest possible appointment. Mr Stephen's assistant remembered her. 'Mrs Redenhall's little friend? Come at four. He'll squeeze you in.'

She left work early to be in good time.

It started well, a vigorous hair wash ridding her of London grime. And then she overheard something that trampled her peace of mind and threw her future into doubt.

Chapter Eighteen

Stuart, the shampooist, massaged a pulp of fuller's earth, linseed oil and vinegar into her hair, made her a turban from a towel and asked her if she'd like refreshment. 'Ginger beer, if you have it.' He brought it with a back copy of Time Life magazine and Vanessa settled down to let the oils penetrate. She was reading a piece on the actress, Vivienne Leigh, when Mr Stephen brought a client to the mirror next to hers and began removing her over-sized hair rollers. The woman, a stranger to Vanessa, was talking about a friend.

'. . . not even enough to buy herself a hat or a pair of gloves. Her selfish, selfish husband has spent the lot.'

'Awful, but what can she do?' Mr Stephen murmured, teasing out a curl.

'Plenty. It's not the Dark Ages. We women have choice now.'

Vanessa listened with half an ear, more interested in Miss Leigh, until she heard –

'He's violent, did I say? Hit her in a churchyard of all places. She kept a brave face.'

Mr Stephen tutted. 'No woman should have to tolerate that. And she has no money, you say?'

'Old money, but that's a fancy way of saying it's run out. She's having to do her own cleaning.'

'No lady should put up with that. Shall we try a softer style today? A parting would be a start.'

'I don't like them. I mess them up.'

'A parting for them, not for your hair. Has she got another man in her sights?'

'There is an admirer.' The client's voice dropped, and Vanessa missed a segment until the woman spoke up again. 'The title will come to him in due course, and naturally, she'd like to be safely hitched to him before it does.'

'Naturally,' Mr Stephen echoed. 'I'm glad we trimmed a little off the back. You'll get a nice bounce on the shoulders. What do you call the people who invest in theatre shows?'

'Angels?'

'Because if the lady you're talking about is who I think she is, her husband's angels are about to take flight. One of my regular ladies has a husband who manages a bank, and the rumour is —'

Vanessa didn't learn what the rumour was as she gulped her ginger beer too fast and had to cram her hand over her mouth to stop herself burping. Stuart came to her at that moment and unwrapped her head. 'Time to rinse, Mrs Kingcourt.'

She left the salon with her hair restored to sleek waves, and without any actual proof that she'd overheard a warped version of Fern and Alistair's lives. But there couldn't be many theatre managers in the throes of marital strife. What she'd heard was sickening and worrying. Alistair was relying on outside investors to fund *Lady Windermere*. His angels must not take flight!

The following day, a memo appeared on the stage door notice board.

To all cast and staff
Thursday, October 3rd, 1946

The date for the opening of *Lady Windermere's Fan* is the last Thursday of November. The first technical rehearsal is scheduled for November 21st and the first dress rehearsal for the day after. The final tech rehearsal will be Monday, November 25th, and the final dress rehearsal the following day. Crew start-time on each occasion is eight a.m. Cast start-time is nine-thirty. There are fifty-two days to go to opening.

B Bovary on behalf of Cdr A Redenhall

A copy had been pushed under her door. Alistair had added a line: 'Have you heard from Hugo? Please report.' The memo proved that Alistair still had faith in his show. Faith that proved short-lived.

He was at his desk and looked as though he'd been punched. Seeing her, he rose and held a letter towards her. 'The knives are out.'

The letter came from the chairlady of The Elizabeth Farren Society informing Commander Redenhall that, after detailed consideration, they had decided not to invest in his latest production. The writer cited 'Moral objections, and Management's failure to take an appropriate stance on the matter of divorce.' She concluded that, 'The play's subject matter seems bound to invite a controversy that we, as a society, would not wish to partake in.'

'This is bad,' Vanessa said, passing the letter back.

'I'd like to know how they're so well-briefed on my private life. Have you let anything slip, Vanessa?'

Vanessa asked him kindly not to insult her, then told him what she'd overheard at Mr Stephen's.

He sat back, issuing a heavy breath. Of relief or disgust, she couldn't tell. 'You're saying that all the stuff that slews around about me emanates from a hairdresser's salon?'

'It's possible. The Chairlady of the Elizabeth Farren Society might be a client.'

Alistair screwed up the letter and lobbed it towards the paper bin. 'They aren't the chief backers. We still have funding. Any squeak from Hugo?'

Vanessa reported her fruitless search. As a sop, she described her visit to Stage-Stock, only to be discouraged when Alistair shook his head.

'Too late. Aubrey Hinshaw is sold on Hugo's creations. It's changed the way he's directing the play. We can't jettison Brennan's genius now. How much would it cost to hire, as a matter of interest?'

He winced when Vanessa told him. 'Shame The Farren's costumes were destroyed. We could have made a fortune hiring them out. This poor theatre has had a run of terrible luck.' He came round his desk, clasping Vanessa lightly on the shoulder. 'Don't flinch. I'm not going to kiss you. I shouldn't want to put Patrick Carnford out of a job.'

'He's a very good kisser,' Vanessa agreed. This time, she wasn't going to apologise for something that hadn't been her fault.

Alistair shrugged. 'Close the door on your way out, Mrs King-court.'

Alistair listened to her retreating footsteps. He knew he was being inconsistent with Vanessa. Kissing her, dancing close, then sending her off with a flea in her ear. The trouble was he wanted her very badly, but he was still sufficiently in control to know the dangers for both of them. One incautious embrace and she'd be head-first in the barrel of his divorce. Tarnished by his 'objectionable morals'. He'd never forgive himself.

In the days following, more 'angels' dropped out, leaving only one large investor, Mr Blandford, a London stockbroker with an independently wealthy wife. On the evening of October 14th, Blandford's secretary telephoned to express her employer's doubts as to whether the play should go ahead. Robin Amery, The Farren's Public Relations Officer, took the call and asked the secretary to hold while he fetched Alistair.

Alistair invited Mr and Mrs Blandford to visit. 'Let them meet the cast. They'll see how the sets are shaping up, and we may put on a costume display for them.'

Robin Amery, listening, mouthed, 'We have no costumes.'

Alistair ended the call, saying, 'Sunday the twentieth? Perfect. We look forward to seeing them then.'

Used to making decisions under fire, Alistair felt no panic. He went to find Vanessa. 'Costume display' required her input.

She wasn't in, and her door was locked.

She wasn't in because she was finally cornering Hugo.

He was in his atelier, the lights off, a hunted look on his face. In place of his usual Bohemian garb, he was squeezed into a 'demob' suit, brown pinstripe, too narrow across the shoulders. He'd combed his hair down over his eyes and looked as though he hadn't shaved for days.

'Why are you chasing me, Nessie?'

'You need to ask?' An empty kitbag lay on the table. Otherwise, the studio was bare. 'Hugo, I feel like a lobster dropped in a pan of boiling water. I can't costume *Lady Windermere* on my own.'

'You're not on your own. Alistair's behind you.'

'Not sure. He caught me kissing Patrick Carnford.'

'For pity's sake, what's wrong with you? Can't you see when a man cares, and when he doesn't?'

Uncertain how to interpret that, Vanessa put the kettle on. Hugo looked undernourished. As she passed him, she smelled sweat. 'You need to go home and have a bath.'

He waited till she returned with tea before saying, 'I can't. The police are watching my place.'

'Are you a friend of Mrs King?'

'Fuck,' he said. 'You know?'

'Hugo, I haven't a clue. Will you tell me?'

'Mrs King . . . Queen. I'm a queen, darling. I suppose they didn't have them in the RAF.'

'You're forgetting I went to art college before I joined up. You could have confided in me.'

'No, I couldn't. My life is illegal. Breathing is illegal, the way I do it.' Hugo pushed his hair back, revealing eyes blasted with exhaustion. 'Tell Alistair I *want* him to succeed. And I'm sorry it had to end like this.'

'You're not planning anything stupid?'

'Dear idiot, nobody "plans" anything stupid. That's the whole point of stupid. I'm bolting to Paris. What irony, to follow in the footsteps of Oscar Wilde. He died there, three years on. I don't intend to.' Hugo looked past her, to the window where passers-by appeared as fast-moving stripes. 'I should never have come back to The Farren. It has an atmosphere . . . I thought it was just Cottrill who believed in that Back Row Flo rubbish.

He's mad. Did you know, the first time he saw you, he thought you were Flo, manifesting on stage?'

'Nothing of the sort! Cottrill saw me as an intrusive female.'

'Poor fellow spent the war down the coal mines. Confined spaces turned his brain. The Farren is doing the same to me. When I was younger, working sixty hours without sleep wouldn't have bothered me. I'd have taken Benzedrine and sailed through. But nobody sells Benzo any more. So I'm drinking brandy, glass after glass, but it's unlatched something in my head. My terrors have come back.'

'What terrors, Hugo?'

'Stuff I went through in the war. I can't explain. Then a week ago, I broke a golden rule and kissed a friend in an alley – only a peck, honest, m'Lud – but a policeman was walking past. The bastard blew his whistle, and I ran home. The copper saw me go in, and now I can't go back there. I've kept moving, a night here, a night there, but I can't hide for ever.'

'It's not illegal to kiss a friend on the cheek.'

'In Soho, in an alley next to a club that gets raided twice a year? 'Course it is. I might serve two years, and how d'you imagine the prison warders and the other lags will treat an Irish homosexual who designs theatre costumes? Forget I risked my life for this country.' He put a hand on her shoulder, an echo of Alistair. 'The show will go on. The carpenters will build the sets and you, my diminutive darling, will get the costumes made.'

'How? I am way out of my depth.'

'The man I rent this place from is Mr Rag-Trade. Actually, he's called Doll. No, really, he is. Toddy Doll, *so* Dickensian. You'll find him on Duchess Street.'

'Miss Bovary's sure to bring in that Mrs Yorke.'

'Well, maybe.' Hugo pulled out a wallet and extracted a

cheque, which he gave to Vanessa. It was for a hundred and twenty pounds. 'The upfront payment for my work. I'm running out on the job and I'm not bastard enough to take the money.'

The cheque was issued by 'Rolf Associates' and the signatories were 'Mr & Mrs T Rolf.' 'Your contract is with them,' Vanessa asked, 'not with the theatre?'

'They were determined to employ me over Alistair's head. They knew I'd bugger up and they want the play to fail. I'm difficult, controversial and I misjudge the mood of audiences and critics.'

'Not this time.'

'Bless you. But nobody has offered me work except Terence and Sylvia Rolf. Though I never got round to signing their contract, so I suppose I don't even work for them.'

'If you haven't cashed the cheque or signed the contract, the designs are still yours.'

He tipped his head, agreeing.

Taking out her chequebook, she wrote a draft for sixty pounds. 'Made out to you.'

'What for?'

'It's my savings. I inherited the money from my husband, and I've never felt it was morally mine. Something *I* can't explain.' She tore a sheet from a notepad and handed him her pen, then dictated a short note. Hugo's hand shook.

'Sign and date it.'

'Slow down, bossy-boots. What is the date, by the way?'

As he signed his name, there came a hammering at the door followed by a shout of, 'Open up or we'll force it!'

Hugo turned ashen.

Vanessa asked, 'Is there a back way out?'

He nodded.

'Grab your kitbag. I'll stall them. See you . . . one day. Send me a postcard of the Eiffel Tower.'

It wasn't hard to act the part of a frightened half-wit with two plain clothes men and four uniformed officers cannoning past her. As they pushed past, one of them elbowed Vanessa in the mouth. She shouted, 'He fought for this country! Show some respect!'

She heard crockery smashing in the kitchen. Grabbing the paper Hugo had signed and the keys he'd left on the table, holding a handkerchief to her lower lip, she left them to it and headed to Mr Doll of Duchess Street.

When she returned to The Farren, it was dark and she was staggering under the weight of a heavy package. Approaching the building from Russell Street, she was rewarded by a light in Alistair's office window. *Let him be in a mellow mood*. She'd made decisions that he might be inclined to swat down.

She found him adjusting his clock. Without turning, he asked if she'd been 'Hugo hunting'.

'I have news. Um . . . quite bad.'

'Only "quite"? Then it'll be better than mine.' He set the hands of the clock to nine-twenty and closed the glass. 'You first.'

She told him about the police raid, Hugo's flight.

Slumping in an armchair, he waved her to the other and said nothing for so long that she was stirred to defiance.

'If you want my opinion, the law is criminal.'

'If you want *my* opinion, I agree, but that isn't going to bring our designer back.' He rolled his head lazily to look at her. 'Any brilliant ideas, Kingcourt?'

She opened up her parcel and showed him white silk crepe, a

slab two doorsteps thick. 'Forty-two yards, and they're getting more in next week.'

'"They"?'

'A company called Doll & Saunders, only "Saunders" is a phantom partner, because customers like to think there's more than one person in charge. So Mr Doll said.' Vanessa had found her way to Duchess Street, which lay off Portland Place. Lights on in all the windows, sewing machines whirring, the proprietor in his office. Hearing her explanation that Hugo had been 'called home to Ireland' – a justifiable lie, she believed – Mr Doll had reacted furiously.

'What about my rent?'

When she explained her role at The Farren, adding that she'd like to take over Hugo's lease, Mr Doll had simmered down.

'It's a nice little premises. Just the thing for you.'

He was a manufacturer and wholesaler of ladies' fashions, therefore no use to her as a costume-maker. She pressed him for the name of someone who could make costumes and he came up with one. 'She might do – if you're desperate.'

'I am.' Mr Doll had been sent by heaven. He had access to French silk. The best.

All this, she told Alistair.

He looked at her cut lip and she explained about the policeman's elbow. 'How much?' He meant the silk.

This required a deep breath. 'Eighty shillings a yard.'

'*Eighty?* So this lot will have cost –' he worked it out. 'How did you pay?'

'I haven't, it's on credit. Look – it's real French silk, in dreadfully short supply. French mills are only now exporting again, and customs slaps on a huge tariff, so four pounds a yard is . . . well, what it is. I will dye it.'

Alistair looked sceptical.

'In small batches, to match Hugo's colour schemes. Mr Doll has a man who'll advise me. And the woman he recommended comes with a team of seamstresses.' Vanessa knew she was over-selling. She wouldn't have taken the silk, but Mr Doll had said, 'The next lot coming in will be double the price. Take this batch and you can have whatever you need afterwards at the same price. If it has to be silk, it has to be French – unless you want to make your costumes from old parachutes.'

Alistair was still frowning. 'Hugo said he'd need one hundred and twenty yards for the Second Act dresses, so at my reckoning, that's eight hundred pounds.'

She'd worked that out herself, on the bus-ride here. 'It's prob-ably more than the budget. And that number doesn't include hiring in corsetry and accessories.'

Alistair stretched his arm to Macduff, who had slunk out from under the desk. 'Let's not pretend that putting on a show is cheap. All right. Keep a tight eye on costs.' He told her about the latest investors abandoning ship – some associates of Terence Rolf's - and about the Blandfords who must be wooed and won all over again. 'If they pull the plug, we go dark. I always thought myself quite well off, but I can't bankroll a show on my own. The money my Uncle Bo left in the current account has been pretty much eaten; there wasn't all that much. The bulk of his fortune is tidied away in a trust to which I do not have the key. Have you had dinner?'

She hadn't even had lunch.

'There's a little place down the street. They do an after-the-atre menu.'

'I'm not properly dressed.' She'd run on wet pavements and her stockings were spattered. 'My lip must look stupid, too.'

'It looks bee stung, but if it makes you happier, we'll take a shadowy corner table.'

'Thank you. I'd like to.'

At the stage door, Alistair spent a moment speaking with Kidd, the night janitor who was as short and wiry as Doyle was beefy and broad. Whenever he went out, Alistair handed Macduff into the care of a trusted member of staff with the words, 'Don't let him out of your sight.'

Kidd touched his cap. 'I'll stick to him like glue, sir.'

Their meal was simple and well-cooked, the wine excellent. They talked shop, and Vanessa soon grasped what lay ahead if new investors could not be found.

'I'd have to declare the theatre company bankrupt and I'd be at risk of losing the building,' Alistair told her.

'The Rolfs and Miss Bovary would celebrate. I'm sure, now, that it's their strategy to sink you. Don't you?'

'I'm heading that way. At any rate, they'd most certainly try to buy The Farren, without its debts, from the Receiver. And it would be such a waste. We have a good company, a brilliant director and four leading stars —' he was opposite her, close enough that she saw his pupils dilate — 'and I'm generous enough to include Carnford in that.'

Two glasses of wine and a hypnotic candle made Vanessa bold. 'Thousands of girls would give a year's salary for a kiss from Patrick Carnford.'

'Thousands probably already have.'

She laughed. 'Kissing is free. It's what it leads to that can be costly.'

Alistair touched her sore lip. 'You know the best remedy for bee stings, don't you?'

'Vinegar. Or is it bicarbonate of soda? I can never remember.'

He leaned forward and brushed her mouth with his. A moment's contact, then he sat back. 'We met at the right time.'

'The right time?'

'For friendship. We're a good team.'

'Oh.' That was it. Friendship and the indeterminate postponement of the love she was beginning to feel she couldn't survive without.

He called for the bill. 'I have a request. Can you have a dress made by Sunday?'

She was jarred into saying, 'Definitely. Whose dress?'

'Clemency Abbott's. I'll ask her to come to you for a fitting tomorrow, after rehearsal.'

Chapter Nineteen

The war had driven into the national character a sense that anything was possible. When bridges had been built in days and runways repaired within hours, 'a dress by Sunday' was a cinch.

During a break in the Tuesday rehearsal, Alistair asked Miss Abbott to surrender an hour of her time and go to the wardrobe room. She pouted. 'I was taking my cat to be groomed this afternoon.'

'Shall I write a note of apology to the cat?'

'Mm. Or come in person and say sorry to Mr Whiskers. Oh – and if that pert little Wardrobe Mistress cheeks me, the fur will fly.'

'Understood.' They were at the green room door. Declining an invitation to join the actors for tea, Alistair signalled to Rosa Konstantiva that he'd like a private word. He asked her if she'd attend the fitting.

'Vanessa could do with a helping hand. I know it's a lot to ask.'

'You want me to hold the other end of the tape measure?' Rosa laughed. 'Why not. It'll bring back old times.'

*

In the wardrobe room, Vanessa knew her basic skills were about to be tested and her hands wouldn't stop shaking. She thrust the tape measure under her blouse to warm it.

A knock. Vanessa cleared her throat and called, 'Do please come in. Oh, Miss Konstantiva, how lovely to see you!'

'Isn't it equally lovely to see me?' Miss Abbott walked into the room, stopping in astonishment when she saw Hugo's sketches. 'Are those the costumes?'

'Yes. Beautiful, aren't they?'

'Mm, show me mine.'

Vanessa did so. Miss Abbott stared for a very long time. 'Who is going to make my gowns?'

'Um, it's in hand, Miss Abbott.'

'You have red cabbage stuck to your lip.'

Vanessa automatically touched the split in her lip. No amount of lipstick would cover it. And yes, she knew it looked as if a sliver of cabbage had stuck to her.

Miss Abbot turned to the mirror, inspecting a powdered cheek. 'The other morning, you were insolent to me and I am irreplaceable. So if I say "Jump" you say, "How high?" Understand?'

Vanessa perfectly understood. She also understood that Miss Abbott had an enticing, white neck and that her tape measure would fit four times round it. Five if pulled very tight. 'I had intended to apologise again, Miss Abbott, but you've beaten me to it.'

'So that's the pleasantries over.' Rosa Konstantiva pointed to the clock. 'You now have only forty-seven minutes till we're needed back on stage, Clemency. Get your kit off.'

Laughing, Miss Abbott presented her back to Vanessa. 'Take care with my buttons. They're bone, hand-carved.'

When undressed, Clemency Abbott's underwear reminded Vanessa of the cow parsley that frothed in Stanshurst's lanes in springtime. Physically, the girl was flawless. Her measurements would be text-book perfect. Vanessa asked, 'Would you please raise your arms?'

Miss Abbott raised them a couple of inches. Putting the tape measure around the slender waist, Vanessa dropped one end, which swung against Miss Abbott's stockinged leg.

'You'll replace these nylons if you ladder them.'

The second time, Vanessa jotted down the measurement. Thirty-one inches.

Clemency Abbott screamed. 'I'll sue you. Twenty-three inches. You're holding the tape-measure the wrong way!'

Rosa came over. 'Mrs Kingcourt, you are rather short and Miss Abbott is rather the opposite. No wonder you're struggling. Allow me. You take the notes.'

Rosa manipulated the tape measure this way and that, reeling off figures. She wasn't afraid to say, 'Arms higher, please, Clemency. Head straight. *Straight.* Leave the mirror alone, you'll wear out your reflection.' She took measurements Vanessa hadn't even considered: nape of neck to small of back, hip to the point of the opposite shoulder. As she worked, her accent slipped deeper into French.

'*Et voilà,*' she said at last. '*Ca y est c'est fait. Just in time. Est-ce qu'on remercie les autres pour leurs efforts?* Mademoiselle Abbott?'

Clemency's quicksilver tone slipped. 'What?'

'Say thank you, darling, or we'll imagine you have no manners.'

Clemency Abbott said to Vanessa, 'I hope you got all that down.'

'Every last inch, Miss Abbott.'

'If I don't like the dress, I won't wear it.'

When she'd gone, Vanessa flopped on to a chair. 'Thank you, Miss Konstantiva. You must have done this before.'

'I worked for a couturier in Paris. A *couturière*, I should say. A girl younger than you. Darling Alix, but don't get me started on that. Who's doing your making-up?'

Vanessa fetched the card Mr Doll had given her. 'She's called Mrs Farrah-Digby. Very good, and she's free. I mean, free to take on a job.'

'Why, if she's good?'

'An unexpectedly cancelled order.'

Rosa grunted. 'All right, but next time, find somebody who is snowed under. They're always the ones to ask. Right, want a lesson in how to make a block pattern from somebody's measurements?'

Vanessa would for ever after think of Mrs Farrah-Digby as 'The Cat-Keeper.' It took her over four hours to find the costume-maker's home on a Victorian-gothic street in Sydenham, one of London's southeast extremities. Jumping off the last of three buses, Vanessa laboured up a hill that gave a stunning panorama of London and far-off Kent. The wind whipped at the skirts of her coat. The house was a handsome villa, but dirty windows and an unkempt front garden dragged it down.

Still, everyone's windows were dirty and many gardens were wildernesses, as people had left London in droves. She rang the bell, and read the tarnished brass plate by the door: *Farrah-Digby, costumier.*

Vanessa had written, quoting Mr Doll's name, saying she'd be calling today at eleven. She had no idea if her letter had arrived. As the bell clanged in the heart of the house, Vanessa adjusted the satchel that was cutting into her shoulder. She rang again and the lusty clangs eventually brought footsteps. The door opened narrowly and a woman with curling-rags in her hair stuck her chin out. 'Who and why?'

Vanessa got a waft of smells, none pleasant. The fingernails around the edge of the door were stained dark yellow. Vanessa explained her business, repeating 'Mr Doll of Doll & Saunders' and 'The Farren Theatre' several times. 'There's a big order to come, a production's-worth, but we absolutely need a first dress by Sunday. He thought you could do it.'

'Who thought?'

Vanessa repeated 'Mr Doll' loudly.

'Why didn't you say?' Mrs Farrah-Digby opened the door another inch or two. 'Come in, but don't let the cats out.'

Vanessa squeezed through. With her satchel swinging, she felt like a camel passing through a turn-style. The door shut and she was in a dark hallway, four plaintive cats winding around her ankles. Two more regarded her from the stairs. The primary odour was of feline male.

'You must love cats,' she said, to break the ice.

'I feed them, they repay by killing mice. Come on through.' A haze of cigarette smoke caught Vanessa's throat. There must have been a party here last night. On a dining table cluttered with glasses and ash trays that Mrs Farrah-Digby pushed to one side, Vanessa laid out a detailed drawing of Lady Windermere's morning gown which she'd copied from Hugo's original. To that she added the template she and Rosa had created from Clemency Abbott's dimensions. Then, very carefully, she took out her silk. There'd been no time to dye it to the prescribed colour, a mid-lilac, but Vanessa had acquired lace that colour, and a separate length of antique ivory lace to trim sleeves and neckline.

The Farren needed a dress capable of seducing Miss Abbott into the performance of a lifetime, and the wealthy Blandfords into taking out their chequebook.

She'd also brought some of the violet coat linings she'd unpicked. A resourceful seamstress ought to be able to create a passable replica of Hugo's design from all these pieces. Mrs Farrah-Digby turned them over. She wore a candlewick dressing gown over silk pyjamas.

When I rang the bell, she was in bed, smoking. Vanessa thought of Mr Doll's whirring, clattering workroom and wondered – where's the noise? The activity?

The woman sniffed. 'By Sunday, you say?'

'I'd need it by Saturday afternoon. By five p.m. at the latest.'

'Sunday it would have to be. My head-woman collects work from me at seven. Her girls won't start on it till tomorrow: Thursday to cut, Friday to sew. Lace-covered silk is two dresses. Saturday for the trimmings, Saturday night to hem and finish. And it won't be cheap. Period styles aren't like modern clothes. Your average girl-who-sews wouldn't have a clue.'

It'd be a lot less effort to hire from Stage-Stock. 'You do have period patterns? This is a gown of the late 1890's – '

'Modern clothes fit to the body,' Mrs Farrah-Digby cut in. 'Period clothes are built to sit over underpinnings. You've brought the corset that goes with it?'

'No.' Vanessa was going to Stage-Stock later for that. She'd had an illuminating conversation with their corset mistress a few days ago, who had advised on the correct shape. Wasp-waisted 'swan-bill' and 'S-bend' corsets had come in a few years after Lady Windermere's era, the woman had advised. The look Vanessa required was more 'ice cream cornet', straight-sided.

Vanessa asked Mrs Farrah-Digby about her charges.

With more speed than Vanessa would have attributed to someone still in pyjamas at eleven-thirty in the morning, Mrs Farrah-Digby presented a chit for Vanessa's signature, asking for an upfront payment of twelve guineas. 'Just so we know where we stand. Can you let yourself out?'

Walking downhill to the bus stop a few minutes later, Vanessa couldn't stop thinking about French silk and antique lace between those yellow-stained fingers.

Choosing Lady Windermere's accessories from Stage-Stock took a couple of hours. There was a long discussion as to which shape of fan would be historically accurate. In the end, Vanessa selected ostrich feather, as it was the most dramatic. Vanessa also hired shoes and earrings, a pearl choker, engagement and wedding rings. On her way back to the tube, she bought a meat-and-potato pie – mostly potato – from a butchers on City Road, eating it fast as she walked. It was now pitch-dark, and when she reached Farren Court, she was glad of her torch. Alistair was having the path reconstructed, so as well as the usual pot-holes, there were unlaid paving blocks to avoid. The wind keened eerily along the theatre's flanks and she was glad when a powerful beam illuminated Caine Passage. It was Alistair coming alongside her, lighting the way with a signalling torch. He had Macduff on a lead beside him.

He said, 'Advance warning, the Rolf-Bovarys are here in force.' He fished out his keys at the stage door. 'I've given Doyle orders to lock up whenever he's away from his post.'

She accused him of fastening the stable door after the horse had bolted.

'Where has the horse bolted, by the way?' Alistair took her satchel, giving her macduff's lead in return.

'Paris. Why are the Rolfs and Bovarys here?'

'To gloat. They've heard about Hugo's defection. Will we have our dress in time?'

'If we don't, I'm running away to Paris too.'

In the auditorium, a cleaner was polishing the ashtrays on the backs of the seats. Once the show opened, a team would come in at dawn each day, but right now, it was a lonely job. Peter Switt was swabbing the stage boards under Cottrill's direction. Doyle came down the side aisle, touching his cap to Alistair and Vanessa. He must have worked out that they'd let themselves in. 'Call of nature, sir, ma'am.'

Alistair told him they didn't need the minutiae. His attention shifted upwards, where Neptune's trident pierced the painted waves. He said slowly, 'Terence Rolf wants The Farren, but he doesn't love it. At Bo's wake, I sat a moment in the dark and overheard Rolf and Miss Bovary talking. They expressed no grief. It was all about how they would run this place now they had a free hand. And they spoke of Bo's money, how they might get it, afraid someone else would beat them to it.'

Vanessa hissed at Alistair to say no more. The Rolfs, their son and Miss Bovary were a few yards away. *A Royal Flush*, she thought, though a better collective noun might be 'a Stealth of Rolf-Bovarys' as she hadn't heard them enter the auditorium. They appeared dressed to go out, the ladies in fur and rhinestones, the men in evening suits. Edwin wore his red-lined cloak with a magician's flair.

'Oh – ' Vanessa almost flew off her feet as Macduff lunged towards the newcomers, halting short of them, haunches low.

Edwin Bovary shouted, 'Redenhall, do something!'

Alistair retrieved the dog, rolling the lead round his wrist for extra grip. 'I wonder why he dislikes you all so deeply. You in particular, Edwin.'

'Because I don't like dogs and refuse to fuss him.'

Later, as Vanessa was putting her acquisitions away in the wardrobe room, Alistair came to her, Macduff with him. The dog was panting, open-mouthed. A sign of stress.

She filled a bowl with water and the dog lapped gratefully. 'Have they gone?'

'They're having aperitifs in the green room. After you escaped, I withstood twenty reasons why I should terminate this dog's life. Oh, and they're planning to gate-crash the Blandfords' visit.'

'Can't you ban them?'

'I could. I have adequate reason, but I'm biding my time.' Alistair scowled. 'I can feel them fingering concealed daggers, like Borgias at a wedding feast. Watch your back, Mrs Kingcourt, because Miss Bovary intends to call in Mrs Yorke to take over your job.'

'Too late.' Vanessa took Hugo's cheque from her bag. 'He's waived his fee, and signed the costumes over to me. Miss Bovary and Mrs Yorke can go jump.'

It was way past home-time, and Alistair accompanied her down to the stage door where they saw the Rolfs and their son departing just ahead of them. Vanessa asked angrily, 'Why does Edwin wear that cloak?'

'It's a device to show that he is a serious, successful actor, in the footsteps of his late uncle.' He caught her expression. 'What have I said?'

'The last time I saw it, my dad was wearing it.'

Alistair shook his head. 'With respect, Vanessa, your father probably bought his things second hand. If he wore a cloak with a red lining – and they were part of the actors' uniform a generation ago – he either bought it cheap or it was a discarded prop.' They reached the door. 'Would you like an escort home?' It was very dark, no moonlight.

She accepted. At the door of the Calford Building, Alistair said, 'I'm taking Macduff back to my flat tonight. He hates my stairs, but I want him under my eye for a while.'

'They wouldn't hurt him?'

'Who knows?' Leaning forward, he kissed her cheek. 'Good night.'

'You too.' She watched him go, matching his pace to the dog's. She almost called him back, but obscenities shouted from an upper floor window reminded her that her lodgings were eccentric, to put it mildly. Besides, she felt suddenly rather queasy.

As she searched for her door key, two men came down the stairs. Each carried a tea chest laden with household goods. They were followed by a woman clutching a bundle of personal items. The landlord brought up the rear saying, 'I warned you, Betty. I won't have monkey-business on my premises.'

'Sod you,' the woman chucked back. 'You were happy enough to take rent off me all these months.'

'Because you told me you were an exotic dancer. What you do for a living ain't exotic and it ain't dancing.' The landlord noticed Vanessa desperately trying to fit her key in her lock. 'I've got a better class of tenant now.'

The woman flung at Vanessa, 'You've had it in for me from the start, you stuck-up bitch. Don't forget, your window's right on the pavement. Funny how bricks fly out of a person's hand.'

'Sorry about that, dear,' the landlord said after the woman had stormed away in pursuit of her possessions.

'You must have had some idea what she was up to.'

'There's "having an idea" and there's having it shoved in your face. One of her "gentlemen friends" came up to my flat at four this morning and relieved himself on my door mat. I don't sleep soundly and I caught him at it.'

Vanessa grimaced. Betty — she hadn't known the woman's name until now — had robbed her of many hours' sleep and she wouldn't miss her. But what if she followed through on her threat? She was compelled to ask, 'Will you show me her room? I'd feel safer one flight up.'

'You fancy Betty's room? All right. Follow me.'

Each floor of the Calford Building contained four rooms, and each level had basic lavatory and washing facilities. Other than to bash on Betty's door when the groaning bedsprings had threatened to unhinge her, Vanessa had never climbed the stairs. She'd never discovered if the room directly above hers was number seven, the one her father had occupied. She was relieved to discover it was six-A. All at once, she felt nauseous. It must be due to climbing the dirty stairs and touching the greasy handrail.

Betty's abandoned room was no better appointed than Vanessa's, except that it had small oven and a vanity unit around the sink. 'I'll take it right away. Will you help me swap my furniture around?'

The landlord saw no reason why not, saying he'd help her on Saturday.

'Now — tonight. Betty might come back after a few drinks and bring friends with her. Lots of men have guns. They were meant to hand them in when they left the services, but they didn't always.'

Perhaps fearing a second death on his property, the landlord immediately fetched extra hands from a nearby pub. Two hours later, Vanessa was in her own bed, in a new room. 'I've gone up in the world.' This room's atmosphere felt heavy. Along with nausea, she had shooting pains in her stomach.

She woke in the early hours with the worst headache of her life, a steel clamp to her brow and a sweat-soaked nightdress. That meat pie she'd eaten earlier after Stage-Stock –

She got to the corner sink in time to be grossly sick then crawled back to bed. Though the sickness eased, the headache didn't. Fever took over her limbs.

What if she died too? She was a terrified five-year-old again. *What if she, Vanessa, was put into a hole as dark as this room, as cold as the night outside?* She reached into the darkness for her father's hand but there was no answering warmth. Not there for her. Never there for her.

Chapter Twenty

'Tanith?' He found the girl in the green room, reading a magazine. Now officially cast as Lady Agatha Carlise, 'Miss Stacey' had adopted lazy ways. 'I need you to do something.'

It was Thursday, mid-morning, and Alistair had been twice to the wardrobe room. Walking away last night on Long Acre, he'd felt Vanessa's silent call and despised the pig-headedness that had stopped him turning around. Throughout the night, he'd woken repeatedly with the Rolfs' and Miss Bovary's faces in his head. Vanessa thankfully hadn't noticed, but yesterday, they'd stared at her as if they were writing a script and she was the page. They hated her. It had made his skin creep and now she hadn't come in. He would have gone himself, but he had a fire inspection this morning, and he didn't trust Cottrill to handle it. He gave Tanith Vanessa's address and asked her to go right away.

'She may be visiting cloth wholesalers, but she normally tells Doyle where she'll be.'

Tanith kept her magazine open, a finger marking her place. 'Couldn't Peter go? It's more his job now.'

'Miss Stacey, I wouldn't send Peter Switt to knock on your

door if I thought you'd overslept. Second point, I still pay your wages. Get going.'

Forty minutes later, Tanith reported that she'd peered through Vanessa's window from the pavement and seen only an empty room. 'Totally cleared out.'

'Sure it was the right room?'

'Perfectly. That day you took us home from the Wishbone Club, we waited for her to go inside, don't you remember? We both know where she lives.'

Tanith was being deliberately provocative. He felt his temper shortening. 'Did you knock at the door, try to raise somebody?'

She nodded. 'It's the sort of building where the residents hide when they hear knocking, because it's either the police, social services or a debt collector. D'you think she could have run away with Hugo?'

'Don't be simple.' Hugo Brennan wouldn't invite a woman into exile with him. Vanessa had spoken about running away to Paris if she couldn't deliver Miss Abbott's dress in time, but that had been in jest. Anyway, to get to Paris you needed a passport and currency. There was only one logical place she'd have gone. He put a call through to Lord Stanshurst. The butler answered, informing Alistair in his pinched, over-polite, way that 'his Lordship is currently unavailable.'

'Out all day? Gone abroad? Be specific, man.'

'Walking the dogs in the park, sir.'

'When he's back, ask him if Mrs Kingcourt has arrived home.'

'I haven't heard that she has, sir.'

'Would you mind walking over to her mother's house? Mrs Ruth Quinnell, isn't it? But don't alarm the woman. Call me when you've seen her.'

Alistair oversaw the fire inspection, cutting the officer short when he tried to make conversation. Back at his desk, he caught up with the accounts but his mind wouldn't settle. He didn't suspect Terence Rolf or his wife of leaning towards violence. Too buffed, too well-fed. Miss Bovary, on the other hand, had the impulses of a predator. Edwin was an enigma. When, after four hours, no word had come from Stanshurst and his calls went unanswered, he walked Macduff to Vanessa's lodgings, and saw the cleared-out room for himself. Possessing a more stubborn fist than Tanith, he raised a response. An old, rough-looking man put his head out of an upper window.

'The girl in room two, have you seen her?'

'Scarpered,' came the reply accompanied by a gobbet of phlegm, which Alistair jumped to avoid. 'Got kicked out.'

Alistair felt a nerve jump in his throat. The old man was either drunk or barmy, but it put the cherry on his anger. He should have found Vanessa decent lodgings. He could have made her believe it was a perk of the job.

'Any idea where she's gone?'

'Nah.' The window was slammed shut.

An hour later, he and Macduff boarded a train at Charing Cross. Getting out at Hayes, they got a lift in a coal lorry; its driver lived in Stanshurst. He dropped Alistair and the dog at the bottom of Church Hill and pointed. 'Straight up. White cottage on the right, green gate.'

If Vanessa had turned up at the Hall, Ruth Quinnell declared, Lord Stanshurst would have sent word. Hugging a worn house-coat around herself, she created a deliberate barrier in the doorway. When Alistair requested water for the dog, she went wordlessly to fetch some. While he waited, Alistair willed Vanessa to pop out from behind a hedge. The front of Peach Cottage was dominated by a gnarled fruit tree from which, presumably, its name sprang. It had a picket gate and fence and was postcard-pretty with its white weather-boarding. Two small bedrooms he guessed, the interior low with beams. Doubtless, Vanessa could glide through it without hindrance. A closer inspection showed that the cottage was falling into disrepair, its thatch rimed with green, window frames rotting. He thought of Vanessa sending half her monthly earnings here . . . Come to think of it, the cottage probably belonged to his father-in-law. Most of Stanshurst did.

As Macduff quenched his thirst, Alistair tried to make conversation with Ruth Quinnell but she answered in monosyllables and after a while, started coughing.

'Vanessa coughs quite a lot,' he said, seeing her use a handkerchief she had at the ready. 'When she's anxious.'

When the spasm passed, Ruth Quinnell said hoarsely, 'Aviation fumes. I've been like this since Biggin Hill became operational.'

Macduff had drunk all the water. He'd be hungry by now. 'I'll walk up to the Hall,' Alistair said. 'If Vanessa should arrive – '

'She won't. Her life's in London now. She's on a wild goose-chase after her father's shadow. I wish her joy.'

'Why don't you love your daughter more, Mrs Quinnell?'

Shock shimmered over her face. 'Who do you think you are?'

'Withholding love is a fool's game, you know.' He looked at the fruit tree whose black-spotted leaves spoke of exhausted roots. 'Come on, Macduff.' He turned his back on Peach Cottage. Hearing the door slam he thought, *Now I know why you believe in very little, Vanessa Elizabeth. But where the hell are you?*

At the Hall, his father-in-law was surprised but welcoming. No, his butler hadn't mentioned a telephone call earlier in the day. Or perhaps he had. Trouble was, Borthwick was growing daft, and he, Lord Stanshurst, was becoming forgetful. 'We're like the man who can't throw playing cricket with the man who can't catch. Will you stay for dinner?'

'So long as you feed the dog too.'

Dinner was tinned fish and boiled turnip. Lord Stanshurst and Macduff wolfed theirs down, while Alistair found himself nostalgic for wardroom fare, corned beef and carrots. The butler served a 1928 Château Cheval Blanc from a crystal decanter. During a moment when Borthwick was fetching a dessert of late windfall apples, Lord Stanshurst mentioned Ruth Quinnell.

'A good woman but whenever I see her coming, I feel like a spider who has just spotted the feather duster. She makes apple pies with the peelings on, did you know that?'

'It doesn't surprise me.'

'She was Margery's choice.' Lord Stanshurst referred to his late wife. 'Efficient and incurious, a marvellous thing in a social secretary. Margery liked theatrical friends but demanded dull sobriety in her servants. Ruth's relentless devotion was something of a chore, I'm sorry to say.'

'What of Vanessa? Is she like her father?'

'Eh?' Lord Stanshurst blinked, and Alistair fancied he could hear cogs whirring. 'To look at, you mean?'

'Is she a bolter, like Johnny Quinnell?'

The old man shook his head. 'He was despicable. The way he'd come to me for money, rasping his fingers with the pad of his thumb . . . Vanessa's a steady sort, though she changed after her husband's death. Blames herself.'

'Shot down, wasn't he?'

Lord Stanshurst nodded. 'They called it battle fatigue, twenty-two sorties in ten days. Those lads got so exhausted, they ceased caring if the enemy killed them or not. They'd had an argument – more than a newlywed's tiff – and she told him to leave. Hours later, he was down in flames.'

It offered an insight into Vanessa's anxieties, the constant apologising. Alistair thought of roses on a church memorial and his clumsy feet. It must be coming up to the anniversary of her husband's death. Had she fled on some kind of pilgrimage?

He rose from the table, declining an invitation to stay the night. 'I'll get the late train back.'

'I don't know how you'll make it – I can't drive you to the station as I've no fuel. I could lend you a bike, but the dog won't fit in the basket. We did have a pony and trap, but the old cob died and his replacement doesn't come till next week. You'd have to walk.'

Alistair would have done so gladly, but Macduff wasn't up to five miles of road. Reluctantly, he accepted the offer of a bed. He asked to use the telephone, calling Doyle from whom he learned that Vanessa had not shown up at the theatre. He told Doyle to check her lodgings again. 'Call me at Stanshurst if she's there.'

Doyle did not call back.

'Do you know how Vanessa's husband came to grief?' Lord Stanshurst asked from the sideboard where he was un-stoppering the port decanter.

'Not really, no.'

'She denied him his conjugal rights and kicked him out into the cold. Those boys had fought the whole summer and autumn long. You'd think she could have found it in her heart to comfort him. So destructive.'

'We can't know the circumstances.'

Lord Stanshurst grunted and poured each of them a measure of port. 'Before we turn in for the night, I'd like assurance that your anxiety for Vanessa does not overshadow your loyalty to Fern. Whatever Vanessa's claims here, Fern comes first.'

'You know Fern wants a divorce?'

Lord Stanshurst's hold on the port decanter was shaky, but in other respects he was still the ruler of his house, the patriarch. 'Divorce does not happen in my family. Live apart if you must, but do not expose my name to disgrace.'

Respectful but implacable, Alistair replied, 'Unfortunately for you, Nigel, I'm incurably middle class. I won't spend my life sustaining a civilised lie. Fern either comes back to me, or she may have her divorce. *If* she goes to court and asks for it.'

Lord Stanshurst looked appalled. 'My daughter, taking the stand, incriminating herself?'

'If she wants her freedom, she must pay the price.'

Alistair was put that night in the east wing, in a single bed in an undusted room reserved for guests of modest status. The curtains had an ugly horse-chestnut leaf weave. The same fabric had been used for the chairs. Had Ruth Quinnell used this room in the past? He wondered because along with faded prints of Stanshurst dogs and horses, there was a photograph of Vanessa. She was sitting in the passenger seat of Lord Stanshurst's 1910 Rolls Royce, dressed in an old-fashioned duster coat, her arms folded as if she was saying, 'Hurry up so we can get going!' Her hair seemed lighter than in real life though the curls were familiar, as were the eyes. Alistair knew the car, which had fetched Fern and himself from the station on their first visit here as a married couple. It was the colour of the port wine he'd just drunk, and since 1940, it had been up on blocks, its fuel tank dry.

After a wretchedly bad night, Alistair collected Macduff from the kitchen and they walked down the long avenue to the lane, where an approaching rumble promised the possibility of a lift. A military vehicle rounded the corner, stopping as Alistair flagged it down. A khaki-clad shoulder leaned out of the driver's side. 'Something up?'

'Commander Redenhall, RN – and dog – requiring a lift to Hayes railway station.'

The driver papped his horn and a pair of squaddies jumped over the tailgate. Macduff was bundled into the back, while Alistair got up beside the driver's mate. He glanced back towards Stanshurst Hall, nestled among winter trees like a sheltering dove. He was sorry to lose his father-in-law's friendship. Sorry to be seen as a bounder who wouldn't play the game.

Though he sensed this wasn't goodbye. Stanshurst's roots coiled around him, around Vanessa, Ruth, Johnny Quinnell and Fern. They might never be cut.

The early London train was pulling in as the army truck drew up at the station. One of the squaddies kept it waiting while Alistair and another soldier hefted Macduff into a compartment.

Another bout of knocking at the Calford Building finally brought the landlord down. It wasn't the man who had told him that Vanessa had scarpered, though this one smelled as unpleasant as the last one had looked. Alistair's fist itched to make contact with the blue-veined nose. If this bastard really had thrown Vanessa on to the street –

The man put up his hands in swift surrender. 'Throw out Mrs Kingcourt? She's a lovely lady. Though come to think of it, I haven't seen her for a while.' A deep tuck appeared between his brows. 'She moved upstairs. I did warn her – '

'Upstairs. Bloody hell. Just take me to her. Do you have a key?'

Chapter Twenty-One

Alistair was shocked by the heat radiating from Vanessa's skin. That colour was fine for a shrimp, but not for a young woman. His priority was to get her out of this place. In the doorway, the landlord stood dry-washing his hands, saying over and over, 'She was fine two days ago. Wednesday night, she was right as ninepence.'

Unsure if she could hear, Alistair told Vanessa, 'I'm taking you where you can be looked after.' Wrapping her in bedclothes, he carried her downstairs. She was no heavier than a set of golf clubs. He'd fetched his car from a street behind Cecil Court, where he generally parked it, and settled her in the passenger seat. Macduff had the back seat. From Long Acre, Alistair drove fast down Charing Cross Road and along Whitehall, turning into the lattice of streets that terminated at Ledbury Terrace. The drawing room lights were on at number twelve. He knocked. Fern answered.

'Now what?' She looked ready to use her fingernails should he try to push past.

'Vanessa's ill. I want you to call our doctor and look after her.'

'Oh, God, where is she?'

'In the car. Can I take her straight upstairs?'

'I – yes. I'll just – '

'I don't want to see him, or even know he's here. Tell him to stay where he is.'

It was strange, but from the moment Alistair put her in his car, Vanessa's headache ceased. When he laid her on the guest-room bed at Ledbury Terrace, she felt as weak as feathers, but the pain in her joints vanished too. She was able to croak, 'I'd like water. And to wash. Let me wash.'

Fern leaned over her and pushed a strand of hair off her forehead. 'I'll run you a lovely bath. How about some hot black-currant? And later on, toast and Bovril?'

'Just toast, thank you. Thank you both.'

When she woke to morning light, her bedsheets smelled of spiced orange from Fern's bath oils. She felt heavy-limbed, hot-eyed, but otherwise well. She dozed until Fern came in with a tray.

'Darling thing, what have you been doing to yourself?' Setting the tray on a bedside cabinet, Fern plumped up Vanessa's pillows. She answered her own question. 'Over-worked and harried. We heard about Hugo Brennan's midnight flit.'

'Who told you?'

Fern murmured, 'Oh, you know, the grapevine spreads deep and wide.'

'Mr Stephen spreads deep, for sure.'

Fern poured tea. 'Darrell has donated his sugar ration.'

'None for me.'

'Oh, stuff, you need the energy.' Fern stirred in two teaspoons' full. 'I won't lie, Vanessa. The word on the avenue, Shaftsbury Avenue, is that The Farren is in trouble, and I planted the seeds. It's war, d'you see? Though I pity Alistair. Wilton Bovary left him a theatre without the money to run it. Selfish old man, hiding a fortune in trust so that everybody fights for it. Like throwing a bone to starving dogs. The sisters want to break into the trust. They want to break Alistair.'

Vanessa sipped her tea as Fern talked. Sweetness slid into her veins. Money didn't interest her, except as the means of enabling life, but she knew that not everyone viewed it in the same way. 'You're the first person I've heard speak badly of Wilton Bovary. Alistair loved him.'

Fern laughed. 'Darrell says that you groom Alistair with your eyes.'

'"Darrell says". Are you two living together yet? You've moved back into the master bedroom.'

'I sleep alone, the pinnacle of respectability. You know ... when Alistair laid you on the bed, I watched from the door-way. If he'd cherished me half as much, things might be very different. Did you know he raced down to Stanshurst, trying to find you?'

She blushed. She'd had no notion of it. 'He *cares* about me, that's all.'

Fern picked up a bowl of porridge. 'Feed you?'

'Certainly not!' Vanessa wriggled up straighter. 'I wish I understood you. Are you bad, or just taking a holiday from goodness?'

'I'm fighting for what I need. I told you that.'

Vanessa sighed. 'Can I borrow something to wear?'

Fern brought her an outfit and underwear, then left her to sleep. When Vanessa woke, Alistair was at her bedside.

She blinked. She was wearing a powder blue silk night-dress that had wrapped around her like a mermaid's tail. One of Fern's, too generously cut for Vanessa. The straps had slipped down her arms. 'Is it Saturday?'

She had to repeat the question.

'Don't think about work,' he said after a moment.

'But tomorrow is the Blandfords' D-Day, and if I'm not there to dress Clemency Abbott, Miss Bovary will take over. I will fight her on the beaches.'

He smiled bleakly and she wondered if he was annoyed at being put to such trouble. 'How much petrol have you used on my behalf?'

'A third of a gallon. Does it matter? I'll chauffeur you wherever you'd like to go – just not to that repulsive building, unless it's to pack your things. I'll find you somewhere else to stay, or put you up in a hotel. I don't care what you say – '

'It's all right. I'm never going to sleep another night there.'

He put his hand on her forehead, like a doctor. 'When you didn't come to work on Thursday, I imagined all sorts of things. You could die in the Calford Building, and nobody would notice.'

'Don't!' It had taken at least two days for her father's death to impinge on the same residents. 'I shall take over Hugo's flat, then he'll have somewhere to come back to.'

Alistair leaned forward and put his arm around her. She nestled into him and his lips found her open mouth. A hand slid to cup one of her breasts, freeing it from its silk. In a muffled whisper against his lips, she admitted, 'I want you so very much!'

'I know, I – '

'Alistair?'

The summons came from the doorway. He broke away and Vanessa attempted to cover herself. Fern stood in the doorway, a black object obscuring the upper part of her face. There came the click of a shutter. Another and another.

Fern lowered her camera, a neat little pre-war Voigtländer. She was wearing her Paris suit with the big pockets. 'I know a man who'll develop this film in four hours. Nessie, didn't you once advise me to consult a good divorce lawyer? I have one. He's called Mr Cloud. Isn't that charming? With chambers on The Strand.' Fern smiled as if freedom were materialising in front of her. 'He told me I needed proof of my husband's adultery, and now I have it.'

Vanessa pulled the bed covers up and whispered to Alistair, 'What have we done?'

'The blame is mine.' He took and held her hand.

Fern said musingly, 'I wonder what the Blandfords would say if I showed them candid shots of you and the Wardrobe Mistress in my house. They'd say that at the very least it implies a lack of gratitude.'

'Don't make threats, Fern. Say what you intend to do.'

'Do? Nothing. I used the last exposures months ago taking pictures in the park. One still can't get a decent roll of new film. The camera shop sells government surplus but it jams this model.'

'Are you saying there's no film in the camera?'

'Darlings, you're off the hook, but my goodness, your faces. I won't ask if you're in love. *Lust* is written all over you.'

As soon as she'd dressed, Alistair drove Vanessa to Long Acre and they packed those of her belongings that would fit in the car. She had Hugo's keys, and intended to move straight in to his flat. The owner of the dance-wear shop was the landlord, so she saw little problem in having the tenancy assigned to her. Tomorrow, members of The Farren's stage-crew would shift her larger items.

Before leaving room six-A for the last time, Vanessa made a

sweep of every corner while Alistair opened an alcove cupboard. 'Nothing much here,' he said. 'Empty beer bottles. And this.' He passed her the beginnings of a letter. Written on cheap, lined paper, it was dated, 'February 9th, 1945.' But '9th' was crossed out, and '10th' was written in its place, suggesting the letter had been begun after midnight.

In Johnny's familiar, left-hander's writing was, 'Dear Toots, I'm so sorry our meeting miscarried – '

Vanessa said, 'This must be where he died, though I used to write to him at room seven.'

At the door, Alistair traced a shape with his finger. 'This is room seven. See? Someone's unscrewed the original number and replaced it with "Six A". You can see seven's ghost in the paintwork.'

She shuddered. 'Let's go.'

That night, Vanessa slept in Hugo's flat, which was warm and smelled pleasantly of furniture oil. She was woken early by the clopping of hooves outside. Pressing her face to the window, she saw a horse-drawn gig going by, full of family in their Sunday best. On a jaunt out of town? She spent a moment relishing the fact that she was alive and well, though still weak.

She washed in Hugo's tiny bathroom and threw on her clothes, eager to get to The Farren. Miss Abbott's dress was due for delivery at seven a.m.. The Blandfords would arrive late morning. Mr Kidd, who worked here on Sundays, let Vanessa in at the stage door, pushing out a clipboard.

'Sign, please, Miss, and jot down your arrival time. You're a pair of early birds.'

He must be referring to Alistair whose name the only other one on the list. He'd arrived at five-forty. '"None shall sleep",' she murmured.

In the wardrobe room, she boiled water and wished she had a telephone extension so she could call Alistair and say, 'Tea's up.'

Would he come to her? Looking back on their embrace of the day before, Vanessa tried to see it as a turning point in their relationship, though it felt more of a power shift in the battle between Alistair and Fern. She made tea for one and munched on salted biscuits. All she could do now was wait for Mrs Farrah-Digby's girl.

Seven a.m. came and went.

At eight, she heard feet on the stairs. She ran out and saw Rosa Konstantiva.

'Your face tells me I'm not what you wanted,' Rosa said.

'If the dress doesn't arrive soon – '

'It will, and Clemency Abbott will keep us waiting. Make me some tea, darling. I've brought the remains of a French apple tart. A friend of mine bakes them.'

The dress arrived at nine-twenty. Kidd brought up a sullen creature with pudding-bowl hair and thick ankle socks. In reply to Vanessa's, 'You're two hours late!' the girl muttered, 'Madam said you'd give me my bus fare and something for my time. She said not to leave without you paying her bill. Six guineas.'

Vanessa dug into her petty cash tin. 'Five shillings cover your bus fare?'

'I want fifteen.'

'Five. And tell "Madam" that I'll pay her balance when she invoices me. Put the parcel on the table. Wait – ' the girl had flung down a brown paper package and stomped to the door – 'I want to check it before you go.'

'Madam said to tell you it's as you asked, and she doesn't do refunds.' The girl kept walking.

'Sounds ominous,' Rosa muttered.

Vanessa cut the parcel string and Rosa sniffed.

'Your seamstresses smoke. Though so does Clemency, so perhaps she won't notice. When I worked in couture, tobacco was *maudit*.' Rosa put her nose to the packaging. 'It isn't just cigarettes.'

Vanessa pulled out the dress. It held the creases of its folding, even when she shook it. 'Cat,' she wailed in disgust. 'It smells of fags and tom cat!'

She and Rosa took it between them. It seemed the right shape with puffed 'elephant' sleeves tapering at the elbow to a tight cuff. It had a high neck, a sharply-defined waist and a short train. All the signatures of an age of fashion extremes. But –

'Something's very wrong,' said Rosa.

Instead of the eighty-shillings-a-yard French silk Vanessa had supplied, the under-dress was of shiny, artificial taffeta. The top lace had been used skimpily while the Brussels lace was nowhere. It wasn't in the parcel at all. Vanessa realised that Mr Doll had been warning her, in his way, not to use Mrs Farrah-Digby. Not to be too desperate. She hadn't listened, and now she'd been swindled.

Rosa laid the dress on the table, lifting the hem and exposing raw edges. 'She has a workroom, this Mrs Farrah-Wotsit?'

'No.' Vanessa was sure of it now. The smell, the rushed look. 'She's gone at it herself, stolen my cloth and I'm going to kill her.'

Rosa turned the dress over, holding the skirt up to the light. 'What's this stain?'

Vanessa looked. 'It's coffee. No, it's gravy. No! The bloody woman's scoffed her dinner at her sewing table.'

'At least the mark is on the back.'

They heard the lift hydraulics grinding just then and sooner than they liked, Alistair was ushering in Miss Abbott. Greeting them in his detached way, he said, 'I've had a message from the Blandfords' secretary.'

'They're not coming.' Vanessa sagged with relief.

'They're attending a matins service at St Paul's and will be here at eleven-forty, curtain up at eleven-fifty. Did you see the set?' he asked Vanessa.

She hadn't. She'd come straight to her room. 'Is it good?'

'The scenery men have done a nice job. Ronnie Gainsborough's coming, and James Harnett too. They and Miss Abbott will perform an opening excerpt from Act One. Don't worry,' he smiled faintly at Vanessa's expression, 'both men are bringing their own costume. Is that the dress?' He moved as if to inspect it but Rosa snatched it up and flapped it.

'Best way to get creases out. Scoot, please, Commander. Let's try it on you, Clemency.'

Alistair left and Vanessa fetched the hired corset, a chemise and drawstring pantalettes. Clemency Abbott was at the mirror, trying out different angles for her burgundy velour hat. Her nail colour was a perfect match and Vanessa couldn't help wondering how the woman managed to be a fashion plate so early in the day. A personal maid, perhaps?

'Miss Abbott, if you'd kindly go behind the screen and don your underpinnings? Rosa will help.' Vanessa scratched the back of her neck. Nerves usually made her cough, not itch. A moment later, she dug under her waistband to scratch. It wasn't nerves; it must be bed bugs from her short stay in room six-A. Betty of the squeaking springs must have had an infestation.

'Corset, please,' Rosa called.

Vanessa passed it over the top of the screen. Shortly afterwards, Clemency Abbott emerged, waist pinched to an authentic *fin-de-siècle* nineteen inches. Vanessa opened out the dress for the actress to step into. It was only-just across the bosom. When re-laced, it would flatten the famous Abbott contours. We'll keep it loose, Vanessa decided.

'What horrid material.' Clemency stroked her hips. 'And what's wrong with these sleeves?' She tried vainly to raise her arms. 'I'm trapped.'

Rosa said without missing a beat, 'I can tell you from personal experience, it was considered aristocratic at the turn of the century to be pinioned.'

'But I need to arrange roses. I need to act, damn it.'

'We'll make an incision under the arms, and put in a gusset.' Vanessa almost laughed. She'd been storing up the word 'gusset' and hadn't realised why. She was loosening the dress when Miss Abbott spun around so violently, the cheap taffeta split. 'Something's eating me,' she screamed. 'Get this vile thing off me!'

'If you'd just stay still, Miss Abbott – '

'Don't "Miss Abbott" me! This dress is crawling! The room needs fumigating. You need fumigating. How *dare* you?'

Eventually stripped to a chemise over pantalettes, Clemency Abbott shoved her arms into her coat, not bothering with her dress. As she searched for her shoes, she shouted, 'I'll call my agent. This is a violation of my contract.'

Vanessa stood numb, while Rosa opened the window and hurled the dress out.

'Cat fleas,' she muttered to Vanessa.

'Cat, yes. I wronged Betty.'

'Who?'

'Never mind. I'll have to resign. If I don't, Miss Bovary will demand Alistair sack me. And what about the Blandfords?'

Vanessa leapt back to avoid being hit by a chair. Clemency was flinging them aside as she tried to find her shoes.

Rosa said, 'There's always a way out, whatever the situation.'

'We don't have a dress and in a minute, we'll have no actress. I suppose you could – '

'Be Lady Windermere for the day? If Ronnie Gainsborough has to make love to me, he'll walk too. Clemency?' Rosa threw her voice. She occasionally gave ballet classes and had developed a tone that could bring a lake of swans to a stop, instantly.

Clemency Abbott dropped the chair she'd been about the chuck. 'Where the hell are my shoes?'

'I have a horrible feeling I may have thrown them out of the window, with the dress.'

'Miss Konstantiva, I'll have you – '

'Applauded for quick-thinking? Darling, how generous. Do calm down, or you'll burst veins in your cheeks.'

'Fetch my shoes!'

'I'd rather not, dear.'

'Then she can fetch them.' Clemency stuck a finger at Vanessa, who could see the shoes on the sink drainer. Clemency hadn't spotted them yet through her red mist.

'Good idea.' Rosa smiled as if she knew that Vanessa would somehow salvage the situation.

Heaven alone knew how. The only solution would be to provide Clemency with a dress so perfect that it would melt her anger and sweep away malice. Leaving the room, Vanessa acknowledged that even if she found such a dress, by the time she came back with it, Clemency would be gone. Though that could be rectified. Vanessa locked the door behind her, and strode away, thinking, *Might as well be sacked for two crimes rather than one.*

If she was to save herself from being out of a job and, inevitably, out of Alistair's life, she had to pull a cat out of the bag. Unfortunate phrase, in view of what was biting her under her blouse. She stopped halfway down the stairs. 'I wonder . . .'

Chapter Twenty-Two

There was no certainty that Tanith had been telling the truth about her grandmother's Worth gown, and the chances were that Lady Ververs would flatly refuse to lend it anyway. But there was nothing to lose by asking.

One problem – Vanessa didn't have Tanith's telephone number. Alistair was also unlikely to have it.

But how about a fanatical record-keeper who knew everything about everyone? In the poky room where she'd made tea with Hugo on her first day, she located the keys and opened the drawer labelled 'R-S-T-U'. It took her a few moments to find 'Stacey, Tanith'. There was an address, 4 St James's Park Terrace, and a telephone number. Tanith had told Miss Bovary the truth about her domestic circumstances, at least. Relocking the cabinet, Vanessa tried Alistair's door in hope of using the phone, but it was locked. She could hear the dog snoring inside. Miss Bovary's room was not locked and she crept inside and dialled the operator from the desk telephone.

As she did so, she discovered she'd accidentally brought two cards out of the cabinet. The second one belonged to Eva St Clair. As she waited to be connected to Lady Ververs' residence, she read what Miss Bovary had written about The Farren's tragic Wardrobe Mistress.

"Accomplished. Roman Catholic, a priest's sister, unmarried. Has a scandalous understanding with Johnny Quinnell and others." Was 'others' code for Wilton Bovary? The record continued: "Gave birth out of wedlock, at The Farren, having hidden her condition. Disrupted opening night of "The de Vere Mystery". Child small and frail." A pulse ticked in Vanessa's neck. Eva had given birth . . . There were no clues as to the child's gender or its fate. An entry dated 12th September 1940, in different ink stated: 'Eva gravely injured in last night's bombing. Not expected to live.' A final, chilling line had been added on the 1st of September 1946. The September just gone: "Eva St Clair is dead."

Lady Ververs' butler answered just then. After learning Vanessa's situation, he gave his opinion that there was indeed a Worth gown stored away in the house, and that her Ladyship might oblige if the correct degree of gratitude were shown.

'I'm willing to open a vein and give her a goblet of my blood, Mr Tucker.'

The butler suggested that a private box on opening night would be more acceptable, and Vanessa recklessly agreed. Reading confirmation of Eva's death had lent her the courage that sometimes accompanies shock. 'Tell Tanith it's for Miss Abbott and to bring it in a taxi *now*.'

On her way out of Miss Bovary's room, she snatched a moment to look for the photograph that Hugo had stared at the last time she'd been in this room. She fancied that one had been removed, the others shifted around to cover the gap. There must be a hundred or more, recording The Farren's repertoire right back to the late Victorian era. She was intrigued by a picture of a near-naked trapeze artist caught in mid-flight across a painted sky. A thin girl with elfin features. A young Barbara Bovary! Beside that hung the cast photo of *The de Vere Mystery*. She recognised Johnny at once. He was playing a gardener, or similar, wearing a leather jerkin and bowler hat. A caption read 'Opening Night'. It was dated May 29th 1920.

That was the very day that she, Vanessa, had entered the world.

Her watch said eleven-fifteen. Miss Abbott was due on stage in thirty-five minutes. Vanessa shook off the cold chills to concentrate on rescuing her career.

'You locked us in,' were Miss Abbott's first words as Vanessa returned to the wardrobe room.

'Did I? My poor brain! But I've found you a fabulous dress.'

The room smelled of acetone. Rosa explained, 'I persuaded Clemency that she couldn't play Lady Windermere with burgundy fingernails.'

'I'm not playing her,' said Miss Abbott with cold finality. 'When I get home, I shall invoke the clause in my contract that says I mustn't be physically endangered, or my health threatened.'

'But you haven't been threatened,' Vanessa protested.

'Cat fleas,' Clemency said with triumph. 'You can catch plague from them.'

'Not cat, dear, rat. You obviously weren't listening in history lessons.' Rosa returned the nail polish remover to the wardrobe. 'Oh my, what have we here, Mrs Kingcourt?' She held up a box. 'If not a wealthy French lover, then a black market chum?'

She'd found the Chanel perfume that Vanessa had still not given back to Fern. 'It has the boutique label on it. My dear, you could sell this for twenty pounds.'

In a flash, Clemency had taken the box from Rosa, her fingers melting around it. She gave Vanessa a naked glance.

'Ten pounds,' she said huskily.

'It's not for sale, Miss Abbott.' The door to the room bumped open and Tanith stumbled in, breathless. She had a bushel of oyster-white silk over her arm.

'Granny's gown!' she announced.

'Fifteen pounds,' Clemency said.

'The perfume isn't for sale.' Vanessa put it back into the cupboard then helped Tanith lay the dress on the table. Silk-satin rustled like sweet papers. Pale skirts were embroidered with humming birds whose tongues were embedded in lush camellia flowers. A poem without words. An erotic poem.

'She was a lass, your granny,' Vanessa said, stroking the silk. Though not the morning gown the script called for, it would make a powerful statement. *If* she could persuade Clemency Abbott to put it on.

Rosa made a long 'mmm' as she fingered the cloth. 'Genuine *Worth*. They don't make glories like this these days.'

'When granny wore it to her box at the theatre, people in the stalls rose and applauded,' Tanith said.

Clemency hardly looked at the dress. 'I will have that perfume. Twenty pounds.'

Vanessa held up the gown, reverently. 'I swear it's a seventeen-inch waist. Too small for you, Miss Abbott.'

That got Clemency's attention. 'I can get mine to sixteen inches.'

'But the neckline is so low you'd be in danger of giving Mr Blandford an eyeful he hasn't seen in a month of Sundays. It was a good idea, but sadly, it's not to be. Miss Abbott?' The actress was regarding Vanessa keenly. 'I won't sell you my perfume. I want you to take it as a gift.'

The gleam in Miss Abbott's eye filmed over with suspicion. 'And in return?'

'Prove you can achieve a sixteen-inch waist.'

Clemency laughed, saying, 'Play Lady Windermere? Deal!'

Rosa pretended to fan herself in relief. 'I've volunteered to play the piano,' she said, 'to bring up the scene. I'll go down now and give you a nice, long lead-in.'

At eleven fifty-one Vanessa and Tanith stood in the wings as Clemency took her position behind a circular table draped with lace. A delightful set had been put together. On the table was a blue rose bowl and a basket of roses – artificial ones, as real flowers on stage were considered by some to be ill-fated. The fan Vanessa had hired was propped against the rose bowl. The placing wasn't in the script, but it was a nod to the play's title.

Peter Switt faded the lights to darkness.

'Good luck,' Vanessa whispered as Clemency picked up a rose and presented a demure and thoughtful face.

Tanith poked Vanessa. 'Never say "good luck" in the theatre! You say "break a leg". Now you have to turn round three times and shout something rude. You *have* to!'

With a disdainful huff, Vanessa did so, finishing with 'Kiss my ass,' learned from Canadian pilots. Rosa played 'Comes the Broken Flower' from the operetta 'Trial by Jury'. The curtains opened to a ripple of applause and the lights flooded Lady Windermere's London drawing room with the impression of sunshine. Alistair, Miss Bovary and Mr and Mrs Rolf sat in the sixth row back, alongside an elderly couple. The lady – who must be Mrs Blandford – was peering through a lorgnette. Her husband ogled Clemency Abbott through a monocle. They looked so much like characters from comic opera that Vanessa had to smother giggles. Clemency arranged her roses, the model of a domestic angel circa 1895. Beside Vanessa in the wings, James Harnett straightened his neck tie and rolled his jaw to loosen the muscles. Ronnie Gainsborough, in the wings opposite, regarded Clemency Abbott as if lightning had struck him.

Chapter Twenty-Three

Afterwards, Vanessa locked herself into her room and washed with carbolic soap to banish the cat fleas. That done, she sent out for buns and made tea for Rosa, Tanith and herself. Clemency and the male actors had been invited into the green room for a champagne reception with the Blandfords.

'Up the Workers,' Rosa said, lifting her tin mug. They pulled chairs from the table and sat in line like factory workers on a break. 'Victory wrestled from the jaws of defeat. Or should I say, "the drawers of defeat". Is it your job to wash underwear before you send it back to Stage-Stock?'

'I rather think so. Thank you, Rosa, thank you, Tanith. Day saved.'

'Commander Redenhall was smiling,' Rosa said thoughtfully. 'And even Miss Bovary acknowledged you'd done a good job, though I had the impression she wished you're flunked it. I like Alistair. I feel, if I closed my eyes and fell backwards off stage, he'd catch me.'

A knock at the door brought Peter Switt with roses. Real ones. Red for Rosa, ice-white for Vanessa and pink for Tanith.

Rosa cooed, 'Six stems each – Doyle must have bribed

somebody at the market, or else some West End hotel has been robbed of its table decorations.'

After her friends left, Vanessa put her roses in water, burying her nose in petals that smelled of tea and bergamot. How did Alistair know her love of white roses? She'd spent two months at the RAF command centre at Bawtry, south Yorkshire. A gracious country house, its surviving gardens had held a ravishing display of white, Yorkist roses and she'd loved to walk among them.

That June and July of 1943 had been a time of healing for her. Two and a half years on from Leo's death, long enough for hope to poke up its shoots. And life was hopeful. The story of the Worth gown would ricochet off every wall of the theatre. Actresses would knock at her door, demanding to know what wonders were in store for them. Five-and-a-half weeks to go before the opening night. She had to appoint a costume maker. Today.

She took Eva St Clair's personnel card from her bag and words leapt out, in Miss Bovary's voice. 'Accomplished. Scandalous. Child small and frail. Eva dead.'

Lighting a candle, she held the card in the flame's heart until Miss Bovary's judgments returned to the universe as wispy smoke. The ashes went down the plug hole. 'I wish I could have seen you again, Eva. You might have told me who I am.'

You already know. A voice, inside her head. She quelled it. Having failed abysmally with Mrs Farrah-Digby, who now would she call on to make her costumes? Turning, she saw that her roses had responded to the winter sunshine streaming through the window, opening another fraction of an inch. White roses. Yorkist roses.

Mrs Yorke had costumed past Farren productions. If she'd

agree to do so again – well, even Miss Bovary would approve, having recommended her. Vanessa couldn't wait to talk to Alistair.

She found him on stage, Macduff at his feet. The actors had all gone and the theatre was showing its abandoned soul, though from the fly tower, a vocal duet told her that Tom Cottrill was overseeing the riggers returning the lights to their Friday positions. Alistair was staring into the theatre's unlit depths.

'Those roses are lovely,' she said, emerging from the OP wings. Macduff levered himself to his feet and put his head under her hand.

'You earned them.' Alistair kept his gaze straight ahead. 'Rosa tells me the first dress was given a flying lesson.'

'I was done. Turned over. Cheated. I've decided to call in – '

His glance cut her off. 'Cheated. I know the feeling.'

Was that disappointment in his voice? 'Did the Blandfords . . . I mean, are they going to . . .'

'Invest? They liked what they saw. Who wouldn't? They intend to honour half their promise, pay fifty per cent of what they agreed. I can get no more. Once they've made up their conjoined minds, it seems they cannot change them.' He smiled, mocking himself. 'Don't you hate those rigid types? The immovable fence posts, stuck fast in the clay?'

Vanessa placed her fingertips against his chest.

'What are you doing?'

'Seeing if you're capable of moving. Often, people think they're stuck when really, they just need a good shove.' He covered her hand so she felt the rise and fall of his ribs, the beating of his heart.

He said, 'I might fall, and take you with me.' Their eyes met and the warmth in his was like winter sun sweeping a glacier. Vanessa knew then what power she had, what she might unlock.

She freed her hand. 'Don't flirt, Alistair. People will mutter that I'm more than just the Wardrobe Mistress.'

'That will happen anyway. Fern won't waste what she saw.'

'There was no film in the camera, she said.'

'Of course. Vanessa.' He threw her name into the auditorium. 'What else can you summon up? See, over there?'

She discerned a figure. Greyish-black, seated in the middle row of the auditorium. 'Who is it?'

Alistair called out, 'Excuse me, Madam, are you waiting for somebody?'

Macduff's hackles rose. Tom Cottrill was just coming down from his ladder and stumbled on to the stage, his face bloodless.

'It's her, there, look!' His voice caught like a double violin note. Peter Switt followed and stood beside Cottrill, open-mouthed.

'If it's Back Row Flo, somebody really should give her a geography lesson.' Alistair sad drily.

The figure rose and side-stepped to the end of the row. As it reached the point where the stage lights cut into the darkness, Vanessa saw that it *was* female, wearing a grey, belted coat and a felt hat. A hat to keep out ill weather and for bending over graves. Vanessa went to the foot of the stage. 'I didn't expect to see you. Nobody told me you were coming.'

'So this is where you work.' Ruth Quinnell's eyes outlined the stage, and briefly wandered up to the seascape ceiling. 'This is what lured Clive away.'

Vanessa stared down at her mother in dismay. Ruth was not a woman on whom clothes hung smartly. The best that could ever be said of her was that she was tidy. But today, her coat was buttoned up wrongly. She'd screwed her hair up under her hat, and her face, hollow with anger and misery, had more of the grave than good health about it. She stared unblinking at Vanessa. A no-sleep blankness in her eyes spoke of grief or terrible shock. By contrast, her mouth did double duty, twitching, jerking.

The best thing would be to take her up to the wardrobe room. Vanessa made for the pass-door beside the prompt box but Ruth moved surprisingly fast and a moment later joined them on stage.

'Is that him? Is that Commander Redenhall?' Ruth pointed at Tom Cottrill, who laughed. A disturbing sound.

'No, Mum. This is the Commander.'

Ruth turned her gaze. 'Yes, of course. You are the rude one who came to my door looking for my daughter.'

Alistair said, 'How do you do, Mrs Quinnell?'

'I do badly. Badly.' Ruth undid her coat and something spilled out, making a pattern of shiny, monochrome squares over the stage boards. Photographs. Small. Six in number.

Peter Switt picked up one. He snickered, looked at Alistair and dropped it. Alistair glanced at another before handing it to Vanessa.

The camera had captured a slice of unveiled intimacy. She in bed, he leaning across, his handsome, honed face in profile. 'Fern promised – '

'She didn't promise,' Alistair said gravely. 'She only implied there was no film. One might call it "lying".' He gathered up the prints and held them out to Ruth. 'Are they intended as keepsakes?'

Ruth looked flummoxed by Alistair's calm. 'I don't want them, dirty objects.' Clasping her hands behind her back, she faced Vanessa. 'Miss Fern brought them to me. What will her father say? What will Lord Stanshurst think of you, like that, with his daughter's husband? He'll say I've brought you up wrong. It'll be all over the village. I'll be a laughing stock. It's been hard, Vanessa, winning back respect.'

'I know. Let me explain, Mum – '

'Don't call me that. You've broken up Miss Fern's marriage. You, who fed from that family's hand all your life. You can't keep a man, so you took another woman's.'

Alistair was watching Ruth Quinnell; his look was cold, a little contemptuous and even pitying. He said, 'Your daughter cannot be blamed for a situation that is private to myself and Fern.'

Ruth hissed in contempt. 'She'll be named as the "other party" when Miss Fern brings divorce proceedings.'

'That won't happen, Mrs Quinnell.'

'It'll be in the newspapers, every disgusting detail. How will I walk up to the church, with my head high?'

'I'm so sorry, Mum.' It flashed through her mind that after today, she might never call this woman 'Mum' again.

'Sorry? It's over, Vanessa.' Ruth left the stage, striding towards the foyer.

Vanessa shouted after her, 'You may hate me, but you can't stop being my mother.' It was a test and she waited, breath held, to see how Ruth would react.

Ruth marched back towards the stage. 'Stop? I never started. I'm not your mother, Vanessa. You aren't mine. Your father paid the bills and your mother was a whore.'

PART THREE

I am not your mother

Chapter Twenty-Four

In the days that followed, Vanessa avoided company, and Alistair in particular. Then, on Monday, October 28th, she woke up from a dream in which she was flying naked above The Farren's stage, suspended from a wire. The audience was throwing stale Chelsea buns at her. That same morning, she made contact with Mrs Yorke of Mayfair. Costumes must and would be made.

Far from being the snooty dragon Vanessa was expecting, Daphne Yorke was gracious. More than that, she was kind. She'd always had an affection for the Farren, she said. Was anything ever heard of Eva? Ah, how very sad, such a loss. How was dear Barbara? Still thin from the shock of her brother's passing? And what of naughty Hugo? In Paris . . . ah, well, genius cannot be chained. Costuming Lady Windermere would not be cheap, warned Mrs Yorke. Gowns for an entire female cast, under current restrictions . . . then again, designs by Hugo Brennan did not slip under the door every day.

Work-hands could be hired. Women released from war duties were queuing to get back to their old trades. But where to accommodate them? Her own workroom was bursting like an overcooked sausage.

'What about Great Portland Street, Hugo's *atelier*?' Vanessa suggested.

Mrs Yorke clapped her hands in delight. 'Yes, why not. Though do call it a "workroom", or the girls will get French delusions. They'll expect commission and to be allowed to parade on St Catherine's day.'

Mrs Yorke could not personally oversee the project, sadly. Her private commissions were overwhelming now that the diplomatic set was back in town. Christmas parties galore this year in Mayfair and Kensington. But . . . her niece had recently joined her business. Miss Penny Yorke had served a New York couture apprenticeship before the war and knew how to block a pattern. She perfectly understood how to set a sleeve. Facings, darting, seam allowances, kick-pleats and closures were no mystery to Penny.

Miss Yorke called at The Farren two days later, bringing notebook and pencils. A chic young woman with a slight transatlantic accent, she listened while Vanessa presented Hugo's drawings. Vanessa watched for signs of dismay, but Miss Yorke remained unruffled.

'Exquisite,' she said, then reminded Vanessa that period costume began with corsetry. 'Your Mr Brennan has put the emphasis on the waistline. Spot on for the era, though I guess he'd have done it differently if he had to wear the corsets himself! If the hire companies can't provide the correct underpinnings, we'll have to— what have I said?'

'I feel that a concrete rucksack has been cut from my shoulders, Miss Yorke.'

'Penny, please. And if I may –?'

'Yes, call me Vanessa.'

'I'll introduce you to our Mr Stanley. He's been in corsets all his life, so to speak. Getting the materials will be the fiendish part. Seen any whale baleen lately?'

Busy days followed, decisions made, costings worked out. 'Operation Windermere' was born on messy tables, lines drawn on cardboard and rolls of *toile* muslin. A couple of the stage crew paid Mrs Farrah-Digby a visit and — using the power of polite conversation — reclaimed most of Vanessa's lost materials. As Penny took on new staff, Vanessa formalised a year's rental of Hugo's premises with Mr Doll. Her mind then returned to other obsessions. She'd come to London in search of a father, and now she must search for a mother as well. Eva St Clair, *whore?* That vile word had one positive effect: after a lifetime of tip-toeing around Ruth's unpredictable temper, Vanessa now felt no compunction in asking for clarification on one vital point. On the evening of November 2nd, she sat down to a supper of onion soup and wrote a short letter.

Dear Ruth,

If you intend to end contact between us, then this will be my last letter to you, though I hope you can forgive the pain I have caused you. I have a request: allow me to know who my real mother is and please explain the circumstances of my birth.

Yours,
Vanessa

The Monday following as she left home to meet Penny Yorke's corset maker, Mr Stanley of Berwick Street, the postman hailed her.

It was early and cold, and too dark to read the handwriting on the dog-eared envelope the postman gave her. Its stale smell gave away its origins, however. She recognised the musty stink of Peach Cottage's under-stairs cupboard where Ruth kept her stationery supplies. Deciding that Mr Stanley and his corsets could wait half an hour, Vanessa ducked into a café whose blinds were being pulled up. While her coffee was brewing, she slid out the contents of the letter. There was only one item. Her birth certificate.

Her pulse skidded as she read the 'who, when and where' of her entry into the world.

Who: Girl, Vanessa Elizabeth
Where: The Farren Theatre, Farren Court, London
When: 29th of May, 1920
Father: Clive John Quinnell. Profession, Actor
Mother: Eva Elizabeth St Clair. Profession, Theatre employee

So now she knew. She couldn't put a name to feelings that were a tangle of hooks in her throat.

The cheery waitress poured black coffee into Vanessa's cup. 'That'll hit the spot.'

Vanessa declined the breakfast, which was scrambled powdered egg and reconstituted mushrooms. Sipping the bitter liquid, a question towered over her. Why had Eva let her go? Why had Johnny returned to Ruth taking her along with him?

Eva was loving, a natural mother, while Ruth . . . Vanessa pressed the gold key against her breast bone. There must be somebody in this world who knew why Eva had given her child away.

She called for the bill. Mr Stanley wouldn't expire if she missed her appointment with him. She was going to church.

★

At the Church of the Blessed Robert Drewrie, she learned that Father Mannion was visiting a sick parishioner. A nun working in the church office invited Vanessa to wait in the sanctuary. 'Would you be here to request a wedding?'

'No.' Vanessa had her birth certificate ready, but didn't immediately show it. 'I'm hoping – I mean, I'm seeking – more information about Miss Eva St Clair.'

'Ah. Sister to our own Father Joseph, God rest him. God rest her soul too.'

'So it's true she's dead?'

The nun inclined her head. Her lined face was framed by a linen coif and veil, the white not quite white, the grey worn shiny. Her brows were faded but the eyes fixed on Vanessa with guarded concentration. 'Miss St Clair passed away on the last day of August, this year, in an alms house run by my own order. It was a release.'

Vanessa's mind soared away to a frosted graveyard where a maimed woman acted a dumb-show beside a grave. A show of tearing out her heart, casting it into an open pit. At the time, Vanessa had assumed it was grief at the loss of Johnny. But what if Eva had been demonstrating the loss of her child. Or the *removal* of her child?

Sucking the idea back into herself, Vanessa murmured, 'I think I am Eva's daughter. I was fostered . . . brought up by a woman who was no relation.'

The nun's sympathy evaporated at her words. 'You're suggesting Father Joseph's sister bore a child out of wedlock? You will un-say it.'

'She did.' Vanessa thrust out the birth certificate but the nun stepped back, arms crossed.

'I will not hear it.'

'Then at least tell me where Eva's buried, sister.' Vanessa needed something, anything! 'At Kensal Green? That's where London's Catholics are buried, I think.'

In an act of concession, the nun took the birth certificate. Twice, she looked from the page to Vanessa, her eyes and mouth refuting what she saw written there. Finally, she handed the paper back, shaking her head. 'Put this aside, child. Go and be a daughter to the good woman who brought you up.'

'That "good" woman never even liked me. What is good, exactly? Tell me. I want to know.'

'Some things it is better not to know.' The grey nun said a firm 'goodbye' and retired to the shadows.

Furious, frustrated, Vanessa set out immediately for Kensal Green. The journey took nearly two hours, but it was early still, the frost silver on the ground. Leaves crunched underfoot like sugar crystals as she quartered the Catholic cemetery. A mean wind worked away at her ears. Soon, she was stumbling from the cold, her eyes weakening so that she had to lean closer to the graves to read their names. Telling herself that she'd check just ten more rows, and then return to the theatre, her eye fell upon the name 'St Clair.'

'Father Joseph St Clair, beloved of his parishioners, resigned this life 23 March 1944.'

This was Eva's brother. Her own uncle? Beside it was a grave to the memory of an Elizabeth St Clair, but she'd died in 1900. There was an Edith and numerous Marys, but no Eva. Nor was there undisturbed ground to suggest a recent burial. Eva wasn't here, so where was she?

Making her way back to the railway station, Vanessa reached out mentally to Alistair. She hadn't confided her belief that she was Eva's daughter, for fear he'd despise her. After all, that birth certificate proved she was illegitimate. Perhaps she'd suggest they have lunch. No, too late. She'd been in the graveyard longer than she'd realised. All right, supper together at her flat. She had four rashers of bacon to tempt him with. He could bring Macduff.

At that moment, Alistair was dealing with that day's mail which he'd been too busy for until now. A pagoda of bills soon built up at his elbow, though with the Blandfords' cheque now safely in the bank, these had less power to depress him than they had a week ago. He marked some for Miss Bovary's attention, then turned to the legal-looking envelope he'd left to last.

In restrained language, Mr Cloud of Cloud, Maybridge & Dunch, Solicitors, Finsbury Pavement EC2, informed him that his client, Mrs Redenhall, was petitioning for divorce on the grounds of Commander Redenhall's affair with an un-named female. Photographic evidence of adultery was in existence. The letter went on to say that Mrs Redenhall wished to proceed with all due regard for discretion, trusting that Commander Redenhall would co-operate – 'In which event no third party need be cited as co-respondent.'

In street language – play ball or we'll name Mrs Kingcourt.

Alistair allowed himself ten minutes' silent fury, then put a call through to an old Navy friend. Kip Fuller had been a lieutenant on a sister ship, a 'hostilities-only' man, meaning he'd been commissioned for the duration of war. Fuller was now back in his peacetime profession, a partner in a firm specialising in matrimonial law. Or as he'd described it to Alistair, 'Hostilities still, but on dry land.'

He listened to what Alistair had to say and agreed to represent him, adding, 'Cloud and Maybridge are an expensive outfit. Your best bet is to agree to everything as quickly as possible. We'll organise you a professional co-respondent.'

'Explain.'

'A lady of pliant principles who will act as your short-term sweetheart. She will be the "other woman" to keep the courts happy. You'll pay her.'

'Kip, but this is all so bloody unjust.'

'Until our divorce laws change, somebody has to be the guilty party and don the adulterer's hat. Nobody likes to ask such a thing of a lady.'

'You don't know me,' Alistair growled. 'I'm only agreeing to it because I need to protect an innocent party.'

'In which case, keep the "innocent party" at arm's length for now. Would you jot down a list of your assets so we can plan for the future financial support of Mrs Redenhall?'

'Her next husband can take care of that.'

Kip Fuller chuckled. 'You can't let her go empty-handed. It looks bad. Didn't your godfather leave you a bundle? Somebody told me that Wilton Bovary made a fortune backing Broadway hits.'

'So he did, but he didn't leave the cash to me. Perhaps he meant to, and died before he could put it in writing.'

Kip Fuller sympathised. 'I'll put all I've said in a letter and dig out the telephone numbers of some professional sweethearts. Remember what I said; keep the "innocent party" out of this, even if it means walking past her with your nose in the air.'

Alistair took his friend's advice when Vanessa knocked on his door, asking him to supper that evening. 'Sorry, far too busy.' She responded by looking utterly deflated.

The next morning brought a letter by hand. Alistair rang the operator, and reeled out the first number on Kip's list. It was a Dollis Hill number belonging to a woman named Primrose Duckworth. Mrs Duckworth answered on three rings, listened to Alistair's clipped account of his situation, and said, yes, she'd be happy to help. And yes, she'd sort him out, 'nice and daisy' if he'd be good enough to arrange the necessaries. She gave him the name of a sea-front hotel, the spectacularly unimaginative Sea View in Hove, explaining that they 'knew the routine and only charged an extra five guineas for gents in his predicament.'

Putting the phone down, Alistair felt a strong call to see Primrose Duckworth in the flesh, in case she matched the image conjured by her name; he pictured unnaturally yellow hair and a flat-footed waddle. The thought of explaining such a companion should he meet anyone he knew . . . He rang her back, suggesting a meeting at Euston station, the great hall. 'Will lunchtime suit you?'

'Lord, you're a speedy worker! Lunchtime it is.'

Mrs Duckworth proved to be a plump redhead, ten years older and several shades brighter than Fern. Her suit of red book-maker's check was a size too small. Alistair's instant, ungallant desire to run gave way to a grit-toothed determination to see the business through. He took Primrose for a drink in the badly beaten-up Euston Hotel, where, over pink gin and port-and-lemon, they arranged the next leg on his road to divorce.

She said, 'We'll have to go to bed together, dear. I hope you don't snore.'

At home that evening, he dialled the Sea View, Hove, and booked a room for two for the coming weekend.

That week felt like the longest of his life.

It was pretty much the longest of Vanessa's, too. She saw nothing of Alistair, and knew he was avoiding her. Doyle made things worse on Friday evening by telling her that Alistair had gone off by taxi somewhere, carrying an overnight bag. By Sunday, Vanessa felt so pent up with rejection, she slunk into Cecil Court, stopping to tie her shoe-laces when she drew level with his flat.

If eavesdroppers hear no good of themselves, lurkers see their own deepest fears. In the dark windows of Alistair's flat, Vanessa saw a movie reel of him enjoying a private weekend with some well-connected, sophisticated woman of his acquaintance. Or even, perhaps, with Fern.

Come Monday, Vanessa went directly to Great Portland Street, spending the morning among Penny's seamstresses. She got back to the theatre after lunch and asked Doyle, 'Is he back?'

Doyle didn't trouble to ask who. 'Late last night. He picked the dog up from my digs. A relief to be honest. The old fellow pines for his master. He has this whine –' Doyle imitated it and Vanessa smiled for the first time in many days. It cracked open the cut to her lip which had almost healed. 'Was Alistair alone when he called for Macduff?'

Doyle's careful neutrality did not falter. 'Only him and his suitcase.' He scratched his damaged ear. 'He's up on the stage, if you want to ask him.'

Vanessa had no intention of asking anything, but she couldn't resist heading to the auditorium. There she found Alistair, Ronnie Gainsborough and the director in conversation behind the proscenium. The issue was the casting of Mr Cecil Graham, the minor role that Mr and Mrs Rolf wanted for their son. A newcomer, Jeffrey Mardell, had been given the part and Gainsborough had misgivings.

'Cecil Graham is supposed to be a smiling viper. Mardell smiles as if a loose woman has just made an improper comment to him. Has he even lost his cherry yet? Why aren't we using Edwin Bovary? One glance at that red-lined cloak, my stomach curdles.'

'Well?' Aubrey Hinshaw gave Alistair an impish glance. 'Why aren't we using Edwin, Commander?'

'No military service and his father is the producer, which is bound to ruffle feathers. Anyway, he's up for Iago in a touring *Othello*. According to his mother, he was "born to the Classics".'

Hinshaw laughed. 'We'll work with Mardell, then. Pity we can't whisk the lad off to some of the Cairo nightspots I haunted before the war. He could be deprived of his cherry, fleeced and given a mild dose of a sexual disease all in one night. That would change his smile. Why don't you take him out some time, Ronnie?'

'Corrupting innocence is far more Carnford's style. Perhaps you could oblige, Commander.' Gainsborough picked a hair off Alistair's jacket. Real or imaginary, he held it up to the light. 'Auburn this time. Somewhere good for the weekend?'

Vanessa stopped breathing.

Alistair answered in exasperating style. 'Somewhere bad. One can have a good weekend any time. Bad ones take dedication and effort.'

Vanessa slipped away. Later that week, as she passed the half-open door of the green room, she overheard Lawrie Weston speaking. Weston was playing a florid-cheeked Lord Augustus Lorton. They were discussing the newcomer, Mardell.

'. . . dried completely on his Act Three entrance, poor lad. Can't say I'm surprised, the way Ronnie glowers, though one has to admit that if Mardell has "it", then it's jolly well hidden. Know who'd have done Cecil Graham to a T?'

Pure intuition, but Vanessa knew what was coming.

'Johnny Quinnell. More smiles per mile than any other man I knew – when he wanted something from you. Once he'd got it, the smile was packed away. A brass clock for a heart had Johnny. It ticked, and that's about all.'

'I never understood why dear Bo put himself out for the fellow.' It was Noreen Ruskin's mezzo voice taking up the thread. 'You can measure a man by the number who turn up for his funeral. By all accounts, Quinnell pulled in a crowd of three.'

'Four, darling. The wife, his daughter, Eva and Billy. Don't forget, he was competing against darling Bo.'

Vanessa heard the clink of a bottle against glass, and a woman's sigh. 'That was the strangest Sunday I ever spent, and the saddest. How was it they both passed away the same night?' This voice belonged to Irene Eddrich. Half-Swedish, Irene spoke with a lilt that was stronger off-stage than on.

'The cold, dear one, the cold,' Lawrie Weston answered. 'They say Bo came here on foot the night he died. Cold air can be fatal to ageing lungs. As for Quinnell, blame the demon drink. They say he got the keys to the green room bar the night he died.'

'"They say",' Miss Eddrich echoed disdainfully. 'I was in the audience that night, and went backstage afterwards. I did not find Quinnell to be drunk. He was out of sorts, I will admit.'

'There has to be a reason the theatre paid for his funeral,' Lawrie Weston suggested.

'Miss Bovary paid. Her own money.' This was Noreen Ruskin.

'Miss Bovary paid initially,' Miss Eddrich corrected. 'But she got the money back from an actors' benevolent fund, so it was no charity.'

Vanessa kept out of sight, just close enough to the door to hear whatever came next. She'd finally learned the name of Eva's companion at the graveside. 'Billy.' It hurt, hearing her dad spoken of with casual contempt but she wasn't going to storm in and demand an apology. Johnny had been at best 'good in parts', not universally liked. That was becoming ever more clear.

'Poor Eva is who I feel most sorry for, losing both men that she loved. And she'd lost so much already.' Of those in the room, Miss Eddrich had the highest claim to human kindness. 'I visited her after Bo's funeral, did you know? She hardly knew me.'

'Miss Bovary didn't stump up for *her* funeral, I'll be bound,' Miss Ruskin snorted.

'No indeed. Commander Redenhall paid for Eva's burial.'

Patrick Carnford swung into the corridor, and Vanessa leapt away from the wall. She hopped, pretending she had a stone in her shoe. Patrick kissed his hand to her, saying, 'We must have dinner some night. Name the evening, Mrs Kingcourt.'

She wanted to track down Alistair. He'd known all along that Eva was dead, and had said nothing. But she couldn't walk away from Carnford's flirtatious smile without inciting suspicion. 'You do everything backwards,' she told him. 'We've already had our first kiss, and now you want dinner. What comes next, a stroll in the park followed by a light handshake?'

Carnford laughed. 'Go lest I drown in your eyes. Your mother's eyes.'

'You – you've guessed who my mother is?'

'Within a minute of sharing a stage with you.'

'Then, Mr Carnford, there's so much I need to ask you.'

'Patrick?' Noreen Ruskin came out of the green room and placed a possessive hand on Carnford's shoulder, saying slyly in Vanessa's direction, 'Do we need to beware of hidden cameras?'

Vanessa hurried away. Thanks to those candid pictures, many in the company had marked her down as a temptress, a danger to unwary men. Even Tanith had tutted, as if Vanessa's lapse were a sorry thing from which she was armoured by the wisdom of years. Peter Switt always smirked unpleasantly when they passed in a corridor.

Maybe she was following in Eva's footsteps. An all-too-human Wardrobe Mistress whose heart was doomed to break.

Alistair didn't deny having known of Eva St Clair's death for weeks. He also confirmed that he'd paid the funeral expenses.

'The matron of the almshouse where she was living telephoned with the news. She was concerned there'd be none of Eva's old friends and colleagues at the funeral, but I couldn't help. I was running The Farren pretty much single-handed, and knew nobody.'

'Miss Bovary went?' Invited by Alistair to be seated, Vanessa remained standing.

'No. I went to Brookwood alone.'

'Brookwood?' How she wished people would tell her the truth! She described the thankless trip to Kensal Green that had left her with throbbing chilblains and chapped ears. 'Can you at least tell me who else was at Eva's funeral?'

'A couple of nuns and some nurses. Two men, that being myself and her brother.'

'Father Joseph?' No. That didn't add up.

'Billy Chalker, the comic actor. Eva had two brothers.'

Billy, the man in the bowler hat at Johnny's grave? 'Why didn't you say in front of Father Mannion that Eva was dead?'

'I had other things on my mind. Fern visiting you at the theatre, for one. And because I'd rather walk with the living than constantly look over my shoulder at the departed.'

She produced her birth certificate, almost tearing it in her agitation. She insisted he look at it. 'Now do you see why I want to know about Eva?'

She expected Alistair to express shock, or even disgust. But he leaned back in his chair and there was the same tightness in his face that she'd last seen when he confronted Fern and Highstoke.

He said, 'When we've launched our show and we have more time, we'll talk about this document. But for now, may we let Eva rest? May I lock this certificate away?'

She snatched it up. 'Pardon me, but I want to spend half-an-hour at my mother's grave. If you won't take me, fine. I'll ask Patrick Carnford. He's invited me out to dinner, so I'll suggest a trip to Brookwood instead.'

From being intent on some invisible horizon, Alistair now looked at her with hard contempt. 'Carnford won't waste an afternoon driving you to Brookwood, but I will, if you're so determined. Let's make a day of it.' There was a twist in Alistair's voice that unnerved her.

In spite of it, she accepted his offer. 'Thank you.'

'Don't thank me. Just give me credit for trying to protect you.'

'I don't need protecting.'

'No? Leave me, Vanessa. I'll let you know when I've got fuel for the Alfa.'

On November 14th, the final rehearsal took place under Aubrey Hinshaw's direction. Afterwards, at the farewell drinks party on stage, Hinshaw presented Alistair with 'The Book', a sixty-page document containing the script and directorial notes. From now on, the company was on its own.

Wedged in among a crowd of actors and senior staff, Vanessa joined in the cheers. As she took a glass of sherry off a tray

– a tray carried by James Harnett in full butler costume – she saw Alistair threading towards her. It would be their first conversation since he'd agreed to take her to Brookwood, and his expression made her certain he was regretting his offer.

As he passed, he said, 'I've managed to get a few gallons of petrol. We'll go tomorrow, after lunch.' Not waiting to discover if that suited, he went to speak with a group of cast-members, The Book under his arm.

It took them just under two hours to reach Brookwood, slower than it should have been because they took a diversion past St George's hospital in Tooting, where Vanessa bought a bunch of past-their-best flowers from the seller at the gate. As they reached the cemetery, the sun was low in the sky.

Alistair took her arm and they set off to find the Nonconformists' ground, where the Catholics' graveyard was located. He wasn't certain of remembering the way and in the end, their route was so circuitous, Vanessa feared they'd lose the light.

'We need to stop walking every path twice. Concentrate, Alistair, please.'

'Fine.' Five minutes later, he found the path and soon located the tablet of grey granite that marked Eva's last resting place. Releasing Vanessa's arm, he said, 'I'll be a few yards away. Call when you need me.' *When*, not *if*.

She tightened her belt for courage. Here, both her parents were buried, though far apart. As in life, in death. A nerve jumped below her eye, out of time with the beat of her heart.

She crouched before the stone.

Sacred to the memory of Eva Elizabeth St Clair, born 1st March 1888, died 31st August 1946, aged 58 years. 'Then shall I know as I am known'.

'As you are known, to me, at last.' Vanessa put down her

flowers. There was no vase. 'What would I have called you? Mum or Mother?' Or some other name? Fern had called her mother Marge. Wiping tears away, Vanessa saw that Alistair had come a little closer, an upright, angular shape in his dark blue coat. He called to her, 'Ready to go?'

No, not quite. Vanessa's attention turned to the stone to the right of Eva's. This one was no bigger than the back of a child's chair, green with moss. As she bent to read it, Alistair came up at a robust pace, whisking her around so her feet combed the top of the grass. He carried her some distance before putting her down and saying, 'We need to go.'

She fought off his grip. He was ashen, and it had to be something to do with the little grave. She tore away, falling to her knees in front of it. A moment later, a garbled noise ripped from her throat. Alistair was beside her again. She wailed, 'This can't be true. Read it. It can't be.'

He did as she bid. '*In loving memory of Vanessa Elizabeth, daughter of Eva St Clair. Born 29th May 1920. Taken to God 12th July 1920.*'

'It's me. My name, my birth date.'

'I know. I saw it the day Eva was buried.'

'I was born May 29th, 1920. It's me. Alistair, this is my grave.'

'This is what I wanted to stop you seeing.' He helped her to her feet and took her back to the car. Long shadows doubled the reach of trees, obscuring the path. It felt inevitable that they should get lost, finally reaching the car in darkness.

As they drove off, she said to Alistair, 'You will help me understand, before I go insane?'

From Brookwood, Alistair drove them to the outskirts of Guildford, some fifteen miles, to the hospice where Eva had lived out her last years and where the staff added some flesh to her history.

Though having known her only in the aftermath of her injury, she would always be an enigma to them.

Eva's family had come originally from Waterford in Ireland, the matron told them. That was in the last decade of the nineteenth century. In London, Eva had trained as a seamstress, and had joined The Farren as a wardrobe assistant, aged fourteen. 'Where she met her husband.'

'She wasn't married, sister.'

'To us, she was married.' That informed Vanessa that in this sanctuary run by Catholic nuns, Eva's irregular life was neither acknowledged nor referred to. Nor was the fact that she'd given birth out of wedlock.

'The child buried next to Eva . . . that was her daughter?'

The matron nodded. Indeed.

'Sister, did Eva have other children?'

'No. None. We made enquiries after her death. Her one living relative is her brother, William. Billy, as he's known.' The matron found his address for them. Wild Street, Covent Garden.

Vanessa asked, 'Did she leave anything here? Anything I might have as a keepsake?' But the matron informed her that all Eva's belongings had been sent on to Billy.

As they drove away, Alistair said, 'Billy probably lives in the Peabody Trust buildings. They take up most of Wild Street.'

Parking the Alfa outside The Farren, they walked to Wild Street which lay parallel with Drury Lane. The night was moonless, and Alistair's torch saved them from stepping into craters and fissures in the pavement. The Peabody estate was a residential fortress formed of several blocks. They followed signs into a middle court where heaps of blackened brick described a direct hit during the Blitz, or perhaps from a V2 rocket strike at the end of the war. Billy Chalker lived on the third level of block D.

There was no answer to their knock, and a prim-looking female neighbour told them that Billy was away on tour, up north.

'He went a month ago.' She added a quirk of disapproval. 'Four trunks with him, for all his dresses, I suppose. When will he be back? Soon. The milkman's had notice to start delivering again.'

On their way back down to ground-level, Alistair explained that Billy Chalker was a professional Dame, though he took straight roles too. 'You saw him, come to think of it. He was Nurse Witless in *Sleeping Beauty*.'

'Stripy stockings and red-spotted drawers. His boyfriend always sat mid-row of the stalls, you said.'

'Reputedly. Though you'll have gathered by now, theatre gossip is like an extra member of cast, whose full-time role is to spin yarns.' Without breaking stride, Alistair put his arm around her.

She said, 'Officially, I'm dead. It's a horrible feeling.'

'I have coffee in my office. I'll drop a shot of brandy in it.'

They collected Macduff from Doyle, who was waiting for Mr Kidd to come on duty. Alistair passed his torch to Vanessa and as they walked through the auditorium, she pointed the beam upward, challenging the void. There was something brooding about The Farren in its late night state. Macduff began to bark and growl. Playing the beam along the dress circle rail, she illuminated the torso of a woman in black, looking down. She pulled in a gasp.

The shadow-figure dissolved.

Alistair grunted. 'Doyle didn't mention *she* was in tonight.'

Vanessa shuddered. 'She had no face.'

Alistair affected a stiff-lipped drawl. 'You are unobservant, my dear Watson. That was no spectre, it was our own Miss Bovary.

Haven't you noticed Barbara coming into work wearing a hat with a veil obscuring her face? She invariably wears unrelieved black . . . Her appearance has given many a theatre employee the fright of their lives.'

He was teasing, and it helped dispel Vanessa's sense that death was edging close to her. 'All right, Sherlock. Who was Back Row Flo?'

'Florence Nettles, a Victorian barmaid who loved a leading actor. A misguided fool, in other words.'

Still teasing. Or was 'mocking' nearer the mark?

Alistair opened the swing door to the foyer, which was in darkness. Letting Macduff off the lead, he held the door for Vanessa. Macduff went off to sniff a trail along the floor, perhaps left by the tomcat Doyle had recently acquired to deal with the theatre mice. Vanessa turned off the torch. Such dark descended, they might have been blindfolded. 'Tell me more about Flo.'

'Miss Nettles fell pregnant by the rotter. Actor, sorry. Only to be jilted. In despair, she threw herself to her death from the upper circle balcony.'

'A myth, surely.'

'No myth. Bo had the original newspaper cutting reporting the tragedy. Ever since, Florence has haunted The Farren, placing it among that elite band of West End theatres with predictive phantoms. If she appears during rehearsals, we expect bad reviews and a play's early closure. If she appears on opening night, buy the champagne.'

'Cottrill's been seeing her since day one.'

He laughed. 'Cottrill stays awake all night, writing his play, and suffers sleep-deprived neurosis. If Florence really comes, we'll know. Now let's talk of something else. Death does not become you, Mrs Kingcourt.' Alistair's arms came around her.

Vanessa dropped the torch, but held herself stiff. Her head was too full even for desire.

'How can Eva have had one child, and that child be dead, yet here I am with the same name, and the birth certificate to prove it?'

'A certificate proves nothing.' Alistair said. 'I have a dog license. It doesn't prove my name is Macduff.'

'You're saying – '

'I'm not saying any more. I have no special knowledge. I just know that right now I want to take you to bed.'

She melted. She dipped her head, so that it rested against his chest. She wasn't ready to be kissed, not at least until he'd answered one, desperate question. 'Who did you go away with last weekend? You came back with an auburn hair on your jacket. If it was Fern, don't tell me.'

'I'm not ready to tell you,' he said, his lips against her curls.

'Then it was Fern.' She tried to pull away but he stopped her.

'I'm not telling you *here*. Walls have ears.' Putting his fingers beneath her chin, he tipped her lips up towards his. For a blissful five seconds, their mouths met. Then the foyer lights went on and strident voice blasted down.

'Commander, is that you standing about with the lights off? Answer or I will go straight to my office and telephone the police.'

'That's murdered the moment.' For Vanessa alone, Alistair whispered, 'We never got our coffee and brandy.'

'I can offer you instant Nescafé or Bovril.'

'At yours? Beware, I may not want to leave afterwards.'

She didn't pretend to misunderstand. As she prepared her expression for Miss Bovary, who was switching off lights as she came downstairs, she murmured, 'There won't have been any heating on since eight p.m., so you won't be seduced by the warmth of the welcome. What will we do with Macduff?'

'Leave him with Mr Kidd for the night. Three's a crowd, even if one of them's a dog.'

Chapter Twenty-Five

Taking a chair at the kitchen table, Alistair watched Vanessa set the kettle to boil. He'd chosen coffee, knowing its reputation for disturbing sleep. He didn't want to sleep. He watched her check the ice-box, heard her murmur, 'Damn.'

'No milk?'

'Do you mind black?'

'I prefer it.' He stretched out his legs, which made the room seem absurdly small. Vanessa had plugged in the electric fire, aiming the glow at the table. Even with that and the gas ring going, he decided to keep his coat on a bit longer. She hadn't removed hers either.

'I very often drink a last cup of tea or Bovril wearing my gloves, before crawling into bed with a hot water bottle.' She abruptly fell silent, and he saw shell pink creep into her cheeks. Desire spiralled through him, rising from his groin. That tightening ache that shortened the breath and brought a sensation like feathers falling on the back of the shoulders . . . a long, long time since he'd followed this craving to its natural finish. Was that how the night was going to end? She'd used the word 'seduce' but he wondered if Vanessa had ever seduced a man. Nothing in the way she fastened her hands around her cup to draw in its heat as she sat opposite him, indicated bedroom virtuosity. Vanessa's mystique lay in the total absence of feminine wiles. It was what had caught him from the first. Now she was staring at his hands. Putting down his cup, he extended his fingers. 'What are you trying to see?'

She stroked the base of his ring finger, where lighter skin made a stubborn reminder of a wedding ring. 'Is it really, truly, over with Fern?'

'I've not seen her since you stayed that night at Ledbury Terrace and in that time, I've no reason to suppose she's lived alone. I spent last weekend in Brighton with a Mrs Duckworth.'

Catching a flash of jealousy, he decided a dose of mild teasing might be good for both of them. 'Primrose by name, though by nature, she was no shy flower. A natural redhead and her perfume was *Evening in Paris*. We slept together in room fourteen of the Sea View Hotel, on a grainy mattress that smelled of boot polish. I assume some of the guests sleep with their shoes on. It was that kind of place. What have I said to offend you?'

Vanessa had scraped her chair back and was at the sink, refilling the kettle, though neither of them had finished their drinks. Water jetted off the top, splashing as far as his feet.

'Aren't you curious to know why I went away with Mrs Duckworth?'

'I know why men go to hotels with women.' Her voice was hard as a nib. Slamming the kettle on the burner, she faced him. 'I only invited you back here because of what I went through today. I'm feeling disconnected. I could really do with Hugo right now.'

'No, you couldn't. He'd make off-colour remarks about illegitimacy.'

'Patrick, then.'

'Even worse. He'd say trite things while ensuring none of your emotion spilled on to his jacket.'

'Patrick says my eyes are like my mother's.'

'Really?' He stood and reached for her, drawing her closer. 'Let's not fall into argument. Primrose Duckworth is a professional co-respondent. She hires herself out to men in my position.'

'A prostitute?' Vanessa hit him. A swipe of frustration.

'Far from. Well, perhaps not that far from, but far enough. I'm allowing Fern to divorce me on the grounds of my adultery, and to make that work, I had to be seen to commit some. Hove is the adulterer's first choice, two hours from London with sea air thrown in. "The respondent was witnessed in a hotel bed, m'Lud, during the weekend of the 9th and 10th of November alongside a woman who was not his wife." I paid Primrose.'

'To sleep with you?'

'To pretend to. We got up to nothing whatsoever. We chatted about the weather, and her son who was in the Home Guard and is now a milkman. The key is that the chambermaid saw us. It's how it's done, as Fern was good enough to remind me. When it comes to court, Redenhall versus Redenhall, the chambermaid will swear to what she saw.'

Had he expected Vanessa to fling her arms around him? To sob her admiration and gratitude? Yes . . . a soft tear or two would be a start. But she was stony.

'What about the impossibility of divorce for you, which, apparently, I wasn't clever enough to understand?'

He regarded her in climbing exasperation. They'd been within a hair's breadth of falling into bed, and now she was pumping cold water over them both. But she'd had a terrible day. She was lashing out. 'Have you forgotten Fern's photographs? I've yielded to her demands on the condition she hands the negatives over. I did it to protect you.'

'But she'd already done her worst, showing the pictures to Ruth. What more could she do? Pin them to lamp posts on Shaftsbury Avenue?'

'Possibly.' He rubbed an eye, aware of tiredness creeping into his body. Shrewish argument had that effect. 'You're disappointed that I've compromised?'

Her lip trembled. In the severe light of the kitchen, the split given her by a policeman's elbow looked like a stroke of carnation-coloured ink. He waited for the tremble to deepen, for tears to come, but she bit them back stubbornly. 'Yes.'

'I've ripped up my lifelong, personal code to prevent your name appearing in a dirty divorce case.'

'You didn't need to.'

'My God, Vanessa, I'm beginning to see what Lord Stanshurst was getting at. He said you were destructive.'

'When?'

'When he was speaking of you and Leo, your separation.'

'We didn't separate! There wasn't time.'

'All right. When you kicked your husband out of your bed while he was in the middle of active duty. I knew something of it already, from Fern. Instead of being the loving new wife, you demanded a divorce. True?'

'If Lord Stanshurst and Fern say so, it must be.'

He got up, put his lips to her forehead. This was dangerous ground, studded with 'keep out' signs. 'I've a heavy, burning itch to my eyelids. We need our sleep, both of us. I'll let myself out.'

She trapped him in her arms. 'Don't go. I want you. I'll shut up and apologise in kind.'

He considered her offer with his entire body and buried a long breath in her hair. Deep intuition told him that if he followed her to her bed, it would end badly. He put her aside firmly. 'I don't want to.'

For a full minute after the door closed behind him, Vanessa stared at the space Alistair had occupied. She tried, from the bumps and sighs of the cold building, to conjure evidence of him returning. He did not come back and she slumped with her head on the table, sobbing until dry gulps warned her she'd hit empty. Then, from the table drawer, she took lined paper and a pen and wrote him a letter.

This is the truth of what happened between me and Leo. It was 1940, this time of year. The weather over Kent was atrocious but German bombers kept coming with their fighter escorts. All of us were exhausted . . .

She filled a page, then signed her initials at the bottom. The following morning, she got to work while Mr Kidd was still on the premises, sliding a sealed envelope under the door of Alistair's office.

Chapter Twenty-Six

Alistair read the letter, ignoring a shrilling telephone. Vanessa's jagged handwriting suggested she'd allowed no time for caution to set in. She'd written:

> Leo and his section were flying formation over the Dover strait. Visibility twenty yards, they didn't see the ME 109's coming in over the top of them. A mass dogfight occurred . . . Leo got separated tailing one particular ME 109. He hit it astern and reported black smoke coming from it. How elated he sounded, getting a kill! He came through to me on his wireless, talking, as if nothing bad had happened between us. Nor was he anxious at being way out over the water, on his own. I got his co-ordinates and gave him a weather report. Fog getting thicker, rain squalls coming. I could already hear some of his section coming in to land. He said, 'Message understood, Mrs K.' He was turning back when there was a rattling rush, the sounds of gunfire. He shouted, 'Got me!' I knew he'd been hit from the way his voice swerved upwards. A moment later, he screamed he was burning. The fuel tank is at the front in

a Spitfire; they rupture and within seconds, the cockpit's a ball of fire.

He wouldn't or couldn't bail, though I begged him to. Later, I realised that in my panic, I'd forgotten to press my 'broadcast' button. I could hear him but he couldn't hear me. He was brave, packed to the brim with focussed rage. That's good in a fighter pilot. What made that day different was that he'd gone on duty having had no sleep. Alistair, he – '

The next phrase was crossed out, replaced with:

I had to get out of that marriage but throwing him out mid-tour was unforgiveable. I've only ever shared this story with Fern. I trusted her. Unwisely, it seems. Only I know the burden I carry or the other side of the story.

V K

Unforgiveable. How often people used that word to attract the pardon they were confident of receiving. 'Darling, I forgot our lunch. Unforgiveable!' He believed here that Vanessa had applied it literally. Unable to escape her actions, her confidence had been gnawed away. He picked up his telephone – it had fallen quiet – and asked to be put through to the Ledbury Terrace number.

Fern answered after about thirty rings, the croak in her voice implying she'd been dragged from sleep yet again. He said, 'I want you to tell me something in confidence.'

'What's in it for me?'

'What could there possibly be? I've already conceded every-thing.'

'There's money. I ought to have a share of Bo's fortune.'

Knocked off track, he told her not to talk nonsense. Bo's money was in a trust that was not written in his favour.

'I know. His lawyer guards it.' Fern sighed raggedly. 'Father told me. But if it's just sitting there, you must make a bid for it before it goes to the crown or the tax collector.'

'It will go to Bo's sisters, if nobody else comes forward to claim it. This isn't why I called. Tell me about Vanessa's husband. What kind of man was Leo Kingcourt?'

'I never met him. Dashing and racy, I should imagine. Spitfire pilots were every girl's dream, weren't they? I know what he *did* to Vanessa, though.'

'Tell me.'

Fern did so, matter-of-factly, and he could find no response more intelligent than, 'Shit.' As he replaced the handset, he felt he finally had a window into Vanessa's soul. Too much of a window. What could he say to her now? Something must be said. He was about to go find her when his phone rang. It was Terence Rolf, peeved that he'd been ringing all morning. Miss Abbott's agent had called, complaining of the state of the path to the stage door. 'Wrecking the heels of her shoes, old boy, and that is serious to Miss Abbott. Any chance you can speed up the outside repairs?'

Alistair agreed to accelerate the work, which required more phone calls that amply digested his morning. Civilian life, he was discovering, was a balls-aching tapestry of minor frustrations. When he finally found a moment to call on Vanessa, she'd left to visit Penny Yorke. *Right, I'll pay a call on Miss Yorke myself*, he thought. But Doyle stopped him as he left by the main doors:

a gang of 'funny-looking coves' had just arrived with crowbars to re-lay cobbles in Caine Passage. Did Alistair know anything about it? By the time he reached the Great Portland Street premises, Vanessa had already left.

On the 21st of November, the theatre began to hum early as the crew set up the first technical rehearsal. The flymen raised and lowered back-drops, practicing their cues. Lighting riggers went aloft, scripts in hand to set lamps and spots to opening positions. Peter Switt flitted between the prompt box and the winch that operated the curtains, timing to the second how long it took him to cover the five strides between the two. Tom Cottrill, supposedly the glue holding the performance together, stood in the wings like Moses with his stone tablets – or rather, his copy of The Book – clamped to his chest. He claimed to have seen Back Row Flo in the upper circle the previous evening, even though Miss Bovary had explained that it had been she sitting in the Gods, judging the quality of the orchestra who had rehearsed in situ for the first time.

Terence Rolf knocked at the wardrobe room and in his courtly way, asked Vanessa to sit in the auditorium and be part of the audience. 'Knowing they're being watched gives cast and crew something to bounce against. My wife and the Commander have taken their seats already.'

'Do you really need me?' Vanessa glanced at the rails of shrouded dresses and suits that all needed to be checked, ironed and allocated. Since writing her letter to Alistair, she'd used her workload as an excuse for avoiding him.

'Oh, do join the fun.' Rolf's eyes were on her throat, on the outline of something small and hard beneath her jumper. He lunged without warning, and fished out the ribbon, staring at the golden key. 'Tell me why you wear this?'

'It was a gift.'

'From?'

'Miss St Clair. As she gave it to me, she said it was rightfully mine. I've never understood.'

'But she spoke?'

'With difficulty. Answer a question for me, please, Mr Rolf. Why does your son Edwin wear my father's cloak?'

'Your father's?' Rolf's waggish smile vanished. Giving Vanessa no time to jump back, he gripped the ribbon tightly. In a panic, she grasped his wrists to shake him off, accidentally loosening one of his cufflinks, which clinked to the floor. He released her suddenly and went to find it.

By the time he'd retrieved it, his urbane smile was back. 'Never hang things round your neck, Mrs Kingcourt. I knew of a girl who died getting her necklace caught in the door of a lift. Do come down and watch with us. This will be the first tech rehearsal you've ever seen and first times are always the best.'

She slammed her door on him, but in the end, decided to do as he asked. For the first time at The Farren, she felt scared of being alone. Taking her seat beside Alistair, two rows in front of Mrs Rolf, Edwin and Miss Bovary, she toyed with revealing what had just occurred. Terence would deny it, of course. Or claim she'd somehow misunderstood him. Rolf took his seat just then, calling heartily, 'This is Mrs Kingcourt's first time, Commander, she was telling me a moment back. Oh, to be a theatre virgin again!'

'Ignore him,' Vanessa mumbled. 'Who turned the heating on?' She wriggled out of her coat.

'I did. We can't let the paying public freeze.' Alistair leaned closer and whispered, 'I read your letter. Should I burn it?'

'Paste it to a lamp post on Shaftsbury Avenue.'

He pinched her shoulder gently. 'I deserve that. I was brutal to you the night you took me home. I didn't want to leave. I wanted – '

'Don't.' She sensed the others straining to listen.

The orchestra began tuning up, the snare drummer vamping noisily while the strings scraped. Cottrill, on stage, clasped his hands to his ears and bellowed 'Stop!' The orchestra faltered, then started up again.

Alistair said in Vanessa's ear, 'Was the traumatic end to your marriage the reason you never claimed your widow's pension?'

An odd moment for such a question, an odd connection of subjects, but the darkness helped her answer. 'I never felt I deserved it. Leo's savings came to me too, once his bar-bill was paid. I used that money to buy the costume designs off Hugo. It was a relief to give it away.' She paused to watch Cottrill jig in frustration at the orchestra's off-notes. 'I hope your stage manager makes it to the first night.'

'*My* stage manager now he's going doolally?' Alistair grunted. 'I thought I was doing a good thing, employing a man nobody else would. The idea was that he'd write his plays while also being paid. I sometimes think kindness is a form of delinquency.'

Cottrill began pacing the stage, his gaze fixed on the top seating levels. Searching for Flo? Vanessa was struck by an idea. 'Why not ask Father Mannion to come in and bless the upper circle?'

Alistair chuckled. 'Or I could ask Miss Bovary to hold another of her famous séances.'

Vanessa couldn't resist a glance behind. 'She's a spiritualist? So that's what Hugo was driving at.'

'She and her sister are well known in those circles.'

'Hugo said something bizarre to me, that Miss Bovary prefers the dead to the living.'

Alistair nodded, the movement just discernible in the semi-dark. 'She and Sylvia are convinced we have three ghosts. Flo, Bo and Elizabeth Farren herself. They conduct séances in dead of night trying to reach them. Terence joins in.'

Behind the stage, pacing the crossover, Ronnie Gainsborough could be heard declaiming, 'The steel butterflies, how they torment me.'

From the wings, a male voice called mockingly, 'A little stage-fright is a good thing, Ronnie. An excess is hilarious.'

'They say you never get nerves, Carnford,' Ronnie Gainsborough hit back disdainfully. 'Sign of a complacent soul.'

'I'd rather be infected with calm than with woodworm, dear boy.'

'Ronnie, darling, ignore him,' Clemency Abbott intervened, her voice disembodied balm.

Alistair murmured, 'Dress rehearsal tomorrow, Vanessa. Are you prepared?'

'Ask me again tomorrow night.'

'Is that an invitation to coffee? I'll be better prepared this time. Is this play ever going to start?'

It did, but not for half an hour. After calling for the stage curtains to be closed so that Peter Swit might practice opening them on cue, Cottrill walked smack into the drum-shaped table set for Lady Windermere's opening scene. The blue glass bowl crashed on to the stage, and the table top broke in two, the top section seperating from the stem and rolling like a wagon wheel into the orchestra pit. The lead violinist almost skewered the viola player. Peter Swit marched from the wings, shouting importantly, 'Take care! Broken glass on stage!'

As Alistair left to check that Cottrill was unhurt, Terence Rolf commented gleefully to his companions, 'Flo's up to her tricks. Watch for a run of ill luck leading to an early closure.'

Vanessa guessed she was meant to hear. She turned in her seat, saying in a clear voice, 'We, the cast and crew, will make sure you eat your words, Mr Rolf.'

The carpenter hastily repaired the table and the tech rehearsal finally began. The orchestra came in tightly and the curtain swished back like the sound of the sea. Lights rose on a wittily resourceful set. The first lines rang out confidently, the chemistry between Clemency Abbott and Ronnie Gainsborough swelling like volatile haze. Five minutes in, James Harnett made his entrance as Lady Windermere's butler and Vanessa smiled. Harnett had perfected the senior servant's puffed-out walk, half pigeon, half duck. He'd get a laugh on his first entrance.

PARKER: The men want to know if they are to put the carpets on the terrace for tonight, my lady?

LADY WINDERMERE: You don't think it will rain, Lord Darlington, do you?

LORD DARLINGTON: I won't hear of its raining on your birthday! Bugger! Now what?

The stage lights had gone off with a loud snap, prompting Ronnie Gainsborough to his un-Wildean language. A moment later, there came a crash and a howl of pain. 'Man down,' Gainsborough shouted in the darkness. 'The carpenter put the sodding table back in the wrong position. Idiot! Lights and first aid, please. Harnett's fallen. His breathing doesn't sound too good, either.'

Chapter Twenty-Seven

The lights had gone out because the gang re-setting the cobbles in Caine Passage had put a pick-axe through a power cable. James Harnett was stretchered out by ambulance men and when news came that he'd suffered a broken thigh and was in a special ward due to shock, a jittery mood descended. A chain of ill-luck was forming. Flo's doing?

The tech rehearsal was abandoned, the cast asked to come back the following day.

In a candle-lit green room, Tanith held forth. 'Back Row Flo hexes anything to do with Oscar Wilde because the lover that jilted her made his name playing Lord Windermere. Think about it: when they did *The Importance* last time, Wilton Bovary died and some other actor, too. On the same night.'

Vanessa, who had been walking past, was provoked to a savage response but Rosa raised a pacifying hand and gave a reprimand in her customary, measured way. 'It's loose talk like that which hexes a play, Tanith. Do you intend to wash your first big chance down the plug-hole?'

Groping her way upstairs, Vanessa collected her bag and hat. She might as well go to Great Portland Street and round up the last of the costumes. Before leaving, she ran her torch beam along the costume rails. 'Operation Windermere' had produced four-teen gowns. All that was missing were of the minor characters' ball dresses, and Mrs Erlynne's Act Two dress, which had been sent back for alterations. With the dress rehearsal postponed to allow for another Parker to be engaged, she'd be able to give Penny Yorke an extra twenty-four hours.

Penny would be pleased, but Vanessa wasn't. Tomorrow was the sixth anniversary of Leo's death and she'd been relying on frenetic activity to bundle her through. In Caine Passage, in a spitting wind, she saw Alistair briefing men in boiler suits. Come to repair the cable, with luck. Luck. One large injection, please. Alistair didn't see her slip past, her collar pulled high.

The Great Portland Street *atelier* smelled of hot grease from the whir of so many machines. Vanessa couldn't help comparing today's scene with the barren table tops of Hugo's tenure. She greeted Penny, walking between a double row of energetically treadling women. Heads were bent low over work, fingers pushing seams along at maniac pace, braving the needle-blur. Lemon, ochre and ivory silk spilled over table edges, making Vanessa imagine a mass-production of scrambled egg.

Penny hugged her, and cheered when she learned she had a day's grace. 'Our bobbins are on fire but bless you, darling. I prefer not to make my girls sew all night. I often had to, when I worked for Warner Brothers.' Penny had spent the war years in New York costuming propaganda films. With strong, wide cheekbones and hair falling in graduated waves, she resembled her heroine, the actress Katharine Hepburn. She'd returned to London at the end of the war, after her war-reporter fiancé was killed on his way home from Europe. While her aunt Daphne designed and created from a sofa in their Curzon Street salon,

Penny raced around the satellite shops and workrooms, energising the business. She had high ambitions. 'Yorke of London, Paris and New York. Just watch me.'

Vanessa had never seen Penny succumb to stress. If a task seemed overwhelming, she would interrogate it in her American accent until it yielded to logic. One of her regular sayings was, 'Don't react to troubles, respond to them.'

I should have kept that in mind when Alistair told me about Primrose Duckworth, Vanessa admitted as she followed Penny from machinist to machinist, assessing the quality of each woman's work. *I reacted because I couldn't believe he'd done it to protect me. A* response *would have been to throw my arms about him and kiss him half to death. Next time, next time.*

They went through to the back, where Mrs Erlynne's ball gown was displayed on a papier-mâché dummy. Vanessa caught her breath, as she did each time she saw it. A miracle, its *bustier* bodice was secured with fine gilt chains that would be invisible to all but the front row audience. Mauve velvet, clingy as plum jam, it would elevate Irene Eddrich's Nordic beauty to a different level. 'When she stands under the follow-spot,' Vanessa sighed, 'the audience will gasp. If they've a pulse, they will. Gosh – ' Terence Rolf's attack and a lack of lunch had caught up with her. 'Any chance of a cup of something?'

Penny called her assistant and ordered English tea, good and strong. 'You're feeling the strain. Theatre is tough.'

'It's more than that.' Vanessa described her recent visit to Brookwood, finding her own name on a gravestone.

Penny looked satisfyingly shocked. 'Weird. Do you imagine perhaps the grave was empty? It might have been a ruse, to pretend you were dead.'

'Why would anybody need to pretend that? I'm not a Romanov princess.' Vanessa showed Penny her golden key, describing how she'd come by it.

'A gift from the old Wardrobe Mistress. Wow. And what does it unlock?'

'I don't know. And before you say "wardrobe", I've already tried.'

'How about a sewing box?' Penny chuckled at Vanessa's reaction to the throw-away remark then switched back to business. 'I'll have the mauve gown wrapped so you can take it with you. Shall we agree a time for my girls to deliver the last consignment tomorrow?'

Two miles away in his Mayfair office, Terence Rolf was concluding a telephone call. He'd secured his first choice of actor to take over the role of Parker, though it had cost him, as he'd had to compensate a rival management. But it was worth it. His chosen man was renowned for being difficult, with a roster of human vices that were bound to aggravate his fellow actors. Terence Rolf badly wanted to punish Alistair Redenhall for inheriting The Farren, and wrecking Lady Windermere was his chosen method.

As Rolf terminated his call, the threads linking Vanessa Kingcourt to her married captain, to family members known and unknown, grew tighter. A band of players was gathering to act a final scene on The Farren's stage.

PART FOUR

Home to roost

Chapter Twenty-Eight

Vanessa spent the morning of November 22nd, the anniversary of Leo's death, briefing the stars' dressers on the costumes their ladies and gentlemen would wear. Afterwards, she went out and stocked up on shoe laces, suspenders, men's braces – anything that might be needed in a crisis. Meanwhile, the deferred technical rehearsal played through without hitch.

For the first time since she'd walked into The Farren, Vanessa wore trousers to work. Her day would involve endless trips up and down stairs, and would end late. Seeing her stride past, Doyle ran after her to give her a postcard. The picture was a decidedly phallic view of the Eiffel Tower. On the reverse was scrawled, 'Surviving, just. Break a leg. H.'

'It's from –'

'No names,' warned Doyle.

Later as she snatched a moment to bring her accounts up to date, there came a tap at the door. 'Just a mo!' Alistair was the only person who knocked and waited. Running her fingers through her hair, she hurried to open the door. A stranger stood in the corridor. A stranger until –

'Nessie, I've come to smoke the pipe of peace.'

'Joanne! Good heavens – you've –'

'Gone blonde! We all reach for the bottle in the end.'

Vanessa stepped back to let Joanne come in. 'Tea?' She lit the gas under the kettle, mixing up powdered milk while Joanne opened drawers and stood on tiptoe to peer at shelves and inside the big wardrobe. From her eye's tail as she measured out tea leaves, Vanessa saw Joanne pushing her finger into a box of lead disks used for weighting flimsy hems.

Realising she'd been seen, Joanne grinned. 'You've really got under the skin of this job. Why am I surprised? I remember how scared you were at the thought of promotion in the WAAF, but you passed every exam without breaking sweat.'

'It didn't feel like it at the time. Still like a strong brew?'

'Mm. I've brought something for your emergency drawer.' Joanne presented Vanessa with a paper-wrapped block. 'I asked our wardrobe lady what her most useful cupboard item was and she said, "Gin." I said I didn't think you drank it.'

Little you know, Vanessa thought, *though I like it pink*. Unwrapping the gift, she found a caramel-brown chunk. 'Fudge?'

'Solid beeswax, for when zip-fasteners get stuck. You'll get desperate calls from actors jammed into their costume, twenty-five seconds before they're due back on stage in something different. To free the metal teeth, rub wax vigorously back and forth until release occurs.'

'Golly. I hope I never have to free a man from his pants.'

Joanne gave her smoky laugh. 'I can see you kneeling in front of Ronald Gainsborough.'

'Not I.' Vanessa fluffed Joanne's flaxen waves. 'So, Jean Harlow, what happened?'

Apparently, the director of *High Jinx* had woken up one morning convinced that the chorus line should match head to toe. 'Mr Stephen took three goes to strip out my natural colour.

God knows how long it'll take to grow out. I may have to be blonde till I retire. I flatly refused to have my eyebrows done.'

'Quite right. Who knows where it'd stop?' Vanessa touched her own, disordered curls which were crying out again for Mr Stephen's touch.

'Nessie,' Joanne began as Vanessa said, 'Look, I know we – '

'You go first,' Vanessa said. 'You're the elder. Well, you're the blonder.'

'All right. I was a cow when you lived with me. And you were right, I was envious. You were set up in your new job, everything falling into place. Whereas I – '

'Whoa,' Vanessa stopped her. 'You have a part in a West End show. A flat, a boyfriend. What do I have that you don't?'

Joanne shrugged, embarrassed. 'Hope. If war hadn't happened, I'd have been a leading light by now.'

'If war hadn't happened, I'd have been a commercial artist, designing custard powder packaging, wearing horn-rimmed specs.'

'Is it true, your ASM has been given a role?'

Vanessa handed Joanne tea in a china cup. 'As Lady Agatha Carlise. Complete with an Equity card.'

'That's what I mean.' Joanne blew on the hot liquid, sending a mini wave over the rim. 'Being in the WAAF pushed me down the ladder. I'm hoofing in the chorus line while posh girls who floated around Whitehall doing a bit of typing get the plum parts. Who do I have to sleep with to get into a legitimate play?' Joanne added extra saccharine to her cup from a tin she kept in her handbag. 'I warned you what a beastly, soul-destroying profession this is, yet you strolled into a job.' She laughed humourlessly. 'Listen to me. Lady Jealousy-Green. I oughtn't to have taken it out on you.'

No, Vanessa agreed silently. Nor on Alistair.

'Oh, and I have no boyfriend. The Gorgeous Specimen and I

split up. He was nabbed by the girl who moved in after you, actually. It made me realise . . . well, you can't buy loyalty, can you?'

'Not since the war, dearie.'

They drank their tea, and Joanne announced she must drag her backside to the theatre. 'Afternoon matinee, the two cruellest words in the English language.' At the door, she paused, saying, 'You ought to know – while I was being bleached, Mr Stephen's second-in-command –'

'Stuart?'

'– was shampooing one of your actresses. They were chatting about Lady Windermere. He mentioned Commander Redenhall, that business of the sinking ship and leaving sailors to drown –'

'What the hell does Stuart know about sea warfare?'

'Your actress asked the same thing, in language mighty rich.'

'Was it Miss Konstantiva?'

'Don't know but when she'd finished, Stuart was mincemeat.'

'Good.' Rosa had been dropped into occupied France during the war, Doyle had told Vanessa in confidence. Hers was a distinguished war record, and she admired Alistair.

'Do you want to know who started the slander? It was the lady wife. She's been scattering poisoned nuggets for months. Not very "Honourable", is it?'

Vanessa shook her head – in warning. Alistair was standing in the doorway. Macduff's nose pushed past his leg, seeking out the newcomer. 'Jo, shush.'

Joanne failed to pick up her signals. 'She's dumping him for a man who has a title coming his way, and wants to justify herself. Stephen and Stuart are such remorseless gossips, before we knew it, we were convinced Redenhall was a terrible, bad egg. Well, not you. You stuck up for him.'

'Jo, *shut up*. The man you're speaking of is right behind you.'

Joanne eased around, clearly hoping Vanessa was joking. She sagged. 'Please don't tell me you heard. I'll die!'

'Then I won't tell you.' Alistair looked impressive in one of his grey suits, his Navy coat over his shoulders. 'Are you coming or leaving?'

'Just going.' Joanne produced her heart-stopping smile, while the indefinable 'it' that Vanessa had always envied spread through her like steam through pipes. 'What a darling dog,' she exclaimed, though she couldn't hide her recoil as Macduff flopped on his back, proudly displaying his stump. 'I didn't know dogs could get about on three legs.'

'Macduff can do everything except take corners fast.' Alistair asked Vanessa if she'd mind looking after the dog. 'I'm meeting my financial man. I'll be about four hours.' Tipping his hat, he went.

Shutting Macduff in, Vanessa walked Joanne to the stage door. When she got back, having been delayed a few minutes, the dog had stripped the innards out of a kapok-stuffed cushion. She had to pick the fibres out of his ears and teeth, and because he'd swallowed some, he was sick.

'Another diversion to get me through the day,' she told him. She wondered how much Alistair had heard of Joanne's revelations.

When he returned to collect Macduff, he said only, 'Was that your WAAF friend, the one who lives on Phoenix Street?'

'Yes. I'm glad she stopped by. It takes courage to apologise.' Had Joanne actually apologised? Vanessa supposed she had in her way. 'How was your meeting?'

'Frank and open. If box office takings aren't strong from day one, we're done.'

Vanessa watched the first dress rehearsal from the wings. Ronnie Gainsborough complained that the ladies' immense sleeves were like barrage balloons crossing the sun. At the end of Act One, Vanessa was called on to repair Miss Abbott's morning dress, which had snagged on something sharp.

'Our stays are too severe,' Noreen Ruskin complained as she made her Act Two exit.

The actresses had rehearsed in long concert skirts and frilled blouses, and were suddenly adjusting to corsets, stiff collars, heavy flounces. Some had trouble controlling their breath or producing their lines powerfully.

During the interval break, Vanessa visited Rosa in the dressing room she shared with Gwenda Mason. The women were sipping ginger beer, their dresses loosened, their hair flattened under flesh-coloured wig caps.

'It's always the same with a period play,' Rosa reassured Vanessa. 'It's why it's the *first* dress rehearsal. We'll grow used to our packaging. Have a ginger beer.'

'Miss Ruskin is threatening to change her corset for a liberty bodice.'

'She has cousins in the country who send her butter and eggs. She'll have to loosen her laces or cut down on the scones.'

Gwenda pitched in, 'Trouble is, we spent the war slopping about in siren suits and comfy old skirts. Our middles have relaxed.'

Rosa agreed. 'It's hard getting used to Victorian boning.' Under her cap, her hair gleamed like coconut ice and Vanessa wished she could ask more about her set-to with Stuart. Gwenda's presence inhibited her, so after finishing her drink, Vanessa toured the dressing rooms, collecting up smalls for washing and costumes for mending.

A tall, heavy-set man was waiting outside her room. He had a bowler hat in his hand, a hip-flask at his lips. It was the silent man at Johnny Quinnell's graveside. It was Billy Chalker.

Chapter Twenty-Nine

He spoke first. 'Mrs Kingcourt, I presume.' Ponderous jowls, sprouts of grey hair over his ears, he had the look of a sombre clown.

'You were at my dad's funeral.'

'Not I.'

'You were with Eva. Did you know I'd been looking for you?'

He peered at her. He had loose flesh around his eyes, but his gaze was sharp, and sloe-black. 'You're Johnny's daughter?'

'And you must be Eva's brother.' She stuck out her hand, regretting doing so when he took it in a butcher's grip. 'But you don't call yourself, 'St Clair'?' she said.

'"Chalker" is a stage-name. I'm the family black sheep. With a priest for a brother, a pseudonym was a matter of urgency, though I teased Father Joseph that we both liked dressing up in frocks. Weren't you in uniform when I saw you last?'

'I was.'

'And Eva gave you a key.'

Vanessa pulled it from under her top layers.

Chalker rumbled, '"A very little key will open a very heavy door." Dickens said all the useful things and Wilde, all the amusing things.'

'But do you know what it opens, Mr Chalker? Miss Yorke – our costume-maker – suggested it might be a sewing box.'

'It could. Our brother Joseph brought one back from France, after he spent a few months there at a seminary. A pretty thing. Eva treasured it.'

'Do you have it?'

'No. Perhaps it went with her when she moved in with the nuns.'

'They said everything had been sent back to you.'

'Tricky customers, nuns. My dear, this is all very charming but I'm here for a fitting.'

'Costume fitting?' Vanessa was unable to stop herself imagining Chalker in a frock, cavorting in striped stockings. *Come on, Billy-Boy, show us an ankle!*

'You are the wardrobe lady,' he said patiently. 'I am the new Parker.'

'Oh, I see.' Vanessa detected whisky on Chalker's breath. 'You need –'

'The full butler's rig. The unfortunate chap I've replaced is slimmer than I.'

That was an understatement. Billy Chalker was barrel-chested with wide shoulders. Nothing on the rails would fit him.

As she fetched her tape measure, she heard Chalker say, 'New wardrobe, new mirror. That bomb . . . I came here after Eva was hurt and picked my way over splintered wood and glass. Ah, that might explain the disappearance of the sewing box. Damaged, like Eva, past repair.'

At that moment, Alistair came in. 'I heard you'd arrived, Chalker. Welcome back to The Farren.'

'Goodness, Redenhall, you've grown taller since I saw you

last.' Chalker returned the handshake. 'And handsomer. Did you ask Terence Rolf to engage me?'

'Nothing to do with me.'

'Still, I shan't complain. Playing Parker will be easier than Widow Twankey twice nightly and one can't turn down anything at my age.' Chalker raised his arms to allow Vanessa to take his chest measurement. 'Nobody wanted Dames during the war. Bad for morale. I was too arthritic for ENSA, too ugly for film work.'

Terence Rolf walked in. 'Still complaining, Billy? Glad to see you back here in your proper capacity. Let's introduce you to the cast. Mrs Kingcourt can finish off later.'

From the doorway, Chalker issued a plea. 'No scratchy serge, if you please. Brings my thighs out in a rash.'

'Chalker's more used to wearing cotton drawers,' Rolf chuckled.

'*Au contraire*, I've handled many trouser-parts in my time.' A moment later, Chalker flared at Vanessa, 'Johnny Quinnell was dark-haired, with eyes to match. You're an imposter, trading on his name. Stealing Eva's laurels. Stealing her room.'

Shocked, Vanessa looked to Alistair. Billy Chalker burst out laughing.

'Jesting, dear girl. But don't go round saying you're Johnny's. He treated my sister abysmally. Good as killed Eva and her child. You wouldn't want to be his daughter.'

'Wait!' Vanessa made to follow Chalker into the corridor but Alistair pulled her back.

'Didn't you smell the booze on his breath? I hope Rolf knows wht he's doing, hiring him. If he rolls off the bloody stage –' He urged her to concentrate on the play. 'When it's bringing in revenue, we'll talk all about this. Please Vanessa, I'm ignoring my divorce, Fern's slander and financial pressure. If I can, so can you. Organise Chalker's costume. Tomorrow's the final dress rehearsal.'

'Really?' she said tartly. 'I'd forgotten.'

'I hadn't forgotten that yesterday was the anniversary of your husband's death. I admire you.' He kissed her quickly on the forehead and left.

The second dress rehearsal was a concerto of fluffed lines, electrical fluctuations, blown bulbs and snapped violin strings. Tanith was so overwhelmed, she seized up.

Terence Rolf, acting director now that Aubrey Hinshaw was gone, shouted, 'Young woman, you've the shortest part in the theatrical cannon. All you say is "Yes, mamma".' Tanith shed helpless tears. 'My giddy aunt,' Rolf snorted. 'Chalker, got your hip flask? Give our young amateur a shot, see if it turns her professional.'

Tanith choked on the whisky and Chalker slapped her back, saying in rhythm, 'Yes, mamma! Yes, mamma!'

Though it was his first appearance as Parker, Chalker was word perfect. A drinker he might be, but he was no hopeless drunk. Stage-Stock had provided him with a butler's costume that needed only an inch letting down on the cuffs and trouser-bottoms. Even so, Clemency Abbott objected, complaining loudly, 'He puts me out of scale. Lady Windermere would never tolerate a butler she has to lean backwards to instruct.'

Noreen Ruskin, on her way to her dressing room, soothed, 'Darling, he makes you look cute as a doll.' She then added in a stage whisper, 'Wooden.'

Clemency burst into tears.

Vanessa sat in the wings, needle case ready, because in all this rising tension, accidents happened. Swishing hems and boned sleeves caught on the furniture. Rosa got carpet burn under her chin, snapping open her fan too fast. Clemency's morning gown tore yet again, on something projecting from the table where she arranged her roses. The carpenter blamed it on a rogue splinter.

Act Two began with missed cues. Patrick Carnford whispered to Vanessa, 'If Ronnie pulls any harder on his hair, he'll open up a second bald front.'

'The worse the dress rehearsal, the better the opening night. Isn't that what they say?'

Carnford laughed at her. '"They" say anything to stave off despair. We still haven't had our dinner out, Mrs K. How about being my date on opening night?'

'Um – I'm not sure I'm even . . .'

'Coming to the after-show party? Of course you are. I shall order us a taxi.'

'Do I feel like Eva's daughter?' Vanessa asked herself. It was evening, November 27th, the day before opening night. She was steaming up the windows of the wardrobe room. She'd washed the actors' shirts and because the weather had turned damp, she was having to iron them dry.

'Am I Eva's child?' she asked her misty reflection in the mirror. 'I am,' she intoned. Then made a face. 'Billy's right, if Eva was Mum and Johnny was Dad, why aren't I dark? And how come I'm so small?'

She put on a child's voice. '*I was made from the last bit of pastry when there wasn't enough for a whole pie.*'

She continued the self-interrogation as she plied her iron over damp linen, her busy reflection keeping her company. 'I'd never felt such love in my whole life as I felt in my few moments with Eva. Explain that, if I wasn't hers.'

She tried to see this familiar room through a five-year-old's eyes. She and Johnny had sat through *Sleeping Beauty*, Johnny cat-calling Billy Chalker who'd been playing the Dame. Up the steep stairs, knocking at the door. Eva had risen in shock. Young as she was, Vanessa had sensed Eva's distress. Yet Eva had greeted Vanessa as a fellow-soul. She'd stolen a curl and put it away. An image opened in Vanessa's mind, a tantalising glimpse. 'She put it away in a chocolate cake.'

Vanessa rested her iron and focused on the table. The memory she'd summoned in was of a circular, chocolate brown work box.

She searched the room, knowing perfectly well she'd find nothing. In frustration, she took the golden key from around her neck and hung it on the door hook, with her scarf and greatcoat. Perhaps some things were not meant to be found.

After hanging up her shirts, she settled down to repairs. The tear in Lady Windermere's gown was beyond her skill; tomorrow, she'd have to have one of Penny's girls mend it. Her last, least enjoyable, task that night was to remove the cotton underarm pads, which protected the costumes from the actors' perspiration. She dropped the soiled ones into washing suds and added rose-water. As they soaked, she sewed in new ones. This would become a nightly chore. Eleven on the dot came a call from Doyle.

'Taxi's here, ma'am.'

Another day over, the last insulated from reality. Tomorrow night, the curtain would rise on a real play, with a real audience and hard-nosed reviewers. By this time tomorrow, they'd know if they had a hit or a flop.

Lady Windermere's Fan opened on Thursday, November 28th. A sustained publicity effort in the run-up had generated high excitement. The PR Officer, Robin Amery, had bravely teased the press about the onstage chemistry between the star actors. He'd written up the lavish costumes and his reward was a phone that hadn't stopped ringing for days.

During the afternoon, the technicians did a run-through under Cottrill's direction. The actors began arriving from six o'clock. Vanessa checked costumes and accessories so many times, she was in danger of worrying perfection to the bone. Tearing herself away, she toured the dressing rooms, wishing the cast good luck in her own way. She preferred 'You're going to be wonderful!' to 'Break a leg', for all Tanith had told her that the phrase had nothing to do with cracked bones but referred to curtains called 'legs' which masked the wings from the audience. To 'break a leg' implied a glut of curtain calls, putting a strain on the infrastructure.

Fifty minutes before curtain-up, Vanessa changed into a black dress with a buttonhole of white gardenias that Patrick had presented to her. She had erected a card table in the dressing room shared by Rosa, Gwenda, Maxine Shadwell and Emmeline Perkins, which would be her station during the show. Setting out the tools of her trade, she muttered, 'This is what answering ads in *The Stage* gets you.' She'd seen Alistair pacing the corridor, hands clasped behind him, a deadpan expression on his face. Nerves, his style.

Rosa arrived, pulling off her hat and coat. 'The rain it raineth.' She looked at Vanessa's table. 'Five of us in here will make a tin of sardines look roomy.'

Gwenda came in, her Macintosh gleaming. 'It's running rivulets on Farren Court with a surface of sludge from the bomb site.'

'Doyle's sprinkling sand on the footways,' Vanessa assured them.

'Good. I love winter, except for the dark nights and the weather.' Gwenda switched on the lights around her mirror. 'Crikey, here it comes. The gut-shimmie. The intestinal two-step. Pray silence while I recite the actors' prayer: "Dear Lord, make me good, the audience kind and the critics human. Amen".'

Rosa handed round tiny shots of pre-war vodka. 'Never get nerves myself.' She had to be lying. Her cheeks were bloodless as she downed her liquor in one, then crammed her hair under a band and applied Max Factor pancake. 'I heard we've critics coming from *The Times*, *Telegraph*, *Daily Express* and all viperous shades in between. Coming to the after-show party?' she asked Vanessa.

'With Patrick, yes.'

Gwenda whooped. 'Is he behind that fragrant buttonhole?'

Vanessa touched the gardenias in embarrassment. 'They have to have come from abroad. I hate to think how much they cost.'

'Then don't think,' said Rosa, 'or you'll start imagining you have to repay him somehow. Let him see you home, but do not ask him up for coffee.'

Heck, Vanessa thought. *What have I let myself in for?* A note had accompanied the posy. 'Prince Charming requests the company of Cinderella.' Vanessa had deduced from it that the party was an evening-dress occasion and had nearly cried off because her one long frock was blue dimity, made for her while she was still at school. In the end, Penny Yorke had saved her. Calling with a good-luck card, Penny had read Patrick's note and snorted. 'Any man who calls himself Prince Charming deserves his date to turn up in a fertiliser sack. But you, precious, shall go to the ball.' At tea-time, a parcel had arrived. It contained a dress.

The tannoy announced the half. Thirty-five minutes to go.

Rosa went into a breathing routine, exhaling long, sibilant streams while Gwenda gargled and began her vocal exercises.

'Moo-mah-may. Moo-mah-may. Jiggety-jiggety-jog. Jiggety-jiggety-jug.'

Five minutes of that, then it was corsets on.

As Rosa and Gwenda got into their gowns, Maxine Shadwell and Emmeline Perkins swept in with cheerful 'Darlings!' Not needed until the second act, they sat around in robes, drinking tea, comparing notes on their journeys in. They discussed if, to be classed as 'cats and dogs', rain had to be bouncing out of the gutters, or if 'teeming' was enough.

Gwenda, reddening her lips with Leichner, asked in dismay, 'What if it stops people coming?'

'We get to eat the ice-lollies the usherettes don't sell. I hear it's a choice of frozen carrots or rhubarb pulp tonight.' Rosa skimmed corn silk over her makeup, put on her flesh-coloured cap and lowered her wig over it. Instantly, she was a Duchess. 'Fan. Hell. Where's my fan?'

'By your elbow, darling.'

The tannoy crackled and a strangled voice announced, 'Fifteen minutes, please, ladies and gentlemen.'

'Who's been giving that Switt boy elocution lessons?'

Miss Eddrich's dresser poked her head round the door. 'All the boxes are occupied. Lots of flash-bulbs in the foyer. Lady Ververs has assumed the place of honour, her butler in attendance.'

'Lady Who?' Maxine Shadwell demanded.

'Tanith Stacey's grandma, Dido Meredith as was,' Emmeline informed her. 'I've heard that when they play the National Anthem, she bows and waves. Ooh, listen.'

They could hear a rumbling, like potatoes tumbling into a hopper far away. An audience was gathering. Alistair came to wish everyone well, and Vanessa was able to appreciate him up close in his evening-wear. He told them he'd be watching from the Bovary Box. He'd sent flowers to all the cast and to Vanessa. Early snowdrops. Vanessa's were in water, on her table upstairs to enjoy later. Alistair's glance at her buttonhole prompted her to mumble, 'Your flowers were lovely. Are, I mean. They'll last. These won't.'

He raised an eyebrow. 'Are you in my party tonight?'

'I – I don't know. I'm with Patrick.'

'Then I will see you later.' The tannoy summoned the beginners to the stage and Alistair went.

Patrick Carnford came next to wish them 'Merry times.' Hair slicked to dark gold, he looked supremely elegant in a grey morning coat, his silk cravat pinned with a pearl spike. He wasn't among the beginners so could lounge against the doorframe and smile at their bustle. 'Remind me,' he said to Vanessa, 'is it *The Importance* or *Lady Windermere* tonight?'

'*Lady Windermere*,' she told him, horrified.

'Patrick is teasing.' Rosa told him to shift so she could get out. 'Though anyone who slogged eight shows a week with ENSA might forget who they're meant to be on any given night.'

'Or they might wish to,' Patrick came back with feeling. Rosa laughed and went on her way. Billy Chalker emerged from his dressing room, and a moment later, Ronnie Gainsborough and Clemency Abbott passed by on their way to the wings.

A minute later came the opening bars of the overture. It dawned on Vanessa that she hadn't seen Tanith.

Chapter Thirty

In the tiny upstairs dressing room that Tanith shared with the female understudy, Vanessa found panic. Tanith had knocked over a bottle of wet-white. Liquid makeup.

'I didn't put the top on. Do something, Vanessa!' Glycerine and zinc oxide trailed down Lady Agatha's costume. 'I'm on in five minutes!'

More like two. Vanessa hustled Tanith down to her station, where she scraped the mess off the skirt. She then sponged the silk with diluted white vinegar, which she'd bottled for such an eventuality. The wet-white came off, leaving a damp patch on the lemon yellow silk.

'I smell like a chip shop,' Tanith wailed. 'I look as if I've wet myself. Mr Rolf will sack me.'

Peter Switt came running up, red-faced and sweating. 'Tanith, you nut-case, get going! Beginners are on stage already.'

'"Miss Stacey" to you,' Vanessa corrected. 'And she will make her cue, never fear.' Grabbing a diffuser of lavender water, she sprayed Tanith's skirts, masking the smell. She ruched up the silk. 'Hold your skirt as though you're keeping your hem off the floor. Show the lace of your petticoat. There. Aren't you meant to have a reticule?'

'It's upstairs!'

'Here.' Vanessa tore off her gardenias. 'Hold these over the stain. Nobody will know. Run!'

'Bless you, Nessie.'

Noreen Ruskin was watching from her dressing room doorway. 'A worthy successor to Eva.'

'I hope so, Miss Ruskin.'

The actress came into the corridor, head forward, eyes narrowed. 'I'm absolutely certain I know you from somewhere else.'

As applause rang out at the close of Act One, Vanessa crept backstage, curious to see, to hear and absorb. She found Patrick awaiting his Act Two cue.

'How's it going?' she whispered.

'They're laughing in the right places, and sometimes in the wrong places, which is so much nicer.'

'How's Mr Chalker doing?'

'Got a big clap on his entrance, which will please him. I daresay people expected him to come on in a spotted frock.'

Miss Ruskin, sucking on an aniseed ball, glared. Roy FitzPeter, playing the Australian, Mr Hopper, stood silently, as if in prayer. Clemency Abbott stroked a stuffed, plush kitten. Everyone dealt with stage fright in their own fashion. Out of sight of the stage, a gramophone attached to loud-speakers began pealing Strauss waltzes to imply a ball in progress off-scene. Tom Cottrill was guarding it.

Devilment made Vanessa go up to the stage manager and murmur, 'No sightings of Back Row Flo?'

Cottrill kept his gaze on the spinning centre of a vinyl disk.

'I saw her, actually. I nipped out into the auditorium and there she was, two levels up, selling choc-ices.'

'Good God. Where on earth did she find choc-ices? I haven't seen one of those since 1940.'

'Touché, Mrs Kingcourt, touché.'

Vanessa couldn't imagine what had altered Cottrill's attitude until it struck her that, for the first time, she was wearing black. Neat, self-effacing, as a female employee should be. Cottrill wasn't a deep soul; he was just a man. On stage, Tanith delivered her line with boisterous confidence. 'Yes, mamma.'

Vanessa projected silently to the unseen critics – we need this to work. Please love us. Irene Eddrich would make her entrance shortly in the mauve gown, and nothing would have dragged Vanessa away, though it meant enduring Ronnie Gainsborough tutting about 'interlopers' backstage. Miss Eddrich took up her position. She wore a velvet cloak, for warmth, and her dresser hovered near. On cue, the dresser held her arms and Irene let the cloak go. Neck, shoulder and arms gleamed like marble.

'Well?' Irene breathed, noticing Vanessa. 'Will I do?'

'Absolutely.'

Moments later, Vanessa heard an audible gasp, followed by spontaneous applause. She wished Hugo could have witnessed the effect of his creative vision.

When the curtain fell at the end of Act Four, applause went on for four minutes, twenty-two seconds. Cottrill timed it. There were five curtain calls. After the final curtain, the dressing-room corridor filled with well-wishers, with pressmen and photographers.

Vanessa squeezed through the crush, collecting up items of costume. She piled them on her table for the morning. Locking herself in, she prepared for her date. She would be one of the party booked to dine at Pinoli's. Alistair would be there, and Irene but not, thankfully, Ronnie Gainsborough or Miss Abbott.

The dress Penny had loaned her had been made for a petite client who'd then declared its flame-orange colour 'impossible to wear'. It was ankle-length and sleeveless, with straps just wide enough to cover a brsserie, and was the sexiest thing Vanessa had ever worn. A nipped-in waist made the most of a skirt as full as the Board of Trade allowed. As Fern's mustard-gold hat had done before, the colour seduced amber notes from her eyes and warmed her skin. Vanessa wasted several minutes trying to coax her curls into a bun. In the end, she brushed them vigorously and pushed them back over her ears with diamante clips. Checking her reflection, she decided the deep neckline needed to be filled. A diamond pendant or a gold dog-collar would be perfect . . . in her daydreams. At home, she had a string of cultured pearls, but no time to fetch them. In the end, she dried off Alistair's snow-drops and pinned several to her bosom, then hung her gold key on a blonde ribbon so it nestled in the cleft of her breasts. She'd felt naked without it.

Coat or no coat? Rain hammered against the window, but not hard enough to extinguish vanity. Cramming on her san-dals, grabbing her bag, an umbrella and a filmy, silver stole, she ran to the lift.

'Carnford's gone ahead, didn't you know?' Gwenda Mason called from the stage door where she was waiting with Rosa, Maxine and Emmeline. Elation glowed in her cheeks and eyes. She'd glimpsed a girl in a Victorian bonnet, she said, in the upper circle. For the merest second.

Maxine Shadwell said, 'Patrick waited for you till gone seven.'

Before Vanessa could answer, Alistair joined them. 'Where are the others?'

Maxine repeated, 'Carnford's gone ahead with Miss Eddrich. Roy, Vic and Miss Ruskin are on their way. We're a party of ten.'

Rosa whispered to Vanessa, 'Irene was overwhelmed by the press, so Patrick whisked her out. My dear, it's fatal to be late for someone like him. There's always a rival ready to snatch your place. Oh dear. What became of the gardenias?'

The open stage door was letting in rain and Vanessa wrapped her stole around her shoulders. 'It feels worse, somehow, to be stood up while wearing orange.'

Rosa tutted sympathetically but it was Alistair who answered. 'You'll have to make do with me. Shall we go?'

Doyle informed them that their cabs were waiting on Bow Street, adding for Alistair and Vanessa's ears alone, 'Miss Bovary and Mr Edwin Bovary are to join your table.'

Alistair's expression shifted. 'Why is Edwin coming?'

'Miss Bovary's escort.'

'Can't they go to Rules with Mr and Mrs Rolf?' Alistair shrugged. 'Don't answer that, Doyle.'

The doorman said he'd fetch Macduff down once the theatre was empty. 'We're having fish and chips, being as it's First Night. Enjoy your dinner too, Sir and Madam.'

That, Alistair told him, depended on the reviews. 'The first editions will arrive during coffee.'

Doyle had ordered four cabs, and Alistair and Vanessa found themselves alone in one. They reached the western end of Shaftsbury Avenue without a word wasted between them. His arm lay along the seat back, his sleeve brushing her shoulders.

Their driver made a sharp right into Wardour Street and Alistair's hand came down on her shoulder. She felt its warm weight. Skin never lies and hers felt as if it were purring. Not safe in taxis?

Lethal. She turned toward him. Her lips stung, wanting to seduce a kiss from him before the taxi stopped. Loyalty to Patrick Carnford had fizzled away. After all, he'd jilted her. 'Alistair?'

He was staring out towards the brick ribbon of Wardour Street.

'I wish you'd kiss me.' It was meant to be teasing; it came out fraught.

'I know you do.' He turned a maddened look on her. 'But you're Carnford's date, not mine.'

'I'm wearing your flowers, and I think he was being kind, or flirting.'

'Carnford knows what he wants and usually gets it. Don't look at him as you're looking at me now.'

'Like this?' She bent close, her lips brushing his. Alistair leaned forward and tapped the dividing glass. 'Drop us here, driver. We'll walk the last fifty yards. Do us good.'

Chapter Thirty-One

At Pinoli's, three tables had been pulled together, spread with linen and crystal. Patrick Carnford presided at one end and Irene Eddrich at the other. Thanks to Vanessa's umbrella turning inside out in a gust of wind, she and Alistair arrived rather dishevelled and moments behind Miss Bovary and Edwin. Edwin was being divested of his scarlet-lined cloak.

The same waiter took Vanessa's stole. Noreen Ruskin, frowning in her habitual way, exclaimed as she saw Vanessa's dress, 'You've a dose of courage, wearing a gown that colour. Did you hire it, dear?'

Alistair jumped in. 'Any colour suits a sparkling complexion.'

'You mean "windswept",' Vanessa said.

Quietly, he answered, 'You've bathed yourself in candle-flame. Go sit by Patrick, set him alight. I shall sit by Irene.'

Irene Eddrich made room for him. 'We've ordered as the kitchen has stayed open late for us. Mushroom fricassee, then lamb cutlets. We're all having the same. Miss Bovary, would you like to sit on the other side of me, and Edwin beside Gwenda?'

Patrick rose as Vanessa took the seat beside him. 'How cruel, arriving with another man.'

'Sorry. I spent too long titivating in front of the mirror.'

'Not one second wasted.' Patrick gave her exposed shoulders

and cleavage a leisurely appreciation, though he frowned faintly at the snowdrops. 'I had to dash. A pushy type with a notebook was asking Irene how it felt to share a stage with Clemency Abbott. "The mature actress and the rising star". Quite uncalled for.' He kissed Vanessa's hand. 'You look utterly charming. Do I?'

'Of course, but aren't you the third most handsome man in England?'

'Fourth. I've slipped, but Ronnie's at number six so I can bear it.' He studied her ersatz necklace. 'That little key hints at much to be unlocked, Mrs K.'

Vanessa's glass was filled by a waiter, and she savoured the champagne, leaning forward to chat with Roy FitzPeter who confessed to being in agony.

'At this moment, a dozen reviewers are penning judgement on us. It only takes one to have toothache or a gouty knee, and we're slain.' FitzPeter had left his Australian accent at the theatre.

'It's so much worse for you than me,' Vanessa admitted. The hardest part of her job was over. Until a new play was chosen, she had only to maintain the costumes in her care. She felt a sudden prickle and discovered that Miss Bovary was staring at her.

Miss Bovary hadn't touched her champagne. She was out of place among these jubilant, over-excited actors. Why come at all, Vanessa wondered? She formed an idea why when Miss Eddrich proposed a toast.

'To Commander Redenhall, who brought us back together.'

Everyone raised their glass, except Miss Bovary. Edwin got to his feet with an air of superior indulgence. Each cast-member was toasted in turn, more champagne ordered as the bottles ran dry. Tanith, the last to be feted, thanked them all for being so 'wonderful and lovely and kind'.

She blushed as Roy, her onstage fiancé, said, 'Thank *you* for

bringing such corking swagger to the words, "Yes, mamma"!'
FitzPeter had reverted to broad Australian.

Patrick tapped his glass with a spoon. 'Someone else deserves a
toast. She slips between the corridors, quiet of tread, yet without
her we would be – '

Miss Bovary arranged her features.

'Quite naked,' Patrick went on. 'I give you Mrs Kingcourt.'

'Oh, don't.' Vanessa shook her head.

Rosa put in softly, 'Not everybody loves the limelight, Patrick. Leave Vanessa be.'

Patrick was not to be deflected. 'A few weeks ago, I watched
a provincial production of The Scottish Play.'

'Bad luck,' Vic Pagnell commiserated. J Victor Pagnell was
well cast as Mr Dumby. Plump, affable.

'It was all right, but the costumes . . .' Patrick made a face of
pain. 'The ladies' frocks were cut from battlefield-surplus lavatory tents. The men sported belted hessian sacks and leggings
knitted from unravelled dishcloth. We, on the contrary, have
postured in silks and velvets and could not have done so but for
this girl.'

'It was Hugo,' Vanessa insisted. 'Hugo Brennan's work.'

'And Yorke of Mayfair,' Miss Bovary cut in. 'Without dear
Daphne and her niece, you would indeed have been naked, Mr
Carnford.'

'It's true,' Vanessa agreed.

Patrick wouldn't have it. 'Vanessa led the unit to victory after
the commanding officer was shot. As darling Bo would have said,
"No false modesty".'

Alistair raised his glass. 'To our Wardrobe Mistress, who stumbled into a job she was born to.'

'Well, we know the two of *you* get along rather well,' Miss

Bovary said. She stood up, murmuring something about the ladies' room but took a moment to address Alistair. 'Praising Mrs Kingcourt does you no credit. A man on the threshold of divorce should not arrive at a public place with an unattached widow, unless he wants to wipe the floor with her reputation. Poor judgement, Commander.'

'Leave my private life alone, Barbara. Leave Vanessa alone.'

Miss Bovary sniffed. 'We know about those photographs.'

Alistair's eyes grew cold. The dinner guests tensed. 'What do "we" know?'

'You two were caught in bed together.' Miss Bovary shifted her contempt from Alistair to Vanessa.

Vanessa knew she had a split second in which to rise above the accusation, or be buried. 'I've seen photographic stills of you wearing a lot less than I was on that occasion, Miss Bovary. I believe there's one of you dangling over the stage in nothing but fleshings and three sequinned hearts.'

Laughter greeted this, but Irene Eddrich silenced it. 'Go powder your nose, Miss Bovary. When you return, we will have changed the subject.'

Edwin Bovary drawled, 'I don't care for the mixing of actors with backstage. It never works.'

'Neither does my watch,' Vic Pagnell snapped, 'yet it tells perfect time twice a day. Shall we raise our glasses to Mrs Kingcourt, then sit down?'

The toast was given. 'Mrs Kingcourt!'

Noreen Ruskin leaned over the table, saying to Vanessa in a wondering voice, 'I *knew* I knew you. Knew the first time I saw you, at Wilton Bovary's funeral. You were in uniform, a clumsy colt of a girl.' Miss Ruskin nodded, certainty growing. 'You have your mother's eyes.'

'The colour of a good Amontillado sherry,' Patrick Carnford agreed. 'Too unusual for there to be any doubt.'

'Doubt about what?' Edwin Bovary demanded.

Patrick waved vaguely. 'Never mind. Here comes our food.'

Waiters came with trolleys. Hors d'oeuvres were served. Good humour spread around the table and Miss Bovary's return was hardly noticed. When the first course was cleared, Noreen Ruskin beckoned to Vanessa, who reluctantly went to her.

The older woman whispered, 'Your mother was my very dear friend, but she broke rules.'

'By not marrying my father?'

'She couldn't, could she?' From Miss Ruskin's painted eyes fell three or four tears. She fiddled for her handkerchief. 'We too shall be friends now. The past is our secret.'

'Yes, Miss Ruskin.' Vanessa had no idea what she was agreeing to.

Midnight struck. Champagne flowed up from the cellars, and by the time their main course had been removed, faces were flushed, the volume of chatter high. Dessert was mint fondants and coffee. A shout of 'Commander Redenhall, Sir!' went unheard.

A young man in woolly hat and muffler, trousers caught in with bicycle clips, stumped up to their table. 'Sir?' he bellowed. 'I've got them.'

Peter Switt dropped a wad of newsprint next to Alistair. 'The early editions, Sir. I've been all along Fleet Street, got the lot.'

Silence fell. Alistair's mouth tightened.

'Mr Cottrill's taken another lot to Rules,' Switt said. 'I biked here like a tornado.'

'Sink or swim, Commander,' Edwin Bovary murmured. 'I watched the play sitting next to the *Telegraph*'s reviewer. He scribbled furiously and sighed a lot.'

'I'll start with *The Times*.' Alistair flipped broadsheet pages till he found the review page. Vanessa could hardly breathe. She wanted to go to him, to be ready if, as Miss Bovary and Edwin clearly hoped, slaughter had been committed. Alistair was reading silently.

'Well, what does the blighter say?' Vic Pagnell demanded. 'Stop torturing us!'

Alistair finally looked around the table. He let the paper fall. 'Ladies and gentlemen, I'm deeply sorry – '

Patrick Carnford groaned. 'They've stuck the dagger in. We'll close, won't we?'

'Deeply sorry to tell you – ' Alistair locked eyes with Edwin Bovary – 'that we have a triumph on our hands.'

The Times, Thursday, November 28th, 1946

I went to The Farren tonight mourning the passing of Wilton Bovary, expecting I know not what. As the curtain rose, my rationed eye was seized by a spectacle of silk and the scene-painter's art. What followed was Wilde, pure but never simple. Like the best of trifles, *Lady Windermere's Fan* is sweet, filling and with a dash of dry cynicism. Irene Eddrich as Mrs Erlynne thrums with the complexity of a woman who knows herself to be bad, yet dares hope that the world might mistake her ravishing figure for virtue. Miss Eddrich's voice charms like a nightingale in an orchard at dusk. Patrick Carnford lights a fire under the part of Lord Windermere, a more seductive aristocrat than is generally served. One wonders why her Ladyship would entertain the darkly presumptuous Lord Darlington in her drawing room when her suave, wedded lord awaits her upstairs. Ronnie

Gainsborough as Darlington offers us a superb variant of Ronnie Gainsborough. Clemency Abbott is a pretty Lady Windermere, a good woman wronged. She has enough depth to remind us that Wilde was an Irishman, a grain of sand in the English oyster. This production is a pearl.

Only the *Daily Express* gave a lukewarm rating, calling the play 'frothily old-fashioned', but everyone agreed that *Express* readers would expect Wilde to be nothing else. After every review had been dissected and wrung dry, and the last champagne drunk, Roy FitzPeter suggested they all move on to a jazz club.

Rosa shuddered. 'I to my bed. Shall we share a taxi, Vic?'

Victor Pagnell took her up on it.

Vanessa looked at Alistair. 'Fancy it?'

'Ask your boyfriend.'

Patrick was keen, as were Irene and Gwenda. Miss Bovary declined, and took Edwin as an escort home for Miss Ruskin and herself. Edwin looked so deflated, had he been anybody else, Vanessa would have felt sorry for him.

It was a party of seven who crammed around a wobbly table in an upstairs room of a pub off the Strand. On a postage-stamp stage, The Solomon Risco Quintet was tuning up. They were a modernist jazz ensemble all the way from New York. The new, big thing according to Roy FitzPeter.

'Is Solomon Risco deaf?' Patrick demanded when, after ten minutes, it dawned on them that the band, far from tuning up, was playing its repertoire. A distonal segment reached its climax. 'This your kind of thing, Commander?'

'Not exactly. Whenever I sailed the *Quarrel* out of port, I played "The Teddy Bears' Picnic" over the loud speakers.'

People were standing to applaud. A man in a tweed jacket,

pebble glasses glinting, called out in old Etonian accents, 'That was burnin', man.'

Vanessa started to giggle. Nerves. Whenever Patrick reached for his glass, his leg slid against her thigh. A touch that her dress was too fine to repel. *He knows what he wants and usually gets it.* When the same old Etonian applauded a steel guitar solo and shouted, 'Blow that thing, man,' she convulsed with laughter. It was too much for Patrick too. Roy FitzPeter hissed, 'Luddites.'

Alistair apologised. 'But I don't think I could dance like that girl in the corner.'

A young woman with severe, black bangs, in denims and a man's shirt, was doing an impression of somebody swimming to the top of a cylindrical fish tank.

'If you children are aching to dance, we grownups won't mind if you go elsewhere.' Gwenda smiled at Roy. Whatever she made of the music, she clearly liked him. So did Tanith, who chirped, 'I'll stay, too.'

'Go, go,' Gwenda urged. 'You know you want to.'

'All right – so long as Roy undertakes to get you both safely home,' Alistair said. Outside, he asked Irene, Patrick and Vanessa, 'Can I choose the next place?'

His choice was the subterranean Wishbone Club where he'd once taken Vanessa, Hugo and Tanith. As they walked downstairs, the band was playing 'Stormy Weather'.

They got a table from a party just leaving. Vanessa was alarmed to see Alistair remove five pound notes from his wallet and order more champagne. She'd have preferred a cup of tea.

He and Irene took to the floor immediately. Vanessa sat alone while Patrick visited the men's room. She didn't want to watch

Alistair with another woman, but it was like trying not to watch a high-wire artist take a leap. Irene had reached the boneless state, letting Alistair take her weight.

Patrick returned, misreading her expression. 'Been a long day, hasn't it?'

'I'll say. But now we don't have to be up at dawn. We can lie in bed until eleven.' She made a face. 'I mean – '

'*One* can lie in bed until eleven. But one shouldn't, you know. It's bad for one's circulation. Shall we, Mrs Kingcourt?' He led her to the floor.

Vanessa discovered what it was to be partnered by a trained dancer. Patrick talked nonsense, his breath warm against her ear. He masked her less steady footwork. 'How well you stood up to Babs Bovary,' he said. 'Was she really dangling from a wire wearing nothing but a smile?'

'She was about seventeen, I should think. Patrick, did you like my father?'

'Very much. He taught me to act, how to time a comic line. How to raise a single, sardonic eyebrow.' Patrick demonstrated. 'His death pulled down a pillar of my world. I miss him.'

'So do I, though I never knew him. Thank you for saying good things about him.' She reached up and kissed Patrick lightly on the lips.

He stopped her moving away and kissed her slowly, an invitation to a night together, but when the kiss ended, he said, 'That was sisterly. Am I to take it that we won't be waking at eleven tomorrow, in each other's arms?'

'No. I'm sorry.'

'So am I. But not entirely surprised.'

She followed his glance to where Alistair and Irene swayed.

Patrick said, 'Barbara Bovary was right, a man on the cusp of divorce is a man about to take a murky, public bath. Don't join him in it.' He looked at her. 'I think I will invite Irene to dance. Shall I, Vanessa?'

She understood the code. 'Ask her.'

When the four of them returned to their table, the men took off their jackets and bow ties. When the music started again, Patrick extended his hand to Irene.

'Fancy kicking a trotter?'

'Why not, Mr Almond-Soap.' Irene gave the bent smile that had made her famous. 'Let's see if it's still true, what they claim.'

'Remind me?'

'"Atkinson's Almond Shaving Soap, smooth as butter in moments".' Irene explained to Vanessa, 'He was the face on the advertisement.'

'Until I turned thirty. It lathers up beautifully at room temperature. The company still sends me several bars a month.'

'Now we know why you have so many girlfriends.' Irene shot Vanessa a look. No spite in it, no triumph. It said simply, 'leave your apple on the table, someone else will eat it'. On the dance floor they melded perfectly because their heights matched. *I hope I never regret this*, Vanessa thought, picking up her wine glass.

Alistair said, 'Well?'

'He wanted more than I was willing to hand over.'

'And now he won't dance with you.'

'Actually, I turned him down. It's all up to you now.'

'I'm thinking of sitting out the rest of the evening.'

'Perhaps you don't like my dress. You prefer *greige* to candle-flame.' It was a reference to Irene's dress. *Greige* was this year's 'must have' shade from Paris. 'Must have' because it was pretty much the only one on offer.

'I told you before, I don't notice clothes.'

'Then why on earth did you imagine you and Fern were suited?'

There was a cooling in his eyes. Pride touched, etiquette offended – but not terminally because he rustled up a smile. 'I rather liked her without clothes.'

She mauled her wine glass. 'So, for all you care, I could have turned up tonight in trousers?'

'You could, but I wouldn't have danced with you.'

'I'm not wearing trousers.'

'Are you asking – or waiting for me to ask you to dance?'

'I'm asking, Alistair.'

The last time they'd been this close, she'd been in stuffy day clothes. This time, it was silk, perfume and make up. And no Fern between them. The music was blue-tinged, a clarinet solo stirring their hair roots. Every couple danced cheek-to-cheek. When Alistair's fingers flexed against the small of her back, she pressed her pelvis against him so he knew she wanted him.

To hell with the world and its opinions.

A singer came to the microphone, crooning 'Fly to the Stars', expressing everything Vanessa felt: "To be loved and held and missed by you – To fly to the stars and be kissed by you . . .'"

She drew his face towards her and her mouth brushed his.

'I'm not a celibate saint. I can't repel you forever. You know where this ends, Vanessa.'

'Take me home.'

'Whose home?'

She thought about it. 'Yours. I've never seen it.'

Cecil Court was pitch black, as were the stairs to Alistair's flat. From habit, living through the blackout, they felt their way, only turning on lamps when they reached the lounge. Soft light fell on athletic bronze nymphs, wood-veneer cabinets and side tables. A sofa and armchairs upholstered in tobacco brown velvet promised a deep embrace.

'Bo's taste,' Alistair told her. He went to the Georgian fireplace and turned on an electric stove. Dusty coal fires requiring the attention of house-maids and chimney sweeps had gone out of fashion in the 1920s. The decade, Vanessa guessed, when this flat had last been decorated. As the stove's filaments turned amber, she studied the room. Until this moment, Bo Bovary had been a name. A face in a portrait. Here, she felt the man's shadow.

'That must be yours.' She pointed to a framed photograph of a ship carving a creamy path through the waves, its deck cluttered with guns and masts.

'It's the *Quarrel*. Taken from on board a tug in Liverpool Bay. What's it to be, Vanessa?'

He wasn't asking what she'd like to drink. From nowhere came Leo's voice. *You don't know how to satisfy a man, so I'll damn well show you.* She wanted Alistair to make the opening move and erase the scars of her past.

He wanted her. Desire had lived in his eyes since they'd danced to 'Fly to the Stars'. But she knew that his complex code of honour would make him hold back even if it killed him. He would not risk being accused at some later date of seducing her.

'Could you tell me the way to the bathroom?'

'Down the corridor, the door with the fancy finger-plate.' *Don't imagine you can dodge this all night,* his gaze warned as she passed him.

*

The bathroom was a temple to masculine luxury. The jewel on the altar was a tablet of Imperial Leather soap. Vanessa filled the bath no higher than the statutory four inches, a wartime rule to save water and heat. Hitching up her dress, she immersed feet that felt sticky from The Wishbone's dance floor. Then, deciding it would be criminal to waste water, she gave herself a swift, all-over wash. As the water drained away, she put on a white towelling robe she found hanging behind the door. It was surprisingly snug. It must have been Bo's rather than Alistair's. Vanessa checked herself in the mirror. Her hair curled mistily against her shoulders. Running her hands over her breasts, stomach, narrow hips, she took pleasure in the firm contours. Imagining Leo standing behind her reflection, she whispered, 'I've every right to a second tilt at love. You abused ours and now I love someone else.'

A seed sewn in a frozen graveyard had born fruit. Nothing mattered right now but her and Alistair.

His cleaning woman had laid his post on the kitchen table, and Alistair noticed the pile as he put slices of bread under the grill. Ignoring personal letters and those that felt like bills, he sliced open a small, cardboard package. It seemed empty, but when he tapped it on the table, photographic negatives fell out. He held one up to the light and saw that Fern had kept her word, returning compromising evidence to him. Her lawyer must have assured her that divorce proceedings were beyond the point of no return. He'd have to trust that she'd sent them all.

He shoved them into the cutlery drawer and turned the toast over. From nowhere came a deflating doubt.

What was love? Was it, like kindness, a form of delinquency? Marrying Fern, he'd felt every kind of uncertainty about the world they lived in, but of her love, her loyalty, not a single misgiving. Her betrayal still rocked him at unexpected moments.

What if Vanessa proved the same? Sometimes, he feared he'd lost the power to judge. He heard a door clicking shut, and counted the seconds until his ears picked up her light tread. A slight scrape, an agitated breath, told him she was watching him from the kitchen doorway. 'Bovril or Gentlemen's Relish on your toast?'

'Gosh. How did you know I was here?'

He turned and looked down at her bare toes, pink rosebuds under the white hem of the robe. 'ASDIC.'

'Sorry?'

'Sonar detection. I carry a form of it in my head.'

'But I'm not a submarine. I travel on the surface.'

'I heard you opening and closing doors.'

'I couldn't resist checking out your bedroom on the way. I adore the Chinese silk eiderdown.'

'Bo bought it in Shanghai.' He checked the progress of the toast. A few seconds more would do it. 'I hope the water was hot enough.'

He saw her take a steadying breath. 'Alistair, I love you. I always have, straight out of the gun-barrel.'

He knew that at this moment, a man like Patrick Carnford would say something bone-meltingly debonair and they would dissolve into each other. All he managed was a dry cough that sounded like embarrassment. 'Don't you think we should take a step back from this?'

Vanessa rushed forward so fast, he had to save himself from crashing into the cooker. She pressed herself to him and he felt an immediate stirring in his thighs, his groin. He turned back to his toast, but she laid her hand on his stomach, finding a flat band of muscle, pushing between the buttons of his shirt to discover the light scrim of hair. The heat of the grill warmed him, and must have warmed her too.

He covered her hand, controlling the direction of her touch. 'We don't have to end up in bed.'

'Too late. You invited me home.'

'You invited yourself, to be truthful.'

'*To be truthful*, you put the desire in my head.'

'It's been a numbingly long day, Vanessa. I can't think straight.'

She could. Vanessa leaned her cheek against his spine. Daringly, she undid all the shirt buttons, feeling her way. Undid the cuffs and pulled the shirt off him. Her teeth inflicted a row of gentle nips. She felt arousal swell and his hand clamped harder on hers. He wanted her, and she wasn't going to let him waste this moment because something – she didn't know what – wasn't quite right.

Her free hand delivered cobweb caresses as her breath skimmed his shoulder blades. 'You're back-tracking because . . . you believe – hope – that Fern is coming back to you?'

'Bit late for that. Why mention Fern? Shall I mention Leo? Oh, God!' Alistair hauled out the grill pan, slamming it down on top of the cooker as smoke filled the kitchen. He'd incinerated the toast. 'Let's talk about the men you fell in love with after Leo.'

He's snatching for excuses. Hitting the ball off the field but all right, I'll go fetch it back. 'Did Fern tell you that I went down like a skittle for every man in uniform who asked me out?'

'Pretty much.'

'I didn't, actually. When you're with a man who might be dead by the next night, you can't help but love him. It's human instinct. Did Fern also tell you how desperately tame my affairs were? Dancing and kissing and lots of talking. So don't dare use that as an excuse to reject me. You wanted me, now you don't.'

His breathing was changing. Perhaps because she was stroking his belly where his body hair concentrated, creating turmoil. She sensed he was desperate for her to stop, and famished for what she offered.

'I can't sleep with you while I'm in the throes of divorce.'

'Because the world will call you a rotter and me a tart? Sod the world.'

'It's not in me. I need to do the right thing.'

'What is the right thing? You're like the captain of a sinking ship who won't jump off, though he's the last man on board and there's room in the lifeboat. You'll go down just to make some damn stupid point?' She wished him luck. 'It's going to be a long, cold stretch, the rest of your life as a monk.'

He turned in a movement that flung her hands away, the desolation in his eyes proving that she'd painted a vision he'd already seen for himself. 'I was on a ship that went down and I jumped in the end or I wouldn't be here. Plunging into the freezing water, I imagined myself swimming towards Fern.'

'Has Fern's muck-spreading got between us?'

'No, because you stuck up for me. Your friend with the platinum hair said so.' Alistair unscrewed his facial muscles enough to smile.

'You were at war and the rules were different.' She sat down at the table, because she'd suddenly grasped that something bigger than divorce, hurt and exhaustion lay between them. Until it was exorcised, they'd bicker and argue. 'Tell me about the *Monarda*.'

He said nothing for a moment, cutting the blackened crusts from the toast, scraping the charred surface over the sink. Then he fetched in a long breath. 'The first year of war was a slaughter-ground, every convoy losing up to half its ships. We welcomed stormy weather because calm seas made us sitting targets.

Sometimes we seemed to be waiting our turn to die. When a sister ship or a tanker was hit, we'd hear the impact, see a ball of orange fire a thousand yards away. I'd give the order to steam closer and we'd carve a path through charred bodies to find survivors burning in the water. We rescued all we could, most of whom died anyway from their injuries or cold. I kept sane, Vanessa, by handing over my soul. I handed it over in exchange for killing the enemy in sufficient number to help bring the horror to an end.'

He rinsed his hands under the tap, then came to the table, gripping Vanessa's wrist, his fingers cold to her flesh. His eyes searched hers, demanding proof she understood.

'Go on,' she said, looking up at him.

'Fern was my Holy Ground, where I dreamed of returning. I imagined her waiting, a glorious full-stop to the hell I'd been through. And yes, I was an idiot, but I needed something. Decisions I made cost other men their lives. It's right what Fern says about the *Monarda*. It was my utter low point.'

'She's no right to an opinion!'

'It doesn't stop her having one. The *Monarda* was a corvette. By this time, I was captain of the *Quarrel*, in command of the convoy. *Monarda* was astern of us, following close, and we'd warned her there were enemy U-boats on our tail. It was an intensely bright, starlit night as only mid-Atlantic nights can be. When she was struck and exploded and began to sink, we saw every detail, even the men on the bridge struggling into life-jackets. She put up her flares. I ordered my ship to sail away from her because *my* orders were to pursue the submarine that fired the torpedo. Those men swimming towards us, shouting, drowning, will always haunt me.' He engaged in a brief nightmare. 'Some of my crew would have lynched me if they could. But we finished off the closest U-boat, and by doing so, saved maybe ten other ships. If I'd slowed our engines, we might have picked up fifty survivors, of whom forty would never have made it to port. I'm just saying – ' he lifted Vanessa to her feet to bring her nearer his eye-level, 'that I can't make a crucial choice one day then say, "to hell with it" the next. Abandoning the _Monarda_'s crew would then be just another duff choice. Leaving the Navy, taking on The Farren, hiring a nervous wreck like Cottrill . . . hiring you, my pushy little darling . . . would be up for argument. If I can't stand by my decisions, what's the point of me?'

'If we become lovers, we hurt no one.' Reaching up, she kissed the place beside his mouth where beard-shadow was breaking through.

Hard resolution melted in his face and she thought she had him but he resumed control with a self-mocking smile. She'd seen the inner struggle, the forward step, the retreat. 'I appreciate your honesty, Alistair. Let's have that toast.'

Had Macduff been there with them, he'd have had the lion's share of their supper. Vanessa's throat could hardly swallow as she formulated a plan. Alistair wanted her. Let him be complex. Let him be honourable. She would resort to trickery. She wiped her fingers on a napkin. 'It's too late for me to make my way home. Is there a spare room?'

'Yes, the bed's made up.'

'I'll be gone before you wake.'

In the poky bedroom, she turned down the bed covers, felt the cold sheets. In her dad's jaunty voice, she whispered, 'See, Toots? If you want something badly enough, it happens. It's not wrong to want something so badly, it hurts.'

In the lounge, Alistair swigged down colourless liquid. Water. He'd given up drinking entirely during hostilities because he'd seen other ships' officers going headfirst into the rum barrel, or the gin bottle. He sat down, reflecting that he'd never smell burned toast again without recalling the ardour in Vanessa's eyes. *I love you. I can't help it.*

He'd been brought up to believe in fidelity. His parents had loved each other – so deeply, it excluded him. His mother had accompanied his father on every voyage and had died two weeks after her husband. To dispel the memory of his childhood isolation, he reached for his glass. As he bent, something under the chair caught his eye. It was the script of Cottrill's first play, shyly handed to him a few days ago.

Unreadable, un-performable. But within it, an unlit fuse of talent. He intended to tell Cottrill, 'You've got out all your rage and disappointment. Now write about what's good in your life.'

Perhaps Vanessa should write about her marriage, though her script would be short and brutal. Her letter had sketched that unhappy interlude, and his subsequent telephone call to Fern had added human layers.

Fern had told him, 'In the days before he died, Leo and his section had been flying sorties to exhaustion, from first light to midnight. His best friend had crashed on the runway, asleep at the controls. One can understand if his personality changed.' Fern recalled Vanessa describing Leo's home-comings, the few hours' snatched leave, when he'd arrive like a coiled spring, dangerous and angry. On the last, fateful night, the spring had snapped. 'Vanessa was sleeping and he woke her. She immediately smelled another woman's perfume on him, but he wouldn't say where he'd been. He just wanted Vanessa's flesh. She turned her back. He pulled her out of bed and had her on the floor.'

Had? 'Raped?' Alistair had stumbled over the word. This could be Fern exaggerating.

'Not technically, since they were married. He got into bed

while Nessie stayed curled on the lino. When she was finally able
to get up, she kicked him out — even though it was the middle
of the night — and flung her wedding ring at him, telling him to
sell it to pay for their divorce. The next day — '

Leo Kingcourt had been shot down. Vanessa's violated love
had been reborn in terrible guilt. He wondered what it had cost
her to fall in love again.

He washed, brushed his teeth. In token good manners, he
wrapped a towel around his waist and went to the spare room.
The thought of her separated from him by a single door brought
a hardness to his groin. His hand strayed towards the handle. In
his urgency, he might forget to be gentle. 'Vanessa?'

He listened for breathing, heard none. He went in and found
the bed empty. Surely, she hadn't gone home? 'Damn idiot. I
don't love you — '

He found the front door locked, from the inside. That meant —

He went to his bedroom. Throwing off his towel, he pulled
back the covers and slid in to bed, into a body-warm aura that
smelled of Bo's Imperial Leather.

'Vanessa?'

Arms wrapped around him, and a flat belly and slim thighs
rolled against him, sweet salve to burning skin. Fingers slewed
along his shoulders, along his neck, into his hair, as lips opened
against his mouth. She breathed, 'I don't care if you can't love me.'

'I don't love you, I adore you.'

As a young midshipman, he'd witnessed a deckhand being
punched overboard by a freak wave, hurled into the deep and
lost. Alistair went the same way.

PART FIVE

And now, face to face

Chapter Thirty-Two

They played to packed houses through December. Audiences flocked to a play that guaranteed laughter and a gorgeous spectacle. Alistair whistled as he moved between the theatre's compass points – until he was heard doing so and made to turn round three times and swear. His naval obscenities were agreed – by Patrick Carnford and Billy Chalker, who witnessed them – to be among the best they'd ever heard.

A new vein of optimism ran through the company and even Tom Cottrill admitted that he might have over-reacted to the shadows in the upper circle.

Vanessa and Alistair kept their love secret. Not easy. A theatre has eyes front, back, high and low. They met clandestinely, like agents in enemy territory. Alistair's divorce was moving through the legal system, in his words, 'like an over-loaded coal freighter through mud'. Until he was free he refused even to hold Vanessa's hand in public. She continued to call him 'Alistair' while he stayed with 'Mrs Kingcourt'. The masquerade was an aphrodisiac.

Christmas was celebrated on the 22nd of December, a Sunday, with carols sung on stage and dinner cooked on gas burners in Doyle's office, shared with members of the company who had nowhere else to go. Twelve of them, including Gwenda, Billy Chalker and Doyle, dined in the foyer. Vanessa invited Joanne. They all wore hats from the wardrobe room, except Macduff, who donned Doyle's blue seaman's cap.

Christmas Eve was business as usual, with a matinee and evening performance. On Christmas Day, they closed. Vanessa and Alistair went to morning carols at St Martin-in-the-Fields, then back to his flat. Together, they helped Macduff up and down the stairs and walked him through near-deserted streets. As the light faded, they ate dinner in front of the fire. Christmas week felt like a honeymoon, which ended the following Sunday when Alistair woke her and murmured in her ear, 'Would you like a trip out to Epping or Chislehurst, to walk in the woods?'

Her fingertips strolled across his groin and he hardened at once. She stroked his inner thigh and he sighed. She asked, 'Have you got fuel?'

He pulled her on top of him. 'Plenty, darling.'

'In the Alfa! Take me to Brookwood. I want to see my mother's grave again. And Dad's. And the other Vanessa's.'

'Doesn't sound fun.' But he took her there, for all that.

On their return, Alistair parked the Alfa in a street off Leicester Square, and they walked to Cecil Court in silence. The weather had turned to chill, a light sleet stinging the skin. Alistair broke convention, keeping his arm around Vanessa because she looked close to fainting. At Brookwood, they'd found Billy Chalker tidying the grass in front of Eva's headstone, kneeling to his work. Seeing them, he'd got painfully to his feet. The pouchy eyes had been hostile.

Vanessa explained why they'd come and Alistair's heart had bled for her as Billy put up a hand, silencing her.

'I don't know who you are, Mrs Kingcourt, but I know who you're *not*.' He'd indicated the child's grave beside Eva's. 'There was only one Vanessa and she died.'

She'd had tried to get a word in. 'I *am* Vanessa. We were born the same day and – '

'No.' Anger had crimsoned Chalker's face. 'That's my niece under the turf. I carried her tiny coffin. I can even tell you what it said on the death certificate. Neonatal death. She was born at The Farren and survived a couple of weeks. Johnny Quinnell was to blame.'

Vanessa had refused to believe it but Billy persisted.

'It *was* his fault. Eva was having labour pains but instead of calling for help, or taking her to the hospital, Johnny told her to sit tight. It was the first night of a new play, and we both had a part. I was worried, Eva didn't look good but Johnny wasn't going to waste his big moment taking care of a woman in childbirth. "You'll be right as rain, my sweet." Very persuasive, Johnny, when he wanted to be.'

That was when Vanessa turned on her heels. Alistair had remained with Chalker long enough to hear how Johnny Quinnell had responded to his baby's death.

He bolted, or rather he was fetched away. 'Redeemed, like a watch from the pawn shop,' was how Chalker had described it. '*The de Vere Mystery* had ended and we were rehearsing the next thing. A female calling herself "Mrs Quinnell" turned up at the rehearsal room at the back of the Nun's Head demanding a private talk with Johnny. The next thing we knew, he was following her out of the door. Eva tore after him, beside herself. I followed them and I grabbed Johnny in Farren Court. "What are you doing?" Know what he said?'

Of course, Alistair had no idea.

'"I'm sad about the baby but you know me. I follow the money." *Follow the money.* I watched the bastard join the woman calling herself his wife in the back of a motor car, driver at the wheel. A Rolls Royce, colour of blood.'

Alistair offered no comment, except to add, 'He abandoned his wife in turn, a few years later.'

Billy had spat in disgust. 'I never understood why Eva took him back or why Wilton Bovary gave him more work . . . until I met Mrs Kingcourt. You know as well as I, she's not Johnny Quinnell's girl.'

Alistair had walked away then to find Vanessa, his mind turning over Billy's revelations. If Ruth Quinnell had fetched Johnny back home, the blood-red Rolls Royce had to be Lord Stanshurst's. How else would Ruth have got the use of such a car? And if Vanessa was neither Johnny nor Ruth's child, then Lord Stanshurst had to have had some role in the business.

In the flat, Alistair made food, insisting that Vanessa eat, but the steamed carrots and tinned ham he put in front of her was too much. She said, 'I feel I don't really exist. I died at birth, and was buried.'

'No, you weren't. Another child was.'

'I've had a life-long nightmare about being buried alive. Now I know why!'

'You exist. I'll prove it.' Taking her to the lounge, he turned the fire to its highest setting and pulled cushions from the sofa to make a nest on the floor. He made her lie down with him and unbuttoned her blouse and her waistband, then slowly peeled her clothes off. When she was down to her underwear, he took off his own clothes.

When their flesh met he proved to her that she was as alive

as he was. Stroking her hair from her forehead, he told her that her brow was white and smooth as a letter unwritten. Her eyes potent as the last inch of whisky in a glass. Her brows jinked in the middle, asking perpetual questions. Her mouth – with his tongue he traced its shape – turned up each side like a double-ended canoe. Except when she was angry, when it went the other way. 'Capsized.'

Her eyelids fluttered. Reluctantly, she smiled. 'You want me to grin like the Cheshire cat? Didn't he disappear, leaving only his teeth shining in the air?'

'You aren't disappearing, Vanessa. If anything, you're growing more vibrant by the day.'

Entering Vanessa now, as hard as he'd been at eighteen, but with the control and patience of a man in his thirties, he briefly pitied the Alistair who'd pushed her away. As her lips raided his mouth, his throat, demanding more from him, the hurt, confused girl changed into the arrow-straight woman who knew how to please herself and her man.

She slept afterwards, and he laid a rug over her. He needed to retrieve Macduff from Doyle's patient care.

In the comfortable chair in his niche, Doyle snoozed. Macduff snoozed. As it was Sunday, the theatre itself dozed. Outside, the temperature was dropping. A dense fog was taking hold.

Macduff growled.

'Easy boy,' Doyle mumbled. 'There ain't nobody here but us chickens.'

But Macduff kept growling and Doyle, imbued with naval discipline, eventually went to see why. In the pitch-black auditorium, he heard whispering high above and the blood shunted in his veins. He wasn't superstitious, but he wasn't deaf either. He hurried back to his office and telephoned Alistair.

'Something mighty odd is going on here, Sir. Reinforcements would be appreciated.'

Chapter Thirty-Three

Fog bore down between the buildings. Alistair would have preferred to drive himself and Vanessa to The Farren, but in the slippery dark it was safer to walk.

At the stage door, they were greeted by Macduff and Doyle who looked relieved to see them. 'Something's creeping around in the upper circle.'

'You're on duty all night?' Alistair asked, then remembered that Kidd's bronchitis, having abated earlier in the week, had made a crippling return. Doyle was holding the fort day and night. 'We'd better hire you a helper. Wait, Vanessa.'

She'd stridden ahead, with Macduff. 'Follow me,' Alistair told Doyle grimly. 'Let's find out what's disturbing the peace.'

Vanessa hadn't turned on the auditorium lights, and Alistair shone his torch up at the chandeliers whose sparkling tiers made him think of starlit nights at sea. He raced the beam as far as the upper circle rail and captured a movement. Macduff growled, sensing his master's rising tension. Doyle was right. There was something up there.

Vanessa came to stand by him. 'I'd rather ghosts than rats.'

'You can stay behind if you wish.'

'Not on your life!'

They took the lift to the management corridor, then up to the topmost landing. They listened at the door to the upper circle, unwilling to acknowledge that the supposedly empty space beyond was pregnant with whispers. The dog had no doubts. As Alistair pulled open the door, Macduff flew past. He grabbed the dog's collar while his torch beam revealed, as well as the usual raked seats, a table laid with glass tumblers, four chairs around it. And white faces above black bodies, a slash of scarlet, a gold brooch, the fleshy gleam of hands. Alistair instantly knew Miss Bovary by her mushroom-stem throat. It took him a moment to recognise Sylvia Rolf behind a veil.

Employing all the strength of one hand, Alistair held Macduff who was straining on his hind legs. His torch beam jerked, showing two males cowering like cornered quarry. In a flash of understanding, he shouted, 'The dog will pin you down unless you take off that cloak, Edwin,'

Edwin broke the ties at the neck and hurled the garment. Alistair caught it. Macduff fought him for it, though the moment Alistair let him have it, he subsided. Alistair summed up the scene. Absorbed the furtive atmosphere. 'Were you conducting a séance?'

Miss Bovary spoke. 'What if we were? We disturb no one. Bursting in when one of our number is in a trance-state is highly irresponsible.'

'I beg your pardon. Who were you trying to reach? Flo? Elizabeth Farren?'

'Our brother.' Sylvia Rolf's defiance shivered. 'He is close.'

'What's *your* game, Redenhall?' Edwin Bovary demanded.

'Same as yours. To bring the dead back to life, only I won't rely on ectoplasm and etheric vibrations.' He'd been holding back too long, Alistair acknowledged, to spare one person's feelings. He agreed with Billy Chalker that Vanessa was not Johnny Quinnell's daughter and this was as good a time as any to let the truth fly.

He ordered them all down to his office, the pitch of his voice eradicating argument. On the stairs, he asked Doyle to fetch Chalker from Wild Street.

'Why him, sir?'

'I have my reasons. Bring him to the wardroom. No, leave the dog with us.'

In his office, Alistair checked the dog's water bowl, put a match to the ready-laid fire and unlocked the top drawer of his desk, removing a typed document.

'What are you up to, darling?' Vanessa asked nervously.

'Did you know, the last time Chalker played the role of a manservant, it was here, in *The Importance of Being Earnest*? He was Bo's understudy.'

'He was here the night Bo and Dad died?'

'Undoubtedly. Billy wasn't a part of The Farren the way Eva was, but he appeared here in a dozen plays.'

'Perhaps he'll tell me what happened after Dad and I separated outside the White Hart.' Vanessa flung the cloak, which she'd prised off Macduff, around her shoulders. 'Bitter, it was that night. "The owl, for all his feathers, was a-cold".'

'Vanessa –'

A harsh cry from the doorway cut Alistair off. Miss Bovary stormed in and dragged the cloak off Vanessa's shoulders. 'You have no right to touch that!' Macduff showed his teeth, but Miss Bovary raged back at him, 'If you were my dog, you'd know some discipline.'

Alistair took the cloak and draped it over the desk where its vivid lining reflected firelight.

Sylvia and Terence Rolf arrived. She looked unwell, her colour high. Alistair invited them to sit, then asked if Edwin were joining them.

'He's stepped down to the green room for a sherry.' Terence Rolf made a show of helping his wife to sit down. 'You bursting in on our gathering may have caused irreparable damage.'

When Edwin eventually joined them, he sank weakly on to a chair though his eyes were bright and alert. Meanwhile, Alistair extended his hand to Miss Bovary. 'Your keys, Barbara.'

'I beg your pardon?'

'I want them. You've exceeded your rights in this place.'

'By conducting an innocent séance?'

'By diverting Farren money. When Eva St Clair died last August, instead of stopping her pension payments, you instructed the bank to pay them into your brother-in-law's account. It's theft.'

'It's legitimate expenses.'

'A chat with my accountant will confirm that. I have his home number.'

With a hiss, Barbara Bovary threw her keys at Alistair's feet.

Sylvia Rolf asked plaintively, 'Why is Mrs Kingcourt involved in this meeting. It is a meeting, I suppose?' She'd kept on her coat, and sitting nearest the fire, she sweated.

'Our Wardrobe Mistress is the reason for our gathering.' Alistair picked up the typed document. It was the coroner's report into Bo's death, which had lain in his desk since he took up the reins at The Farren. He'd asked for a copy before his godfather's funeral and had studied it on the train journey to Brookwood, at the time unwilling to accept that his beloved friend had collapsed without pre-warning. In the end, he'd found nothing to contradict the medical opinion that Wilton Bovary had suffered a heart attack, brought on by the freezing temperatures of the night. He still questioned the co-incidence of Bo and Johnny dying in unison, however. Gut instinct said that the deaths were linked and he feared he was looking at the link.

Vanessa.

'You aren't planning to re-run the inquest?' Edwin demanded. 'This is distressing to my mother and aunt.'

'Alistair likes tying up loose ends.' Vanessa was frowning at her key, stroking its ribbon.

'There are no loose ends,' Terence Rolf said sharply. 'A coroner's inquest is a final verdict.'

Alistair suggested they go back in time to the 9th of February, 1945, the night tragedy had struck. *The Importance of Being Earnest* had been running for three weeks to good houses. 'On Friday the 9th, curtain-up was at seven-thirty, yes?'

He repeated the question until he got a response – from Miss Bovary as the others were scowling at the floor. Curtain-up was always seven-thirty, she said, and by ten o'clock, the play was over. 'Actors in their dressing rooms, removing their makeup.'

'And by eleven, the safety iron was down, stage lights off, the theatre all but deserted,' Alistair concluded. 'Then what?'

'I cashed up,' Miss Bovary answered impatiently. 'Every night the same.'

'You collected takings from the box office and bar, counted and bagged them while Bo took Macduff out to stretch his legs.'

'You appear to know the routine remarkably well, Commander.'

'A routine night, yet dawn rose on two corpses.'

'Two?' Mrs Rolf demanded.

'The fellow the doorman was forced to eject,' her husband reminded her. 'Quinnell, remember him? He died from alcohol poisoning in his digs.' Terence Rolf addressed Alistair. 'After the show, Quinnell took root in the green room until everyone had had enough of him. I was sorry for the man, sorry for how it ended, but what can you expect when a depressive type steals a bottle of best Haig whisky from the cabinet to drink alone?'

'Quinnell invariably lived down to expectations,' Miss Bovary agreed, 'and I never could fathom Bo's soft spot for him. Unreliable, adulterous with our wardrobe woman.' She sent Vanessa a pointed glance.

'He and I were due to meet.' Vanessa got to her feet. She was within a hair's breadth of quitting the room, Alistair could see. 'We hadn't seen each other for twenty years. I was sick with nerves, and he'd have been in a state too.'

Miss Bovary sniffed contemptuously. 'No backbone.'

Alistair intervened. 'Johnny wasn't so drunk or depressed in the hours before he died that he couldn't write to Vanessa.' They'd come across the beginnings of a letter the day she moved out of the room on Long Acre. Alistair was relieved to see Vanessa sit down again. Evidently, she meant hear this out. He continued, 'What drove Johnny Quinnell? What lay behind his ties to Wilton Bovary? You could hardly meet two men less alike, yet whenever Johnny needed a part in a play, he only had to knock at Bo's door. Why?'

'It wasn't his towering talent, for sure.'

It was Billy Chalker, declaiming from the doorway, Doyle behind him. Chalker wore a thick overcoat and muffler and to

Alistair's eye, he seemed a mite unsteady but perhaps that was down to being brought out on a foggy Sunday night.

Pausing beside Vanessa, Chalker said, 'I wish I could spare your feelings, Mrs Kingcourt, but Johnny was a ham actor. A hearty ladle-full from the stock pot who got better parts than he deserved. But whereas Miss Bovary flounders in confusion, I know precisely what Bo had on Johnny, and what Johnny had on Bo.'

'Keep it to yourself.' Alistair asked Doyle to fetch another chair. When Chalker was seated, he said, 'You never mentioned, Billy, that you were here the night Bo and Quinnell died.'

'You never asked and I admit, I'm not proud that I was forced to understudy in order to pay my rent.'

Vanessa burst out, 'They're saying my Dad was drunk when he arrived at the theatre, but I know he wasn't.'

Chalker removed his muffler and angled himself to face to Vanessa. 'Have I ever said he was? I loathed the man but I won't deny, Johnny was sober when he came and sober when he left.'

'That's what Miss Eddrich said!'

Chalker reached across and patted her hand. 'After news of his death reached us, a story emerged of him drinking himself to the floor in self-destructive frenzy. But that entirely misses the point of Johnny Quinnell. He was destructive to others, but loved himself too well to ever jeopardise his own life. Yes, yes, Terence, go on, glare at me,' Chalker said wearily. 'I'm not so grateful for a spit-and-a-cough part that I'll perjure myself. Sack me, and I'll go back north and be Widow Twankey for the rest of the season.'

Barbara Bovary said through clenched teeth, 'An empty spirit bottle was found in Quinnell's room. That is a fact.'

'Let's pass on.' Alistair smoothed out the coroner's report. 'Bo suffered his heart attack some time after eleven p.m. as he returned from taking Macduff for his final trot around the block. The dog was found at first light, lying by his master's body, am I right, Miss Bovary?'

Perhaps Chalker misheard and thought the question was for him. At any rate, he answered it before Miss Bovary could. 'The doorman, a chap called Jenkins, found them outside the stage door. He gave the dog warm milk. Nothing to be done for Bovary.'

'Why did it take the doorman so long? Doyle –' Alistair threw his voice towards the corridor, 'how far is your chair from the stage door?'

There came a return shout; 'Nine feet, sir.'

'Was Jenkins deaf, then?' Alistair asked Chalker. 'Because, surely, Bo would have tried to knock, or have made some sound.'

'I've no idea if Jenkins was deaf, but he was certainly very old and another of Bo's charity cases. He'd lock up, retire to his niche and push cotton wool into his ears. We knew his foibles, Miss Bovary, didn't we?'

'I've no memory,' Miss Bovary said icily, 'of anything but my brother's tragic death.'

'That's a shame, Barbara,' Alistair said gently. 'I was hoping you'd answer a riddle. I'll ask it anyway. The night Bo died, you counted the takings in your office, as per routine. Did you, at any point, ask yourself why Bo hadn't returned from walking the dog? On a night so deadly-cold, you'd surely want to check?'

'We didn't realise he hadn't returned.'

'We?'

Miss Bovary closed her eyes. She'd blundered.

Alistair concluded for her. 'You, your sister and Terence?'

'And young Edwin,' Chalker butted in. 'He was on the premises. He covered the role of Algernon Moncrieff that night, due to Carnford being ill.' Chalker's wide smile shifted between Edwin and Alistair, giving the impression of a man nourishing long-standing ill will. 'You knew that, Commander. You know everything.'

Alistair shrugged. 'I've studied the books. I came across Edwin's fee in the payroll ledger.' He asked Miss Bovary, 'What of the dog?'

'What of him?' Miss Bovary demanded, tight with suspicion.

'I won't believe Macduff hunkered on icy cobbles as his master died without making a sound. That dog is vocal. Didn't you hear anything amiss as you totted up the money?'

'No.'

'No. Because you didn't count it that night, did you?' Studying The Farren's ledgers, Alistair had discovered that February 9th, 1945, had been an aberration. A night when routines lapsed. A blank page in a cash-book speaks volumes. As did a separate entry in the petty cash book showing that two taxis had been ordered on the theatre account for three a.m. on February 10th; one to go to Bloomsbury, the other to a Mayfair address. 'You didn't sit down in your office all that night, Miss Bovary,' Alistair suggested. 'You and Mr and Mrs Rolf were up in the Gods, holding one of your damnable séances.' He didn't try to keep the disgust from his voice. 'While your brother perished outside, you were bothering Back Row Flo. Had you left by the stage door, you'd have found him, but of course, you prefer to come and go by the front.'

The *Quarrel*'s more fanciful crew members had put it about

that Commander Redenhall could see into men's souls. Sylvia Rolf seemed to share their belief. She sobbed, 'We weren't "bothering" Flo. She was trying to communicate with *us*.'

Alistair let a short silence pass. Now to the crux of this conference. 'Vanessa, was it Johnny who arranged your meeting on Drury Lane?'

Vanessa nodded. 'He had something important to tell me. Naturally, I couldn't drop everything and go. I had to request a Form 295.' She explained; 'Official leave. I needed forty-eight hours and the journey took an age. Then I couldn't find the White Hart. I realised too late that I'd met Dad as he was leaving the pub. We stood so close, I smelled his hair oil and a whiff of cigars. He called me sweet nymph. No, "gentle nymph".'

Edwin chose that moment to reach across for the cloak, but Alistair stalled him. 'Don't. It's why Macduff hates you. You come on to his territory swathed in borrowed scent, a walking betrayal.'

From his desk drawer, Alistair took a framed photograph, saying to Miss Bovary, 'One of the cleaners brought this to me, thinking it was in with the rubbish by mistake. You should have burned it.' He turned the picture so they could see. It was of Bo and Johnny under a bleaching stage light, their khol-lined eyes expressing emotion to some long-ago audience.

'"The Pearl Fishers"' Terence Rolf supplied, after studying it. 'A rotten potato. I lost money on it.'

His wife frowned. 'Isn't that the picture Hugo Brennan was gawping at the day we all took tea in Barbara's room?'

Miss Bovary looked daggers at her sister.

Alistair said, 'I could talk about Bo's dimple and lop-sided smile, his flamboyant soul and zest for every new part he played, but –' Billy Chalker was revving up to interrupt. Putting the picture aside, Alistair seized the cloak. 'This was made for Wilton Bovary by his tailor. Vanessa, you met your father outside the White Hart. The tragedy is, neither you nor Bo realised it.'

She stared as if he'd punched her. Her voice a desiccated thread, she asked, 'You're saying I'm –'

'Bo's child.'

'His and Eva's?'

The others erupted, until cut short by the peel of the telephone. Edwin Bovary got to it ahead of Alistair. After a terse exchange, he rammed the receiver down and said to Vanessa, 'I'm to say that a person by the name of Quinnell has suffered a fall –'

'Ruth's hurt?' Vanessa cried in alarm.

'She's in a poor way at Stanshurst Hall.' Edwin laughed, an ugly sound. 'Bo's daughter? No. You don't look a bit like him!'

'Oh, but she does,' Sylvia Rolf said unhappily. 'The chin and nose. I didn't see it until Terence pointed it out. He said from the first –'

Her husband advised her to shut up. Edwin sneered at his mother. 'Next, you'll be waving her in the direction of his money.'

'I wouldn't touch it,' Vanessa hurled in reply.

Billy Chalker tapped her shoulder. 'You really should. My sister told me who you were at Johnny's funeral. Eva knew all Bo's secrets. And Johnny's.'

She asked, 'Including how he came to poison himself with whisky?'

'Ask him that.' With a sweep of the hand, Billy Chalker framed Edwin Bovary. '*He* raided the green room bar that sorry night, not Johnny. *He* was seen traipsing down Long Acre with a bottle of black market Scotch under his coat.'

Edwin accused Chalker of being insane. Vanessa looked into Chalker's big, blue-veined face. 'Edwin called on Johnny after the show?'

Chalker inclined his head. 'Hoping, I imagine, to find out why his uncle had spent an hour that evening at the White Hart. True, Edwin? Was Johnny writing a letter when you knocked at his door? Shivering, alone, pitifully grateful for any friendly overtures?'

Edwin swore. Chalker shook his head witheringly. 'You went, you poured, you watched him drink. You might have put a coin in the electric meter before you went. Even I would have spared a shilling to prevent a fellow creature from freezing.'

Vanessa scraped back her chair and stumbled to the door. Chalker called after her, 'Eva wanted you to know the truth. You're a good sort, Mrs Kingcourt, but you are not her child.'

Alistair had the last word, ordering everyone by the name of Rolf and Bovary to get out. Out of his theatre, now, and never come back.

Chapter Thirty-Four

> *You have your mother's eyes.*
> *Your mother was a whore.*
> *You're not Eva's girl.*

Vanessa's first impulse had been to run to Charing Cross station and take a train. It was Alistair who had pointed out that it was Sunday. No trains. She then remembered the costumes needing her attention and panic surged up. 'I've got to wash off grease paint, sew on buttons. Miss Abbott's torn her morning gown *again*. Oh, God, Alistair, what can I do?'

'Sleep,' Alistair ruled. 'We'll go to Stanshurst first thing tomorrow. Ruth will survive the night, she's not at death's door.' From his office, he put a call through to Penny Yorke at home, arranging for some of her women to take over from Vanessa the following day.

'How will they get in?' Vanessa fretted. Her world had been spun so violently, trivialities had landed on top.

'Doyle has a key to your room, hasn't he? Let's find him. I'm going to dump Macduff on him again.' Alistair gave Doyle Stanshurst Hall's telephone number so he could call first thing in the morning and arrange for somebody to pick them up from the station. Finally, he told Vanessa, 'Relax, we have good people around us.'

They took the early-bird train the next day, racing through a countryside buffeted by biting winds. Memories of trying to reach her father . . . no longer her father. Of trying to reach Johnny Quinnell through the snow.

At Hayes station, one of Lord Stanshurst's estate workers was waiting with a pony trap, and that next few miles were the coldest of Vanessa's life. Instead of her WAAF greatcoat, she'd worn Wilton Bovary's cloak, an act of bravado she regretted, even when Alistair wrapped his arms around her. To the clip of the pony's hooves, she asked herself, 'Who is my mother?'

By ten-thirty, she was being shown up to the Hall's east wing by Borthwick while Alistair waited in the morning room for Lord Stanshurst to come in from his morning walk.

In a suite of rooms, whose chill was partially dispelled by a room-heater, Vanessa saw a woman reading in an armchair. At their approach, the woman dropped her book and got up.

It was Fern who laughed, 'Only highwaymen wear cloaks in the countryside. Did Black Bess cast a shoe?'

Vanessa explained, 'We couldn't get down last night. Not enough fuel to drive.' Anxiety, tiredness, made her careless.

'"We" being you and Alistair?'

'Yes, um, he's been very kind.'

'Well, good of you to come at all,' Fern said brightly. 'Let's see if our patient is strong enough to talk.'

Vanessa followed Fern into a small bedroom that was warm and bright. Brocade curtains with a broadleaf design were drawn back to give a vista of Hunter's Copse where, months ago, she'd walked with Fern. A nicer, softer Fern.

She asked, 'How did Ruth – my mother – hurt herself?'

'Missed her footing at the top of her stairs. She was bringing a bundle of sheets down to wash.'

Vanessa could easily believe it. She'd fallen down the narrow, dog-leg stairs of Peach Cottage a few times in her life. 'Who found her?'

'I did.' Fern had been at Stanshurst since last week. Yesterday she'd walked to church for morning service. 'People were concerned when Ruth didn't show. She never misses, apparently. We let ourselves in to Peach Cottage. Poor thing's in shock and very sore.'

An understatement, Vanessa discovered. Ruth's head was bandaged like a medieval cadaver's, her features swollen. Vanessa reached for one of the bony hands. The other was in a sling. 'You should be in hospital.'

'But we're a stubborn lady, aren't we?' Fern was clearly enjoying her nurse persona, or amusing herself with it. 'We don't like institutions. Five minutes, doctor's orders, lest she get agitated. Shall I go?'

'If you don't mind.' When Fern left, closing the door behind her, Vanessa apologised for visiting empty-handed. 'I came as quickly as I could.'

'Water.' Ruth found it hard to move her lips.

Vanessa filled a glass from the bedside jug and held it to the injured lips. Ruth sipped. Vanessa asked, 'Why did you call for me? I thought you'd cast me off.'

Ruth mumbled something that sounded like 'lettuce'.

'Oh – "letters"?'

'Home,' Ruth answered.

'In your bureau?'

Ruth breathed, 'Father. Need to say – too late.'

Years too late, Vanessa reflected, trying to stay calm. 'I was told yesterday that my father was Wilton Bovary. Any comment?'

Ruth sighed, 'Actor.'

'So it's true?'

The word 'yes,' slipped between Ruth's lips.

'And there are letters for me . . . from him? From my father?'

'Yes' again.

'I'll stop by Peach Cottage and collect them. Ruth, I need to know who – '

'Half a minute left, dear,' from the other room. Fern was still acting the bossy nurse, still amusing herself. *She must be very bored at Stanshurst to be spending her time in a sickroom. Where was Darrell Highstoke?* Though Vanessa didn't really care. 'Who is my mother?'

Ruth sketched a denial. 'Can't say.'

'Can't or won't?'

'Twenty seconds, then I'm coming in,' Fern called.

She hurried out a different question. 'Why does my birth certificate call me "Vanessa Elizabeth"?'

'Johnny brought it with him.'

'When he left Eva and came back to you? Please don't tell me it was his dead baby's?'

Fern came in, tutting. 'Look at you, leaning across the patient. I said she wasn't to be upset, didn't I? Someone will fetch you a nice cup of tea, Mrs Q.' Fern opened the door wide for Vanessa. 'I saw Pops walking across the lawn a moment ago. I'm sure you'd like a word.'

'Are you trying to get rid of me?'

'Ruth will be all right, but she needs sleep and good feeding. Tormenting her about the past isn't fair.'

Fern must have had her ear to the door. Vanessa promised Ruth she'd return as soon as she could. 'Thanks for taking care of her,' she said as Fern escorted her back to the stairs. The corridors on this side of the house were a maze of identical doors.

'Don't thank me,' Fern replied. 'I sit up here in case Ruth calls out, but Mrs Blaxill comes up from the village twice a day. She was a nurse years ago and is good at the bedpan-and-gruel routine.'

'Even so – ' Vanessa offered more thanks, causing Fern to say harshly, 'Ruth was loyal to my mother for years. Marge would have insisted we take care of her.'

'Fine. I won't thank you again.'

They walked on, until Fern stopped, snapping her fingers to release her feelings. 'I dare say you'll dig out those letters Ruth was talking about. If so, can I ask one thing? Whatever they reveal, keep it to yourself. Promise?'

'I'll take a view.' Fern had lied to her, humiliated her. The time for promises was over. Vanessa asked instead, 'How's Darrell?'

'At his uncle, Lord Chiddingford's. He's meeting his mother there, to tell them formally of his intention to marry me.' Fern's tone altered and she was suddenly the polished, finishing school version of herself, chic in a dress of olive wool with a collar of yellow plaid that brought out the fiery tones in her hair. The metamorphosis made Vanessa feel drab. Why had Alistair let her wear this damn cloak? It trailed on the floor. It was dangerous on the stairs.

'Will Darrell's family accept you?' she asked, letting Fern go down ahead of her. 'A divorcée?'

'They will in the end, because the moment my court case is settled, I intend to get pregnant. Lord Chiddingford is desperate for his line to continue and even Darrell's mother would stop short of allowing the birth of her grandchild to be illegitimate.'

'All's fair in love and war? Giving Ruth those photographs, *darling*,' Vanessa aped Fern's hyperbolic style, 'was scraping the barrel.'

'When you want something, you fight for it.'

They crossed the downstairs hall where Vanessa stopped. 'Alistair was never unfaithful to you, Fern, was he?'

'You tell me. He had every opportunity.'

'He's fidelity made flesh and I love him.'

Fern made a sound of disgust. 'I try so hard to hate you.'

'You showed those photos to Lord Stanshurst, I suppose?'

'Absolutely not.' Fern shot a horrified look at the morning room. 'He has no idea what you . . . oh, do take off that cloak! That ridiculous man wore it when he put on his plays here.'

'My father, you mean?'

'Wilton Bovary. It flared behind him as he strutted around, overpowering us all with the whiff of bay rum. Everyone thought he was wonderful. His darling actress-chums cuddled up, Marge doted. Pops and I couldn't bear him.' Fern strode into the morning room where Lord Stanshurst and Alistair stood either side of the fireplace.

Alistair said, 'Good morning, Fern.'

She replied, 'This is the last time you'll call me Fern. Next time, it will be "Lady Chiddingford".'

'I will call you Fern, or nothing at all.'

A pair of spaniels broke the tension, racing up to greet the newcomers. 'Down Sprout, down Hermes!' Fern ordered. The creatures swerved on Vanessa, depositing mud on her stockings.

Lord Stanshurst sent them to their baskets, then came forward and shook Vanessa's hand.

'Hello, stranger. What a mess your mother is. Her poor face.'

For a stupid moment, Vanessa thought he was about to reveal her mother's identity. It was only when he said, 'Fern says that the only sustenance in her cupboard was pudding rice and mustard,' that she realised her error. She nodded. 'It's how she chooses to live.'

Lord Stanshurst agreed. 'Fern, darling tug the bell. Tea, all? Take a seat, Nessie.'

Vanessa sat on a sagging sofa while Fern pulled the bell sash connected to the kitchen. 'It's awfully good of you to have Ruth, Lord Stanshurst,' she said, 'but it feels like an imposition. I could look for a convalescence home for her.'

'Stanshurst looks after its own, Vanessa, so don't feel in any rush.' Lord Stanshurst explained to Alistair, 'We put her back in her old room. She prefers the abandoned side of the house.'

'It's where you put me when I stayed last,' Alistair replied.

After an awkward silence, Vanessa said, 'You must at least let me pay for her nursing, Lord Stanshurst.'

'Don't you already send Ruth half your wages? You'd better keep something for yourself. Dratted expensive place, London.'

Vanessa felt Alistair's quizzical glance. She hadn't mentioned that she was still helping support the woman who had disowned her. After a few minutes, Borthwick brought in the tea tray. In his dark coat and wing-collar, he reminded her of Billy Chalker, walking on stage as Parker. Vanessa jumped to her feet, offering to take up Ruth's tea as an excuse to leave the room.

Ruth had fallen asleep, so she drank the tea herself. There wasn't much in the room to distract her, other than pictures of dogs and horses. Fern shared her father's disinclination for country pursuits but Lady Stanshurst had bred gun dogs and had been a fine horsewoman, though at some point in her life, ill-health had forced her to give up. Vanessa remembered Ruth saying that 'Her Ladyship' was lonely at Stanshurst, and regretted giving up her pre-marriage profession.

Vanessa noticed a picture laid face down on the bedside table. Picking it up, she almost dropped it again. It was a framed sepia photograph of herself.

Herself in the passenger seat of Lord Stanshurst's Rolls Royce. She couldn't recall ever sitting in that car, and certainly not in an old-fashioned duster coat. Nor had she ever worn her hair rolled up in a voluptuous bun. She gently roused Ruth and held the picture in front of her. 'Who is this?' Ruth shut her eyes again tightly.

'Please tell me who my parents were.'

'Your parents were an actor and a whore.'

Vanessa heard her name being called from downstairs. She put the picture face down and fled.

Chapter Thirty-Five

Catching the eight minutes past one train depended on how fast the pony could pull the trap. Alistair and Vanessa walked round to the rear of the house, to the stable yard. They'd said their goodbyes to Lord Stanshurst. Vanessa was so silent that Alistair asked if she was feeling ill.

'A headache.'

The stable yard was mournful with its empty loose-boxes, the coach-house losing its tiles. As they passed its gaping door, Vanessa saw a glint of red. Inside was a majestic, outdated car, its bodywork speckled in frass from the coach-house roof. It had no wheels. Mice had been at the seats' leather. The Royal Automobile Club badge on the radiator grille was mittened in spider-web, as was its double 'R' insignia.

Alistair looked over her shoulder. 'A Silver Ghost. Lord Stanshurst can't bear to sell it though he can't afford to run it either. Billy Chalker described this car coming to London to fetch Johnny away from Eva.' He gazed at it thoughtfully before pulling his attention back. 'If you want to take a detour through the village, we need to get moving.'

'A moment.' She reached under the steering wheel, where a

pair of goggles hung. Drivers' goggles for the road. 'Did Lord Stanshurst have a chauffeur?'

'While his wife was alive, but he told me he always drove this beauty himself. It was his pride and joy.'

She dropped the goggles. 'If this car fetched Johnny away, Lord Stanshurst was at the wheel. Let's go.'

The door key of Peach Cottage was kept under a brick. Alistair stayed in the pony trap with the driver, telling Vanessa to be quick.

Inside the dark and chilly cottage, Vanessa took stock of the living room. As ever, it was surgically tidy, plant holders, candlesticks and sparse mementoes arranged symmetrically. In this front parlour, she'd read during interminable evenings. She'd sketched and done her homework in front of the fire. It had been her job to bring in the coal and black the grate. And to scrub the herringbone bricks of the floor. There were spots of blood by the stairs. Poor Ruth. Alone, angry, abandoned. What had she ever gained by inducing Johnny back to her?

Vanessa searched the bureau but found no letters. She searched the parlour, the bedrooms. Alistair was calling to her to get a move on. She'd have left, except that she was thirsty. She went into the kitchen for a cup of water. On the drainer next to the copper which was laid with coals to heat the water for washing, Vanessa found a bundle of letters. Each was addressed in the same flourishing hand. 'Vanessa Quinnell, Peach Cottage, Stanshurst'. She opened the first of them and read:

My dear Vanessa, I am breaking an embargo I was rushed into twenty-one years ago. When you were born, I pledged not to contact you, nor to write or in any way invade your life. But times change. I would never have imagined back then that this country would be at war again, or that I would long painfully to have a child, a daughter, at my side. And so, as you have come of age, I have broken that pledge. I am your father and I want to know you. Would you like to know me? If so, write to Johnny. He will arrange everything. My dear girl, I do hope your answer is "yes." Yours,'

It was signed 'W Bovary' and dated 29th May 1941 – the day of her twenty-first birthday.

Alistair spoke her name and she passed the letter to him, unable to express what she felt. After a moment, he said, 'Johnny didn't tell you, did he? I expect he was hoping to manage the affair to his advantage. He wanted to be the broker. Are there others?'

Subsequent letters were dated at six-monthly intervals after the first, and all were invitations to Vanessa to get in touch. In each, Bo had written his address. *The Farren, Farren Court, London*. That both Johnny and Ruth had, by different means, kept her in ignorance was impossible for Vanessa to deny. In fact, what were the odds that Ruth had intended to burn these letters when she lit the coals for the water? Had she not fallen bringing sheets down from the bedroom, this paper would have been ash by now. Alistair put a hand on her arm.

She turned to him and he frowned at what he saw in her eyes.

She said, 'I know who my mother is. I'm going back to the Hall, Alistair.' She gave him Bo's letters and ran out of Peach Cottage and down Church Hill, taking a path through the park that was too narrow for a pony-and-trap to follow.

Chapter Thirty-Six

Walking back into Stanshurst Hall, she heard voices from the morning room. Fern and her father.

Vanessa crept up the stairs, intending to return to Ruth's bedroom, but instead, she found herself in what must once have been a private, upstairs sitting room. A woman's room with watered silk walls and pastel carpets. Furnishings were draped in Holland covers. She lifted the corner of one and found a French-style ottoman upholstered in striped silk. The sound of hooves took her to the window. She saw Alistair jump down from the trap and run towards the house.

They'd all be here in a while, but she wanted a few moments alone with her discovery. She'd have another go at finding Ruth's room, she decided, and the picture of the young woman in the Rolls Royce. But something in the room's shrouded silence tempted her to linger. She walked through an open arched doorway into a sitting room.

And she saw the portrait.

It was above the fireplace. A slight young woman with coppery hair and pale skin peppered with freckles. The mouth was sensual. The eyes' lively expression was accentuated by arched brows. The irises were a rare, unusual shade of amber. 'It's me,' Vanessa breathed.

'It's Margery.'

Lord Stanshurst stood in the archway, Fern behind him. To Vanessa's relief, Alistair followed them into the room. He looked windswept, suggesting a hectic dash to get here.

Lord Stanshurst continued, 'It was painted in 1913, for our marriage, when we were the young lord and the brilliant stage star.' Cynicism misted his expression. 'Christopher was born the month after war was declared in 1914. In March, 1917, I accompanied my unit to France, leaving Margery expecting Fern. Some months after Fern's birth, I had a letter from my mother, telling me that Fern was here with her nurse-maids and that Margery was in London. With somebody else.'

'With Wilton Bovary.' Fern's mouth twisted. 'You wouldn't give her a divorce, would you, Pops? In your world, marriage is for life. I wish you'd challenged him to a duel!'

'A duel? Your grandmamma would have had a fit.' Lord Stanshurst gave his daughter a sad smile. 'She forced Margery back here and wrote telling me that my family was together again. I trusted all would be well, as up to then, I'd escaped serious injury but I caught the tail-end of a gas attack in October '18, a few days before the end of the damn show. They put me in a sanatorium, and I didn't get out for over a year. By then, Margery was back in London with her lover. Pregnant. His, obviously. What to do?'

It was Alistair who asked, 'What did you do?'

'A secluded house on the south coast, on the salt marshes. A private nurse and Ruth Quinnell in attendance. Margery was registered with a doctor under the name "Hunter" so nobody would know that it was Lady Stanshurst giving birth. The child was to be whisked away and adopted incognito.'

'But that didn't happen, did it?' Alistair looked at Vanessa.

'No,' Lord Stanshurst admitted. 'Margery wanted to see the

child grow up. She asked Ruth to adopt it, but Ruth refused. Damn right. A lone female, whose husband has been away at war can't suddenly go home with an infant.'

Vanessa said, 'You must have orchestrated things very carefully.'

'Ruth wanted her husband back. She wanted Clive. Johnny, whatever he called himself. But he'd hunkered down in London, refusing to leave some woman he was living with.'

'Eva,' Vanessa said. 'She wasn't "some woman".'

'I understand she was quite a girl,' Lord Stanshurst said dryly. 'Margery kept a correspondence going with an actress friend, a Miss Ruskin, who told her that Quinnell was acting at The Farren and co-habiting with their wardrobe woman. They'd recently lost their child and the relationship was in trouble. That was our lever to get Quinnell to return to Ruth and adopt the child.' He nodded at Vanessa. 'You, I should say, m'dear.'

'You drove Ruth to London,' Alistair suggested.

'On a burning day in July. I parked in Bow Street, by the magistrates' court. Kept my coat and goggles on so the blighters swarming in and out wouldn't see my face. Dear God, I sweated!'

'How did Ruth induce Quinnell away?' Alistair asked. 'Not charm, I daresay.'

'Five hundred pounds down, another five hundred when Vanessa reached her sixth birthday. From Bow Street, I drove Quinnell and Ruth to Euston station and sent them up to my Scottish estates near Crianlarich. That's even more remote than the salt marshes. I drove Margery's baby up with her nurse a few days later. By the time the Quinnells returned to Stanshurst, nobody questioned Ruth and Clive having a little daughter. War has its uses. It muddles the picture.'

'You make it sound so easy,' Vanessa said bitterly.

'It was easy, really,' Lord Stanshurst said, almost in surprise.

'When Johnny— Clive, I mean, left again on my sixth birthday, did he collect his five hundred pounds?'

Lord Stanshurst nodded. 'I gave him the cheque myself.'

Of course! She'd seen a record in the payroll ledgers during her stint as Lord Stanshurst's secretary. 'And my name – '

'You were baptised Margaret.' Hearing Fern's gasp, Lord Stanshurst reached out to his daughter. 'Margaret Mary. Those were Margery's given names.'

'Why did she get Mother's name and not me?' Fern's face pinched with anguish.

'You were named Frances for my mother. Chris called you "Fern", of course, but your baptismal name was my gift to you.'

Fern nodded fiercely. 'Better than Margaret. Better than *Toots*.' *She's my Tootsie-Wootsie*. An echo from years ago.

Fern rounded on Vanessa. 'Don't think this makes you my sister.'

'It does, I fear.' Vanessa's anger wasn't with Fern. 'Did you know before now?'

'Not until I found that photograph by Ruth's bed. I knew it was Marge sitting in the car, but it was you, too. Chris told me she'd been unfaithful to Pops and once, when she was ill, she'd hinted at another child. We're telling nobody about this, you understand?'

'Nobody will hear of it from me.' Vanessa turned to Lord Stanshurst. 'Why am I called Vanessa? Why steal a dead child's name?'

Lord Stanshurst put his hands to her shoulders. 'We couldn't have you called Margaret, it would have given the game away. Quinnell acquired his deceased child's birth certificate after he left that wardrobe woman.'

'Eva.'

'You took her name, birth date, everything.'

On the brink of retching. Vanessa walked out of the room. She'd been living another girl's life, having another girl's birthday, for twenty-six years. She'd taken the name of Eva's little dead scrap. Alistair came after her.

'We need that poor pony again,' he said. 'Or shall we walk?'

'We'll miss the matinee.'

'Damn the theatre. Bugger Lady Windermere.'

'Then let's walk. I want to go, now.'

At the end of the avenue of bare trees alive with chattering rooks, Vanessa looked back at Stanshurst Hall. A mother she'd never really known had been lonely here, and found solace with a beguiling actor-manager.

She stopped. 'Heck. I left Bo's cloak in the pony trap.'

'Shall we fetch it?'

She thought a moment. 'I'll keep it as a memory. The night we met, I amused Bo, I think.'

'You'd have liked each other.'

'I made him late.' Playing Lane the manservant, Bo was one of the beginners on stage in *The Importance of Being Earnest*. Curtain-up was at half seven. 'He bumped into a shivering WAAF and we enjoyed a verbal tussle. I went into the saloon bar and looked for Johnny. I saw workmen, and an ARP warden. A man monkeying around at the piano wearing a flat, check cap. His hair was grey, his face worn.'

'That was Johnny.'

'I hadn't reckoned on how the years would have changed him. I walked out.' Her fingers dug fiercely into Alistair's arm. 'I delayed Bo by talking. Do you suppose he burst his heart running to the theatre?'

'No,' Alistair said with absolute finality. 'It was mischance. Or fate. You said it yourself. "Fate is co-incidence with strings attached."'

He kissed her, and when she met his eyes, they glittered. 'None of it was your doing.'

'Do you mind me being Marge Stanshurst's daughter? Ruth called her "a whore". And I always thought she worshipped her mistress!'

He put his arms around her. 'I suspect Ruth's adoration was actually for Lord Stanshurst. You know, I didn't think you could be more precious to me, but knowing you're Bo's daughter . . . if we have children, he lives on.'

She shivered in his arms. 'My parents were Margery and Wilton and my given name is Margaret.'

'Now we need to prove it,' Alistair said. 'So you can inherit his money.'

'I don't want to.'

'If you don't claim it, Sylvia Rolf and Barbara Bovary will eventually get it. And after them, Edwin. Think about it, Edwin Bovary spending your inheritance.'

Chapter Thirty-Seven

Three weeks into the new year of 1947, a letter arrived for Vanessa.

Gilmore & Jackson, Solicitors
South Audley Street, W1

Dear Mrs Kingcourt,

In response to Cdr Redenhall's letter asserting your claim to the late Mr W Bovary's residual estate, I would urge you to present proof as soon as you are able. Proof would consist of papers of adoption, the sworn testimony of your birth-mother and the doctor attending, or a person in a position of trust, such as a magistrate who was party to your fostering by Mr and Mrs Quinnell. A birth certificate alone is insufficient. Letters sent to you from Mr Bovary do not constitute evidence, as it is too late to confirm their provenance.

Yours faithfully,

P Jackson

Vanessa passed the letter to Alistair at the breakfast table. He read it, then frowned, saying, 'Lord Stanshurst won't back up your claim. Ruth might – '

'She won't go against Lord Stanshurst. He owns her home and pays her a wage still.'

'Then we need to find proof positive. Show me that key.'

Vanessa pulled Eva's key from under the four jumpers she was wearing. Penetrating, Arctic cold had arrived on January 21st, gripping the country. Though they moved the electric fire from room to room, Alistair and Vanessa felt they were living outside in a cave.

'When Eva gave you this and talked about your "rights", did she give any indication she meant Bo's wealth?'

'She couldn't say much at all. Billy thinks Eva may have left something for me in her sewing box, but –'

'We don't know where Eva's sewing box is. Chalker thinks she left it at the theatre.'

'Darling, there's no point setting our hearts on this money.' Vanessa reached for the marmalade, which she was going to spread on a slice of cold Yorkshire pudding. They were out of bread. 'Things are going well enough, aren't they?'

'We're level in cash,' Alistair agreed. 'But there will be a lull come February. The weather will be in command then.'

If that was a premonition, Alistair was spot on. In London, temperatures plummeted further and the streets became perilous. Deep snow blanketed even the main thoroughfares and their evening performance on Friday, January 23rd, played to a crowd of thirty. The usherettes encouraged a straggling audience into the centre of the stalls, to give the actors a focus. Alistair then cancelled the Saturday matinee as only one person turned up. The green room echoed with dark mutterings. 'This is worse than the war!' Forty souls made it to the evening performance.

Gas pressure got so low, the central heating struggled. On stage, the actors' breaths solidified like dandelion clocks.

'I'm wearing three vests – I only wore two when I toured Scotland in '43.' Ronnie Gainsborough's teeth chattered as he awaited his cue. On stage, Clemency, Rosa and Tanith shivered so violently in their silk and lace that they couldn't project their voices in a low register. Vanessa had run up under-shifts from stockinette fabric. To accommodate the added bulk, corsets had been let out. All the ladies looked as if they'd had a surfeit of Christmas pudding.

When a power cut shut down central London, the riggers substituted battery-powered spotlights. Alistair said to Vanessa during the interval. 'We need kettles on, hot cocoa backstage at all times.'

Trains had ground to a stop, stranded in sidings from Scotland to Cornwall. Buses were at a stand-still. The only people moving freely in the capital were Scandinavian ex-patriots who happened to have skis with them. Spirit burners in the dressing rooms kept the mist off the mirrors and allowed the actors to soften their makeup.

Alistair, Vanessa and Macduff spent Sunday the 26th wrapped in rugs, huddling in front of a wood fire in Alistair's office. Coal had run out. Every two hours, they'd dash round the theatre to check the pipes. On Monday, at dawn, Doyle came on shift. Of all the employees, he seemed least perturbed by the misery, the hardship. When Vanessa commented, his answer was simple: 'It's no worse than being at sea in winter.'

The following Monday's matinee brought in a respectable house, the audience bundled into mufflers, pom-pom hats and double overcoats. They drank soup from Thermos flasks. The usherettes doled out cocoa.

As they geared up for the night's show, Alistair showed Vanessa their latest financial position. 'We'll survive the month on current takings.'

'I can't believe this bitter snap will outlast the month.'

'Can't you?' he smiled. 'The Russian convoys were breaking ice in June. Your place or mine tonight?' A joke. They would sleep once again in Alistair's office. Getting back and forth twice a day, even a short distance, had become dangerous and energy-consuming. They slept together on a mattress, Macduff across their feet. Only Doyle knew of the arrangement and his lips were sealed. His old commander could do no wrong.

Glacial January culled the cast. Some through illness, others through sheer exhaustion. New faces came, rehearsed by Patrick Carnford, who took over as Producer once Terence Rolf's forced resignation took effect. Patrick put in two hundred pounds of his own money, and waived his January salary. Under Carnford, the understudies got their chance. Clemency Abbott produced a doctor's note stating that she had pneumonia.

'A star fades, the world turns,' Patrick said on reading the note. Joanne Sayer, out of work following the closure of *High Jinx*, made her Wildean debut as Lady Windermere on the first of February. She was a hit with audiences, less so with Irene Eddrich, who believed it to be *her* role to smoulder dangerously.

'Lady Windermere is supposed to *douse* Lord Darlington, not arouse him.'

Ronnie Gainsborough, missing Clemency, compared Joanne's performance with that of a 'pert chambermaid who has success-fully seduced the son of the house'. Joanne snuck into his dressing room and filled his shoes with snow. Patrick gave her private rehearsals, teaching her how to project innocence. A dramatic reversal, Rosa Konstantiva observed, of his usual habit.

Billy Chalker trudged in each day. 'General Winter won't see me off.' Off-stage, he dispensed hot toddies wearing a flowered house-coat and yellow ringlets. One time, late for his cue, he dashed on without taking them off and won a roar of applause. He and Vanessa avoided each other. Knowing that she hadn't caused Johnny Quinnell to drink himself to death freed her though she was no less alarmed by the true cause. Johnny would have been miffed at her lack of appearance. Through the years, he'd acted the role of a cheerful dad. While all along, he'd had a plan and the plan involved money. Bo's money.

As the first week of February limped by, The Farren became famous for its 'We Won't Close' spirit, though they cut the matinees, as it took all day to heat the auditorium and defrost the water pipes in the cloakrooms. The seventh of February was a Friday.

Vanessa hung costumes in dressing rooms, then checked the props because the Props Master had given up the struggle to get in. Ironing had become a favourite pastime because it stopped her fingers freezing — when there was electricity to do it by. She cleaned makeup marks off with Thawpit, and brushed and mended, keeping moving.

As she walked by the green room an hour before curtain-up, Patrick Carnford sang out, '"Fresh lavender, buy my fresh lavender!"' in the geriatric squawk of a street seller.

Ten or so actors were inside, drinking tea and smoking. She told Patrick, 'I rub lavender oil in your seams, as I can't wash anything.' All she got from her tap was a dribble of water. She couldn't dry anything either. 'Better to stink of lavender than other odours.'

'Take tea with us, dear.' Noreen Ruskin made room for her

on a banquette. The revelation that Vanessa was Wilton Bovary's daughter had swept through the theatre like Yellow Fever. Neither Vanessa nor Alistair had spoken of it, so who was the culprit? Miss Ruskin was prime suspect as she had recognised Vanessa's resemblance to her dear friend Margery.

No longer a Backstage Bessie, Vanessa had become everyone's pet, Noreen's most particularly. It had its advantages! Vanessa gratefully accepted the hot tea and a slice of cake made with butter from Miss Ruskin's cousins' farm.

'Darling, you don't wear your amulet.' Noreen's painted nail tapped where Vanessa's key had hung until the previous day.

'I have put away childish things.'

From the doorway, a voice boomed the remaining lines: '"For now we see through a glass, darkly; but then face to face".'

'Knock the snow off your boots, Billy,' Rosa Konstantiva chided.

Vanessa said, 'You put those words on Eva's grave.'

Billy found the largest, empty chair. 'My brother Joseph explained them. It's about the value of love, without which nothing profits a man. Or woman. Wear your little key. It unlocks your fortune and was a gift of love.'

'Bo died loaded, I heard,' Roy FitzPeter said from behind his two-sheet newspaper. 'I'd try every keyhole in London, Nessie.'

'Bo made his money transferring a show to New York,' said Miss Ruskin. 'Many tens of thousands.'

'Anything would help,' said Rosa, sadly. 'Once a theatre goes dark, reviving it is the devil. I doubt even Commander Redenhall could do it twice.'

'Do what twice?' Alistair, on his way out to walk Macduff, paused at the doorway. 'What's the weather report, Fitz?'

'Snow,' answered FitzPeter. 'On snow. On snow.'

'I'll walk with you.' Vanessa drained her tea, burning her tongue.

'"They may be some time",' Patrick quipped.

Joanne arrived just then, swathed like a Muscovite and Vanessa slipped out with Alistair.

That night, they had an audience of over a hundred. 'Somebody upstairs loves us,' said Patrick, who had called at Rosa and Gwenda's dressing room to let them know. Vanessa was at her table, as usual. A few minutes later, Patrick was back. 'Tanith hasn't come in.'

'Have you telephoned her?' Rosa asked.

'Her line is down.'

Peter Switt announced the half. When he called, 'Fifteen minutes, please,' there was still no Tanith. When the five-minute call came, Patrick said to Vanessa, 'You'll have to go on.'

'Me? I'm not allowed. I haven't a card.'

'To hell with that. Who will know? We cannot proceed without a Lady Agatha.'

'What about Anne?' Vanessa meant the understudy, Anne Aisleby.

'She's playing Lady Stutfield and she's in Act Two with Lady Agatha. Nessie, just get into the dress, follow Rosa and say, "Yes, mamma" when she prods you. For me?'

Why not? The audience would be semi-comatose anyway. Vanessa ran upstairs for Tanith's costume. Rosa and Gwenda helped her into her corset and Vanessa discovered what it felt like to be reefed in like a sail and still have to move and breath. They dropped the dress over her head, put the wig on her. Rosa pinned on her hat.

As she stood with Rosa in the wings, Vanessa discovered the reality of stage fright, the gut-shimmie Gwenda had described.

'We're on,' whispered Rosa. 'Now remember, look out into the audience. Imagine you're addressing one person right in the centre. When you say your line, open your mouth wide or nobody will hear. And enjoy yourself.'

Vanessa walked on behind Rosa, and her nerves left her. With no time to think about how to be Lady Agatha, Vanessa simply recalled her own shy, frustrated youth. She clamped her eyes on Joanne, playing Lady Windermere, because, surely, a smothered, over-mothered girl would stare at a beautiful, sophisticated society leader. When Rosa, as the Duchess of Berwick, addressed her, she answered in a bell-like voice, '"Yes, mamma".'

Coming off stage a few minutes later, she ran into Patrick.

'I did it!'

'Course you did. You're the total sum of Wilton Bovary and Margery Bowers. Next month Lady Macbeth, and St Joan after that.'

The following morning, Lady Ververs' butler telephoned to say that Miss Tanith had stumbled on the steps at home, and had strained ligaments in her ankle. She was unlikely to come to work until later in the week. 'You're on again,' Patrick told her.

Alistair thought it hilarious. 'You're ten years too old to play the part, you know that.'

'Yes, Papa!'

That night, disaster. Vanessa made her entrance with a sweep of a flounced skirt. Smiling at Lady Windermere, she walked straight into the table with the rose bowl. For the second time in its fragile life, the table broke in two. Vanessa saved the bowl, a papier mâché replacement of the original, and was left holding it, along with the lace cloth, for the entire scene. On her cue to exit, she faced the dilemma of walking off-stage clutching Lady Windermere's possessions.

Joanne helped not one bit. She smiled angelically, then leaned out towards the audience and ad-libbed, 'Poor Lady Agatha! She is a known kleptomaniac.'

Vanessa walked over and plonked the cloth and vase into Joanne's hands.

'Heaven be praised,' Joanne declaimed, 'she is reformed!'

Vanessa exited to unearned applause. She reported her mishap to Patrick who cursed the table, explaining that it was what antique dealers called "a marriage": two bits of furniture muckled together. 'A bad marriage. It collapses at the most inconvenient moments.'

'And its sharp bits rip Lady Windermere's dresses,' Vanessa said with feeling.

'Yes, well, our carpenter thinks it was rescued after a bomb, and glued together from salvaged parts. I'd have him make us a new one, but he's snowed up at home. God, this hellish weather!'

Salvaged from a bomb blast? Though she was due back on in the next act, Vanessa raced up to her room and retrieved something from the corner of the mirror. What if . . .

Her heart thudding, she sailed through her next scene, hardly aware of getting on and off. Later, when the safety iron was down and the actors were filing out into the snow, she slipped back into the wings. Alistair saw her and followed. He was in evening dress, as he was for every performance.

'You shimmered, my star,' he said, with irony, as he caught up with her.

'Rewriting Wilde? Lady Agatha as an habitual thief is far more interesting. Never mind that.' Switching on lights, she pulled Alistair on stage with her, handing him the blue vase, rose basket and lace cloth. Someone had repaired the table with yards

of string and she turned it over cautiously. 'It's "a marriage",
Patrick said . . .'

'"Marriage" and "Patrick" are not words I like hearing
together.'

'Shush. May I have your torch?'

It hung from his wrist by a loop. He handed it to her. 'Why
are you trembling?'

'Years ago, I saw Eva using a sewing box that reminded me
of a big cake because . . . well, look.' She pointed the beam at
the table's drum-shaped top. Aged cherry wood had gained the
hue of molten chocolate, along with the nicks and scratches that
might have resulted from a bomb exploding nearby. Within its
rim was a small, gold keyhole. Alistair grew suddenly tense.

'Your key . . . you have it?'

In answer, Vanessa fell to her knees and jabbed Eva's key into
the hole. It fitted perfectly.

Chapter Thirty-Eight

Wilton Bovary's lawyer, Mr Jackson, was asking Terence Rolf to kindly refrain from telling him how to do his job when Alistair and Vanessa entered his office. Besides Terence in the small room were Edwin and Miss Bovary.

Alistair apologised for their lateness, which was owing to them having walked from Covent Garden. Temperatures overnight had dipped to minus ten and the tube was not running.

Jackson welcomed them. Terence Rolf barely acknowledged their 'good day'.

Edwin smirked and inclined his head. 'Sorry for your trouble, Redenhall. And you, Mrs Kingcourt. You've had a wasted journey as we're here to claim my uncle's fortune. My father has been reminding Mr Jackson of his legal duty to release the money in trust.'

Miss Bovary, hatted, coated and gloved and as poker stiff as a guardsman, echoed her nephew. 'I am co-heir to my brother with my sister.'

'You would have been,' Alistair said equably, 'had Mrs Kingcourt remained ignorant of her parentage, as no doubt you hoped.' Sylvia Rolf was absent, he noticed. He'd heard she'd had some kind of nervous collapse.

Penry Jackson requested silence. 'Commander Redenhall, is Mrs Kingcourt here to substantiate her claim?'

Vanessa spoke for herself. 'Yes, Mr Jackson. I found something in the theatre which proves . . . I *believe* proves . . . that I am Wilton Bovary's daughter.'

Alistair was struck by her calmness. She was on the verge of owning – or losing – a fortune, yet she might have been discussing an embroidered teacloth at a sale-of-work. He watched her take a large brown envelope from her shoulder bag and ask the lawyer for clean paper.

When white paper was placed in front of her, Vanessa emptied the envelope over it. Out first was a curl of light brown hair. Child's hair, tied with a filet of sea green ribbon. Next, a photograph of an attractive, though weary-looking, woman holding a tiny baby. The infant was wrapped in a shawl, only its face showing. The woman was Lady Stanshurst, formerly Margery Bowers, actress. She met the camera's intrusion diffidently. For all that, there was pride in the way she held her child.

'That picture was taken by the sea,' Vanessa said huskily. 'You can see the patterns of light on the room ceiling.' The photographer was reflected in a mirror. He was positioned behind a portrait camera, a hand raised as if he'd just said, "Smile". The man was a youthful Wilton Bovary.

'The baby in the shawl,' Vanessa said, 'is me at a few days old. On the back somebody's written, "Margaret Mary" and my mother's name.' Vanessa passed the photo to Mr Jackson. 'Don't read her name out, please. Her identity mustn't be revealed.'

The lawyer stared a long time at both sides of the photograph. He was seeing 'Margery with Margaret Mary, July 16th, 1920'. Jackson was also seeing Bo's handwriting, of which there was a great deal in existence.

The lawyer frowned. 'It's a lady with a baby, with Mr Bovary present, but how do we know that baby is you?'

Vanessa reached into her bag. 'This is what I've been looking for, without really knowing. It's my birth certificate. My real one. My birth was registered the day before this picture was taken and I agree, alone it's no proof that I'm Margaret Mary Bovary –'

'So why waste our time?' Terence Rolf was trying to see the reverse of the photograph, which Jackson put down when he realised what was happening. 'Where did you find this stuff?'

Vanessa pointed to the key at her throat. 'In Eva St Clair's sewing box, on stage at The Farren. Hidden in plain sight.'

'What's that confounded woman to do with anything?'

Alistair answered. 'Eva loved two men. She kept the secret of Bo's affair with a lady, but also concealed items on behalf of Johnny Quinnell, who had a strong motive for ensuring Vanessa's eventual recognition. He foresaw this moment and made sure that proof of the baby's identity was preserved. Show him, Mrs Kingcourt.'

With a jolt, because she'd forgotten what it felt like to be addressed so formally by Alistair, Vanessa turned the birth certificate to its blank side. She pointed out a row of purplish-black blotches. 'I made those,' she said.

Penry Jackson angled his desk-lamp for better clarity. 'I take it that these are infant fingerprints?'

'The tiny ones are my baby prints. The larger ones were made when I was five, when I was taken to the theatre to meet Eva. Johnny rolled my fingers in ink. "Five little piggies". Eva took the certificate to my father, Mr Bovary, to sign. See, there's his signature against each set of prints. And the dates. He's written, "These are the marks of my daughter, Margaret".'

'Utter rubbish!' Miss Bovary pushed Vanessa aside, reaching for the certificate, but the lawyer prevented her from taking it. She slapped the desk in frustration. 'Babies don't have fingerprints!'

'Mine did,' said Jackson. 'I spent half my life cleaning greasy little dabs off the lenses of my spectacles and the dashboard of my car. Have you compared these with your adult prints?' he asked Vanessa.

'Not officially.'

Jackson took a magnifying glass from his desk drawer. 'Would you kindly hold out your hands?' He studied Vanessa's fingertips, then used the glass to look closely at the prints. 'The loops and whorls match, to my unprofessional eye. It will have to be proved, perhaps in court.' Jackson folded the certificate into its grooves. 'Mrs Kingcourt, can anyone testify to the circumstances of your birth?'

'My foster-mother . . . I believe Ruth Quinnell could be persuaded. And a titled gentleman could be ordered to do so, but I'd rather not.'

'Very good. In the meantime, shall we put these precious items in the safe?'

Vanessa picked up the certificate, the curl of hair, and the photograph, while Penry Jackson unlocked a cupboard door that proved to be the false veneer of an iron safe. He turned a dial in sequence.

Alistair saw Edwin Bovary tense. Predicting his next move, he seized Edwin's shoulder, but a three-mile walk in compacted snow had slowed his reflexes. He got only a handful of Edwin's coat. Vanessa's enraged 'No!' told him that Edwin had seized something precious. A second later, came a howl of pain. Vanessa ran to the safe, and thrust her birth certificate inside. Penry Jackson closed the door with a snap and secured it.

Edwin was hopping and Alistair tried to imagine what martial manoeuvre Vanessa had employed against him – until he noticed that she was wearing her doughty RAF beetle crushers. Edwin's foot would be bruised for a month. Alistair smiled.

'I take it you want Bo's money after all,' he said.

'I want The Farren to have it.' She came to him. 'I want you to have it.'

'On one condition.'

She laughed. 'Granted, probably.'

'That when I'm free, you'll marry me.'

The freezing winter of 1947 persisted into March. When the final thaw came, one hundred thousand properties were rendered uninhabitable through burst pipes and flood damage. The Farren's pipes burst, as did the water tanks in the roof. Suffering a catastrophic deluge, it was declared a dangerous building, its doors and windows clad in metal sheets to keep intruders out. Restoring it would dig deep into Wilton Bovary's money.

Three years later

May 29th, Brookwood Cemetery, Surrey

Butter yellow roses for Eva, bought that morning from the market. For Eva's infant daughter, a bunch of fragrant pinks. Vanessa laid the flowers on each grave, then trimmed the grass. She took care that no part of her cinch-waist 'New Look' suit came into contact with grass clippings. Alistair waited nearby with two bouquets of roses. Packing away her things, she told Eva, 'As of today, I'm Mrs Redenhall.' She smiled across at Alistair, who didn't know that he had confetti on his collar.

When she walked over to him, he gave her his arm. 'You couldn't have chosen worse shoes for this.'

Her pearly stilettos had left a trail of heel-marks in the grass. She made a rueful face. 'Wearing flatties with a Paris-made suit is a crime.'

'Says who?'

'Rosa, Gwenda and Joanne. One of them hid my beetle-crushers.'

They walked through the grounds, the air fragrant with pine needles and tree blossom. One last task, after which they were being driven to the coast, where they'd sail to France to begin a honeymoon that would end in Rome.

In the actors' corner, Alistair placed roses on his godfather's grave. 'Hello, Father,' Vanessa said to the headstone, which was a marble book, open at a stanza of verse. After a moment's silent respect, she went to another grave nearby. This one had a simpler stone that read 'Clive Johnny Quinnell, Actor'.

Laying the final bouquet, Vanessa said again, 'Hello, Dad.' Childhood emotions have deep roots. Johnny had been the only father she'd ever known. She'd promised him a better grave, and she kept her promises.

She wondered what either father would have made of the brand new, modernist theatre that Wilton Bovary's fortune had built on a barren stretch of Thames riverbank. While The Farren went through its slow, expensive renewal, the New Wilton Theatre was building a reputation for cutting edge drama. They'd opened with Tom Cottrill's play, *Higson's Choice*.

Vanessa and Alistair were jointly manager and producer and their head designer was Hugo Brennan. A competent woman with two assistants ran wardrobe and hired in seamstresses when she needed them. Vanessa would smile as she walked past the studio, hearing the whirr of sewing machines. Uninterrupted electricity, reams of fabric, central heating and hot water – some folk didn't know how easy they had it.

'Let's go,' Alistair said. 'It would be very embarrassing if we missed our ship.'

'Aye aye, Sir.' Her fashionable shoes gave her just enough lift to kiss the frown line over the bridge of his nose. He kissed her upturned throat. A flame flickered, before they recalled where they were.

They strolled back towards the road, smartly-dressed married lovers. As they approached the gleaming black Crossley parked at the kerb, Alistair whistled. Doyle stamped out his cigarette and tugged down his jacket before opening the rear door. A dog with a grey muzzle and one leg short of a full set lumbered towards them, his tail beating joyfully.

The Dress Thief

Alix Gower may be poor but she's also ambitious, and she'd
do anything to secure her dream job in one of Paris' premier
fashion houses. But Alix also has a secret: she supports her family
by stealing from the very houses she so adores. Then Alix is
unexpectedly given a break - a way to support her elderly grandmother and a future she can believe in . . . but it comes at a
terrible price. Will Alix risk her reputation, her relationships
and even her personal safety for a dream? And is the handsome
English reporter she keeps bumping into really to be trusted?
The Dress Thief is an award-winning, atmospheric novel about
love, dreams and betrayal.

Winner of the 2014 Love Stories 'Best Historical Read' award.

Winner of the 2015 Public Book Awards.

Shortlisted for the 2015 RITA Awards.

Summer in the Vineyards

*A bittersweet romance set in the rolling valleys of
the French Dordogne wine-making region.*

Shauna Vincent, a graduate from the north of England, has just learned that the job she set her heart on has gone to a socially well-connected rival. Devastated, she accepts an offer in France from an old family friend – to be au pair to the woman's grandchildren. Within a week, Shauna is deep in the Dordogne. With little to do other than organise her two charges' busy social diaries, she has endless hours in which to explore the magical landscape that surrounds her.

Her new home is the ancient Chateau de Chemignac with its vineyards and hidden secrets, including a locked tower room where she unearths a trove of vintage gowns, one of which feels unsettlingly familiar. Then Shauna falls asleep one afternoon in a valley full of birdsong, and has a strange dream of a vintage aircraft circling threateningly overhead. So when she suddenly awakes to find charming local landowner Laurent de Chemignac standing over her – Shauna wonders if the dashing aristocrat might be just the person to help her untangle this unexpected message from the past.